THE
REDEMPTION

THE REDEMPTION

A THORNTON MYSTERY

C.L. TOLBERT

Sandy —
I appreciate your friendship

LEVEL
BEST BOOKS

and support! Love,
Cindy

First edition

ISBN: 978-1-947915-43-5

Cover art by Level Best Designs

Cover photo by Brian Swanner

This book was professionally typeset on Reedsy.
Find out more at reedsy.com

To my husband, Engin, who rebuilt our house while I wrote.

Praise for THE REDEMPTION

"Mystery, murder, and mayhem in The Big Easy; C.L. Tolbert's *The Redemption* is a page-turner guaranteed to keep you guessing until the very end." — Bruce Robert Coffin, award-winning author of the Detective Byron Mysteries

"With *The Redemption*, Cynthia Tolbert delivers another beautifully written and compelling read in her Thornton Mystery series, as law professor Emma Thornton's fight to save a teen wrongly accused of murder endangers her own life in this gripping tale of corruption and crime in the 1990s Big Easy." — Ellen Byron, award-winning and bestselling author of The Cajun Country Mysteries

Chapter One

September 9, 1994

8:05 p.m.

Just before dark on the night of his death, Brother Reginald Antoine stepped out of the cottage where he lived. He slammed the door shut to prevent the soggy heat of the late summer evening from invading the front room. Except for occasional river breezes, the New Orleans climate was swamp-like until late October. His exits had become swift and cat-like to avoid escalating power bills and a strain on the house's only window-unit air conditioner.

He stood on the front porch for a moment, staring at the entrance to the Redemption housing project. All was quiet. No one was in sight.

He was looking forward to the evening. He'd promised to help Alicia Bishop complete forms for a scholarship to Our Lady of Fatima, the top girls' school in the city. He found himself singing under his breath as he locked the front door.

Most of the kids Brother Antoine worked with never finished school, and he was painfully aware that he'd failed far more than he'd helped. But Alicia's story would be different. Her graduation would be her family's first. Clear-headed and determined, much like her Aunt Juanita, the woman who had raised her, she was destined to earn far more than a high school diploma. He believed she was destined for great things.

1

Brother Antoine surveyed the street, familiar to him from childhood. Alicia and her Aunt Juanita lived in an apartment only a few blocks over, but well within the Redemption housing project. Driving such a short distance would be silly, plus he felt like getting a little exercise. It was a good evening for a walk, even though no one felt completely safe walking around any neighborhood in the city at night. At least one person had been killed in New Orleans every day that year, so far. Sometimes more. Too many drugs were on the streets. But he didn't worry about any of that.

He tucked the bundle of papers he'd pulled for the meeting under his arm and headed out. When he was a kid, he'd found the Redemption overwhelming—so vast it couldn't be taken in, visually, from his porch or from any single location. A crowded jumble of russet brick, broken down porches, and peeling army-drab paint, it stretched across the lower garden district from Magazine Street to the Mississippi River. When he was about six he tried to count the buildings, but gave up when he got lost. Everything looked the same to him back then. When he returned to live at the mission house, he realized he'd been wrong. Each place was unique. Every apartment, every stoop, every front door was distinct, because everything inside was different. Every place had its own family, its own problems, and joys. He didn't realize how much he'd missed it until his return.

He passed the community garden planted around the corner from the mission house with its patches of brave sprouts pushing out of the ground. He was proud of that little spot, and equally excited for the people who were involved, especially those few who returned week after week to dig, and prod, and encourage the seedlings to grow. Some of the plants even promised to bear fruit, which was reason enough to celebrate.

As he walked, he could smell urine from a street gutter where drunken men or stoned boys had relieved themselves. A recent rain only added a steamy intensity to the mix, creating a cauldron of odors which would vanish only when the next day's sunlight parched the streets.

The Redemption was teeming with human spirit, poverty, and crime. It was home to many, but with rare exception, no one chose to live there. And everyone who did, even the very young, understood how fragile life could be.

He walked up the steps to Juanita Bishop's apartment and rapped on the front door.

* * *

9:00 p.m.

Sam Maureau pulled his car into the Redemption and parked at a curb at the end of Felicity Street. He was alone. Jackson, his partner, couldn't come. But Sam wasn't worried. He checked his watch. He was right on time. Things were under control.

He turned off his lights and, except for the murky glow of the half-obscured moon, was surrounded by a blanket of darkness. It took several seconds for his eyes to adjust, but even after he waited, he still strained to see. Most of the streetlights on that block had been shot out, and several apartment windows had been boarded over. He peered in between the last two buildings on the corner for any sign of movement.

Sam kicked aside a beer can as he stepped out of his car. He didn't expect any trouble that night. Marcus, a dealer who ran the Gangsta B's, the largest gang in the city, had asked for a meeting to discuss 'some business,' but they'd never had problems before. Their businesses had always co-existed, side-by-side. Sam had begun selling crack in small quantities ten years earlier, when he was twenty-five, and had remained one of the smaller dealers in the city. He figured that Marcus, who was younger by at least ten years, either wanted to bring him and his territory into the Gangsta B's, or he wanted to buy him out. He didn't see the need to change anything right now, unless the price was right. He was making pretty good money. His clients were happy with him. But he didn't mind talking with Marcus.

Sam patted his jacket pocket. The gun was still there. It never hurt to be careful. He locked his car, checking to make certain nothing was in the back seat. Marcus had asked him to meet around the corner.

Sam made his way across the grassy common area, dodging the few mud puddles he could see reflected in the wan moonlight, to an old iron bench across from Marcus's grandmother's apartment where they had met once before. He sat down to wait. The bench hadn't quite cooled from the daytime heat. The faint breeze from the river ruffled what scant remnants remained of his once luxurious surfer-boy hair and sent greasy paper bags and random debris scurrying across the sidewalk. He absent-mindedly patted his bald spot to make certain it was covered.

He couldn't see them, but their chatter floated over to his bench. Even though the words were indecipherable, Sam heard three distinct voices. Then he heard Marcus speak.

"Go get Louis."

Out of habit, Sam felt his jacket pocket again, reassuring himself that his piece was still there. Marcus and one other young man came into view. Sam nodded as they approached.

Marcus was a commanding presence. Tall and athletic, intricate tattoos of black ink wove across his dark skin, tracing his biceps, and emphasizing his ropy, muscular arms and powerful shoulders. His long hair, pulled back into a ponytail, flowed down his back. No one questioned his authority.

"We're gonna wait a minute for Louis." Marcus pulled out a cigarette from his back pocket and lit it, blowing billowy clouds into the night air.

"Yeah, sure. But what's this all about?"

Marcus ignored Sam's question and pulled hungrily on his cigarette, blowing smoke rings, refusing to make eye contact with Sam.

Several minutes later, a tall young man and a boy who couldn't have been over sixteen joined them.

"You and your people gotta go. You're right in the middle of my territory. I'm claiming it, and I'm taking it—now. Ain't nothing you can do about it." Marcus threw down his cigarette and stomped it into the grass.

Sam stood up to face Marcus. "Fuck you, Marcus. You don't need my three blocks. I've had it for years, and its outside your territory, anyway. You can't just take it." Sam clenched his left hand into a fist and shoved his right hand in his jacket pocket where the gun was hidden.

"That's where you're wrong, motherfucker." Marcus grabbed another cigarette and rammed it three times against the pack. "I got business coming to me from uptown all the time now. It's time for you to give it up." Marcus nodded to the three boys, who formed a circle around Sam and Marcus.

"No way, bro!" Sam's hand instinctively tightened around the gun.

Surrounded by the group of young men, Sam saw an opening, turned, and simultaneously pulled the gun from his jacket. As he stepped toward his escape, he saw something moving along the sidewalk next to the street. It appeared to be a man dressed in dark clothes, but it was impossible to be certain. Sam heard one shot and felt it whizz by him. The distant figure dropped. Sam twisted around and aimed his weapon toward the sound of the gun fire. Then he heard another shot.

Feeling something hot in his chest, he crumpled to the ground. The last thing he saw was the young kid, the one they called Louis, running toward the river.

* * *

Brother Antoine said goodnight to Alicia on the front porch of her aunt's apartment and started his walk back home. He was feeling good, lighthearted. He and Alicia had completed her application, and she had nearly finished her essay. He was certain she was a shoo-in for the scholarship. He'd only traveled a few feet down the sidewalk when he saw a group of men and a few boys gathered together in the grassy area next to one of the buildings. The cloud-covered moon offered enough reflection to allow him to make out the scant silhouette of the tallest member of the group. There was no doubt. His swagger and perpetual cigarette were unmistakable. Marcus Bishop. They had to be up to no good.

Brother Antoine followed the curve of the sidewalk, which brought him a little closer to the group. He noticed there was movement, perhaps a scuffle. He heard a shot, then felt a searing pain in his chest. He placed his hand on his shirt where he felt dampness, and, struggling to breathe, fell to the ground. He grabbed the scapular around his neck, praying, as he lay there, someone would come administer the last rites.

Chapter Two

September 15, 1994

Professor Emma Thornton doctored her ice coffee at the creamer station. The morning ritual with other What's Perkin' regulars reminded her of beasts at a watering hole, each avoiding eye contact as they quietly poured packets of sugar and containers of cream into their grandes and ventis. Emma wasn't human before caffeine. Instead, before she'd had her morning coffee she was closer to the dried-out horseshoe crab the twins found on the beach at summer vacation—empty-headed, vile, and somewhat monstrous.

She took a sip of her sweetened caffeine mixture and felt her mind and body come back to life. She had an early meeting with the dean, and knew she'd need a brain, or at least half a brain. She didn't have time for a second cup.

* * *

Emma scanned the indictment. Two counts of murder in the first degree, and two lesser included charges of murder in the second. Two dead guys. One shooter. And a juvenile at that. Louis Bishop. This kid must be a regular Wyatt Earp. She heard Dean Georges Munoz shuffling papers at his credenza and glanced up.

"What do you think about taking on this case through the clinic, Emma?"

The clinic was the Legal Clinic for the Homeless at St. Stanislaus University Law School in New Orleans, where Emma had been an assistant professor for the past four years. Munoz started the clinic, but these days, Emma ran it, supervising students who provided free legal services to the city's ever-growing homeless population.

"It isn't a typical homeless case," Emma said. "This kid doesn't live on the streets."

"That's never been a requirement."

Emma knew Munoz was right. You didn't have to live on the streets to be homeless. Louis didn't have a home. He drifted around from one relative to the next. He didn't have a permanent address, so that was good enough to fit within the program. It wasn't Louis's lack of a home that was making her hesitate. It was the nature of the charges.

"Emma?" Munoz said with an encouraging tilt of his head.

Just by looking at him, Emma knew the dean wanted her to take the case. Seventy-five-year-old Munoz defied old-man stereotypes. Physically fit, with an imposing build, Munoz was a kind man who regularly advocated for the disenfranchised. He especially cared about kids in need. He'd been Emma's Criminal Procedure professor and mentor in law school in Georgia. She admired him. He'd been an anchor for her in New Orleans. Someone she knew she could rely on in an unfamiliar city. She didn't want to disappoint him.

"The problem is, Louis is sixteen. The DA will seek the death penalty since more than one person was killed. Plus, I couldn't try the case by myself if I wanted to since the Louisiana Supreme Court requires that two attorneys defend an indigent in a capital case. Louis falls into that category. Plus, I don't have any death penalty experience."

"That problem's easily solved. I can be first chair," Munoz said, "but I'd need you to do the leg work, and handle most of the trial prep and trial. I understand you're nervous, but you defended a guy charged with murder in Georgia. This isn't that different. And if we don't pick up the case, someone from the public defender's office will. They're way over-worked. This Louis kid's got to be scared. A lawyer who could devote a little more time to his case—like you—could give him a better shot. And, if everything goes to hell in a handbasket, there's always the Death Penalty Clinic to bail you out."

"Gee, thanks. They only handle appeals, right?"

"I was kidding." He smiled. "You're going to be fine. Like I said, you can count on me. I've tried a few capital cases in my career." The dean began organizing the papers on his desk.

I'm going to be fine. He'd already decided for her. For them.

"If I take the case, I'll need help. The new law is a bad one. Kids shouldn't be subject to the death penalty." She shook her head. "A child shouldn't be treated as an adult, no matter what the crime is. Wonder if that law will ever come off the books?" Emma set the report back on the dean's desk. "You know the DA's office will make a big deal of this case." She took a sip of her ice coffee. The ice had melted, but she drank it anyway. "One of the victims was a Catholic Brother, and the accused is so young. It's a very sensitive case, and it could easily get a great deal of press. Don't you think?"

Dean Munoz nodded. "I can see that. We don't want the case tried in the press. But don't be afraid of them." He hesitated. "So, you'll take the case?"

Emma hesitated. She wasn't anxious to take this case on. The death penalty was a serious issue, especially since a juvenile was involved. She couldn't live with herself if things didn't go right. The only thing that gave her any consolation was the dean's promise to be the primary lawyer on the case, first chair. "I'll do it, but I'll hold you to your promise. You'll not be first chair in name only."

* * *

September 15, 1994, 3:30 p.m.

"Do any of you keep up with the local news?" Emma scanned the classroom for a show of hands, her mouth moving slightly as she counted to herself. "Did you happen to catch the report of the arrest of a sixteen-year-old boy for the murder of two adult men? It was down at the Redemption housing

9

project."

She hesitated as late arrivers drifted in. Emma met with the entire clinic group, including all clinical professors, and students on a weekly basis in the large lecture hall, but had smaller break-out sessions three times a week with her homeless clinic students in one of the smaller classrooms. Today was a regularly scheduled session with her group. She was looking for about three or four third-year law students to volunteer to work on trial preparation in the Bishop case. She wasn't sure how the students would react to taking on a capital case. It was so different from the usual landlord-tenant/ homeless issues they were used to.

When all students were seated, she nodded to a student who had raised his hand.

"What would you think about working on that case, Josh? I'd need for you and two or three others to volunteer to do the investigation in the case and the legal research."

"Yeah, I'd like to work on it." Josh Delcambre scribbled down a few notes on his legal pad. "I think one of the guys shot was a Catholic priest, right?"

"He was a Catholic Brother. Technically, they're not ordained as priests. But he was a member of the Catholic religious community, and lived at the housing project, or close by."

"Anyone else interested? Louis Bishop, the sixteen-year-old who was charged, drifts from home to home. One week he may be at his grand-mother's and the next will find him at this aunt's or a friend's. But, technically, I believe he'll qualify for our program. He certainly fits into the poverty guidelines."

Two more students, Melissa Granger and Lauren Acevedo, raised their hands.

Emma was pleased with her volunteers. Raised in Mid-City New Orleans, Melissa had an ease with the city and culture that was all still new to Emma. Melissa's father was the first African American neuro-surgeon hired at Tabor Medical Center and was now the head of the department. Melissa was a good law student, a warm and empathetic person who understood, in a beat, the emotional energy that ignited a case. She'd make a great trial attorney, to the regret of her father. He'd hoped to sway her toward the medical profession. His loss was now Emma's gain.

Josh was equally impressive. Married, and the father of two, Josh's background included a Master's of Social Work. He was thoughtful, thorough, and eager to learn. The energy he brought to the classroom was infectious.

Emma had interacted less with Lauren, but she knew she had a background in TV journalism. Lauren was poised and charismatic. Emma suspected she was still polishing her skills for the major TV networks and a law degree would enhance her ability to land one of those jobs. Emma also had a feeling Lauren would be great at questioning witnesses and thought the case could benefit from Lauren's skill set.

"Good. We have our group. One other thing, article 305(A) of the Children's Code provides that the jurisdiction of the juvenile court disappears when a juvenile, who's at least fifteen years old, is accused of certain crimes, including murder. Juveniles charged with committing those crimes are tried as adults. In Louis's case, the DA chose to push through a quick indictment with the grand jury. Their finding of probable cause immediately divested jurisdiction from juvenile court and transferred it to criminal court, so Louis will be tried as an adult. And the DA could seek the death penalty." The class began to murmur. "St. Stanislaus doesn't allow law students to try capital cases. But, if the DA chooses to pursue the death penalty, you'd do all of the trial prep, and motion practice. You'd interview the client and witnesses, help work the case up, do research. And you could attend the trial."

Emma scanned the classroom for signs of confusion or distress. Seeing none, she proceeded.

"Today we'll need to drive out to Orleans Parish prison to meet with Louis and get his authority to proceed. I also want to drop by the St. Francis of Assisi Mission house and visit the scene of the crime. Does anyone have time in their schedule to come along?"

Josh raised his hand again.

"Okay, Josh. Looks like it's just you and me. We'll gather all we can and report back to Lauren and Melissa.

"Before we go, I'd like you to keep a few things in mind as you make your way through the discovery process and conduct your investigations. What possible connections could there be to sixteen-year-old Louis and the two men who were killed? Did they have a relationship of any kind? Did they even know each other? If the men were murdered, what could the motive have been? Maybe it was a random act, instead. But we should all look for any thread that could tie Louis to Mr. Sam Maureau, and Brother Reginald Antoine."

Chapter Three

Emma and Josh headed out to view the scene of the murder, and even though an alternative route down Magazine Street would have been a little shorter, and traffic may have been lighter, she ignored Josh's curious glance, and chose the drive down St. Charles Avenue.

Emma relished the elegant old boulevard, some of which was still paved in cobblestones. The canopy of two hundred-year-old oaks that lined the street, dappling it with shade on the hottest of days, and its stately homes, had once defined New Orleans to her. She loved the city and its clanging street cars bringing people to work in uptown mansions or to downtown high-rise buildings. But she couldn't square such beauty with the sort of poverty which could be found right around the corner from nearly any destination in the city. Whether by design or accident, a pattern had developed in New Orleans's neighborhoods. One street would host dozens of mansions, painted in candy-like shades, or in creamy-white Greek-revival tones. All behemoths called the "Painted Ladies," the homes carried annual property taxes that exceeded the yearly take-home pay of most middle-class families. But around the corner from the charming opulence of St. Charles, many families lived in destitution. The disparity of wealth was alarming.

Emma and Josh were headed to see Brother Moore of the St. Francis of Assisi Mission House, only a few blocks from where the shootings occurred at the Redemption before meeting with Louis. Emma was not looking forward to the visit.

"Are we expected?" Josh flipped through his scant notes.

Josh's question jolted Emma back to her task. "Yes, I spoke to Brother

Moore before class today. He has to be upset by Brother Antoine's death, but he told us to come by anyway. I have a few questions for him."

Emma was glad Josh had agreed to come along to meet Brother Moore and to interview Louis. In his thirties, Josh was a little older and more mature than most of the other students at the school. Yet he still appeared boyish, with tousled sandy hair, and a freckled, upturned nose. He always had a ready smile. Emma met Josh's wife, Tracy, at one of the law school Christmas parties. She worked as a nurse at a local hospital and supported the family financially. She'd overheard Josh's complaints about finances and knew they were tight. Yet, even though he was the primary caretaker of their two toddlers, he still managed to have the time he needed to prepare for class and exams. He and his wife were a good team.

Emma spent her law school days frazzled from too little sleep, too few hours devoted to study, and dashing between her work schedule and time with the twins. But that was life as a single mom. If you were a mom, and had goals or ambitions, something was going to suffer, and it was usually sleep.

Emma kept an eye out for marriages that worked, and Josh's clearly did. She knew there wasn't a formula for a happy relationship, but she liked to watch for clues in the successful ones. Josh and Tracy respected each other. Law school was their mutual goal, not Josh's alone. Their relationship gave her hope—a feeling that she and Ren, her boyfriend, might just make it after all. She'd like that. She'd certainly like to see him more. Have him in the same town. Develop mutual goals.

Emma and Josh rounded the corner of St. Charles to First Street and its Creole townhouses, sophisticated and lovely, even in states of disrepair. Some of the homes were beautiful, even though they were falling apart. Stopping sometimes, even in the middle of a run, Emma would stare at them for minutes at a time, studying every detail. She never tired of the city's architecture.

She and Josh took a left on Magazine and drove down the shop-filled street to Felicity, at the edge of the projects. The mission house was across the street from the Redemption.

The St. Francis of Assisi Mission House, which stood at the entrance of the Redemption, had seen better days. Home to an order of Christian Brothers since the 1950s, the small home had once been painted a vivid white and trimmed in a cheerful apple green. Most of the levity of its earlier years was gone, leaving behind a residue of flakes and chips and the sagging bones of its former self. The outside of the home was covered with community announcements and faded, once-cheerful banners proclaiming past events. Living, working, and counseling at the Redemption, the Brothers were dedicated to the community, never failing in their endeavor to promote goodwill, but struggling to make a difference.

"Come on in while I speak to Brother Moore. You need to meet him, too."

Josh nodded and stepped out of the car.

Brother Moore came to the door after two quick knocks. He was as pale and colorless as the faded house where he and his order lived. Even his eyes were a pallid and watery blue. But he welcomed Emma and Josh with an outstretched hand.

"We've been expecting you, Professor Thornton. Sorry you had to come here in such tragic circumstances." Brother Moore shook Emma's hand, then Josh's.

Emma stepped into what was once the living room of a cozy home, noting that it was now an intake facility for a growing number of community concerns and organizations. Catholic Charities funded the majority of the programs offered there, and financial assistance was the motivation of all but a few who entered the building.

"We're so sorry for your loss." She grasped Father Moore's hand again. "Juvenile Services notified us of the murder. I believe it was a few blocks over?"

He pointed with his thumb. "It was off Felicity Street. A block and a half from here."

"Dean Munoz suggested that I speak to you before we officially agree to take the case. Josh is one of the clinic students who has agreed to help."

"There's not much I can say that juvenile services hasn't already told you." Brother Moore rubbed his chin. "The other man who was killed along with

Brother Antoine was in his mid-thirties, I believe, but I don't know him. Louis Bishop's grandmother lives close to where the murders occurred, right there on Felicity Street." He moved his hand in the direction of the street, then gestured for them to sit down.

"What was Brother Antoine doing out at night in that area, or do you know?" Emma walked toward an over-stuffed chair and sat down. Josh and Brother Moore sat down across from her.

"He was visiting a young lady who had asked him to help her complete forms for a scholarship to Our Lady of Fatima High School. It was the sort of thing he did."

"Do you know any of the people involved other than Brother Antoine—Louis, the young boy they've arrested, or anyone else?"

"I don't really know Louis, but I know something of his family. Louis's cousin, Marcus, is one of the biggest drug lords in the city. You can always bet drugs are involved, one way or another in a shooting here, and there are rumors drugs were involved in this one."

"You said something about rumors. Did you speak to people in the neighborhood about the shooting?"

"There's always a lot of talk, some of it you can rely on, some of it I'd take with a grain of salt. We've lived here a long time and have gotten to know a lot of people. So…" Brother Moore shrugged. "It's not so unusual they'd talk to us."

"Can you give us any names? Do you think they'd also speak to us?"

"What I can do is get together with them and see if they'd be willing to speak with you. But I have to warn you, not everything you hear will be reliable. Consider yourself forewarned." Brother Moore managed a weak smile.

Emma nodded. "Can you give us directions to where it happened? We're on our way to see Louis, but thought we'd check out the scene of the murders first. We're going to drive over to save time. We're going by to see Louis afterward, and Josh needs to get back home by a certain time. So do I, really."

Brother Moore pointed in the direction of the area. "Once you're in the projects, take the first left, and then your next right. The shootings took place between the first two buildings on your right. Louis's grandmother's apartment is the building on the right."

* * *

As Emma walked to her car, she scanned the neighborhood. It was late morning, and there was little activity on the streets. It was a school day and there were no children playing outside. A few younger mothers were out pushing baby strollers. Two women passed next to Emma and eyed her suspiciously.

Emma had seen her fair share of crack addicts at the law school's homeless clinic and had developed an ability to spot the users. Most were thin. Their skin took on a gray and dusty appearance, as if they were about to crumble. Sometimes their mouths were burned or peeling from the pipes. The two women passing Emma reminded her of the addicts she'd known. She watched them meander down the street, hollowed out, mere shells of themselves, moving in strange off-kilter gaits. They were vulnerable, easy targets for drug dealers, sex traffickers, pimps, and loan sharks, all those who preyed on the poor.

She detected the aroma of sizzling Andouille sausage nearby, and it could be her imagination, or the fact that she was hungry, the smell of biscuits baking in the oven. The front steps of an apartment off to one side was graced by an older woman braiding a squirming toddler's hair, paying no mind to the wincing face below her masterpiece. Begonias and toys dotted porch steps here and there in colorful little patches—tiny flags of personal identity in a sea of monochromatic, shabby, uniformity.

They drove to the scene of the crime. Emma had asked Josh to bring along a camera and a measuring tape so they could conduct an abbreviated investigation. They'd get a forensics report from the DA, which should contain a sketch of the site with measurements, but it never hurt to get a good look of the actual location.

When they pulled up, Emma knew forensics had completed their tasks, or a guard would still be on duty. Most of the tape and crime scene paraphernalia had been cleaned up, although a few yellow plastic remnants still fluttered on the ground. Josh popped his Cannon in his jacket pocket and they walked over to the sidewalk to take a look at the scene. Blood stained the porous concrete, its rusty color partially faded by sunlight and recent rains. Only a faint remnant of the light blue chalk lines which had once traced the body of Brother Antoine remained. Emma pointed to the tracings and Josh snapped several photographs of the sidewalk.

Emma waved her hand at the ground. "I'll also need you to measure the distance from the bloodstain to the curb, then to the edge of the sidewalk."

Emma crept onto the grassy section, keeping an eye out for any clue which could indicate where the other body may have gone down. Then she saw a tiny blue flag and realized it must have been used by forensics to mark the second body's location. The grass in the area of the flag was flattened, and she also noticed dark markings, perhaps blood, on the ground close by.

Emma motioned again to Josh. "We'll need a few photos from this area too. Make sure you get a close up of the flag and the grass around that area. You'll need photos and measurements of the distance between the two bodies."

"Understood." Josh walked through the grassy section, and using the bench in the area as a fixed point, focused the camera on the scene, and took a series of photographs at various angles. He took measurements. Then, getting as close to the ground as he could, snapped photos at various angles between the bloodstain and the blue flag.

"Got it." Josh slipped the camera in his front shirt pocket.

"Think you'll be able to find where the bodies fell if everything fades and the flag blows away?"

"Yeah, I should be able to."

Emma motioned for Josh to follow her and began walking back to her car. She could hear distant laughing and the ruckus of children at play.

"We were lucky to have gotten those photos. We'll have to get a ballistics expert on board to see if it was possible for one shooter to pull this off. I'm also wondering if the body that landed on the sidewalk was accidentally in the line of fire—an innocent bystander. We'll have to see what the reports have to say."

Chapter Four

Emma rounded the corner at Tulane Avenue. Orleans Parish Criminal Courthouse was on her left, and the parish prison, known as Central Lockup, was located behind the older, monolithic structure. Even on the brightest of days, that two-block stretch of the city made Emma feel as if the sun had never bothered to crawl up the sky.

As she turned, the courthouse loomed overhead, casting a dark shadow over the parking lot. Bail bondsmen lurked on the outskirts of the lot in tiny wooden shacks, open for business, twenty-four, seven. The rust-stained Art Deco exterior of the courthouse conjured up images of Gotham City or Chicago in the 1930s. Emma half expected to see Batman swinging from its towers or Al Capone peering around one of the pillars of the place.

In contrast, the prison, set a block behind the courthouse, was a modern, institutional structure. It seemed less imposing, although its reputation was far more severe. Housing as many as 6,500 inmates, the prison had a reputed history of cruelty and neglect. It was no place for a sixteen-year-old boy.

"So, they just brought him straight here? They didn't even start at juvenile court?" Josh unclipped his seatbelt as Emma pulled into the parking lot.

"He may have been brought to the juvenile holding tank when he was first arrested, but since he's already been indicted and charged with two felony murders, they brought him over here." Emma raised her eyebrows as she glanced sideways toward Josh. "That's the law now."

Emma parked the car and locked up. Passing through the metal detectors as they entered the building, she showed the intake officer her bar card and asked to see Louis Bishop. They would meet him in the area reserved for attorney-client visits.

Emma was startled by the room's expanse and its stark white floors and walls. She squinted in response to the glaring neon light hanging overhead. The room looked and felt like the inside of a refrigerator. She'd have to remember to bring a jacket the next time she visited.

"Josh, I'll need you to take notes while I speak to Louis." Emma sat down on a cold metal chair, wishing she'd worn trousers. "But, jump in if you have a question, too."

There were a few additional metal folding chairs scattered about the room. Josh dragged a couple over, placed them next to Emma, then sat down next to her.

Emma heard a shuffling sound and glanced up. A shackled young man entered the room wearing an orange jumpsuit. He glared at Emma and Josh for a moment, then hung his head and continued his shuffle toward the chairs. The name "BISHOP" was scrawled across the right front pocket of his uniform in crude black magic marker letters. The young man kept his eyes fixed on the floor as he walked across, only glancing up when he approached the chairs.

Emma immediately noticed the flat look in Louis's eyes, as if all feelings had been drained from him. Strange for a sixteen-year-old, but perhaps not for one charged with the murder of two men. His deep russet skin tones made the downy soft fuzz along his upper lip nearly disappear. He was so young he hadn't started to shave. His face, slightly marred by teenage acne, would be handsome someday. Although he hadn't reached his full adult height, he was beginning to develop what was sure to become well-toned, muscular strength. Obviously unbathed for days, pieces of dust and debris were stuck in his closely cropped, densely curly hair. Emma's heart ached at the sight of him.

The deputy brought Louis over to his chair, then lumbered back to the entrance of the room. Indicating that he should sit next to them, Emma moved her chair and squared it in front of Louis's so that she could speak directly to him.

"I'm Emma Thornton, and this is Josh Delcambre." She hesitated and smiled, trying to assure Louis that she was a friend. She knew he had to be frightened. "Do you agree that Josh and I and other students from the St. Stanislaus University Law School clinic can represent you in the charges filed against you by the Orleans Parish District Attorney?" She could hear the clanging of an iron-barred door closing, and people shouting in the background as she spoke.

Louis nodded.

"Is that a 'yes', Louis?"

"Yes."

"There are three students assigned to your case. Josh is one." Josh extended his hand to Louis. Louis solemnly shook it. "All of the students are supervised by me. I assign tasks to them, like research, or motion writing. Sometimes, they'll file documents in the court too. But, I will be the one who will go to court for you, and so will the dean of the law school, Dean Georges Munoz. I will introduce him to you later. He couldn't come today because he's out of town. Do you agree that students can work on your case?"

He nodded. "Yes."

"Do you have any questions?" Emma moved in an attempt to make eye contact with Louis.

"Do you know when I can get out of here?"

"That's a tough one. Because you've been charged with two counts of first-degree murder, the judge set your bail at $250,000, which is high. You'd have to raise quite a bit of cash just to pay the bondsman. I calculated it at about $32,500. Do you or any of your family members, your mother or father, have access to that kind of money?"

Louis shook his head.

"Then making bail is not possible. And paying the bondsman back might be very difficult for you down the road, too. I think you need to prepare to stay here until we can get you out. I'm sorry, Louis." Emma clasped her hands in her lap. "But we're going to do everything we can to help you. First, we need to get some information. I'd like to make sure that you understand why we're here. Can you tell me?"

Louis nodded.

"In words. What do you think we'll do for you, Louis? As your lawyers."

"You'll get me out of here."

"Well. Maybe. We'll try. What we'll really do is represent you in court. And we'll defend you. Do you know what that means?"

Louis shook his head.

"We need to find out from you what happened that night, and then we'll conduct our own investigation. Once we're at trial, we'll show the court and the jury everything that might help them understand why you're not guilty of the crime. Do you understand?"

Louis nodded.

"Let's start by having you answer another question. Do you understand why you're here?" Emma flipped through a few pages in her legal pad.

"Yeah, cops think I shot a man." Louis cracked his knuckles.

"The cops think you shot two men. Did you know that?" Emma jotted down notes as he spoke.

Louis nodded.

"Well, did you shoot Brother Antoine, or Sam Maureau?"

"Nah." He sniffed and rubbed his nose.

"Do you know why the cops think you did it?"

Louis made eye contact with Emma for the first time since they'd arrived, holding her gaze for several seconds. Emma was unnerved. There was something in his eye she couldn't place. A secret? Something he didn't want her to know? It was obvious he wasn't going to volunteer much, and Emma could sense he didn't trust her. He had the same guarded manner as some of the homeless war veterans she'd met through her clinic.

He shook his head.

"Can you tell me what happened that night, Louis?" Emma picked up her pen, poised to take notes.

"I don't know nuthin.'" Louis hesitated. "The gun the cops got from under the apartments wasn't mine. I threw mine in the river." He cracked his knuckles again.

"Let's back up. Who was there that night?"

"Marcus, and my cousins Dwayne and Georgie. And that guy Marcus wanted to meet. I don't know his name."

"Was Brother Antoine a part of your group?"

"Nah. He wasn't."

"Do you know Brother Antoine or the other man who was killed, Sam Maureau?"

"No, I don't. I never met either one of them."

"But you know who they are?"

"Yeah. Alicia, my cousin, hangs out sometime with Brother Antoine, and my other cousin, Marcus, hangs out with the other guy. But I don't know them."

"How do you know what gun the cops got, and why did you throw a gun in the river? What happened?"

"I just know they didn't get my gun. Marcus said he'd meet me at my grandmother's and to make sure I had my piece. But I didn't use it." Louis wiped the palms of his hands on his orange jumper.

"If you didn't use it, why did you throw it in the river, Louis?"

"Mmm. Got freaked." He shrugged. "I knew the cops would be looking for everyone that was there that night. Someone like me can't be caught with a gun on 'em."

"Why did you have a gun in the first place? Where'd you get it?" Emma peered at Louis but couldn't make eye contact.

"I always had a gun," he said, casting his eyes toward the floor. "I had one since I was a kid. Marcus gave it to me. Said I might need it and learnin' how to use it was the first step to becomin' a man."

"How old were you when you got the gun?"

He cocked his head to the side. "Ten. Somethin' like that."

"Have you ever used it?"

"Nah." He shook his head. "Never had to."

"What happened the night of the murder? Why did Brother Antoine and that other man get shot?"

"I don't know nothin' about what happened." He cracked his knuckles, turned around and pretended to look at writing on the wall.

"What about the gun the cops found? Whose gun was that?" Josh interjected as he scribbled furiously in his notebook.

"All I know is that crack 'ho, Tamika Jones, told them cops I threw it under Mama Ruby's apartment. She told them where the gun was. I'm telling you I ain't had nothin' to do with that gun they found, and I didn't kill nobody."

"Mama Ruby is your grandmother?"

"Yeah."

"Who is Tamika Jones?"

"She's always hangin' around Marcus. If Marcus around, she around. And like I say. She a crack 'ho."

"Was Tamika there that night?"

He shrugged. "I dunno."

"Wouldn't she had to have been there to have said that to the police?"

"I don't know. She could've just been watching from somewhere."

Sweat beaded along Louis's upper lip. Then small drops appeared along his forehead and hairline. He wasn't telling her everything. Marcus probably warned Louis not to speak to anyone about that night. It wouldn't surprise Emma if Marcus had threatened Louis, too. Unless she could work some kind of miracle, she wasn't going to hear any of the specifics of the night from this kid. Not yet, anyway. But if she played it right, that would change.

"Do you know any telephone numbers for Marcus, or Tamika, or any of your other family members?"

Louis nodded. "I know some."

Emma ripped off a piece of paper from her notebook and handed it to Louis along with a pencil.

Louis hunched over the paper and wrote down a couple of telephone numbers, one for his mother and another for Mama Ruby.

"What about Dwayne and Georgie? Do you have telephone numbers for them?"

"You can get 'em at Mama Ruby's. Just call them there."

"How about Marcus? Do you know his number?"

"Nah." He shrugged. "But you can try this." He wrote down another number on the sheet and wrote Marcus's name next to it. "It might not work."

* * *

On the ride home from work that evening, Emma couldn't help but think about Louis. She hadn't been able to reach him during the interview. He was nervous. So nervous she'd been afraid he was going to break the bones in his knuckles, he'd cracked them so many times. There were many layers to his life, and right now she could only imagine what they were. It was obvious, if only from his facial expressions and reactions, that he'd known some cruelty, some pain. Exposure to drug dealing and murder would have a tendency to age a person beyond his years. But it was more than that. And the problem extended beyond fear of reprisal from Marcus. Something had happened to Louis. Something very hurtful.

His mother seemed to care about him, but she hadn't been there for him for one reason or another. Who helped him with his schoolwork? Did he even go to school regularly? Where did he sleep at night? Who made sure his clothes were clean? His grandmother prepared some meals, but did he eat there every day? What happens to a kid who grows up in an environment where no one seems to care?

Emma had had problems with Billy and Bobby's father. He didn't keep in touch with them, and there were consequences to that. She'd always thought one parent who cared would be enough, but she'd discovered that wasn't true. She was often working or tired. She left the boys by themselves for a few hours while she was at work. They occasionally acted out, she suspected, because their dad wasn't around. She knew the lack of his presence hurt them. And it was cruel. Emma blamed his absence for some of the trouble the twins found themselves in over the years. Lately, they'd been sneaking out of the house when she wasn't there, which was strictly against the rules, and dangerous. She thought she smelled cigarette smoke in their room the other day. And they were only twelve.

She pulled into her parking space next to the sandwich shop. She and her sons lived in the apartment above the shop on the second and third floors. The boys loved it since it was close to the parade route during Mardi Gras and had a balcony. Floats passed close by the front of the place, insuring them a good spot along the parade route even if they slept late. They always caught their fair share of beads. The boys also had the entire third floor to themselves, which they thought was cool. Still, this was New Orleans; no place was safe after dark these days. She and the boys never walked outside at night except to hop in the car if they were leaving to go somewhere, or to take out the garbage. The Big Easy was only easy during daylight hours.

* * *

Emma pulled out her favorite copper pot. She decided to make one of Billy and Bobby's favorites. Shrimp creole. They loved it, and she found cooking therapeutic. Chopping onions, in particular, was cathartic for her, and shrimp creole called for four medium. Lost in thought as she chopped, tears flowing down her face from the sting of the onions, Emma realized Louis's life was hanging by a thread. The death penalty was a serious reality in Louisiana. She and the students had their work cut out for them.

After she added basil, oregano and garlic, the aroma filled the apartment. Billy and Bobby scrambled down the metal staircase.

"What's wrong? Your face looks all red and puffy." Billy walked close to Emma, staring at her eyes and face. "I can tell you've been crying."

"It's nothing. Onions." Emma smiled and ruffled his hair.

"What's for dinner?" Bobby lifted the lid on the pot and peered inside.

"Your favorite, but it won't be ready for hours yet. So, go do your homework. No TV until it's done."

She got kisses from both boys who clambered back up the stairs. She dumped the contents from several cans of tomatoes into the sautéed onion mixture and stirred. Dinner would be ready in a couple of hours. She had time to relax and watch the news or read a book. But all she could do was think about Louis and his upcoming trial.

She decided to see what the twins were doing and trudged up the spiral staircase, something she did periodically to clean their smelly boy things and air out the place. When she reached the top, neither twin was at his desk. She knew immediately where they were. There was access to the roof of the old gabled building through their bathroom window. Emma walked to the bathroom, looked out of the open window, and sure enough, she could see the edge of a blanket stretched across the ancient tile roof and the boys' feet resting against a downspout as they lay watching the sun start its descent across the horizon. She had to admit the Episcopal Church across the street looked beautiful awash in the glowing colors of the sunset, especially from their angle. But their angle—dangling from the roof—was dangerous, a fact which didn't faze them one bit.

"What in the world are you two doing up here again? I've told you to stay off of the roof. Get on down, right now."

"Oh, Mom." Bobby turned around and scampered back through the bathroom window. Billy followed, dragging the blanket they'd been lying on behind him.

Emma knew her boys well, but there was a certain something in them that was foreign to her. She instinctively sought safety, at least where they were concerned, but a little danger excited them. They would always cook up something when they were together.

"The next time this happens you're grounded."

Emma suspected Louis's motivations were far different than her boys'. She doubted danger excited him as much, but thought, instead, he merely responded to his environment. Survival was Louis's primary goal. He lived in a world that was more dangerous than she or her boys could ever imagine. And that danger was not of his making.

Chapter Five

Lauren Acevedo was seated at the front of the small classroom where Emma met with the students from her homelessness clinic. She raised her hand.

"Even though I volunteered to help work up Louis's case, I'm wondering whether we should help out a sixteen-year-old who, I would bet, is a crack-head." Lauren's words stopped Emma as she was writing the day's assignment on the board. Emma had never trusted Lauren's intentions. She'd always suspected Lauren signed up for the homeless clinic to get her poverty law credit out of the way. But she hadn't anticipated Lauren's reaction to Louis. Lauren was a journalism graduate. Emma had assumed she shared a more open-minded view typical of most people her age. The fact that she didn't was surprising. A couple of years ago someone making a statement like Lauren's might have upset her, but she'd learned to deal with arguments like that. Now she knew if she asked the right questions, Lauren could show everyone why a case might be important. If Lauren learned anything in the process, that was lagniappe, as they said in New Orleans—a little something extra.

"Louis is as entitled to a defense as any other criminal defendant, don't you think? Someone give me the name of a well-known criminal case." Emma scanned the range of hands flying in the air. "Melissa?"

"There are the O.J. Simpson and the John Gotti trials. The Simpson trial was even on TV."

Emma turned around and wrote "O.J. Simpson" and "John Gotti" on the board.

"Does anyone here believe that the wealth of either of those men made them more entitled to a fair trial or representation than Louis Bishop?" Emma noted the heads shaking no around the classroom.

"Lauren? What do you think?"

"I guess not."

"We don't know that he's the 'crack-head' you described, but even if he has that problem, wouldn't you say he's entitled to a fair trial?" Emma moved out from behind the podium.

"I guess I think people should pay their own way." Lauren flushed. "Why should we provide a free defense for a drug addict? Both Simpson and Gotti paid for their defense. That's the difference." Lauren crossed her legs and began swinging her left foot.

Emma nodded. "I understand, but you missed the sense of what I was saying, which was not as much about money as it was about something else. Can anyone identify what's missing here?"

Josh raised his hand. "Everyone's entitled to a fair trial and representation. But you can't get a fair trial unless you're represented by competent counsel. Both O.J. Simpson and John Gotti could afford excellent attorneys. Louis Bishop can't. So unless he gets help from us or from the public defender's office, he won't get a fair trial."

"That's right." Emma walked to the whiteboard and picked up a marker. "The Sixth Amendment provides for the right to effective assistance of counsel, and lawyers must be appointed for defendants unable to afford attorneys. You should have known that, Lauren. That's basic constitutional law. There's a slew of cases on the issue. We have one hundred and twenty days after the arraignment to get ready for trial, and there's a lot to do. Those of you who agreed to work on Louis's case will get no more credit for it than for any other, even though it's complicated, and could be more time-consuming. So, I've decided to lighten the load for the three who've agreed to take on Louis's case by eliminating some of their other class assignments." Emma wrote *Josh, Melissa* and *Lauren* on the board. "If you three are certain you'd like to work on the case, which means not objecting to the fact that Louis may or may not be addicted to crack cocaine, I'd like you to stay after

30

class for a few minutes. If you have any reservations about this work, it would be best if you withdrew now."

* * *

When class was over, Emma glanced over the room, surprised to see that all three students were still in their seats. Motioning for them to move forward to the front of the classroom, she handed them a page of names and phone numbers. Although she suspected the students were ready to go home, they appeared alert and eager to participate, even Lauren.

"Louis gave us the information you see on the sheet. Some are witnesses. Some are family members. I'm going to assign a few to each of you.

"The DA could send out the Death Penalty Notice in Louis's case any day now. It's rare that anyone other than a physician holds a person's life in his hands. But lawyers who represent defendants in death penalty cases do just that. Everything we do in this case could impact Louis's life."

Emma moved to the whiteboard and wrote *Stages in a Capital Case*.

"You already know the first stage, even if you haven't taken the capital punishment seminar. It's the same stage as all criminal trials. What's that, Josh?"

"Whether the defendant is guilty?"

"That's right, the guilt phase. The prosecutor must prove Louis is guilty, beyond a reasonable doubt, of first-degree murder. A lesser verdict carries a lighter sentence. It should be obvious to you at this point what we'd have to do to work up that phase of the trial. Melissa, want to give us the run down?"

"Talk to the witnesses that were at the scene. Maybe talk to some forensic experts on ballistics, and whether they can match up the bullet found at the scene to the gun the police have."

"Yep. We'll need to challenge the state's evidence. For instance, we may want to work on ways to show that Brother Antoine's killing was accidental, that he was an innocent bystander. That no one had any intention of shooting Brother Antoine. That could be an important defense in several ways."

"Does anyone know the second phase of a capital trial? It's not that different from a regular criminal case, either."

The students exchanged glances as she wrote *Penalty Phase* on the whiteboard.

"During this phase the prosecution may put on evidence of 'aggravating circumstances.' Who can tell us what that means? You should know this from criminal procedure."

Melissa raised her hand.

"Aggravating circumstances are really bad crimes which accompany the murders, like a kidnapping and a murder, or an armed robbery and a murder."

"What do you think the prosecutor might put on as evidence of an aggravating circumstance in this case?"

The three students exchanged glances. Melissa shook her head.

"More than one person was killed. In Louisiana, the capital punishment statute can be triggered by the 'knowing killing' of more than one person. And Louis has been charged with two murders. So, what do we need to do?"

"Show that Brother Antoine's death was accidental? That he was an innocent bystander?" Josh said.

"That's right. Now you're thinking like a defense attorney."

"Defense attorneys also get to put on mitigating evidence. This will explain to the jury factors they must consider before deciding whether to give the defendant the death penalty or a life sentence. If a defendant suffered abuse as a child, or if he was under the influence of another person, the jury may take those circumstances under consideration when they make their decision about sentencing."

Melissa raised her hand. "Is mental illness also considered mitigating evidence?"

"This is a mitigation of sentencing issue, not a 'not guilty by reason of insanity' standard of proof. So, we can put on proof of learning issues, intellectual disabilities, mental illness that doesn't rise to the level of mitigating guilt, and something called 'deprived backgrounds.' What do you think deprived backgrounds would mean?"

"Maybe proof that a person grew up in a family that didn't show him love, or didn't show him right from wrong? Something like that?" Melissa said.

"That would work. Anything we can use to show how or why a person would have difficulties making good choices can be used to show a solid reason for the jury to consider a mitigation in sentencing. In Louis's situation, what might that be?"

"Louis doesn't have a home, or a certain place to stay every night. He floats around from house to house. That would make life difficult for him." Josh glanced at the board and jotted down a few notes.

"Yep. Absolutely. Anyone else?"

Melissa raised her hand. "Louis doesn't have his dad in his life, so I'm thinking it would be easy to fall under the influence of an older cousin."

"Good point. Also, we can use the fact that Louis doesn't have a prior criminal record. That can mitigate against the death penalty. All of these factors can be used. If Louis has learning disabilities, we can use that too. He's still considered guilty, but these factors mitigate against the punishment of death. Are y'all with me?"

Emma surveyed the small group for signs of confusion. Seeing none, she continued.

"So, we'll need to speak to Louis's family members, school teachers, and counselors to see if we can develop a theme for our mitigation argument, right?"

Emma walked around the classroom. "Don't worry. After we start digging in, it'll all come together."

Emma handed out an interview schedule with the list of witnesses and assignments to each student, hoping she hadn't overwhelmed them with the gravity of Louis's case. Their job was sobering and it could be heartbreaking. She hoped they were up to the task.

"I'm going to interview Louis's mom in the morning. If I can get the name of Louis's school and her permission to get his records, I'd like to go there tomorrow afternoon and interview his counselor. Would anyone like to come along with me on either interview?"

Josh raised his hand. "I don't have any afternoon classes and can make the school interview."

"Okay, Josh. If I get what I need, we'll head out tomorrow." Emma paused when she noticed Josh's frown.

"Do you have a question?"

"What about Marcus?"

"What do you mean?"

"Why isn't he on the list? He was at the scene of the shooting, wasn't he?"

"He was."

"Then shouldn't we meet with him?" Josh crossed his arms across his chest, his body language immediately giving away his defensiveness.

"I thought about it, but can't imagine he'd agree to see us. I also wouldn't want to jeopardize your safety by having you contact him. He's a known drug dealer, supposedly running the largest gang in the city. It wouldn't be safe."

"But it's necessary."

"I'm not so sure. What's he going to tell us? He'd hardly tell us who shot the victims. And I don't think we have his actual phone number. It's probably a pager. So I didn't put him on the list."

"I don't think we're doing our job if we don't interview him. We could try going by his pawn shop."

"Nope. We're not doing that. If we do anything at all, we'll set up an appointment with him here. I see your point. But right now, I don't want to jeopardize the well-being of any student by scheduling a meeting with Marcus. The less he knows about what we're doing and who we are, the better. What's he going to tell us—that he'd planned the murder of Mr. Maureau all along? That Louis had nothing to do with the shooting? I don't think so." Emma crossed her arms and shook her head. "But I'll think about it."

Chapter Six

Sandra Bishop, Louis's mother, stepped into Emma's office at the clinic, holding the hand of a beautiful child Emma mistook for a girl.

"That happens a lot," she said, quietly correcting Emma's blunder. "I just like long hair." Ms. Bishop gently caressed the multitude of shoulder-length braids that flowed along the little boy's back.

Sandra Bishop's face and hands were tinged with gray, and cracked, especially around her mouth. She kept her large, heavy-lidded eyes downcast. Scarcely moving her lips when she spoke, her voice barely rose above a whisper, as if she was afraid to speak. Her clothes hung from her body, draped and sagging, at least two sizes too big for her tiny frame. Her frazzled, rumpled appearance was in stark contrast to her fastidious young son's. Her hands, tender and kind, touched the little boy's back.

The tyke, who appeared no older than four, was dressed in the latest style of the day, a brightly striped, long sleeved polo shirt and baggy pants, complete with miniature suede boots, untied ever so fashionably. He looked up at his mother and smiled.

Emma was stunned. Louis was so unkempt. His hair hadn't seen a comb in months. His nails were jagged and dirty and his face hadn't been washed in days if not weeks. Sandra Bishop must have spent hundreds on the hair and outfit of her younger son. But, to be fair, Emma wasn't sure how often Louis got a chance to shower in prison. Somehow she doubted it was a daily occurrence.

"His name is Myron." She smiled proudly.

"Ms. Bishop, I'd like to ask you some questions about Louis." Emma directed Louis's mother and younger brother to take a seat in the two chairs placed in front of her desk.

"I don't know much about him over the past five to six years. He hadn't lived with me since he was ten."

"Why not? Have you been out of touch?"

"When Louis was ten or so, I hit some bad times. Started usin' a lot. It wasn't good for him to be around me." She looked down at her hands. "So Mama Ruby said she'd have him come live with her. And he stays there most days, unless he sleeps on Juanita's couch. That's my sister, Juanita Bishop."

"But things are better now?"

"Yeah. I met Myron's daddy and things got better." She smiled.

"Why didn't you have Louis come back to stay with you after that?"

"He didn't really want to." She clenched her hands together. "He likes it at Mama Ruby's. And by that time, he was old enough to choose."

"Do you know why he stays at Juanita's house some nights?"

"I think he gets picked on a little."

Myron pulled a toy car out of his pocket and started scooting it along the arm of his chair.

"Who picks on him?"

"Mostly Marcus."

"Do you know why Marcus picks on him?"

"Marcus can be mean. He can be good sometimes too. But not always. And he don't like Louis drawin' and stuff. So he make fun of him."

"Louis likes to draw?"

"Yeah! He's real good. Especially at drawing clothes—fashion things. He and my mama even used to draw out patterns for clothes. My mama was a seamstress for D.H. Holmes—downtown—for a long time. Then she retired and moved into the Redemption. Louis learned a lot from her."

"Do you know if he still works on making patterns with your mom?"

"That stopped, I know."

"Why?"

"Marcus told him that was a woman's job. But Louis kept on doing it.

Marcus kidded him for a while, then it got kinda nasty."

"What do you mean?"

"He started punching Louis when he saw him doin' stuff for Mama Ruby. Then one day, my sister told me Marcus beat him up. Called him names and all 'a that. Louis has pretty much stopped working with Mama, but I bet he still draws all those clothes."

Emma jotted down notes in her notepad. "Does anyone else stay at your mother's house?"

"Well, there could be a whole bunch of people there. Sometimes Alicia's there. She's my baby sister's child. She comes over to practice the piano some, but she usually stay at Juanita's. Marcus's at my momma's a lot, but he don't sleep there. He got his own place. There's Dwayne and Georgie—there's a whole lot of them. I can't name 'em all. Kids is coming and going all the time."

Myron hopped down from his chair and scooted his toy car across the floor. Emma watched it crash into the wall next to Ms. Bishop.

"How often do you see Louis these days?"

"Every once in a while. The last time I saw him, I thought he was using."

Crawling across the floor, Myron retrieved his little car, pivoted about on his seat, and slammed the tiny vehicle into the opposite wall, making a loud crashing sound effect. Ms. Bishop never flinched.

"Why do you say that?" Emma asked.

"He was real jumpy, shaking his knees up and down when he was sitting at the table."

"That could have been something else, couldn't it? Maybe he was nervous, or maybe he didn't feel well."

"It could be, but I don't think so."

"But you've never seen him using drugs, right?"

Sandra Bishop nodded. "That's right."

"What do you think he was using?"

"Crack. And that's somethin' I know about, like I said." She looked at the floor. "I been clean four years now. Since I had Myron." She glanced at the four-year-old and smiled. Even though Myron was well cared for, Ms.

Bishop was oblivious to his behavior, almost as if she was numb.

"Can you tell me what school Louis attends? I'd like to speak to his teachers and get his records, if that's okay with you." Emma handed Ms. Bishop a release to review and pointed to the signature line.

"That's fine. He goes to Fortier, when he go." She reviewed the release and signed it.

"Do you know the names of any of Louis's teachers or counselors, or the principal of the school?"

Ms. Bishop shook her head and placed the pen back on Emma's desk.

"Did Louis have any learning challenges as a child?"

"He had some struggles with readin'. He didn't like to sit still and do stuff at school. Unless he was drawin'."

Myron began scooting his miniature car along the windowsill and waving to students as they walked past.

"Did you know Marcus gave Louis a gun?"

"I don't know about no gun. I ain't never see Louis with no gun."

"Do you know if Louis has ever worked for Marcus?"

"I don't know. He might do a little work for Marcus sometimes. You know, Marcus have that pawn shop. He sees Marcus over at my mama's."

"What sort of work does he do for Marcus?"

"I wouldn't know."

"Would the drugs Louis uses be from Marcus?"

Ms. Bishop shrugged. "If he usin', I'd think that's where he got them."

"Is there anything else you'd like to add about Louis's childhood, or his learning habits?"

"No." She folded her hands in her lap. "'Cept, he don't mean no harm to anyone. He wouldn't a shot no one. He like to kid around and stuff, but he's not mean. He was never a mean child. And, even though he don't want to live with me anymore, I understand. He saw me during some bad times, and I don't blame him. I love him. He's my special boy. Always will be." She wiped a tear from her face.

"I'm sure he is, Ms. Bishop. Thanks so much for coming in today. I'll call if anything develops and we need to speak to you again."

Ms. Bishop nodded, stood up and indicated it was time to go to Myron, who retrieved his tiny toy car from under Emma's desk. They walked out of the door holding hands.

* * *

Dean Munoz was in his office when Emma knocked on the door. He still taught Federal Jurisdiction and constantly researched ideas for upcoming journal articles or new texts. Despite his age, he showed no signs of slowing down. He'd always fought for the underprivileged and had made it a part of his life. He wasn't afraid of a battle, not in war, after having served in World War II, in a courtroom, or in a room full of drug dealers.

"Do you have five minutes?"

"For you, anytime." The Dean waved her in and moved a stack of books from a chair in front of his desk.

"I assigned several witnesses in the Louis Bishop case to my students today. Except for Marcus Bishop. I didn't assign him to anyone, and one of the students is questioning why."

"It's a good question. Why not?"

"I didn't think it would accomplish much of anything. He's not going to admit to shooting anyone, or seeing anything, and I can't imagine he'll give us any valuable information. I wouldn't mind talking to him, but I don't want the students to, and right now they're the ones conducting the interviews. Louis gave me a number for him, but I'd bet it's a pager."

"Why don't you want the students to speak to Marcus?"

"I feel responsible for the students. I have a feeling he might not want us to know everything that happened that night."

"The students all agreed to assume the same responsibilities and duties as an attorney for any of the cases they're assigned to at the clinic, right?"

"That's correct."

"Then you're okay to let them speak to Marcus. But if you still don't want to, you need to go ahead and try that number, even if it's a pager. Why don't you call it and find out?"

"Guess I could. What do I have to lose? The worst he could do is lie."

"That's not true. But just talk to him. At the very least, he's an eyewitness to the shooting. You'd always interview one of those, right?"

"That's right. But we suspect he's much more."

"Any defense attorney would contact and interview an eyewitness to a crime or tort. If Marcus had witnessed a car wreck, you'd interview him, wouldn't you?"

"Of course."

"And, you'd always interview anyone who witnessed a shooting. It just makes sense, doesn't it?"

Chapter Seven

Emma eyed the cracked sidewalk, bulging and lopsided with oak tree roots, careful not to trip, as she and Josh made their way toward Alcée Fortier High School. They had an appointment with Louis's guidance counselor for one thirty. Emma could tell, even from a distance, that the school's once grand façade was crumbling and stood unrepaired, nearly in ruins. Within walking distance of the Redemption, Fortier had much in common with the public housing project. Half of the windows of the school were broken and boarded up, or covered with burglar bars. Vandalism had made its mark in the form of colorful spray paint displays on its outer walls and doors. Emma and Josh passed two hundred-year-old oaks lining the sidewalk to the school's entrance, which provided some relief from the late September heat. A slight breeze from the Mississippi River blew silver-gray clumps of Spanish moss from a great oak's lowest branches as they climbed the steps to the administrative offices.

Emma and Josh entered a tall, dark corridor which belched out the summer's heat and held it, hovering above their heads. They stopped, realizing they weren't certain where to turn.

They approached a group of teachers as students scurried to class before the tardy bell rang.

"Could you tell us where the guidance counselor's office is?" Emma asked a teacher who was leaning against a metal locker.

She directed Emma toward an impossibly crowded hallway and an equally crowded corridor toward the right. Emma felt like a salmon swimming upstream as she walked against the flow of students rushing to class. She was glad she was able to schedule a meeting with Jesse Branson. He sounded genuinely interested in Louis. She saw a "Guidance Counselor" sign on a door and knocked. The door opened immediately.

He was a tall, lanky man who moved with the effortless grace and rhythm of an athlete. Even though his glasses gave him a more academic appearance, Emma would have thought he was a professional basketball player. Emma liked his kind brown eyes and gentle hand shake.

He gestured for Emma and Josh to sit down in his sparsely furnished office.

"Mr. Branson, can you tell me about Louis's placement at Fortier? What is the 'behavior problem classroom' and why is Louis there?" She prepared her notepad and nodded for Josh to do the same. "Does Louis have a learning disability? Has he been tested for learning or emotional problems?"

Emma stopped her round of questions and paused. "Sorry, I fired out such a string of questions. Do you need me to repeat any of that?"

"No problem. I think I got it." Mr. Branson smiled. "Louis is in a class with a lot of other students who act out in school. And he hasn't received any special testing with the exception of testing for reading levels. He's there because he's disruptive."

"How many students are in the class with Louis?"

"Thirty, or so. Altogether, there are about one hundred and twenty students in the program."

"Good grief. That's a huge group of kids. How many students are in the school?"

"There are around six hundred and thirty students in the school. So almost twenty percent of the students here are considered 'disruptive.'"

Mr. Branson flipped through the folder holding Louis's school records. "A surprising percentage of the Orleans Parish Public School population would test out with some learning or emotional issue. There's just not enough money in the system to pay for psychological testing for all of those special programs." He stopped to read several pages.

Mr. Branson paused and glanced over his glasses. "But, like I said, we tested his reading skills. He reads on a fifth-grade level, which makes him five grades behind. So, he takes remedial reading classes. Do you two want to come take a look at Louis's class? That way you can have a better understanding of what goes on in the program."

"Sure. Does being that far behind in reading qualify him for placement in a learning disabilities program?"

"Technically, it could. But Louis hasn't been placed yet. And he won't be tested further. They've decided to take care of his needs with remedial reading and the behavioral program."

"To save money?"

"You got it."

Emma nodded, and they walked down the hall, out of double glass doors, and down a curving sidewalk littered with dirty bubble gum and candy wrappers to a group of trailers parked along the back section of the schoolyard. The trailers were next to an open baseball field. P.E. classes were in session.

"Louis's classroom is in one of these trailers?" Josh asked.

"Yep. The school ran out of classrooms, and for the past few years has been temporarily housing special classes, including the kids with behavior issues, out in these trailers. Remedial reading classes are out here too."

Mr. Branson walked up the steps of the trailer and rapped on the door. A woman opened the door for them, and they entered the classroom.

"At least there's air conditioning in the trailer classrooms, which is more than I can say about the rest of the school." Mr. Branson turned his back to the classroom as he spoke.

The trailer was filled with thirty high school students stuffed into the two overly crowded aisles of the small classroom. Most were teenaged boys, passing notes, reading comic books, or taking an occasional swing at their neighbor's arm. Some were sleeping. None were paying attention to the assignments listed on the chalkboard at the front of the room. The teacher, sitting at her desk, was writing in a notebook, ignoring her students.

"I've seen enough, thanks, Mr. Branson." Emma turned to walk out of the trailer.

"Not the most positive environment, is it?" Mr. Branson closed the door and walked down the steps with Emma and Josh.

"I'm not sure what's going on in there. Is there anything else that you can tell me about Louis?"

"Louis is a sweet kid, easily distracted, although that's not unusual. His attendance is low and I've tried to contact his parents about that. His father isn't around, and his mother rarely returns my calls. When she does, she still can't bring herself to care about Louis, or his school work, or attendance. From what I've been able to observe, he doesn't do much when he does show up, except draw. He likes to joke around with other kids, but that gets him in trouble. Today they call that 'poor impulse control.' When I was growing up, they would have called him the class clown." Mr. Branson smiled. "Most people like Louis."

They walked back into Mr. Branson's office and sat down.

"He likes to draw?" Josh pulled out his notebook and pulled back a few pages so he could take notes.

"Oh yeah. He draws all the time."

"What sorts of things?"

"Believe it or not, he has a thing for men's fashion. And he's really good at it.

Especially hoodies and shoes. He's got some wild shoe ideas."

"Is there any way we could see any of his drawings?" Emma asked.

"There are a few up on the bulletin board in the school cafeteria. We had a showcase of the kids' talents the first week of school, and Louis's designs were included. I was impressed."

"I'd like to see them on the way out." Emma paused. "Would you be willing to testify at trial about some of the things you just told us about—Louis's lack of family support and his reading problems?"

"Sure. Louis is a great kid, but he's lost and wants to belong to something. I'm sure he wants to please too." Mr. Branson flipped back through Louis's file, stopping to read an entry.

Emma paused again, waiting until Mr. Branson finished reading. "We're in the process of analyzing the case right now, so we don't know many of the facts. But all you'd need to testify about, ever, is what you've been able to observe here at the school. We can hire a psychologist to evaluate him for emotional or learning issues."

"I don't have a problem with that. Just let me know what I need to do, and when I need to do it." Mr. Branson closed Louis's folder and cleared his throat. "One other thing, lately I noticed that he's been cutting slashes in his eyebrows."

"What does that mean?" Emma had noticed Louis had two tiny scars on his left eyebrow.

"Louis is in a gang, or at least, he wants people to think he's in one." Mr. Branson leaned toward Emma. "Gang members often slash their eyebrows to identify themselves to each other."

"Do you know anything about New Orleans gangs? I'd guessed kids Louis's age might be involved with gang activity."

Jesse Branson raised his eyebrows and nodded. "Ms. Thornton, if you and the students in your program are going to represent Louis, you'll need to understand what's going on here." He cracked his knuckles. "Yes, kids Louis's age, especially kids living in inner cities, or in low income federal housing projects, could be involved in gang activity. It's possible that a kid from one of the most affluent families in the country could be too. But Louis's cousin heads up the Gangsta B's, the best-known gang in New Orleans. Most kids are involved in gangs because family members are dealing drugs or are addicted, and they either need protection or need to bring in money to support everyone. I suggest you speak to one of Louis's relatives to see what's really going on. It's not unusual to set up a younger gang member to take the rap for a crime, particularly murder, since they can serve time in the juvenile system and get out at age twenty-one." He crossed his arms.

"Well, that won't work so well if he is tried as an adult, and Louis will be."

"I don't know what's going on in this case, I'm just telling you what I know." Mr. Branson cleared his throat again. "I grew up in the projects. I know what goes on there." He folded his hands in his lap.

Emma saw a quiet resignation in the counselor's eyes. "Did you know anyone who was in a gang?"

"Let's just say I'm familiar with them, and if it weren't for my grandmother, who dragged me out of the projects when I was thirteen, I might have been in the same position Louis finds himself in today. I owe her my life. My mom tried to do everything on her own, then she lost her job, and got sick. We ended up at the Redemption. It was a tough time. My grandmother stepped in and made room for us at her home down on Lafayette. Beautiful place. Everything changed after that. I'm still there. She left her home to me in her will." He looked down at his hands. "Everyone could use a hand-up sometimes. I've tried to pay her back by working with troubled kids, but some days it's way larger than I am. I haven't been able to do more than calm a few kids down long enough to help them get through the day. I can't get through to any of them longer than that."

"I'm sure you're doing more than you realize." Emma stood up. "I'd like to see Louis's work before I go."

Mr. Branson led Emma and Josh down the hallway to the double doors that led to the school cafeteria. He opened them and pointed to the bulletin board along the north wall. Emma walked up close to the display, her eyes flitting from one drawing to another, searching for Louis's name.

Mr. Branson walked behind her, his finger pointing to a sophisticated line drawing in the middle of the board. Emma stepped closer for a better look at the meticulously sketched menswear. Oversized jackets were elegantly detailed with cowl necks or hoods. Some were to the waist, some below the knees, with baggy pants, or pants cinched at the ankle. He'd drawn an array of clothing as well as footwear, each more intricate than the next. *Louis Bishop* was firmly inscribed at the bottom of the page.

Emma turned and stared at Mr. Branson, her mouth agape.

"He turns out hundreds of these. He never stops thinking of this stuff. While we're pondering what we're going to cook for supper, or whether the laundry is done, he's thinking about how to stich an inseam on a pair of pants so the stripes all meet in one continual line."

"I thought he was the class clown," Josh said.

"A diversion. He tends to downplay this passion of his. I don't think he trusts his friends to understand. You know. There aren't that many guys who are into designing clothes. Especially in high school. But it's the one thing that calms him down. I watched him sketch out a drawing once. It was as if he'd escaped to an entirely different world."

"Just when you think you've got someone figured out...," Emma said.

"Yeah. This was a surprise, huh?"

"Well, I knew he liked to draw. His mother told me that. But I didn't know he was this talented. But this seems like something more. If a kid doesn't have the family he wants, maybe he needs to create his own world. Looks like Louis creates nice things for himself. On paper. Nothing wrong with that," Emma said as she and Josh followed Mr. Branson out of the school cafeteria.

Chapter Eight

Emma entered her number as soon as she heard the beep. She'd followed through with the dean's suggestion and had placed the call to Marcus. But as she expected, the number Louis had given her was for a pager. In retrospect, she was glad she'd placed the call, but she didn't think speaking to him would accomplish anything that would help Louis or anyone else. She didn't expect to hear back from him.

It was the end of the day. Emma packed up her things and drove home. The house was quiet when she walked in. The boys were nowhere in sight.

"Billy! Bobby! I'm home!" She started the climb up the spiral metal staircase to their third-floor bedroom, feeling the slight rise in temperature as she ascended. The house, which was more than a hundred years old, had never been properly insulated.

As she reached the boys' floor, she could see them poring over homework, their heads bobbing to the beat of a tune coursing from their portable CD players. Sound was coming through their headphones at such a ramped-up pitch that Emma could hear a percussive pounding clearly across the room.

She walked up and pulled Bobby's left ear piece away from his head. "You're going to damage your hearing. Turn it down."

She walked over to Billy, who stopped what he was doing and looked up. "That goes for you too. Turn down the volume." She turned her thumb down. "Better yet, turn off the music for a minute." Emma made a motion with her finger across her neck. Billy and Bobby each turned off their CD players and pulled off their headphones.

"There! That's better. Now I can actually talk to my boys. Almost done with the homework?"

"Yeah, I've got a couple more rows of math to do and I'm done." Bobby flipped a page in his math book.

"I'm almost done too. I'm just answering a few questions in geography. Looking up stuff on a map. Won't take me long."

"You guys want to take a run with me?"

Billy and Bobby looked at each other, but didn't answer.

"Come on. You've been cooped up all day and video games won't do you a bit of good. Finish up and then go change, and I'll race you. First one back home gets an extra scoop of ice cream tonight. We're having red beans and rice for dinner. Get a move on!"

Emma climbed back down the stairs and prepared for the run. The boys hadn't been as enthusiastic as she'd hoped. They were getting older and were already pulling away from her, even though they were only twelve. She could feel their family core transforming.

A few minutes later she heard the boys' tennis shoes beating a quick staccato as they made their way down the staircase, the bolts straining and clanking with each step. Emma closed her eyes, half expecting one of them to slip. The staircase was a menace, old, rickety and slippery. If the twins weren't as agile as a pair of cats, they would have fallen down the twisty steps long ago.

"Let's run down 6th Street to Magazine, then Magazine to Louisiana Avenue, then back home to St. Charles. We'll stay together until we reach St. Charles, then it's each man for himself." They walked down to the outside door and locked it behind them. Emma started jogging at a comfortable lope. The boys followed, keeping up easily. There was plenty of daylight left, so Emma wasn't concerned about their safety. She loved seeing the boys run, their long legs pumping, easily keeping her pace, their cheeks becoming pink with effort and the heat of the early autumn evening. Most of the run was down Magazine Street. Magazine, which in French meant "shop," was just that. A street filled with dress shops, coffee shops, restaurants, grocery stores, antique stores and the like. Emma loved living within walking distance to so many places, especially the coffee shops. The boys were fascinated by a huge guitar store on the corner of Louisiana and Magazine, which was already closed when they passed, making the Louisiana Avenue stretch far less interesting to them. But Emma kept her eyes peeled for any signs of activity at Marcus's pawn shop as the boys ran by.

The neon sign flashed "OPEN" at Louisiana Avenue Pawn. The traditional symbol of the pawn shop, three spheres hanging from a wrought iron bar, was suspended from an eave. Emma slowed to a light trot, allowing the boys to get ahead of her. They plowed their way down the street, bus brakes hissing behind them at stoplights, as she checked out the shop and the cars parked in front of the building. One appeared to be an unmarked governmental car, white in color, its plates announcing its purpose, the word "PUBLIC" written vertically along the left-hand side. The front of the cement block building was protected by a sliding metal door. The handle to the door was wrapped in metal chains clipped together with a padlock. She thought lights were on, but couldn't tell whether anyone was inside. She kicked her run into higher gear to catch up with the boys. When they finally reached the corner of St. Charles, Emma nodded. They turned right and took off, each at their top speed. After a while, she hung back a little and watched them go, delighted to see each boy trying his utmost, spindly legs flying like little pistons. They were great runners, speeding down the street, neck and neck, perfectly matched.

Emma caught up to them, and they all slowed down. She put her arms around their shoulders. "You two did great. You both earned an extra scoop of ice cream tonight! But let's get in quickly before it gets too dark. We don't want to try our luck tonight." She ruffled their hair.

Billy nodded and wiped the sweat off of his forehead with his tee shirt. Emma hooked her arms around their necks and they walked the remaining half block to their home on St. Charles.

After dinner and double scoops of ice cream, she got the twins off to bed and gathered up her supplies for a soak in the tub. One of the greatest features of their apartment, in Emma's opinion, was the fact that she and the boys had separate bathrooms, and she had a clawfoot tub in hers. It was huge—one of those old iron ones that had been splendidly refurbished, staying hot, since it was iron, for the duration of the bath. It was her favorite place to think. Tonight, she wanted to give the Marcus problem some thought. She eased herself into the hot lavender-scented water. Her nagging aches and pains of the day were immediately relieved, and she could focus on the problem that was confounding her.

She wasn't certain what step she needed to take next with Marcus. There was a slight chance he'd call her back, but she didn't think the odds were high. But if he did, she'd set up a meeting with him at the law school. It was the most neutral place they could meet. She'd avoid the pawn shop, although she was dying to know what was going on with the unmarked cop car in front of the place. She realized any effort she made with Marcus would be futile, or dangerous, or both. She needed to proceed with caution.

She dried off, slipped on her pajamas, and walked over to the phone. She hadn't spoken to Ren in several days. He didn't know anything about her new case, and she wanted to talk to him about Marcus.

Emma had met Ren, who was the Chief Deputy of Jonesburg, Georgia, when she was in law school. She'd divorced the twin's father when the boys were very young and had never expected to fall in love again. Certainly not with a deputy sheriff from a small town. After she graduated, she'd wanted Ren to move to New Orleans with her, but he "just wasn't a big city sort of guy." He liked wider spaces and country people. So, she couldn't insist he make a change for her that he would only grow to hate. Plus, he was being groomed to take over as sheriff someday. Even though they were still seeing each other, it was getting more and more difficult to carry on a relationship at such a distance.

But Ren was an excellent analyst. She'd seen him at work on a case she'd been involved with in Georgia and knew how good he was. She liked hashing out problems with him and trusted his instincts. More than that, he was the sort of man who couldn't be knocked off center—he had a built-in gyroscope. She couldn't help but love him, no matter where he chose to live. He was her confidant and her anchor.

She dialed his number. On the fourth ring, a groggy Ren answered.

"Is everything okay? It's a little late for you to be calling."

"Hey. I'm sorry it's so late. Are you okay to talk?"

"Always okay, for you."

She sighed. "It helps me to talk about my cases with you and it looks like I've accepted another one, a murder. My client, a sixteen-year-old boy named Louis, may have been set up by a drug dealer. This drug dealer also happens to be his cousin, Marcus. I'm worried that everyone who's involved in the case, including my students, may be in jeopardy, and that no one, including my client, will tell the truth about what happened that night because they've either been paid off with drugs or they're too frightened." She crawled into bed and leaned back against a stack of fluffy pillows.

"You are in a pickle. See, I told you not to move to New Orleans. You wouldn't be running into drug dealers of that sort in Jonesburg. We have nice drug dealers here. Most of them are farmers. They grow marijuana plants six feet high, all mixed up in their cornfields. It's amazing."

"Very funny, Ren." She was glad he couldn't see her smile. "This is serious. I need a strategy and I don't have one where Marcus is concerned. He has one. And so far, his is winning."

"What's his? Paying off witnesses with crack cocaine?"

"That's one. And I suspect he's also got kids doing anything he wants because they're trying to survive. I'm guessing they eventually hope to graduate to Marcus's gang, the Gangsta B's. Or maybe they're already in it. It's all about survival for the drug addicts and the kids."

"I think you've got to set up a way to watch Marcus for a while. How does he work his people? How do they move around and how does he get them to sell his stuff? Who does what? You've got to figure it all out."

"That would be great if we were undercover cops. But I have law students assigned to the case. I can't jeopardize their safety and I'm not crazy about jeopardizing mine. We'd stick out like sore thumbs if we tried to do something like that." She grabbed a couple of pillows and arranged them behind her back and neck.

"But keeping an eye on Marcus and his people will tell you how he operates. How he uses the other witnesses on your list, if he uses them at all. You need to know his role in the Bishop family, the community. Who is this Marcus person? What are you up against here?"

Emma nodded. "All that would be great to know, but it sounds so cloak and dagger. I know there's a coffee shop about two blocks from Marcus's and Louis's grandmother's apartment, on the corner. That's the area where the murder occurred. I suspect that's where Marcus carries on his drug business, but I don't really know anything other than where the murder occurred. So, if we meet there. it might offer a way to keep an eye on the area and still be safe. But we may spend all day there and accomplish nothing." She shrugged. "Guess it wouldn't hurt to try. God. This is crazy."

"That's what you get for living in a crazy place."

"Must it always come back to this? You sound like a broken record. Marcus also has a pawn shop around the corner from where I live, but I would think everything there would have the appearance of being legal. Don't you think?"

"I don't know. You don't have enough information yet, and it doesn't do any good to speculate. But it's good to know about his business. A pawn business deals in cash. It's perfect for money laundering. I'd bet good money he's doing something illegal there, but you wouldn't bc able to observe what it was from the street."

"Yeah, that's what I thought, too. By the way, I called Marcus's pager today."

"You what?"

"Yeah. Thought I'd try to set up an interview with him about the night of the murders."

"Why all this talk about safety and then turn around and do something like that? That's crazy."

"I don't think he'll call me back, and if he does, I'll meet him at the law school. That's safe."

"No, it's not. It's not safe to have any part of your life, not even your work life, exposed to someone like Marcus Bishop. You shouldn't be on his radar for any purpose."

Chapter Nine

Emma ordered a dark roast with chicory and extra foam. She'd gotten used to the bitter additive since she'd been in New Orleans, and now coffee didn't taste like coffee without it. She grabbed a Danish, and sat down next to the only window that gave her access to a view of Louis's grandmother's apartment, two blocks away.

She blew the foam off the top of her coffee to cool it before taking a sip. Emma and her students had agreed to take turns watching the perimeter of the Bishop apartment for signs of activity. Any activity. No one had made an appearance yet, but it was early. She settled in with some work, keeping one eye on the grassy area surrounding the apartment.

She was lucky to get a table. It was far too hot to sit outside and her shift was for two hours. The coffee shop was filled with an eclectic blend of hippies, goth-types with tattoos, piercings, and spiky black hair playing chess, college kids studying in the corner, and businessmen and women grabbing a quick cup of joe on their way to work. The barista was talented, and the pastries were fresh and delicate. Perched on the edge of one of the grittiest neighborhoods in the city, the shop's offerings were professionally presented and delicious. She would have been quite comfortable there if only she weren't searching for people she didn't know and had never even seen before.

There was one definite plan of the day. An interview of Dwayne Bishop at 11:00. Lauren Acevedo would talk to him. It would be helpful to see what he'd say about the night of the shootings.

* * *

After two-hours had nearly passed, Emma realized Ren's idea, and her execution of it, was, at best, premature, and probably unnecessary. Her view from the coffee shop window was hardly enlightening. It offered a narrow span across Felicity to Mrs. Bishop's building and the bench where some boys had started gathering. There were no trees in that quadrant of apartments. No shrubs had been planted along the sidewalks or porches. There was no basketball goal or area for children to play. The grass had been trampled flat in the middle of the commons area, leaving a fringe of scruffy weeds along the sidewalk. Even though it was a dazzling day, the sunlight that had played so brilliantly along the sherbet-colored uptown houses, illuminating the wisteria, crepe myrtle and azaleas, seemed to have faded, obliterated by a sense of foreboding and an oppressive gloom so great that all color vanished.

Emma searched the faces of the young men who had started to gather, but she knew it was futile. She hadn't met any of the main players from the night of the murders, except Louis. She wasn't sure why she'd thought Ren's plan was a good one. She hadn't learned a thing that morning, except that the bench was a gathering spot for kids.

Emma walked to the counter to order an espresso when Lauren walked in, her strawberry blonde hair casting a glow about her head from the sunlight in the doorway. Emma could never recall whether her eyes were blue, gray or green, but they were an icy, nearly white version of one those colors. Her skin was nearly translucent, with tiny purple veins exposed along her hairline. Emma wondered how all that would look on television someday as she nodded toward her table. "Want anything to drink?"

Lauren shook her head. "No thanks." She set her purse and notebook down and pulled up a third chair.

"For Dwayne," Lauren said as she scraped the chair across the floor. "Let's hope he shows."

At that same time, Emma noticed a young man breaking from the pack of boys. He sauntered down the sidewalk in the direction of the coffee shop and crossed the street. The doorbell tinkled as he entered the building. Lauren walked over to the young man.

"Are you Dwayne Bishop?"

He put his hands in his low-slung pockets and tilted his chin down once.

"Would you like to sit down with us?" Lauren gestured toward the chair next to hers. Her cheeks a little ruddier than usual.

Dwayne followed Lauren to the table and eased into the chair.

Lauren sat down next to him and skimmed her notes. Emma noticed Lauren fidgeting with the pages in her notebook. She squirmed about in her chair and couldn't seem to get comfortable. She was flushed and had begun to perspire. Her hands were shaking. Some pre-interview jitters would be understandable from most students, but Emma didn't expect that from Lauren. She'd spent her undergraduate school years learning how to ask questions of strangers and had prepared hours of on-screen camera interview questions. Emma had overheard her brag about those interviews to students during class. Tough questions should be her specialty.

Lauren had made her feelings about Louis clear earlier. She wasn't sure she felt he deserved a defense since she had misgivings about his drug use. And now, she was showing signs of anxiety at the thought of asking Dwayne a few questions. If she couldn't put aside her personal feelings, she'd have to be taken off the case. Intolerance had many faces, and fear was one. Judgment was another.

Emma grabbed her coffee and walked over to the table. "I'm Emma Thornton, from St. Stanislaus University Law School." She extended her hand, which Dwayne shook, and sat down. "You may already know that Louis Bishop was arrested for the murder of two men a couple of days ago. Several students and I, including Ms. Acevedo here, represent Louis in the case."

"Okay." Dwayne crossed his arms.

"I spoke to Louis right after he'd been arraigned. He told me you were there the night of the shootings. So, we'd like to know what you recall of that evening. Lauren has prepared some questions for you. Go ahead, Lauren."

"First, I'd like to know whether you're related to Louis. You have the same last name." Lauren pushed her hair back from her face and readied her pen. Without giving Dwayne time to answer, she pushed forward. "I forgot to ask you if you'd like something to drink. I'd be happy to get it for you." She glanced at Dwayne.

Emma was concerned. Lauren's face was even more flushed and her questions were rapid-fire fast.

"Nah. That's okay. And we're cousins. Pretty much grew up together." Dwayne leaned back in his chair.

Dwayne appeared to be a little older than Louis. He was taller, as well, and seemed athletic, with long tapered hands. Dressed in brilliant red, white and blue athletic gear, his clothes were immaculate. Unlike Louis, he was well-groomed, as if he'd just stepped out of the shower. Every hair on his head was flawlessly shaped and in place. He was a study in perfection. But Emma strained to hear him. He was soft-spoken and barely moved his mouth when he talked. His eyes darted back and forth, checking out who was coming in the shop as he spoke. He seemed distracted, but when he wasn't checking out patrons, he made steady eye contact. And when he was more relaxed, his body language was confident, self-assured.

"How old are you?"

"I'm seventeen, but I'll be eighteen next month."

"So you and Louis are related on your father's side?" Lauren sipped her coffee and eyed Dwayne over the rim.

"Yeah. My daddy is Louis's mama's brother." Dwayne played with a torn napkin on the table, twisting it into even more little pieces.

"But you don't live with your father, do you?"

"No. Louis don't live with his mama neither. We stay at our grandmother's, Mama Ruby's, over off of Felicity Street, right over there." Dwayne pointed with his thumb toward the second apartment building on the street.

"Do you stay there every night?" Lauren said, her foot shaking up and down like a like a sewing machine needle.

"Yeah, pretty much."

"What about Georgie and Marcus?"

"Marcus has his own place, but me, Georgie and Louis, we stay at Mama

Ruby's most of the time."

"You were there on the night of the killings?" Lauren leaned back in her chair and squinted at Dwayne.

"Yeah." Dwayne nodded and looked down at his hands.

"Where does Marcus live?"

"He got a place right over his pawn shop there on Louisiana."

"And Marcus was at your grandmother's the night of the killings, too?"

Dwayne looked over his shoulder and at the door. He nodded.

"Is that a yes?"

"Yes."

"Do you and Louis and Georgie ever do any work for Marcus at the pawn shop?"

"No. We do some work for him now and then, but not at the shop."

"What do you do?"

"Oh, just odds and ends. Errands, you know."

"Can you elaborate?" Lauren said, rubbing her hands together. Emma wondered if her hands were sweating.

"Huh?"

"Can you give me some details?"

"Nah, not really. Just stuff." Dwayne leaned back in his chair.

"Tell me what happened the night of the murder."

Dwayne sighed. "We were at Mama Ruby's, for dinner, you know?"

"Who else was there that night? I need you to list everyone, to the best of your ability." Lauren hunched over her notebook, poised to record each name.

"Well, Mama Ruby, she cooked for everyone, like always. Marcus, Georgie, Louis, and me, we were all there. Alicia was there for a little bit."

"What did your grandmother cook that night?" Lauren pushed her hair out of her face and jotted down notes as Dwayne spoke.

"What she cook?" Dwayne cocked his head, then closed his eyes. "Pretty sure it was meatloaf. She does the best meatloaf, with those green beans you cook all day, you know? And mashed potatoes. Yeah. Mama Ruby's meatloaf and fixin's. Can't beat it." Dwayne smiled for the first time since he'd walked in.

"What else happened that night?"

"Um. We finish dinner. Then Marcus said he wanted us to go and meet some guy with him. So, we did, except for Louis. Louis was scratchin' around looking for somethin'. Once we started walking out there, he sent me back to get Louis. Few seconds later, we came back out and Louis brought a brown paper bag with him. Then before you know it, we hear two shots and see two guys down. That guy Marcus was meetin', and some priest out by the street." Lauren wrote as quickly as she could while Dwayne was speaking.

"Did you know the guy Marcus was meeting?" Lauren checked off the question from her list.

"No, I never seen him before."

"Did you know what Louis had in the brown paper bag?"

"No, but I could guess." Dwayne looked down at his hands and picked at a little spot on his thumb.

"What is your guess?"

"A gun."

"Did you see a gun in the bag?"

He shook his head. "No, I never did."

"Did you see what Louis did with the brown bag after he brought it outside? Did he hand it to Marcus?"

"No. It was all dark then, and it happened so fast."

Lauren marked another item from her checklist. "Who was outside that night? I need to know who could have witnessed the shooting."

"I don't know who saw what, but me, Georgie, Louis and Marcus, we were all there that night, plus the guys that was shot. After the shootin', I didn't see Marcus. Everyone else was standing there, but Marcus, and Louis. I saw Louis runnin' off down to the river."

"Where do you think Marcus went?"

"I don't know. He just took off. I don't know where he went."

"Was a woman by the name of Tamika there?"

"Tamika Jones?"

"Yes, I believe that's her name." Lauren sat back in her chair and checked her notes.

"Don't think so, but she never too far away if Marcus's around." Dwayne glanced out of the window again.

"Is she Marcus's girlfriend?" Lauren followed Dwayne's gaze out of the window.

"Ha! She wish! But she around a lot. Especially around Marcus. And Mama Ruby don't like it, not one bit."

"Why's she around so much, and why doesn't your grandmother like that?" Lauren suddenly swung her legs around to the other side of the chair she was sitting in and crossed the other leg. She began swinging the crossed leg with renewed vigor.

"You have to ask Marcus, or maybe Mama Ruby." Dwayne looked at the front door as a new patron entered.

"What can you tell me about either Mr. Maureau and or Brother Antoine, the two men who were shot that night?"

"Like I said, I don't know Maureau. I really don't know Brother Antoine either. But I heard rumors about both of 'em."

"Rumors?"

"Yeah."

"What were the rumors?"

"Can't really say. They rumors."

"Is there anyone who might know more than you, or who would be willing to talk about the two men?"

"Yeah, maybe."

"And who would that be?"

He shrugged. "I don't know."

"I've heard that maybe Georgie could help?"

"I don't know." He looked down at the ground. "Maybe you could talk to Georgie. He might talk to you about Maureau. I'm not sure. And Alicia was friends with the brother."

"Do you know if Louis knew either man, either Brother Antoine or Mr. Maureau?"

Dwayne shook his head. "Don't think so."

"Did you ever see Louis talking to either man, or see him together with either man, ever?"

"Nah. I don't think he knows them. But you'd have to ask him." Dwayne crossed his arms.

She tore a piece of paper from her notebook. "Could you draw a circle where each person was that night and name each circle? Make sure you include the people who were shot."

Dwayne took the paper and drew and labeled six carefully arranged circles. He slid the page over to Lauren, who pulled the page over with her fingertip.

Emma leaned toward Dwayne. "One more thing. You said there were two shots. Are you sure? Could there have been more than two shots?"

"I thought there was only two, but everything was happening so fast." He shrugged. "I can't be sure. If another shot was fired, it must have been close to the same time. I know I heard two shots."

Emma glanced at Lauren's notepad. All questions on her list had been crossed off. "You've been a big help, Dwayne. We'll be in touch if we need to speak to you later." Emma closed her notebook.

Dwayne nodded and stood up. He shoved his hands in the pockets of his sweatshirt, eased around the table, and was out of the front door before they had gathered their papers.

Emma watched Dwayne walk out of the room, then turned toward Lauren.

"You did a good job with your questions, but we both made some mistakes today. Do you know what they are?"

Lauren shook her head.

"Well, for one thing, I should have anticipated that Dwayne would be uncomfortable talking to us in such close proximity to his grandmother's apartment and so close to the place where his friends hang out. It's no wonder we couldn't get much from him today."

Lauren nodded.

"What should we have done instead?"

"I guess we should find another place to interview witnesses. Something farther away from here."

"I agree. I'll speak to Father Alfonso about that. I've been told he knows the community pretty well." Emma started packing her briefcase to go. "But I also noticed you seemed uncomfortable around Dwayne. If you were, that's something we can't have. The client will sense your discomfort and will have no trust in our ability to represent them. We also need Dwayne's testimony, his cooperation. If he senses you don't feel comfortable around him, he won't feel comfortable around you. He won't speak to us candidly about the case. So you and your fears become a liability. Do you understand?"

"I'm comfortable around Dwayne. I don't know why you're saying that."

"I don't mean to be unfair. I noticed you were nervous, or anxious, and I know you're very used to interviewing people, even people on camera. So, the only conclusion I could reach was that there was something about Dwayne, or perhaps Dwayne's diverse background that makes you nervous. If I'm wrong, please correct me."

"I'm not sure why you think that. I have no problem with Dwayne and I want to stay on the case." Lauren pushed a strand of hair from her eyes and crossed her arms across her chest.

"I'm not trying to be hard on you. But we can't afford to jeopardize this case. I received a death penalty notice this morning before I came here. We need all the help we can get from our witnesses and they don't know us. If you act skittish, they're going to clam up. But more importantly, I want you to examine your feelings. Know where you're really coming from, what feelings you harbor. When you say you have no problem with Dwayne, is that genuine? It sounds condescending. Apply that same question to Louis and Georgie. We can't afford to have a lawyer on the case who'll do anything but zealously defend the client."

Chapter Ten

Emma gathered her things and headed for the law school. It was still early, and she had much to do. She had to transcribe her notes from the day and get ready for class tomorrow. She hoped she hadn't been too harsh on Lauren, but believed in being direct. After all, Louis's life was at stake.

The campus was nearly deserted when she pulled up to the school at lunchtime. She unlocked her office and threw her purse and briefcase on the chairs in front of her desk, and the phone began to ring. She scrambled to reach it, finally grabbing the receiver on the fourth ring.

"Hello?"

"Who's this?"

"I beg your pardon?"

"I got a call from this number. Who's this?" It was a male voice, deep, husky, as if he'd been smoking cigarettes.

"Is this Marcus Bishop?"

"Who wants to know?"

"This is Professor Emma Thornton. I represent your cousin, Louis Bishop, in his criminal case. I paged you earlier to set up a time to speak to you about the night of the two killings. I understand you were there and may have witnessed what happened."

There was a pause. Emma could hear an exhaling sound, as if they were smoking a cigarette.

"I ain't got nothin' to say."

"Could we meet and chat about Louis sometime, or speak over the phone?"

"I already said I don't have nothin' to say."

"The DA will probably meet with you about that night, but even if he doesn't, he could subpoena you to court to testify as a witness. I need to know what you'll say to him. It's very important that we talk."

Emma could hear Marcus breathing on the other end. Then the flick of a lighter and continued exhaling. He was a chain smoker.

"What about what I'm sayin' don't you understand? I'm not talkin' to you. I know who you are. You been pokin' your nose into my family's business for a few days now, and that's gonna end. I know where you live. I know where your boys go to school, and I even know where your boys catch their school bus. Don't be pushin' at me, because I'll push back. And you won't like it." He hung up the phone.

Emma felt dizzy as bile rose in her throat.

* * *

Shaken from her conversation with Marcus, Emma sat at her desk, trying to clear her head. Her heart was beating so fast she had to take several deep breaths before she could think.

The boys didn't get home from school until 4:00. She still had several hours but wanted to make certain she was at home when the bus dropped them off. It was the best way to protect them. Her parents lived too far away and were too old and frail to be counted on to watch the boys any longer. She had a couple of good neighbors she could rely on for help, but that wasn't a permanent solution.

Billy and Bobby were only twelve, and even though they considered themselves almost grown, they weren't. Before Marcus's veiled threat, Emma had allowed them to stay by themselves for an hour at the apartment after school, but she couldn't allow that to continue, now. She wasn't sure how someone could threaten twelve-year-old children, but Marcus clearly had.

Her only solution was to start the day a little earlier at the law school so she could get home in time for the boys' 4:00 bus. She glanced down at her hands. They'd finally stopped shaking.

* * *

Emma dashed from her office to catch the dean before he headed to lunch, which for him was usually around 1:00. She hit the elevator button to the second floor, hoping he would be on board with her plan.

"How about lunch? My treat if you'll let me talk about the Bishop case."

"Good timing. I was just getting hungry. Let's try that new place on Maple Street."

Dean Munoz was a fast walker, and Maple Street was within walking distance from the school, just across St. Charles and a couple of shady blocks down the road. Maple was one of those storybook New Orleans streets which only grew more charming with age. A sliver of cobblestone, it was lined with pastel-painted Creole cottages, all of which had once been residential, and now were mostly retail. There was a bookstore, a few clothing stores, a makeup studio, and several outstanding restaurants and bistros. Emma had made a point of sampling something from each during the past four years. She loved dining alfresco at any of them, especially on a nice day. But she was focused on her problem today and didn't have an appetite.

Dean Munoz nodded toward the new pizzeria. "What do you think?"

"Looks good to me." Emma knew this restaurant had a reputation for turning orders out quickly.

They chose a spot outside, under one of the fans. Two hundred-year-old oak trees provided a canopy of shade over the patio's pergola. The restaurant was a converted stucco home, which was nearly as old as the trees. Emma breathed in and closed her eyes for a moment. She opened them and noticed the dean looking at her curiously.

"Sorry, Dean Munoz. I received notice in today's mail that the DA plans to pursue the death penalty in Louis's case. And I also got a call from Marcus. He returned my page, actually. He said he wouldn't answer any of my questions and made a threat against the twins. Said he knew where they went to school and where they caught the bus. He said that if I continued to pursue him, he'd retaliate." She exhaled loudly.

"Good God!" He clenched his fist. "I wasn't expecting that! Have you reported it? Something needs to be done."

"Well, I have a plan. But it will need your approval. It was the only thing I could think of. The boys usually get home around 4:00 on the bus. If I could get home around the same time, I'd feel better about their safety. I usually stay at the school until 5:00, but my classes are all over by 2:30. I only stay that late to be available for students. So, I could get to campus an hour earlier than I have been, leave a little before 4:00, and still spend the same number of hours at work. Would that meet your approval temporarily until the Bishop case is resolved?"

"Of course. Anything we can do to accommodate you. I'm so sorry this has happened. But don't you think you should get the police involved? You should call them and report Marcus's threat, at least." The Dean swirled his glass of ice water. "And to think I was looking forward to your conversation with Marcus." He shook his head.

"At least now we know who we're dealing with. And now I understand Louis's situation a little better. I'm sure he wasn't mature enough to figure a way around Marcus. Marcus has too much control of the family and is obviously a bully. And he might even push him around sometimes. But it's clear Marcus supports the family. I think he even enjoys it. I'd bet any of them would retrieve a gun for him if he asked them to, including Louis."

The Dean nodded. "But would they shoot someone for him? You need to know if Marcus asked Louis to do that, and if he carried the order out."

"Maybe I don't want to know that. But one thing's certain, Marcus won't be the one to tell me if he did."

"Right. You'll need to work on getting Louis to tell you what Marcus asked him to do, and I don't expect that'll be easy."

"I don't know if Louis is protecting Marcus, or if he's just scared of him. But the death penalty is a pretty harsh threat, too. Maybe that will inspire him to talk a little."

The waiter sat the tray down on the stand, and the area was immediately filled with the aroma of basil, rosemary, garlic and sundried tomatoes.

"The pizza smells like heaven." Emma sighed. She still didn't feel like eating. She'd get it boxed to go. "And judging from the pungent aroma coming from yours, you'll need to avoid class for a week."

They finished up and true to her word, Emma paid for lunch against the dean's protests. "Thanks for helping me with my schedule. Let's hope nothing comes of Marcus's threats."

Chapter Eleven

Emma needed to step up her plans for the afternoon to make it home on time for the twins' bus. She was scheduled to meet with Father Francis Alfonso about finding a safer place to interview witnesses and began gathering items for the meeting. Emma didn't know Father Alfonso well, but knew he was passionate about the law and certain political issues. He taught criminal law and criminal procedure, and knew the Louisiana Criminal Code like the back of his hand. The dean told her that he also knew more about local goings on than anyone else at the law school.

* * *

Father Alfonso's office was located on the second floor, down the hall from the dean's. It was a corner office with double windows, the sort of place junior partners in large firms would kill for. He had earned this prize space through seniority and absolute respect. Revered by students and faculty alike, he'd taught at the law school longer than anyone else, and had won the Distinguished Teaching Award at the school for the past ten years in a row.

Looking like a clean-shaven Santa Claus in a clerical collar, Father Alfonso was often surrounded by groups of students, either before or after class, engaged in heated debates. He didn't bother to hide his opinions on abortion—he was against it—or capital punishment—he was against that too, stating that the core argument against each act was the same. He lent a hand to the capital punishment clinic when he could. But he was open-minded and welcomed arguments on any side of any legal issue and was known for his after-hour deliberations.

Emma knocked on Father Alfonso's door and entered, following his booming welcome.

"Professor Thornton! What brings you to my little cubbyhole? I'm honored by a visit from such a lovely lady. Sit down, sit down." He gestured toward one of the upholstered chairs in front of his desk.

Emma glanced around the comfortably furnished, but overflowing, room. Father Alfonso's office was bursting with stacks of books piled on the floor, on all chairs, and double stacked on the bookshelves which lined all four walls. A large bowl of M&M's sat prominently to one side of his desk. Emma picked one of the upholstered chairs, moved the unwieldy stack of books which was on its seat to the floor, and eased herself into its well-worn cushions.

"Now what can I do for you?"

"I'm representing the boy accused of killing two men the other night. One of the men killed was a Catholic Brother by the name of Reginald Antoine. Did you know him?"

"I knew of him. He lived down by the projects, the Redemption I believe?" Father Alfonso plunged his hand into his desk drawer and pulled out a handful of M&M's. "Help yourself to those in the bowl. I keep a stash for myself in my desk. Those," he pointed to the bowl on the desk, "are for guests. Chocolate helps me think." He threw several candies in his mouth and turned his attention toward Emma.

Emma shook her head. "No thanks, but yes, he lived near the Redemption."

"He is, was, a good man. That much I know." Father Alfonso dipped his hand into his desk to grab another handful of M&M's.

"One of the reasons I'm here is because a witness has told us that there are rumors being spread about Brother Antoine. But he refused to say what the rumors are. Have you heard them or do you know what that's all about?"

"No, I've never heard anything but good things about him. He's a stand-up sort of fellow. He grew up in those projects, you know. He wanted to go back there to make a difference, to do good work." Father Alfonso popped a red M&M in his mouth.

"I don't know much about Brother Antoine. Anything you can tell me would help at this point."

"I just know he wanted to help the people at the Redemption, especially the kids. He'd started a basketball team, there was even a garden." Father Alfonso closed his desk drawer and sighed. "This is so sad, and his death is such a loss. I remember seeing him at a potluck supper one summer a few years back. He'd brought his guitar to play for the kids. Everyone, especially the little ones, gathered in a circle around him singing. That's the sort of thing he did. He created community wherever he went."

Emma nodded. "I need to speak to others who might know him, too. I'll speak to Brother Moore again. He was in the same order and lived in the same home as Brother Antoine. Can you think of anyone else? I'd like to get to the bottom of this rumor thing."

"I'm sure you realize there may be no truth behind a rumor."

"Of course. I'll check with Brother Moore to see if he knows of anyone else who could give us some insight. Also, I'm trying to find alternative places to meet my witnesses. Is there a Catholic property where we could meet that wouldn't arouse curiosity in case we're being watched? Something inconspicuous. Not a church. I thought a homeless shelter or a thrift shop might work. Do you know of a place like that?"

"A thrift shop might be a good idea. It would be believable for the witnesses to be doing a little shopping there. That's a cool thing to do now, right?"

"I'm not sure." Emma smiled. "I think you may be hipper than I am, Father Alfonso. But a thrift store sounds good. Do you know of one?"

"I have a friend who runs the St. Francis de Paul thrift shop on Carrollton, right before it curves toward St. Charles. You can't miss it." He grabbed a sheet of paper and scribbled on it. "I'll contact him. They have everything there, you name it, from kitchen pans, to couches, to designer shoes. I'll let you know what he says, but I'm sure it'll be fine."

"Did I tell you we got notice our sixteen-year-old client would be subjected to the death penalty? We might need your expertise on this case. Could we pick your brains if we need to?"

70

"If you can keep me supplied in M&M's, I'm yours." Father Alfonso smiled. "Seriously, you can speak to me about your case anytime. I'd do anything to help anyone facing a sentence of capital punishment, especially a kid. It's unthinkable." He shook his head.

* * *

Brother Moore answered the door and gestured for Emma to come into the Christian Brother's well-worn but cozy living area. The paint was peeling from the cracked plaster walls, and the tweed couch was worn, but the room was clean, bright and welcoming. If she wasn't in a rush to get home, Emma would have felt at ease there.

At their first meeting, she and Josh hadn't been invited beyond the front room, which was a common area used for small community gatherings, services, and activities. Brother Moore was ashen that day. Withdrawn and clearly upset. But today was different. Brother Moore gestured for her to sit down on the overly stuffed chair to the left of the fireplace.

"How can I help you, Professor Thornton?" Brother Moore sat down in a chair opposite Emma. At their first meeting Emma found Brother Moore's reserve and rigid manner off-putting. She couldn't tell if his gruff demeanor was a symptom of his grief, or if he was a little shy. But today, he was looser, almost as if someone had untied the strings that held him together.

"We're researching all of the victims and witnesses from the night of the murders. I wouldn't think Brother Antoine would have much in common with Sam Maureau, the other victim, or the witnesses that were there that evening. Still, we need to know everything we can about Brother Antoine, the names of his family, friends, anything you can think of and any connections there may be to the people who were at the scene of the murder that night. Do you know if Brother Antoine helped or worked with any of the witnesses, or the other murder victim or his family?" Emma handed Brother Moore a list of names.

Brother Moore scanned the list. "He and some of the brothers had a community basketball team that practiced at the gym over at the high school.

He could have worked with some of the kids on this list. But you'd have to ask them or better yet, ask his old friend Lionel Boudreaux. Lionel was a great basketball player. Almost made pro. So Brother Antoine asked him to help out with the kids. Lionel's also on our local police force, here in this district."

"Lionel patrols the streets here at the Redemption?"

"He does, along with several other guys in his precinct. You might even see him in his cruiser this evening. He usually has the 3:00 to 11:00 shift."

"Were Lionel and Brother Antoine very close?"

"I think they'd known each other all their lives. I know they went to high school together. But Brother Antoine had his responsibilities with the church, and Lionel had his with the police force. You wouldn't see them together these days unless they were down at the gym with the kids. They did a great job with that, starting from scratch and working their way up to a full-fledged community team. They were good coaches. And they stuck with it, getting the kids involved and dedicated to the team, too."

"Where does the team play? Maybe my boys and I'll go see them sometime."

"I think they practice on Thursday nights. They use the gym at St. Anthony's High School. Brother Antoine secured that for them."

"Do you know anything about Brother Antoine's family members, or other friends I could contact?"

"His mother is still alive, but he doesn't have any other family members. She lives at St. Ann's. I'm pretty sure she's in memory care. Alzheimer's."

"I see. Were you able to get back with some of the people who had spoken to you after the murders?"

"Like I said, some folks around here just like to talk. The one person I think you should speak to is Juanita Bishop. You probably already had her on your list. She was on her front porch at the time of the shootings. It's possible she heard or even saw something. She's a caring and committed aunt and has devoted herself to her niece, Alicia. I think Louis stays over there sometimes too. It would be worth your while to speak to her."

* * *

Emma pulled out of the projects and turned down Magazine Street, lost in thought. Something about New Orleans made her uneasy, and now, after Marcus's warning, she doubted whether she should have brought the twins here at all. It was an achingly beautiful place. She even loved the decay, which was ubiquitous. Dampness and humidity had taken a toll on nearly every structure in the city, leaving a patina on most surfaces, especially iron fences or balconies, or any wooden building not properly kept. It created a lovely effect, a visual feast. Yet there was a current of malevolence in the city she couldn't deny. Even before Marcus's threat, she'd often felt the need to look behind her, even in the middle of the day.

Although its beauty couldn't be denied, it wasn't a very sophisticated town. There was a pelvic thrust energy there, even in most sacred and happiest of holidays. With multiple bars on most streets, it was a tough town to raise boys in. It was a tough town period. She felt the urge to smoke again since she'd been here, especially lately, and she hadn't felt that way in years. She reached for her purse, which was in the passenger car seat, and explored the contents along the bottom of the bag, even though she knew she didn't have any cigarettes.

She had mixed feelings about contacting Brother Antoine's police officer friend, Lionel Boudreaux. She'd read unsavory accounts of New Orleans cops in the newspapers. Several had been indicted recently for their involvement in a drug operation. 1994 had already gone down as the deadliest year in the city's modern history, and the year wasn't even over. A couple of officers had even robbed a restaurant and murdered an employee. She needed to visit the police department to see the evidence in the case and had been putting it off. But she couldn't avoid it any longer. The autopsy report was essential.

She pulled into her parking space at the side of her apartment building. As she exited her car, she noticed two boys, stopped, sitting on their bicycles in the middle of the street, looking up toward her apartment. Even though they were obviously young enough to be in school, it would be at least a half an hour before the twins would be home. She knew instinctively these boys were up to something. She had a feeling, especially after Marcus's threats, that it might not be good. She needed a dog. A full-time, loud-barking, put-the-fear-of-God-in-you, dog.

She grabbed her purse, locked the car and walked around to the side of the street where the boys were lingering on their bikes.

"Can I help you with something?"

The boys scattered.

She started shaking. Realizing she was beginning to come unglued, she sat down on the curb and took a deep breath. This place, this case, and Marcus's threats about her kids were wearing at her, eroding her confidence. She couldn't think clearly. Everything seemed exaggerated. She needed to get a grip.

She stood up, walked to her front steps, and, hands shaking, opened the door to the apartment and walked up the stairs. Once inside, she went directly to the refrigerator and pulled out a Sancerre. After pouring a glass of the cooled wine, she stepped out onto the balcony and sat down on the small wicker chair she'd bought only last week. It fit her body perfectly. The second floor was cooler; there was almost always a breeze at that elevation. The wind blew Spanish moss in the oak tree across the street as the wine trickled slowly down her throat. She felt her body relax. She heard the rumble of a streetcar in the distance and watched traffic lights glitter on St. Charles. She looked down at the ancient street car tracks illuminated by the sun that had already started its descent. It was a grand boulevard. She never tired of the beauty of the place, day or night. She leaned back and breathed deeply until she heard the boys tromping up the stairs.

"Hey guys, want to go to the pound? I think we need a dog."

* * *

Hundreds of dogs were available. Purebreds, mixed breeds of countless combinations. Each one was more tragic and more adorable than the last. Emma wanted to take every single dog home. As she passed their cages, her heart broke, and she was just as certain she was breaking theirs. She didn't know how she could make a choice, and the twins weren't capable of it. They made contact through the cages with every dog they saw. How could they possibly choose?

They rounded a corner and saw two regal heads staring intently at them, little stubby tails wagging furiously. They were females from the same litter, and tracked each other's movements identically, turning their heads, wagging their tails, all in syncopated timing. Then, one made a rogue move and practically climbed up the cage to get to them. They were a year old, house trained, but still had the energy of puppies. German Shorthaired Pointers who'd been abandoned by their previous owners for being way too energetic, they were perfect for Billy and Bobby. Their long, goofy ears couldn't hide the keen intelligence behind their eyes. Their sharply defined muscles twitched at the thought of bounding out of the kennel and running around with the boys. An instant connection was struck up between the four, a dog for each boy and a boy for each dog.

Emma envisioned taking them out for runs, which she knew would be safer with the two dogs in tow. She couldn't believe their luck. They decided to name them before they even filled out the adoption papers. Maddie and Lulu. Maddie was solid brown, which was called "liver," and Lulu had an amazing coat of brown and white speckles. They were gorgeous. Emma and the boys couldn't wait to take them home. Maddie and Lulu's stubby little tails wagged in complete agreement as they were loaded in the car. They were sweet, sweet girls, but it wouldn't hurt if strangers believed they had a menacing bite.

Chapter Twelve

L ouis woke up before the buzzer went off. He pulled the note out from under his mattress and opened it up. It was early. 6:00 a.m. He knew what the note said, even though it was still too dark to read it clearly.

"Keep your mouth shut if you want to walk again."

He didn't have any problem figuring out who it was from. He just didn't know how Marcus was getting to him in prison. He must have people everywhere.

He rubbed his shoulder. It still hurt after being rammed by another prisoner last night as they were fighting their way into the mess hall for dinner. Dinnertime at the prison reminded Louis of a movie he saw as a kid when thousands of knights ran yelling across a battlefield to scare their enemy. Only here, instead of going into battle, the prisoners were vying for the first stab at dinner, when the gruel that was served still resembled food.

He sat up in bed and put his hand over his eyes. He'd love to have one of Mama Ruby's breakfasts. He could just taste her biscuits, all buttery and soft. He shook his head. He couldn't afford to go all soft now.

That guy came out of nowhere last night. Nearly knocked him over. Louis didn't think much of it at the time. But when he discovered the note in his pocket after he was knocked down, he figured it wasn't exactly an accident. And he wouldn't have a problem keeping quiet. He didn't need a warning, really.

He sat up in the cot and placed his bare feet on the floor. It felt gritty under his feet. Mama Ruby would make him sweep a floor like that. He smiled, remembering Sunday mornings at her house, getting ready for her big dinners. It was his job every week to clean up the kitchen before she cooked. Marcus always brought the groceries in early, excited to show off what he'd bought. Sometimes he got a cake or even chocolate chip cookies. They were Louis's favorite. There was a lot of good in Marcus. He knew it. Everyone knew it. Louis just didn't know how to deal with the bad.

* * *

Lionel Boudreaux had asked Emma to meet him at the 6th District before his shift started. There was an interrogation room in the back where they could speak. She and Josh were escorted down a narrow, dimly lit hall to the room, where he was seated at a small table.

Officer Boudreaux wasn't what Emma had come to expect from the New Orleans police officers she'd seen around the city. His demeanor was military-like, spit polished. Dressed in a uniform with creases so sharp they'd draw blood if you touched them. His neatly tucked shirt could hardly contain his shoulders. Donuts couldn't have been a part of his daily diet, unlike the majority of New Orleans' finest. Emma guessed he worked out daily—his physique wasn't possible otherwise.

Emma reached out and shook the officer's hand. "I'm so sorry for your loss. I understand you and Brother Antoine were friends."

Officer Boudreaux gestured for Josh and Emma to take a seat in the two metal chairs on one side of the table. He sat down across from them. "I still can't believe this happened to Reggie. He was one of the best. We'd been friends since junior high school. I played basketball—he played football, but other than that, we did everything together. We both got into college on athletic scholarships, so our lives took us in different directions, but for the same reason. We wanted to help the community, be there for the kids, you know? Maybe even give them something to aim for. There are so many roads to happiness and success. We wanted to help some of the kids from the Redemption find their way there."

"I have to say, you aren't saying what I'd expect to hear from a New Orleans police officer. I don't mean that in a bad way, but I didn't expect to hear anything about 'roads to happiness or success.' Do you know Louis Bishop, the young man who's accused of the double murder?"

"I'm not sure. I know he isn't one of the regular team members. He could have come by a time or two. Sometimes kids do that and then something else in their life pulls them away."

"In Louis's life that something else could have been his cousin, Marcus Bishop. Do you know Marcus?"

"I don't know him, but I know who he is, and what he does. Almost everyone in the area knows that." Officer Boudreaux sat back in his seat and crossed his arms over his chest.

"What do you know about him?"

"It's common knowledge he runs a gang here that's known for selling drugs. He never gets caught since he gets everyone else to do the dirty work, all the buying and selling. And he owns a pawn shop. Gives him legitimacy. So, my guess is the money's laundered through the shop, but I suspect he's hired an accountant to cover that up."

"Do you know if Brother Antoine knew Marcus?"

He shrugged. "Not to my knowledge."

"What about the other man who was killed, Sam Maureau?"

He shook his head. "I doubt it. He was another dealer, but he didn't live at the Redemption. Reggie kept up with the people there, mostly."

"One of our witnesses, a cousin of Louis's, Dwayne Bishop, said there are rumors going around about Brother Antoine. Do you know what that's about?"

"No. Kids are always talking trash. I wouldn't pay attention to that. I think I may know Dwayne. He's a good kid, played with us for a while, but he's pretty intimidated by his cousin Marcus. The whole family is, really. He's the boss. Make no mistake."

"You mean he runs the family?" Josh jotted down notes as he spoke.

"He does, but it's more than that. He makes a lot of money. I'm pretty sure he takes care of them. Gets their groceries and all that. He uses that to get them to do what he wants. He does the same to others. He offers them a little money, but more money than they've ever seen, and gets them to do some of his smaller stuff, none of which is legal, of course. Marcus is a great manipulator, but he's lethal. Poison. Especially to kids."

"So he uses kids. What do you mean by smaller stuff?" Josh said. He stopped writing and glanced up at Lionel.

"A lot of the drug business is hand to hand and kids are good at that. They can carry money or small amounts of drugs, and no one would suspect. Marcus gets them to carry out those small exchanges for him. He promises them membership in his gang in exchange for those favors. I'm sure he pays them too. But gang membership feels like 'family' to the kids. Gives them the feeling they're protected, that they belong. Of course, they're not protected at all. If they join, they're more in jeopardy than they've ever been."

"Right. I've been told kids take the rap sometimes for the gang activity, and I'm thinking that's what Louis might have done, not realizing he was going to find himself in the Orleans Parish Prison with grown men instead of at juvenile."

Officer Boudreaux shook his head. "If that's what happened, it's a shame. Louis is getting a little old to be manipulated like that, but Marcus is intimidating. I've heard he's not all bad. He likes to help folks out sometimes. I know he's helped take care of families who don't have enough food to eat. But there's no excuse for pressuring kids like he does."

"He's probably manipulated Louis his entire life." Emma paused. "Do you know the young girl Brother Antoine was visiting the night he was killed? I believe her name is Alicia Bishop."

"I don't know her, but I think she lives with her mom, who owns a hair salon in the neighborhood, if it's the woman I'm thinking of. The name of the salon is A Cut Above."

"I'm pretty sure Alicia lives with her Aunt Juanita. And that's right, Juanita owns a hair salon. How do you know her?"

"Let's just say Juanita has a reputation for holding her own. She doesn't put up with any crap, not from anyone. She's a strong woman."

"What do you mean by 'crap'?"

"I think that's a question for Juanita. You should pay her a visit. She's earned her nickname. You'd enjoy meeting her."

"What's her nickname?"

"The Queen." Officer Boudreaux smiled.

"And there's one more thing you should know."

"What's that?" Emma leaned closer.

"Reggie was a friend of the police department."

"What does that mean?"

"That's all I can say. Just know he was a friend."

* * *

On their way back to school following the meeting with Lionel, Emma and Josh drove down Magazine Street, past A Cut Above. Emma found an unmetered parking space close to the shop, and pulled in.

The interior of the shop was painted in more hues of purple than Emma thought possible, with swags of hand-painted gazebo-like structures designating each work station. As they waited to speak to Juanita Bishop, Emma perused the salon, fascinated with the work that was going on at each post and what had already taken place on top of the receptionist's head. A Cut Above excelled in architectural-type coiffeurs. Hair was braided, ironed, coaxed, prodded, then molded into various forms several feet high, with geometric, botanical and other design features that would have inspired any of the Renaissance artists. Most were up-dos. Some were cone shaped. There were beehives and precariously perched swoops. All had embellishments of some sort, some as detailed as accordion shaped festoons that looped from one end of the coiffure to the other. The receptionist garnished her look with four-inch chartreuse fingernails and glittery gold eye makeup. Emma, dressed in her navy suit, her hair in a ponytail, felt dull in comparison. A caterpillar among butterflies. She stared at the receptionist, admiring her fastidious sparkles from the top of her head to her shiny opalescent toe nails. There was not one chip or mar on any shiny surface. She didn't know how she managed such perfection. There was no question that the ladies of New Orleans spent a great deal of money at A Cut Above and that Juanita had to be making a pretty good profit. Emma wondered why she was still living at the Redemption.

A tall woman with regal features, flawless umber-colored skin, and towering hair glided around the corner in a billowing caftan. She extended her hand.

"I'm Juanita Bishop. Can I help you?"

"I represent your nephew, Louis Bishop. I'd like to talk to you about the night of the double killing in your neighborhood."

"I don't have a client for another fifteen minutes. We can step in the back to talk if you'd like."

Emma agreed, and they walked through the shop to a small office painted a cheerful periwinkle, with a black metal desk and a couple of zebra striped chairs. Several days of mail littered the top of her credenza, but Emma could tell Juanita deployed order in the management of her business. Behind all of the glamor, glitz, and tall hair in the shop, there was a serious woman. It was easy to see how Juanita had earned her nickname.

"If I understand things correctly, you're Louis's aunt. And Brother Antoine was visiting Alicia at your house the night he was killed?"

"That's right." Juanita picked up her mail and began separating it into organized stacks.

"What is your relationship to Alicia?"

Juanita smiled. "She's my niece. Mama, we call her Mama Ruby, had six kids. I'm the oldest. Alicia's mom, Amy, is the baby. Amy got problems." Juanita rolled her eyes toward the ceiling. "You met Sandra, Louis's mom, right? She had a few things going on too, but not as bad as Amy." She shook her head.

"Yes, I met her. What do you mean by Amy's 'problems'?"

"She got a pretty bad crack habit. It's upsettin' for a lot of reasons, but mainly 'cause Alicia's a great kid. She lives with me because she needs some stability. There's not much at Amy's and my mom's place, even though my mom tries. But the place is overrun with everyone and everything, you know. Too many kids and too many things going down there. My mom ends up cooking for everyone, and tries to hold them all together, but Marcus takes over. It's not a good environment for a kid."

"What do you mean when you say Marcus takes over?"

"Well, he buys the groceries, and he's there every Sunday and a lot of the other days. He's just there too much as far as I'm concerned."

"But he doesn't live there?"

"No, he don't. He got his own place above his shop, down on Louisiana. It's real nice."

Emma nodded as she scribbled in her notebook. "Did you sit down with Brother Antoine and Alicia when they met on the night of the shootings, the night he was killed?" Emma looked down at her notes.

"Well, I was there. I offered Brother Antoine something to drink and, you know, just hung out, in case there were questions. The scholarship is important to Alicia. I hope to move out of the Redemption soon too. I been saving up to buy a house. 'Course, Alicia would come along, you know. She's a part of my family and always will be." Juanita leaned back in her chair and crossed her legs, looking even more regal as her caftan floated around her knees.

"Do you recall anything of the events of the shooting? Did you walk Brother Antoine to the door, see a gathering of men or boys outside in the common area or anything that night?"

"I didn't walk him to the door, but after they were out there, I thought I heard something that sounded like gunshots, and I ran out to the front porch to check. Alicia was already there."

"How many gunshots did you hear?"

"I thought I heard two." She held up two elegant, tapered fingers. "But I'm not sure. There could have been more."

Emma checked her notes. "One other thing—I spoke to one of the police officers who patrols the 6th District. He said that he knows of you and that you don't put up with crap. What does he mean by that?" Emma scooted up on the edge of her seat.

"Who said that? I'd like to know before I tell you anything."

Emma nodded. "Lionel Boudreaux. Do you know him?"

Juanita nodded. "I think I know who he is. He's one of the good guys, and they aren't all so good. I know who the drug dealers are around here. Half of them are relatives. I can handle that. But when cops come calling for a favor, or to put pressure on me for money for 'protective services,'—she made quotations marks in the air with her fingers—after they've already been paid by the city to protect me, that's where I draw a line. I'm not paying a cop to protect me. And I'm not going to fall for their shakedown. I don't need an off-duty cop hanging around my shop. There's no need for that here on Magazine Street. Give me a break." She stood up, gesturing toward the schedule on the bulletin board. "We don't stay open that late." She walked to the back window and looked out. "It gets a little dicey down here sometimes, but you just watch what you're doing." Juanita sat back down and put her hands on her temples and massaged them as if she was trying to relieve a headache.

"Oh my God. I don't blame you. I had no idea this went on. I see police officers standing guard duty at private businesses all the time. Is that what's going on? Are they harassing the business owners for protection money?"

"I can't speak to that. I don't know about no one else. I only know what happened to me. But I think it may have happened to some of the others here on Magazine."

"Did the cops leave you alone after that?"

Juanita sat back in her chair. "No, they didn't. One night, when I was closing up the shop, one of the cops who tried to force protection on me earlier, came up behind me and shoved me against that door, sayin' I'd better be careful, that they was watching me, that they knew about my family. He said if I'm not careful, they might find a health violation at the shop, or even worse. He said if I don't cooperate with them, they might even find some of the stuff like my nephew sells somewhere in the shop. And I could go to jail for a long time."

Emma shook her head. "What did you do? Did you agree to the protection?"

"No. I called the 6th District and reported the cop who shoved me against the door for police brutality."

Emma nodded. "Looks like Officer Boudreaux was right about you. You don't take any crap off anyone. What happened after that?"

"They said they were conducting an internal investigation, but I haven't heard nothin' since I reported it." She sat with her elbows resting on the arms of her chair with her hands, fingertips joined in a steeple-like point under her chin, the picture of composure.

"You know you could file a private lawsuit against the police department."

"I know. That's not really my style. I'd like to see what happens with the complaint. That's all I'd really like to follow up on at this point."

"Do you know if you had any witnesses to what happened or if there were any cameras in the area? Do you have a camera outside your shop?"

"I don't but I'll ask some of my neighbors. I never got one because I've been saving my money to move."

"At this point, the equipment, or a camera, at least, is probably a good idea. You might need some back up."

Juanita glanced down at the ledger on her desk. "You might be right. I'll look into it."

Emma exchanged phone numbers with Juanita and made plans with her to speak with Alicia on a night when her homework wasn't overwhelming. As she was gathering her purse to leave, Juanita sat back in her chair.

"There's one more thing. I'm gonna tell Alicia not to answer any questions about the night of the shootings. If you knew my nephew like I do, you'd understand."

Emma sat back down in the zebra striped chair. Several seconds passed before she spoke. "Are you saying you believe Marcus had something to do with the shootings?"

"No. I'm just saying Alicia ain't gonna answer questions about that night. Period. I'm only doin' this to protect her. I don't even want you coming up to my house. For any reason. Talking to you at the shop today was okay. But never at my place." Juanita sighed as if she was relieved.

"I understand more about Marcus than you know." Emma paused. "What if I set up another place for Alicia and me to meet? Would that work for you?"

Juanita shrugged. "I could think about it. But I'm not too crazy about Alicia speaking to anyone, anywhere."

"I'm pretty sure I have a place, a Catholic Charities thrift shop over on Carrollton. I'll have to set it up—make sure there's a private room to meet in, and all of that."

Juanita nodded. "I'll think about it, like I said."

"Okay. I'll set it up and call you."

"You need to understand I don't know if Alicia saw anything that night or not. But being a witness to a crime is dangerous around here. So, she's not going to know anything about that night. At all."

Chapter Thirteen

Emma heard the sound of skittering dog nails on the wooden floors of her apartment as she made her way up the steps. She was a few minutes past four getting home. She cursed herself under her breath. She had to do better than this. The boys should already be home, or, at least, she prayed they were. And that everything was okay.

When she opened the door, Maddie and Lulu, ran circles around her legs, their back ends wiggling in syncopated pirouettes, signaling that everything was right in the world. They were beautiful, athletic, intelligent creatures who were gentle one moment and playful and full of mischief the next. More importantly, they'd become a barometer for everything that happened inside and in close proximity to the house. If something was askew, they'd know immediately, and unless they were distracted by a tasty treat, they'd let everyone else know.

"Hey mom. You're never going to believe what happened." Bobby's smile was shaky. Billy and Bobby looked like young, blonde colts, all legs and knobby knees. Puberty wasn't far away, their voices had started deepening, but they were still boys, not quite young men, and were at the age where curiosity and adventure were constantly beckoning. Even though Emma was relieved to see Bobby, she was immediately suspicious.

"And what would that be?" Emma sat her purse down, patted Maddie's head, and scratched behind Lulu's ears.

"When I came home today, Maddie and Lulu were on the roof." Bobby's smile became even more tenuous, then disappeared altogether when he saw his mother's face.

"What? That needs some explaining. By all means, get over here and fill me in."

Bobby edged toward his mother, his eyes darting between the stairs and where she stood as if he was planning an escape.

"Do you mean you took the dogs out on the roof after I told you not to? Or did you leave the window to the bathroom open again and the dogs got out on their own? Either situation is pretty irresponsible, you know." Emma folded her arms across her chest.

Bobby looked down at his scruffy, untied tennis shoes, and shrugged. "Yeah. I guess we might have had the window open before we went to school. I don't remember. The dogs were out on the roof when we got home. We looked up and saw them up there, barking at us. Their ears were hanging over the gutters. It was pretty crazy." He attempted a smile.

"Jesus. They could have really gotten hurt if they'd jumped or fallen, Bobby. Or an ambitious thief could have figured out a way to climb into the house while we were out. It wouldn't have taken much of an effort with a wide-open window. You two have got to be more responsible than that. Where's your brother? Billy, get down here!"

"Yes ma'am." Billy crept down the stairs.

"I've told you two a thousand times do not go out on the roof. And don't leave the window open! I would board it up, but that would actually be a fire hazard. The roof is a danger to you and now to your dogs. You two are responsible for Maddie and Lulu. They're a part of our family, and your carelessness could have ended up costing them their lives."

Emma thought she noticed Billy's eyes welling up. She looked at the twins. They knew she was upset, and they always wanted to avoid that, but she wasn't sure they really got it. If they did, they wouldn't have left the damn window open again. Of course, she hadn't told them about Marcus, because she didn't want to scare them. But she also wanted them to be careful.

"Should I look into finding another home for Maddie and Lulu? A place with someone who would actually care for them?"

They shook their heads.

"Then you'd better start paying attention to what you're doing. I'm going to look into getting a lock for that window, and I'll be the only one who'll have the key to it. You've forced my hand on this."

"Yes ma'am." Both boys said in unison.

"Do you two think you can behave yourselves, or do I need to look into getting a babysitter for you?" Emma turned when she heard a noise which sounded like someone clearing their throat. Ren peeked his head from behind a wing-back chair. Emma jumped back, startled.

"Oh my God! Ren! Why didn't you tell me about Ren, guys!"

"We were going to, but we just hadn't gotten there yet. Plus, he wanted to surprise you." Billy said as he grinned at their guest.

"Well, he did! What brings you to New Orleans?" She ran to Ren as he began to stand from the chair and threw her arms around his neck and hugged him as hard as she could.

Ren kissed her, grabbed the small of her back with his arms and pulled her close. "I just wanted to check up on you. See how things are goin'." He released her, held her at arm's length and as he checked her out from head to foot, smiling. "Lookin' good, Miss Emma. I got a friend from the Academy who moved here a couple of years ago. Thought I'd check in with him, too, see how he's likin' it here. But mainly, I just wanted to see you guys." He ruffled the heads of twins and canines alike, all of which were within arm's reach.

"I'm so glad to see you! How do you like the new additions to our family?" Maddie and Lulu danced around Ren, tails wagging, as if they knew they were the topic of discussion.

"They're beautiful, but looks like they tend to get in a little trouble, just like their mom."

* * *

Emma cleared the dishes away and shooed the twins upstairs to complete their homework before lights-out. Ren had already begun filling the dishwasher. They swung back into their old routine as if they hadn't lost any time together. Emma scraped and rinsed the dishes; he loaded the dishwasher and washed the pots. It was a muscle memory of comfort and ease, time worn, and sure.

Emma loved having him in her kitchen. His tall form nearly filled the space. The overhead light caught the golden flecks in his hair, and his kind brown eyes, crinkling in the corners from sunshine and smiles, warmed her heart. There was something sexy about a man doing a little housework.

"How's your case goin'?" Ren threw the dish towel over his shoulder and sprinkled soap in the dishwasher dispenser.

"It's going, but we are only at the very beginning. And I'm running into a few road blocks already witnesses who don't want to talk in "exposed" places like coffee shops, others who don't want to talk at all. I can't even get to the bottom of the rumors about the deceased victims. I don't know anything about anything yet. And." She hesitated. "Did I tell you about Marcus?"

"What about Marcus?"

Emma took Ren's hand and walked him into the living room and sat down on the couch. She pulled him down next to her.

"I ended up calling him after all. He called me back and said he knew about the twins, and where their bus stop is. Scared me to death. I've started making sure I'm here by the time the twins get home, by 4:00."

"What? I told you not to contact that guy. You never give your personal information out!"

"I didn't. But I called his beeper and he called me back on my office line. I guess someone followed me home and figured out where the kids' bus stop is."

"Good God, Emma! This is just what I told you to avoid!" Ren jumped up from the couch and began pacing the room. "This isn't good."

"That's an understatement." Emma massaged her temples.

Ren clinched his fists. "This isn't a joke. You're in real danger. You've been threatened, and even though bein' at your place when the boys get home is a good step, you couldn't fend off a guy with a gun. I remember your marksmanship. A gun in your hands would be even more dangerous to you and the boys."

Emma squinted her eyes and looked at Ren. "Wait a minute. Why are you here? You said you wanted to see your friend who's with the NOPD. You wouldn't be thinking of a move to New Orleans, would you?"

Ren sat down next to her and grabbed her hand.

"Not so fast. Let's not change the subject. This thing with Marcus scares me. What about that open window upstairs? Couldn't Marcus or one of his gang members have crawled upstairs and left it open? If you're not going to be careful you shouldn't take cases like Louis's." He shook his head. "What am I going to do with you?"

"I understand why you're upset. I didn't dream the boys would be a target. It's upsetting to me too. I haven't been sleeping at night. And that's why I got the dogs. Plus I've been hearing some rumblings of corruption on the New Orleans police force. I'm not sure who to trust, except for you and my colleagues at school."

He nodded. "For now, make sure you're here by 4:00, and be here as often as you can. Keep your eye on Billy and Bobby and don't go out after dark. I'm upset, not angry. You know that. My buddy, the guy I'm talkin' to tomorrow, works for internal affairs. So, yeah, he knows about the corruption. It's been in the papers, right? But he can't speak to me about it directly." Ren said.

"One of the witnesses in Louis's case has filed a claim against an officer who threatened her for failing to pay his 'protection fee.' He shoved her around a bit and threatened her shop with health violations, and worse, too." Emma leaned back against the couch and pulled her legs up.

"I knew these things went on, but it's still a shocker when it happens. It's a pretty tough place if the cops turn against you."

"I know. At least I know one good cop. We're going down to the NOPD tomorrow to pick up the ballistics and autopsy reports. Want to come along?"

"Sure. And you're right. I'm exploring a possible move to New Orleans. I just want to see what's open for me here. Do you think we could stop off and get some of those beignets for breakfast on the way down to get the reports?"

"Of course. It'll be an early morning. We should get ready for bed."

* * *

Emma and Ren pulled up at NOPD's 6th District offices at the same time Emma's students, Josh and Melissa were exiting their car. Emma hoped the forensic evidence in the case might unlock clues to Louis's innocence. Fifteen minutes later they were all sitting outside at Emma's favorite coffee shop on Magazine Street reviewing the results.

"I can't believe you can't get beignets anywhere but the French Quarter." Ren said. He'd discovered beignets, a French donut, fried to a golden brown and dipped in powdered sugar, on one of his earlier trips to New Orleans. He'd never forget the experience. Delicate and light, yet crunchy, it was as near to heaven as a pastry could get in his estimation.

"There are a few other places that offer them. The best place is in the French Quarter." Melissa offered.

"Where? Close by?" Ren looked at Emma.

"It's not that far. Nothing in New Orleans is that far away." Emma studied the reports and took a bite of her muffin as she shooed a few hungry birds away from her crumbs. "If you help me with these reports, I'll take you today."

Ren nodded and grabbed the autopsy reports of the each of the victims.

"But first, I have to hire you as an expert consultant. Will coffee and beignets suffice for your pay for right now?"

"Sure."

"Then we can work out something else later."

Ren smiled. Josh turned a shade redder and Melissa grinned.

Emma grabbed Ren's knee under the table and chuckled as he blushed. "But I'm serious. We may need help in this case. It would be great if you could testify about the ballistics issues too, but that's impossible, I'm afraid."

"Right. The DA could have a field day with that. But I could be a consultant. Especially if it's something we can work on while I'm here, or if we can work on it long distance, if I end up going back to Jonesburg." He took a sip of his coffee, eyeing Emma over his cup.

Emma looked up. *"If you go back to Jonesburg?"*

Ren picked up the autopsy report. "This is interesting. Sam Maureau was standing close to Marcus and Louis and the others in a cluster, because they were talking. They had to have been only a couple of feet away from each other, right? But there are no powder burns, or marks, or any indication that he received a close-range shot. Look, the report says, 'No soot or stippling noted.'" He showed the report to Emma, who passed it over to Josh and Melissa. They reviewed it, took a few notes while Ren slurped his coffee.

"One of the shots was fatal. It was to the abdomen and chest." Ren paused, pointing to the language of the report. "It caused '...perforating injuries to the ascending colon, liver, right hemidiaphragm, the pericardium, the heart, and upper lobe of the left lung. A bullet exited the anterior left shoulder area.' So that shot was at an angle, right? The entrance was in the lower abdomen and it exited at the shoulder."

Emma grabbed the multi-paged report and flipped through several sheets until she reached an anatomical drawing on page four. Examining the outlined figure of a generic male, she searched for 'x's' indicating entrance and exit wounds. Three shots hit Maureau, which meant there were six entrance and exit wounds in total, which was more than she'd anticipated. Dragging her finger over the drawing, she located the fatal shot by the chest wall, tracing the imaginary bullet up through Maureau's liver, heart, and finally through the shoulder. The other two wounds were superficial, but at entirely different angles, entering and exiting the body in straight lines.

"Well, that would do it."

Emma scanned the remaining pages of Maureau's report. There were three wounds. Two seemed harmless enough. Only one proved fatal. The others were a shot to the right thigh with a clean entrance and exit wound, which caused little damage, and a grazed right shoulder.

"But look at the angle of that fatal shot, Emma."

"It's pretty weird, huh?"

"Yes. How do you get off a shot at that angle unless it's coming from below?"

"Like from the ground, or a seated position?" Emma angled a pen from the point of the entry wound to a distance away from the sketch.

"Or the shooter could have been squatting down when he made his shot," Josh offered.

Ren raised his eyebrows. "I guess anything's possible. Is there something large enough to hide behind in that common area where the shootings occurred?" Ren sat his coffee cup on the table.

"There's a bench, and I'm pretty sure there's a big green pad mounted transformer in the middle of the common area, too." Melissa scribbled notes reminding herself to check the area for the exact location and size of the electrical box.

Emma moved on to Brother Antoine's report, immediately turning to the anatomical sketch. The drawing was simple, less cluttered than Maureau's. There was only one 'x,' placed directly in the middle of the victim's chest.

"One shot? I've always assumed this was an accidental shooting, that Brother Antoine, a bystander, was just unlucky and got in the way. But even if it was accidental, I still don't see how one shooter could have pulled off all of these shots. Certainly not a kid like Louis. It looks like, based on the angle of Maureau's fatal shot, there was a shooter outside of their group. Maybe more than one. Marcus could have had one planted somewhere. He could have had Louis go get his gun, then pass it off to someone else who did the actual shootings." She grabbed a napkin and began sketching out the common area, placing small circles in the space to indicate where people were standing.

Ren nodded. "There are a hundred scenarios that could work, but that's as good as any. The gun they recovered, the Glock, has a range of fifty-five yards, which is about a hundred and fifty feet or so. The shooter could have been anywhere within that distance from the victims. But, we can also narrow down where it was coming from by the angle of the bullet trajectory."

"By the looks of the ballistics reports, the only casings they found at the scene were tied to the Glock. Is that how you read it?"

"Yep."

"I don't see any reference to bullets found in the bodies, do you?"

Ren scanned the reports. "Nothing was found in Maureau's body, but there was one found in Brother Antoine, see?"

"The bullet found in Brother Antoine was from the Glock?" Emma noted the finding in her notepad.

Ren shrugged. "It's from a Glock. They took test shots from the weapon found under Mrs. Bishop's apartment. But a Glock has polygonal rifling. You can't measure the width of the land and groove impressions on most models because the rifling inside the barrel is rounded. When the bullet is fired, it doesn't leave the usual impressions and you can't tell one bullet or casing from another. So, forensic examination is impossible. In other words, you can't match up the bullet fired to a specific gun. So, test shots don't mean much."

Emma glanced up from her notes. "If Maureau and Antoine were shot from two separate guns, or the same gun, we wouldn't be able to tell?"

"Correct."

"Does that mean there's no point to examining the bullet or the gun?"

"Not really. They've examined both the gun and the one bullet they've found. They couldn't match them up, but they couldn't exclude them as a match either. The prosecution is trying to pin the murder on Louis by claiming the gun they've identified is his, and that a witness saw him throw that gun under the apartment after the shootings. But that's all they've got. They can't prove that the bullet was shot from that gun. All they have is witness testimony against Louis right now."

Emma raised her eyebrows. "I see. They can say he was shot by a Glock, and a Glock was found at the scene, but they can't say, with certainty, that Brother Antoine was shot with the Glock they found under Ruby Bishop's apartment. Right?"

"That's how I see it right now. But I'd like to check out the gun and the bullet they found to be sure."

Emma nodded toward Melissa and Josh. "Let's file a motion for discovery and inspection this week so we can take a look at the gun, the bullets and casings and conduct our own testing. Make sure to include we'll only conduct non-destructive testing, and include a request for the missing casings from Maureau's shooting. Maybe the police picked them up that night, and the DA conveniently forgot to mention it to us.

"Also, we'll need measurements of the common area. We know approximately where people were standing and where the victims fell. We need to find places where a shooter could hide and we'll need to measure the distance between those possible hiding places and where the victims were that night. Could you two locate everything which might provide some coverage, something to hide behind, especially that transformer. And I'd like the measurements of the transformer."

Josh and Melissa scribbled furiously in their notepads as Emma spoke. "And there's one other thing. We need to keep in mind that Tamika was the person who said she saw Louis throw his gun under his grandmother's apartment. Where was she when she saw this? Did anyone else see her? We still haven't nailed down anything about Tamika and she's an essential witness."

"We'll get right on it." Josh said. He and Melissa gathered their things and left. Emma could hear Melissa asking Josh questions about the transformer as they stepped off the sidewalk to the car.

Emma pointed her pen toward Ren as she watched them leave. "Hopefully Melissa will be able to find a pathologist to testify at trial about the angle of the entry, and perhaps even about the fact that there had to be more than one shooter. Also, I like your point about the stippling. We need to look into that too. Seems they were standing close enough that there would have been some gun powder residue on Maureau. But it's too bad we can't use you at trial. You'd be so perfect. You graduated at the top of your class. No one knows more about guns than you do. But I'm afraid it might come out that you and I are in a relationship." She learned back in her chair.

"Yep. The DA could question my objectivity, and he should. 'Cause you drive me crazy." He laughed and grabbed her hands. "But seriously, if I worked as a consultant you wouldn't have to list me as a witness. And, who else would work for beignets." He leaned over and gave her a kiss.

Emma smiled. "I don't see how the DA could find out about us. But, I agree. We can't risk it. So, you're our first expert consultant. Welcome to the case." She hesitated for a moment, and returned his kiss. "I like having you around."

Chapter Fourteen

Emma and Ren found a parking place next to the river. Emma locked her car, breathing in the acrid aroma of the Mississippi, watching as barges and riverboats slowly plowed down the waterway, churning the muddy water in their wake. Emma rarely visited the French Quarter since like most residents of the city she preferred avoiding the narrow, crowded streets and toxic puddles of rain water, horse dung and last night's spilled bourbon. But whenever she made the effort, her love of the place was rekindled.

"I think I can smell those beignets already!" Ren lifted his nose in the direction of a nutty fried aroma.

Emma laughed as they continued walking down the river walk and pointed to a green and white striped awning. "That's where we're headed." The fried donut delicacies were found at the Café Du Monde, at the edge of the quarter, next to the French Market.

"Anyone ever go swimming in the river?"

"Are you kidding? That's a good way to die." She stopped for a minute along the walkway and pointed to the river.

"Can't you see those currents and eddies? That's the problem. I don't know if anyone's ever survived jumping or falling in, but if they have, the water's so toxic and muddy they disappear almost immediately. Most folks who fall in can't even be found."

Ren scanned the swirling waterway. "Yeah, I see them."

"Right. The Mississippi River can't be compared to your little Georgia swimming holes."

"All right, now, Emma. I'm not that much of a small-town boy."

Emma grabbed his arm and squeezed it, and gave him a hug. "I know." She chuckled.

"Thanks for bringing me down here. I know you're not as excited about this as I am."

They entered the café, made their way around the service line to order their food, paid, and found a seat.

"I'm in heaven," Ren said between bites, a white sugary mess all over his face.

Emma stifled a laugh, puffing slightly through her nose, blowing powdered sugar all over the table and the front of her jacket. "Geez. I always make such a mess when I come here, although I guess it's worth it."

"You bet it is." Ren licked the remaining sugar from his fingers. "Delicious! What's next?"

"Since we're here, we can walk through the quarter. Maybe chat about the case? I'd like to pick your brain. I'll bribe you with delicious cocktails, if necessary."

"Lead away!"

Emma's favorite route through the quarter was up Chartres and over to Royal. She liked the clothing stores on one street and the antique shops on the other. But she thought Ren would want to see the glitz and bawdy seediness of Bourbon Street, a block off Royal. They'd wander around a little and when they worked up an appetite, would stop for lunch. She loved playing tourist. And even though New Orleans had a high crime rate, nothing was safer than the areas frequented by crowds. That's what she always told her friends when they visited. "Stay on the streets where all of the tourists are, and you'll be safe. Don't go wandering off on side streets!" She knew she was safer in a busy section of the quarter than she was on her uptown street, especially at night.

They paused in front of an antique shop devoted entirely to kitchen gadgets, marveling at the prices of wine openers, and other items.

"I once found a German wine opener here exactly like one I had at home. It was $800 at this shop and I only paid $88 for mine." Emma shook her head.

"Emma, I can't believe you paid $88 for a wine opener. You can pick one up for a dollar anywhere."

"Not an antique German wine opener."

"Who cares about that, Emma?" Ren rolled his eyes and started down the street.

"So you don't care for my taste in antiquities?"

"I just don't understand it. Why pay more for something just because it's old?"

"The thought is it costs more because it's rare."

"And I think that's a load of crap."

"Maybe."

"The entire city is old and makes money on the fact that it's ancient and falling apart." He stomped down the sidewalk.

"I guess so. But, I like it." Emma scurried to catch up with him.

"Does it remind you of growing up in Savannah?"

"It does, a little. It has some of the same feel, but New Orleans is more decadent in some ways. Are you leaning one way or the other about the move to New Orleans?"

"Not sure." He caught her hand and gave it a squeeze. "I'm thinking about it. If you're on the same page. Would you like me to move here?"

"I'd love it. But what about running for Sheriff in Greendale County when Colson retires? I know he wants you to replace him. He's been grooming you for that position for years."

"I'm not in love with Colson, or the people of Greendale County. I'm in love with you. And you're here."

"Wouldn't you hate it here?"

"I'm not sure, but I know I hate not being with you."

"I love you, too. I just want to make sure you're happy." Emma took his hand and squeezed it as they walked down the street.

They walked for a while holding hands, finally turning to the lights and girly shows of Bourbon Street.

"What a city." Ren rubbed his head as if it hurt.

"You get used to it after a while. When are you talking to your friend?"

"Later on today, after his shift is over. We're meeting somewhere for a beer. I'm not sure this is going to work out, Emma. I just want to see if it can, you know? I can't live with myself if I don't at least try."

She led him toward one of her favorite spots for lunch. "Let's get a muffuletta and a Pimm's Cup." They entered an ancient structure on Chartres, built in 1794, as legend had it, as a residence for Napoleon Bonaparte. Ren and Emma made a bee-line for a cozy table and chairs in the interior courtyard, lured by its dancing banana trees and palm fronds. The patio felt cool even though temperatures on the streets were still hovering close to ninety. Emma glanced up and noticed huge fans working furiously overhead. She leaned back against her chair, and smiled, forgetting for a moment about Louis's defense and the murders of Brother Antoine and Sam Maureau.

Ren reached across the table and grabbed her hands. "What's a muffuletta and a Pimm's Cup?"

Fifteen minutes later the waiter, dressed in a long-sleeved white shirt and black vest, sweating profusely in the heat, swooped in next to them with a large silver tray and stand, and ceremoniously placed a plate with a large round multi-layered sandwich in the middle of the table. It had been cut into several segments. Emma placed a few pieces on their plates. Then he placed a couple of tall frosty glasses that looked like iced tea and garnished with cucumber on the table.

"The muffuletta's an Italian sandwich. See the layers? And the olive spread? It's full of garlic, and all of the Italian meat, salami, and pastrami you could ever imagine." She moved a frosty glass toward him. "And you have to try this too. The Pimm's Cup ... a classic gin-based cocktail."

Fifteen minutes later, neither Ren nor Emma could move.

"Good God, I couldn't get up and walk around now if I had to." Ren rubbed his stomach.

"Yep. It was part of my plan to make you my captive." Emma dabbed her mouth with her napkin.

"No doubt. But I can think of a few other ways you could capture me as well." Ren leaned over to deliver a kiss.

"Before you continue with anymore of that, you have to answer some more questions." She stopped his advance with her fingertips. "Such as, what role you'd see for yourself with the NOPD, if you actually agreed to take a position with the police force here?"

He squeezed her hand. "You need to realize that this may not happen. And, like I said, I really need to speak to my friend. But, if they'd consider my ten years of experience as Deputy Chief toward a Detective position here, I might be interested. I don't want to start at the bottom. I'm sure I'd have to take an exam, and that's okay." He shrugged.

Emma smiled at Ren. "Before we get caught up with packing and getting you on an airplane, can you tell me what your thoughts are about this case, from what I've told you so far?"

"I don't think I have many more insights, really. It would appear Marcus and Maureau were involved in a territorial dispute over drugs and something went wrong."

Emma nodded. "And Maureau was killed."

"Yep. The question is, who pulled the trigger. No witness has reported that they saw Louis actually shoot anyone right?" Ren said.

"That's right. The only evidence so far is the gun they found under Louis's grandmother's apartment, and Tamika's testimony, which won't be good for Louis if she's believable." Emma took a sip of her drink.

"And that's a good question. Was Louis set up, either by Marcus or even Tamika? And keep in mind when you talk to witnesses, or the people who were there that night, there are those who will be loyal to Marcus, for reasons that are apparent to both of us. They're either on Marcus's payroll, or they're dependent on Marcus to supply their drugs. And Tamika could be in both categories. I don't think you can trust them. You're going to have to figure all that out, and I'm sure you will. We don't know if Marcus set up Louis yet, but it looks that way. If Marcus didn't, what happened? Also, was Brother Antoine's death an accident? If not, who would want him dead?"

Chapter Fifteen

Emma got the boys off to the bus, their blonde hair still tousled from sleep. The older they got, the more difficult it was to wake them in the morning. But they made it, shirts barely tucked in and shoes partially tied, laces flying. She breathed a sigh of relief. She kept an eye out when the boys boarded the bus in the morning, and as often as she could, when they got off the bus in the afternoon. So far, she hadn't noticed any unusual cars in their neighborhood. If Marcus or his cronies were spying on her family, they were inconspicuous about it.

Since Ren was visiting, she decided to skip her usual morning run. She got out her yoga mat to work on a few stretches before she hit the shower. Pulling back into downward dog, she sneaked an upside-down peek at Ren as he swigged a cup of coffee. It was nice to have him around. In many ways, he completed their family. But as much as she'd like him to move to New Orleans, the city wasn't his sort of place. And they both knew it. A car horn blasted from the street. Ren stuck his head out of her kitchen window and waved at his friend, Scott McEnroe, below.

"I'll probably be a couple of hours." Ren bolted down the stairs.

Scott worked at internal affairs in the New Orleans Police Department and was picking up Ren to meet with a few other officers. They planned to discuss the openings in the department and whether Ren and his background could be a fit.

After a few more stretches, she stepped on the scale and popped into the shower. She was meeting Juanita and Alicia at St. Francis de Paul's at 11:00.

* * *

Emma glanced around for Melissa as she stepped onto the crooked front stoop of St. Francis's thrift shop. Melissa was usually on time. A bell rang cheerily as Emma entered and introduced herself.

"Father Alfonso called and reserved the room for us. We shouldn't be more than an hour or so." Emma smiled at the clerk, hoping the call had actually been made. She looked around the dusty shop, noting it was filled with an assortment of odds and ends, old china and used clothes, chipped lamps and broken-down furniture, all at "discount" prices.

The clerk nodded toward the back, then scurried ahead of her down the hall to turn on the dingy overhead light. Emma thought the space must have once been a lunch area for employees, but it hadn't been used, or cleaned, in years. There was a small table, four metal chairs, and a refrigerator which stood in one corner. A dead roach lay in the middle of the floor, and old boxes and trash were piled high next to an empty vending machine. Debris and dust littered the room. She couldn't imagine anyone would still use the place for lunch or anything else. She scrounged around in her purse until she found a tissue, which she used to pick up the roach and throw it away. She tidied up the corner as best she could, washed her hands and sat down to wait. Juanita, Alicia, and Melissa should be arriving soon.

She was surprised she'd been able to convince Juanita to bring Alicia in for the meeting. But Juanita took family seriously, and her nephew Louis was in a lot of trouble. Emma was hoping Alicia or Juanita would tell them more about the work Louis and the other boys did for Marcus and the Gangsta B's. And she hoped she could convince Juanita to allow Alicia to speak to them about the night of the murders.

She heard the tinkling of the front door as it opened and some murmurings as people in the front of the shop exchanged words. She stood up as she heard them walking down the hallway to the small room where she waited.

Emma extended her hand as they entered the room. "Thanks for driving all the way out here. Sorry, the place is not quite up to health code. Believe it or not, I've tidied up." She nodded toward the neatly stacked piles in the corner.

"We're a little late because we took the bus. Alicia had practice for junior choir at church after school." Juanita pulled out a chair. "She plays piano for them. And don't worry about that little pile of trash. That's nothin'." Juanita waved her hand in the direction of the mound of boxes and smiled. She had exchanged her flowing caftan for a pair of bejeweled blue jeans, topped off with an embellished, multicolored tunic. Additional sparkle was added with Coke can-sized hoop earrings, hot pink stacked heels, and her signature up-do. She looked like an Egyptian goddess, a towering kaleidoscope of color.

In sharp contrast was Alicia, wearing a navy-blue school uniform with a crisp, white page-boy collared shirt. A tiny gold cross dangled at her neck. Her hair, smoothed into a sleek bob, complimented her studious attire. Her skin, flawless, and as smooth as silk, shone with a fresh glow, soap and water her only cosmetic. Although she was still a child, deep intelligence flashed behind her eyes. She had a quiet presence, but Emma could see she already knew who she was and that she was quite comfortable with it. So unusual for a girl her age. She carried a backpack, which must have weighed more than she did.

Emma gestured for them to take a seat. She heard the tinkling sound of the front doorbell again.

"I believe that's Melissa, one of my students from the law school. If it's okay with you, she'll be asking some questions today, too."

"Sure. Sometimes, two heads are better than one." Juanita looked at Alicia and raised her eyebrows. Alicia nodded, a faint smile flashed across her face.

Melissa entered the room and extended her hand to Juanita, and then Alicia. She pulled out a chair next to Alicia's, scraping it against her backpack, causing it to topple over. A book spilled out. Melissa leaned over to pick it up.

"*The Last Vampire.* I finished this a couple of weeks ago. You're going to love it." Melissa handed the book back to Alicia.

"I can't believe she's reading that vampire trash." Juanita rolled her eyes.

Alicia looked at Melissa with widened eyes while Melissa did her best to suppress a smile.

Emma cleared her throat. "Let's first get an idea about what you're comfortable having Alicia talk about today. We know you don't want her to speak about the actual shootings, but Louis could end up at Angola, on death row. You don't want that for him, either. It will be important to know whether Alicia saw anything that night that could help prove he didn't shoot either of the men. His life could depend on it." Emma pulled out her notebook and pen.

Juanita nodded. "I understand."

Melissa looked at Alicia. "Alicia, was there someone else on the scene who we don't know about? Did you see Louis leave the scene before the shooting began? That's the sort of information we're looking for." Melissa said as she scooted her chair closer to the table and leaned toward Alicia.

Alicia looked at her aunt, who shook her head.

"The DA may also subpoena Alicia eventually, and no one would be able to prohibit her from answering his questions. So, we may as well know what she knows. I realize that sounds harsh, but it will likely all come out in the end."

Alicia nodded and clutched her necklace. "I understand. I think I can help."

Juanita shook her head again. "No, Alicia. I don't want you to testify about that night. Not a word." Juanita laid her hand on the table, her palm flat, then raised it, slicing through the air in a chopping motion, her fuchsia fingernails flashing in the overhead light. "Not for any purpose. You can talk to her about a few things, but she will not be a witness. I'm trying to protect her. I've seen what can happen to witnesses in cases like these, and it's not good."

"Let's just start with some basic questions." Emma turned to Alicia.

"Alicia, do you and Louis attend the same school?"

"Yes, ma'am, but we don't have the same teachers. For one thing, he's in a higher grade, and I'm in advanced classes. And I just applied for a scholarship to Our Lady of Fatima. I'm keeping my fingers crossed." Alicia smiled, her face flushed.

"She's a straight A student. And she never misses school, even when she feels bad. She don't like to get behind in her work," Juanita interrupted, her head held high.

"That's quite impressive, Alicia." Emma flipped a page in her legal pad. "What can you tell me about your cousin Marcus?"

"He can be okay sometimes. He gives Mama Ruby money for groceries and stuff." She paused. "He bosses the boys around. Tells them what to do. But he leaves me alone." She shrugged. "One time a kid was pickin' on me. Followed me from school, and Marcus saw him makin' fun of me. Called me 'Slick' and 'Brainiac', 'cause he thought I was smart." She twisted a small section of hair next to her face. "The kid didn't bother me. He might have been trying to, but he didn't. Still, Marcus came up to him and told him to stop. Said he'd make sure he'd never pick on anyone again if he didn't. I haven't had a problem with anyone after that."

"So, Marcus's been pretty good to you?"

"He usually just leaves me alone. And I don't see him much. I stay by myself at Aunt Juanita's after school most days so I can get my homework done, unless I'm over at Mama Ruby's. I do a lot of reading, too. I'm never in his way. But it's different with the boys, especially Louis. He bullies him. Sometimes he even makes fun of him because he likes to draw. Marcus doesn't think men are supposed to do things like that. Especially fashion stuff. Sometimes Marcus calls Louis 'Hilfiger.' He makes Louis do stuff for him and calls him his little bitch."

Juanita folded her arms across her chest and shook her head.

"He calls him Hilfiger for the designer, Tommy Hilfiger?" Emma looked up from her notepad.

Alicia nodded.

"That isn't so bad."

"But he mocks him. He asked Louis when he was going to start wearing dresses and knitting shawls with Mama Ruby. And, the truth was that Louis really liked doing those things. He and Mama Ruby would get together and cut out patterns for dresses or coats. But Marcus made so much fun of him, he just quit when he got older. But I know he hasn't stopped thinking about designing clothes because he hasn't stopped drawing them. It's his favorite thing to do."

"How does Marcus get Louis to do what he wants?" Emma leaned back in her chair.

"Mostly, Louis does things for Marcus to stop his bullying. Sometimes Marcus even pushes him into fights. Louis would do anything to make Marcus stop making fun of him. But then Louis started getting money for what he was doing for Marcus, and after that, he was a part of the whole thing. Marcus calls his gang 'family.' Now Louis does too." Alicia looked down at her tightly entwined fingers.

"Does Louis like being part of Marcus's gang?"

"I don't think so. Louis is a nice person. Before Marcus made him do so much, he'd hang out a lot more at Aunt Juanita's house. He hid out there to read his graphic novels, listen to music, and draw. I think he needed to get away. Not from Mama Ruby. He loves her. But he likes to keep to himself, and I think he wanted to get away from Marcus. Sometimes he'd make up words to the songs I played on the piano. Silly ones, you know? He doesn't do that so much anymore."

"But Marcus's gang is mostly family, right?" Melissa chimed in.

"No, not really. I think Marcus's gang is scattered all over the city. Dwayne, Georgie, Louis, and probably a few others, take care of the Redemption. Sometimes I see other people who don't live here stopping by to talk to Marcus. But I don't know their names."

"You got to stop hanging around Mama Ruby's. I've heard enough about Marcus and his gang to last me a lifetime." Juanita cleared her throat loudly and shifted her position in the small metal chair.

"What do you mean by take care of the Redemption?" Emma jotted down notes as she listened.

"Something's going on. I don't know if they're selling drugs like crack, or what. I do know that's where my mama got her drugs and probably is where she gets them today."

Emma nodded. "Also, Juanita, even though you've asked us to restrict our questions today, I'd like to know whether Alicia saw Louis throw a gun under his grandmother's apartment. If she could tell me that, it would tell me something about one of the other witnesses."

"I guess that's okay." Juanita leaned back in her chair and looked at Alicia.

"Well, I didn't. I didn't see Louis throw a gun under Mama Ruby's apartment or anywhere else that night."

"Do you know Tamika Jones?"

"I know who she is." Alicia shifted in her chair.

"Why are you asking about that crack head?" Juanita leaned in and scowled at Emma. "And how do you know who she is, Alicia? You shouldn't know the likes of her!"

"She hangs out around Marcus a lot." Alicia hung her head.

"Well, you shouldn't hang out around Marcus a lot. And like I said, that's going to stop, right now."

Alicia straightened her shoulders. "I don't hang around him. I only see him at Mama Ruby's when we're both there at the same time."

"Well, like I said, no more Mama Ruby's." Juanita shook her head.

Alicia sighed. "There is nothing wrong with going over there for dinner. I love Mama Ruby and just like everyone else, I love her cooking. And she's got the piano. Anyway, you love her too. You know she's a good woman, and she loves all of us."

Juanita shook her head. "We'll discuss this later."

"Do you know anything about Marcus's pawn shop business? Do you know if any of your cousins help Marcus with that business?"

"I don't know anything about it. I think he's at the pawn shop in the daytime. He's got other people who help him with that. I don't think the boys, Dwayne, Georgie or Louis, ever did."

Emma jotted down a few notes. "Can you tell me if you saw Tamika on the night of the shootings?"

"No. I didn't, but it was pretty dark."

"That's enough about the night of the shootings." Juanita frowned.

"I know I sound like a broken record, but we may as well get all of the information Alicia has now. We should know as much as she knows. It's important for the case and for Alicia's safety too."

Juanita set her jaw. "Let me get this straight. The DA can force Alicia to talk?"

"He can subpoena her, and if you fail to bring her, you'll be in contempt of court. If he wants to speak to her before he subpoenas her, though, you can insist on being there during the interview," Emma said.

"I'm really against this, but if you promise you're not going to call her to the stand, I guess it's okay. She can talk to you."

"Alright." Emma leaned toward Alicia. "Alicia, how often do you visit your grandmother?"

"I like to go over there for Sunday dinners when I can, if I don't have too much homework. Sometimes I go over on other days too. I like to practice the piano when I can, and Mama Ruby's Sunday dinners are so good. Sometimes, when there's time, I do Mama Ruby's fingernails, too. Painting fingernails is my hobby." She wiggled her fingers in the light and for the first time Emma noticed her nails were painted baby doll pink with little white dots. "I like to try different designs, and Mama Ruby lets me try them out on her."

"Who else is usually there?" Emma flipped over a page in her legal pad.

"Well, usually Louis, Dwayne, Georgie, and Marcus. Sometimes Aunt Sandy and sometimes my mom." Alicia counted off the names on her fingers.

"And your mom is Amy, right?"

"That's right."

"So, pretty much the entire family shows up on Sundays." Emma jotted down a few notes.

"Everyone but Auntie Juanita, who is usually working. And if she isn't at the shop, she needs to rest."

"I see. What happens on those Sundays when you all get together?"

"Sometimes Marcus and the boys get together for a meeting in the back. Then we have dinner. Sometimes Mama Ruby needs a hand chopping, that kind of thing. I help her out if she needs it."

"What goes on in those meetings with Marcus?"

"I've never been in one. They wouldn't let me join them even if I wanted to, and I don't want to."

"Have you ever seen them carrying anything with them in or out of the meetings?"

"Sometimes Marcus carries a bag in with him. Um. I talked to Dwayne about it once."

"Did he tell you what happens in the meetings?"

"Not really, but he did say that Marcus usually gives them their cut on Sundays."

Emma leaned forward. "Alicia, have you ever seen any drugs or drug paraphernalia at your grandmother's house?"

"I'm not sure I'd know exactly what to look for. My mother left a pipe out once. I know what that is. But she's the only one who ever did that. I don't think anyone else ever had anything like that in Mama Ruby's house. Even when my mama was at her worst, she was pretty careful there. No one would want to upset Mama Ruby."

"You never saw any vials or glass pipes, or white rock-like substances, which look like large salt crystals there?"

She shook her head.

"Do you know what are in the bags that Marcus brings in on Sundays?"

"No, I don't."

"Do you know if Tamika is Marcus's girlfriend?"

"I don't know. I don't think so. She just follows Marcus around a lot. She's jumpy, and twitchy, and talks fast. She's got burns on her fingers and lips. She's real skinny too. I've seen it before."

"You've seen what?"

"My mom. She acts a lot like my mom when she's using."

Melissa caught Emma's eye and showed her a question scribbled on a legal pad. Emma nodded her approval.

"Alicia, have you ever seen Tamika talking to the police?" Melissa asked, leaning across the table to get a better look at Alicia.

"When?"

"After the shootings, or any time." Melissa leaned back and nibbled on the end of her pen, which already looked as it if had been chomped to pieces.

There was never any question which pens belonged to Melissa.

"She spoke to them the day after the shooting. I saw that. And I've seen her speaking to them a few other times. You know, before the shooting."

"Do you know which officers she's been speaking to?"

"I haven't really paid that much attention. I didn't get a name or anything like that. But if I see them again, I think I might recognize them."

Emma glanced at Melissa, watching her take notes, impressed with her questions. She knew Melissa was concerned Tamika could be a police informant, someone they used frequently to help solve crimes. If Tamika had provided information to the police that had paid off for them, either through arrests or convictions, they'd have more confidence in what she had to say about the night of the shooting.

"Alicia, I know this might be hard for you to talk about, but can you tell me whether you were able to see anyone out in the common area either before or after the shootings? I'm interested in anything you saw, but especially interested in whether you saw anyone picking up anything from the ground. We think some bullets or casings from shots fired might be missing. But we're not sure."

Alicia nodded and glanced at her aunt. She closed her eyes as if she were visualizing the night of the shooting and took a deep breath. When she opened her eyes, they were misty, as if she was about to cry. "I didn't really look before I heard those shots. I just walked Brother Antoine out to the porch, and said goodbye, and watched him walk down the sidewalk a ways. Then shots rang out. After the shots I looked out and I saw Dwayne, and Georgie standing there, and..." Her hand was shaking as she wiped a tear from her face. She hesitated, searching her aunt's face. "I don't remember seeing anything after that. I was upset."

"What about Louis?"

"I saw Louis running as fast as he could toward the river. And he had something in his hand."

Chapter Sixteen

Traffic on the way to the airport was congested, which wasn't unusual for that time of day. Emma wasn't paying attention to Ren's cheerful chatter as she drove down the highway.

"You okay?" Ren touched her hair.

Emma nodded.

"Scott said he'd give you a call to set up a meeting pretty soon." Ren paused as he looked at Emma. "Did you hear what I said?"

"What? Your friend on the force? Why would he want to call me?" Emma swerved to avoid a car that turned into her lane.

"Haven't you heard anything? I just told you he wanted to speak to you about Brother Antoine, about what you've been able to learn from your interviews so far."

"Why would he do that? I can't talk to him about the case and even if I could, I don't know that much about Brother Antoine."

"I'm not sure. He's probably looking into one of his cases, and Brother Antoine's name came up. Scott's one of the smartest people I know." Ren nodded to a car that let them in the turning lane. "He'd been accepted to law school, but decided to go to the police academy instead, and had the top grades of the class. He's got a good reason to speak to you, I'm sure of that."

"Well, that's interesting. I wonder if he'd tell me about his investigation?"

"No way, Emma. I wouldn't even bring it up."

"It cuts both ways. I can't talk about my case with him, either. It doesn't do any good for him to ask." Emma glanced at Ren from the side of her eye.

"Good point. Just tell him to bug off then."

Emma pulled into the airport entrance, parked in front of the departures gate, and popped open her trunk. She met Ren at the back of her car where she wrapped her arms around his neck and gave him a long kiss. She found herself lingering longer than usual. She loved the man.

"You will be missed, Deputy. Come back soon." She hugged him and watched as he pulled out his luggage from the trunk.

"I will. Who knows? I might call this place home someday. Depends on how you play your cards." Ren grinned as he grabbed the brim of his hat, then turned and walked through the door.

Emma sighed again as she pulled her steering wheel around the sharp curve of the exit lane. She was sorry to see Ren leave. It had been good to have him there. She'd miss his hugs and watching him with the boys. Ren was the best man she'd ever known and was more of a partner to her than anyone else had ever been. When he was gone, it felt as if a part of her was missing.

But she was afraid he didn't belong in New Orleans. He had a home-spun wholesomeness and practical sensibility that didn't jibe with the city. Not that the New Orleans police were more sophisticated than Ren. They weren't. But they were jaded, which wasn't surprising since they worked in a city with a murder-a-day homicide rate. Even so, there was no excuse for the corruption and abuse of several of their members. She couldn't see Ren working on a police force where that was a problem.

Emma ran her fingers through her hair with one hand as she pulled into the law school's parking lot. She had class in the next few minutes. She briefly checked her lipstick in the mirror and slid out of the seat.

* * *

Emma had called a quick meeting of the students who were working on Louis's case. They'd all gathered around a large table in one of the windowless classrooms in the law clinic. The overhead neon light cast a harsh glare on the gathering, giving all participants a gray, haggard appearance. Melissa brought cookies, which immediately improved Emma's mood until she calculated how many miles she'd have to run to work off the calories.

"When he charged Louis, the DA was relying on Tamika's testimony more than anything else. Earlier this week Melissa suggested that Tamika might be a police informant, which makes sense to me. Whether she is or isn't an informant, we'll still need to check out her convictions. We already know her arrest record's a mile long. But arrests aren't admissible. If she's actually been convicted of anything, we might be able to use it to discredit her testimony, depending on the type of crime."

Melissa nodded. "Wonder if it's possible to see if Tamika's name shows up as a witness for the prosecution in any of the *Times Picayune* articles through the years?"

"Great idea! Check that out. Take a look at the law library, or the city library down the street to see if they keep old newspapers on microfiche. Search under Tamika's name and see if you come up with anything. Then get with Josh and set up the meeting with Tamika." Emma found herself walking toward the cookies. "Anyone want to make a coffee run?"

After collecting everyone's dollar bills, Josh took off for the student lounge. During the break, Lauren flipped through her notes. Melissa walked over to Emma.

"Alicia clearly didn't tell us everything that day we all met at St. Francis's," Melissa said.

"I agree. She kept looking at her aunt before she answered. A dead giveaway." Emma had similar concerns and had been thinking of calling Juanita.

"Juanita is clearly calling the shots. Would it be possible to speak to Alicia alone?" Melissa said.

"We can't unless Juanita approves, but I can call and see what she says."

Josh appeared with a cup tray filled with coffees for everyone. Emma grabbed one and moved to the front of the room. She glanced at her notebook.

"Okay. Who can tell us, from the prosecutor's standpoint, the major weaknesses in the case, and what do we need to do about them?" Emma asked, trying to keep the cookies out of her line of vision.

Emma looked at the three students. They were cautious, deliberating each issue before they spoke. No one wants to look like an idiot in law school. All of that was good, but a little spontaneity was necessary sometimes if they wanted to be trial attorneys. They needed to learn to think on their feet. The ability to make a quick decision could save the outcome of a trial.

"Alicia said Louis ran in the direction of the river right after the shots were fired, and he had something in his hands. What do you make of that?" Emma stood up in front of the table where everyone was sitting.

"The first day we interviewed Louis, he said the same thing. Marcus told him to meet him at their grandmother's and to make sure he had his gun. After the shooting, Louis got scared and took off, ran down to the river, and threw his gun in. It didn't really make much sense to me. But that's when he told us the gun under the apartment wasn't his."

Emma stood up and began pacing around the table. "So, why do you think he did that—anyone?"

"Could be he was just a confused and frightened kid who didn't want to be standing there with a gun when the cops came?" Lauren suggested.

"Or he could have been one of the shooters. We thought there could have been more than one." Melissa flipped through her notes. "I've been working on getting a pathologist to verify this and think we might have one. I'll let you know this week. But," Melissa hesitated and glanced around the table, "I wasn't trying to prove one of the killers was Louis." Soft laughter sprinkled around the room.

"Sometimes research reveals things we don't want it to. Are we back to square one? Is Louis a killer, acting at the direction of an older cousin, or is he lying to cover up for that same cousin? Looks like we still need more information," Emma said as she grabbed her notebook and flipped to her list.

"Who's going to interview Georgie? Lauren? You've been pretty quiet today. But you did a good job questioning Dwayne, so I'll assign Georgie to you. Don't forget to ask him if he saw anyone picking up bullets or casings at the scene when you put together your questions. If there were two shooters, there might be a missing gun, right? We didn't know about that when we spoke to Dwayne. Set up a meeting at St. Francis's." Lauren nodded and wrote the details in her notepad.

Emma flipped through her notes. "Looks like that's it for now. Be in touch and give me your interview schedules. I may want to tag along."

* * *

Emma stacked the papers on her desk and arranged them in neat piles. It was a little after 3:00. She needed to leave if she was going to beat the boys home.

She heard a knock at her door, but since her overhead light was on, she knew she may as well acknowledge she was in. She stood and began gathering her purse and other items for her departure.

"Come in."

A tall, dark-haired police officer dressed in NOPD blues appeared. He was handsome. Movie star handsome. Emma nodded him in. He removed his hat and for a moment she stared at him. Something about him was off-putting. He bristled with his shiny badge, nameplate, nickel-plated gun, and the largest mustache she'd ever seen. She hated mustaches and considered them a personality defect.

He strode over to her desk. "I'm Scott McEnroe. I asked Ren to let you know I was dropping by today. Hope I'm not too late." Emma cringed. Not only was Officer McEnroe's voice piercingly nasal, it was at least two or three decibels too loud.

Emma shook his hand. "It's nice to meet you, Officer, but it's getting late. I need to get home before my sons are dropped off by their bus and was nearly out of the door when you knocked. I don't like to leave them alone. It isn't safe these days. I'm sure you understand." Emma stood behind her desk, then picked up her purse as if she were about to walk out of the door.

"This won't take long. I'd like to set up a time to speak to you later this week. But I also wanted to let you know you may want to watch the news tonight. It looks like there's been another death, possibly a murder. We don't know yet. I can't go into all the details right now, but I wanted you to know we found Lionel Boudreaux this morning behind one of the empty buildings on Camp Street. He'd been shot. Just like Brother Antoine. One bullet to the chest. It's under investigation and we don't have any suspects right now. But it looks like a homicide to me."

Emma sat down behind her desk and placed her purse on the credenza. Her knees felt slightly wobbly. "Have a seat, Officer. I can spare a few minutes." She glanced down at her calendar as she tried to compose herself. "I'm sorry to hear about Officer Boudreaux. From what I could tell, he was a good guy. But it's strange that he was killed the same way as Brother Antoine."

Officer McEnroe nodded. "Maybe. I just thought you'd like to know about it. Lionel told me you two had talked about Brother Antoine, and I wanted to ask you about what you two had discussed. About Brother Antoine, that is."

"I see. I don't know anything about Brother Antoine I couldn't answer in less than a minute. There's no need to meet later in the week."

"I thought you were looking into his murder." Officer McEnroe continued to stand behind the office chair, as if at attention.

"I'm not investigating Brother Antoine's murder. I'm gathering facts that might help provide a defense for Louis Bishop. Plus, everything I'm discovering in my investigation is attorney work product and is privileged, so I can't talk to you about any of it, even if it concerns Brother Antoine. I've only spoken to a couple of people about Brother Antoine anyway, and now one of them is dead. Neither person really gave me that much information."

Officer McEnroe grabbed the back of the chair. His cheeks were slightly flushed.

"Please have a seat, Officer. From what I understand, Brother Antoine was a pretty simple man. He wanted to stay in the community he grew up in and do what he could to help. Officer Boudreaux and he had that in common, and the two men worked together in some ways to make that happen. It's such a shame they're both dead. Do you think their deaths are related?"

The officer finally pulled out the worn mid-century armchair and sat down. "We don't know, and we have no leads. It could just be a coincidence."

"But you'd agree that Officer Boudreaux's death makes it seem less likely that Louis killed Brother Antoine?"

"I'm not sure I follow you."

"The shootings were nearly identical. You said so yourself. Couldn't the killers be the same? Louis is in jail. He couldn't have killed Officer Boudreaux. If that's true, it should follow that he didn't kill Brother Antoine."

"Obviously Louis didn't kill Boudreaux. But I couldn't say he didn't kill Antoine. I don't see how that adds up."

Emma nodded and jotted down a few notes on a pad. "But then, this isn't your case."

"True."

"How'd you know I knew Ren?"

"Ren and I are friends from the academy, and he told me you were working on the case. I thought he would have mentioned that to you. Nothing too complicated about any of that." He looked up and smiled.

Emma returned his smile. "I guess not." She hesitated. "Are you going to compare the evidence from the two cases? Officer Boudreaux's and Brother Antoine's?"

"I can't go into that, but I can assure you we'll do all we can to figure out who did this to Officer Boudreaux." Officer McEnroe stood up and walked toward the door. "I'd appreciate it if you could afford me some time this week for a short meeting."

Emma sighed. "I don't see the need, Officer. I'm sorry. I've told you all I know."

Chapter Seventeen

Emma pulled into the parking space behind her apartment building. Her brain immediately began ticking through the contents of her pantry. She didn't think it offered much in the way of nutritional value, and she'd forgotten to thaw the chicken. So dinner was going to be interesting. She unfastened her seatbelt and slid out of the car, startled to see two adolescent boys standing next to their bikes, directly behind her car. They were close in age to her sons, maybe a year or so older. Dressed in blue jeans and t-shirts, they had a scruffy look about them, as if they'd been playing outside in the dirt all day. They must have been waiting on her. Unless she was mistaken, they were the same boys that had been hanging out on their bikes in the middle of the street by her house several days ago. That time they ran when she approached them. Now, it seemed, they wanted to talk.

"Can I help you two?" Emma swung her purse on to her shoulder and squinted into the setting sun, which was directly behind the two boys, making it hard to see their faces.

They looked at each other and then back at Emma and nodded.

"My name's Emma." She extended her hand, which each boy shook solemnly. "Weren't you two here a few days ago? I spoke to you then, and you ran off. What can I do for you?" She moved closer and got a better look at them. They were not street-hardened criminals. She'd taught school long enough to tell the difference between a kid who still wanted to please and do the right thing and those who had long forgotten how. There was a softness in the eyes when someone cared. These boys had it.

"I'm J.C. and this here's my brother Cornelius. Aren't you a lawyer? And you represent Louis Bishop?"

"That's right. But first things first. How did you know where I live, do your parents know where you are, and what can I do for you?"

"We watched you walking around one day. We asked around and found out who you are. We figured out which car was your car. And then from there it wasn't so hard to figure out where you lived. We just had to follow you around a little."

"Why did you do that? Why go to the trouble of following me around and finding out where I live? Isn't it dangerous for you two to be traveling around on your bikes all over the city?" Emma gestured for the boys to follow her to the steps outside her house and sat down on the brick stoop.

The boys sat down next to her. Cornelius rolled his eyes. "Do you always ask three questions at the same time?" His brother laughed.

"Oh," Emma smiled. "I guess I do sometimes. Well, let's start from the beginning. Why did you follow me around?"

"Sometimes we just like to practice our spying skills. But after Brother Antoine was shot, we wanted to ask you about all of that."

"I see. And isn't this sort of a dangerous thing for you to be doing?"

Cornelius shook his head. "We don't think so. We haven't gotten in any trouble yet."

"And do your parents know where you are?"

"We live with our mom. Our dad's not around. Our mom works all night and sleeps all day. She's okay with what we do as long as we don't get into too much trouble. And we hang out at our grandfather's shop a lot," J.C. said.

"What sort of shop does your grandfather have?"

"An antique repair shop. He repairs and sells old stuff. We help him a little. It's down on Magazine. One of the first Black businesses on Magazine, he likes to say."

"Antique furniture?" Emma put her purse down on the steps.

J.C. nodded.

"What's the name of the place?"

"Cooper's Antiques."

"I'll have to go by some day." Emma smiled. "I love antique shops." She paused and looked at the boys. "Are you two friends of Louis? Is that why you're here?"

"Not really." J.C. hung his head.

"Well then, what is it?" Emma leaned back against the brightly painted front door and crossed her feet in front. The warmth of the sun-drenched wood felt good against her back after a long day.

"Like I said. We knew Brother Antoine. He was our coach. He was the best. He spent a lot of time with us. Taught us to shoot hoops and stuff. Everyone is saying what happened to him was an accident, but we don't think so." Cornelius squinted his eyes. Emma thought he was trying not to cry.

"What makes you say that, Cornelius?"

"'Cause lots of times after basketball practice, there'd be a car that would pull out after him and follow him. That car followed him if he was walking or even if he was driving a car. But mostly, Brother Antoine walked everywhere. It's harder to follow someone who's on foot, 'cause you really have to stay back." Cornelius leaned over and wrapped his arms around his knees. "We'd watch that car follow him. It'd pull way back, and then when he'd turn a corner, it'd creep around the same corner but hold back a little, you know? Sometimes we'd follow them, and sometimes we'd watch them from out 'a Pop's shop. That's our granddad. We call him Pop. But we never told Brother Antoine about any of this." Cornelius put his head on his knees. J.C. put his arm about his brother's shoulder.

"We think we shoulda told Brother Antoine about that car. We just didn't know what was going on. We just liked following them around. Sort of like we followed you," J.C. said.

"You followed the car on your bikes?"

The boys nodded simultaneously.

"Would you recognize the car you followed if you saw it again?"

J.C. shrugged. "They were all just big white cars, but different ones, you know? I think some of them were blue and white. I'm not sure I could tell which one we followed. Well, maybe, from the taillights. If you had a piece of paper, I could draw it."

Emma reached into her purse and pulled out a notepad. She ripped off a sheet of paper and handed it to J.C. along with her pen.

J.C. hastily sketched an elongated rectangle with one curved edge and showed it to Emma.

"So that's the taillight as you recall it?"

"Yes, ma'am."

"Do you mind if I keep it?"

J.C. nodded.

"Did you ever see anyone inside the cars?"

"Not really."

"Do you know who Marcus Bishop is? Was he ever at the gym?"

"Yeah, I know who Marcus is, but I never saw him at the gym. Did you, J.C.?" Cornelius said.

J.C. shook his head. "Nah. I don't ever remember seeing him there, but Dwayne and Georgie used to come by sometimes and shoot hoops, remember?"

Cornelius nodded.

"You mean Dwayne and Georgie Bishop, Louis's cousins?" Emma flipped to a clean page in the notepad and jotted down a few notes.

Both boys nodded.

"Do either of you know whether drugs of any sort were ever sold at the gym?"

J.C. and Cornelius looked at each other and shrugged.

"I'm not a cop. You won't be arrested for telling me what you know, but you also don't have to tell me anything that makes you uncomfortable. I just want to help Louis."

"We don't know anything about selling drugs at the gym. At least I don't." J.C. looked at his brother. Cornelius shook his head. "Me either."

"But we did one thing." J.C. pulled a piece of paper out of his back pocket and handed it to Emma. "We got a license plate number from one of the cars."

"Excellent! That will definitely help. I need to get dinner on, but you two are welcome to eat with us, if you'd like. I have two boys who are close to your age. They'll be stepping off the bus any minute. Maybe you'd like to meet them? I'm not sure what I'm cooking yet, but there will be something on the table."

"We can stay 'til 5:00, then we gotta go. Mama'll be waking up and will wonder where we are after that. We eat dinner before she goes to work. If we're not home when she wakes up, we're in big trouble. So, we can stay a little while," J.C. said.

Cornelius looked at his brother and raised his eyebrows. "Two dinners?"

"It'll be okay." J.C. grinned.

Emma heard the squeal of ancient brakes and looked down the street as the school bus pulled up to the corner.

"Here are the boys now. This is perfect timing. I'll unlock the front door for you and you can put your bikes on the landing so they'll be safe." Emma pulled her keys out of her purse and unlocked the front door. J.C. and Cornelius bumped their bicycles up the steps and secured them at the bottom of the landing as Billy and Bobby ran up to Emma.

"Tryouts for field and track are next week!" Billy shoved a schedule in Emma's face as Bobby began making his way up the stairs to the apartment.

"Wait guys. I want to introduce you to J.C. and Cornelius. They're helping me with a case I'm working on. I've invited them for dinner, but they have to leave at 5:00. Why don't you ask them up to your room while I cook? I'll be quick."

The boys stared at each other for a second, then Bobby waved them up the steps. They plowed their way to the third floor, sounding more like cattle than boys.

Before she began dinner, Emma glanced at the number of the driver's license J.C. had given her. The word "PUBLIC" was written vertically along the left side of the plate, before the number, just like the plate on the unmarked car that was in front of Marcus's pawn shop a few days ago. Whoever was following Brother Antoine was a law enforcement official, either a cop or a deputy sheriff. What could that mean?

* * *

The next day Emma heard a rap on her office door and saw Josh's obscured profile through the frosted glass panel.

She put her pen down. "Come on in."

Josh strode in and tossed the license plate number J.C. and Cornelius had given Emma on her desk.

"I couldn't get any information on who this car was assigned to. I don't know whether it's a police car or one of the sheriff's vehicles. You can't trace what cop is assigned to what car by looking it up through the license plate number. I even went down to the station to see if they'd tell me. No luck."

"Well, it was worth a try. Want to stay here while I try to reach Juanita about speaking to Alicia again?"

"Sure."

Emma punched the speakerphone button on her phone and dialed Juanita's telephone number. After a few rings, a woman picked up.

"A Cut Above…"

Emma could hear hair dryers in the background. She introduced herself and was placed on hold. Emma and Josh spent several seconds listening to elevator music, then heard the clicking sound of someone picking up and Juanita's voice greeting them from the other end.

"I know this isn't going to sit well with you, but Melissa and I would like to meet with Alicia again. And this time, we'd like to talk to her without you. Of course, we'd need your permission for that."

"Why do you want to meet with her again, and without me? She's told you all she knows."

"Melissa and I don't think so. We got the sense she didn't feel comfortable talking in front of you about the night of the shootings and don't think she told us everything that happened that night. If we're right, and if she ends up speaking to the DA and everything comes out then, we could be in trouble."

Emma heard a loud sigh. She'd expected Juanita's resistance.

"I don't like it. I told you I don't want her to be a witness."

"We won't call her as a witness. I've made that promise to you."

"Will the DA?"

"We have no way of knowing that. If he interviews her and if he discovers she saw something significant that night, he might. That's why we need this second go-around with her." Emma leaned back in her seat and waited. She could almost hear Juanita thinking.

"Is there anything I could do to keep the DA from talking to her?"

"For one thing, the DA can't talk to Alicia without you or an attorney present. And you can refuse to let him see her, but he can subpoena her, anyway. But, if you explain your fears about Marcus to the DA, there's always the chance that he might provide protection for Alicia."

"God. I can't believe this. I guess you can talk to her again. But I want to know what she says. I need to know everything." Emma could hear Juanita's fingernails drumming with impatience.

"I understand. Also, I never got the name or badge number of that police officer who was trying to intimidate you into paying for protection. You filed a report against him. Do you still have it?"

"Yeah, I've got it somewhere. I think his last name was St. Amant. Kind of hard to forget that. He didn't act like no saint. Let's see if I can find that badge number."

Emma heard rustling sounds, as if someone was shuffling papers.

"Here it is. His badge number, or at least the part of the badge I saw, was 3178."

Emma wrote down the number and put it in her wallet.

"Have you heard from the 6th District about your complaint against Officer St. Amant?"

"No. I was thinking about that the other day."

"Why don't you check up on their investigation to see if you can get an idea when they might be concluding it. Have you seen him since your last encounter?"

"Funny you should ask. I think I saw him walking down Magazine Street right in front of the shop just this week."

"But he hasn't threatened you again?"

"No. Not really. He just looked in the front door window for a second, then walked on by."

Chapter Eighteen

Emma pulled up to St. Francis's thrift shop and turned off her engine. She spotted Lauren's car. They'd planned to meet Georgie that morning, and she and Melissa would get together with Alicia a little later in the day. It had started to rain, and she'd forgotten to bring an umbrella. She threw her purse on the top of her head and made a dash through the gravel parking lot, avoiding puddles until she reached the front door. The bell tinkled her entry as she scooted in. She nodded to the clerk.

"We reserved the back room for a meeting today. Looks like Lauren, my student, is already here. I assume she's in the back?"

The clerk pointed the way toward the lunch room where Emma and Melissa had met Alicia and Juanita earlier. Georgie was expected any minute.

Lauren was seated at the lunch table looking as if she'd made her body as small as possible to avoid touching the room's varied surfaces, each filthier than the next.

"Well, I see the cleanliness of the place hasn't improved since our last meeting."

Lauren managed a thin smile.

"Maybe I can clean it up a bit before Georgie gets here." Emma peered in one of the cabinets and found some paper towels and a bottle of glass cleaner. She sprayed the table top and the empty chairs as well as the counter so everything shone a little and smelled better, at least. She was surprised Lauren made no effort to help. Instead she sat, her elegant limbs pulled together in a tightly wound knot of disgust and disapproval, shooting disparaging bullets across the room with her eyes.

The front doorbell jingled again. Emma knew Georgie had arrived.

Georgie bounced in the room, a study in contrast with his brother Dwayne. Although they both soared well over six feet in height, their physical similarities ended there. Georgie was the younger of the two, yet he was heavier, built with line-backer bulk and muscular strength, while Dwayne was lean and sinewy. Georgie's presence immediately filled up the small lunchroom. In sharp contrast to fastidious Dwayne, Georgie's clothes had a slept-in look, as if they hadn't been washed or even changed in months. His hair was unkempt, and scruffy, and Emma doubted school or homework ever crossed his mind. Yet the brothers shared the same affable smile and warm handshake. Emma couldn't help but like Georgie.

Emma glanced at Lauren. She was concerned she shouldn't have allowed her to continue on the case. Her questions during Dwayne's interview were fair, but she could be aloof and standoffish, so much so that she may have created a situation that made Dwayne feel uncomfortable. Emma couldn't afford to jeopardize the case, especially with something that could be easily adjusted with the removal of one student. It was more important that Lauren get her attitude right today than she put together a brilliant line of questioning. But Emma wasn't going to bet on that, especially after seeing her reaction to the nasty lunch room.

Lauren scooted her chair up closer to the table and flipped open her notepad. She made eye contact with Georgie. Emma noticed her body was curled into a tense coil as if she was a cat about to pounce.

"I understand you were there the night Mr. Sam Maureau and Brother Antoine were killed at the Redemption a few weeks ago." Lauren scowled as she reviewed her notes.

"That's right." Georgie nodded his head, his hands folded calmly in his lap. He wasn't easily shaken. He was as cool and poised as his brother.

"Can you tell me what you remember about that night?" Lauren hunched over the small table, looking all the world like one of the roof-top gargoyles hanging over a balcony in the French Quarter.

"Yeah. Ah. Marcus called us outside, and this guy walked up."

Lauren nodded and flipped a page in her notebook.

"Did he explain why he wanted you to step outside?"

"Not really. He just said he was meeting this guy, and he wanted us to come with him."

"Do you always do what Marcus asks?"

"Most the time." Georgie nodded. "Yeah. Guess we do."

Lauren propped her head up with one hand as she checked her notes. "What happened after that?"

"Well, we got out there, and this guy was waiting for us. Then Marcus sent Dwayne back to the house to go get Louis. When Louis came back with Dwayne, he had a brown paper bag." Georgie leaned forward in his chair.

"How big was the bag?"

"A little one. You know. Like you see kids taking for a school lunch sometimes." Georgie moved his hands into parallel positions, approximately twelve inches apart, to indicate the size of the bag.

"Do you remember what happened next?"

"After Louis came back out, I heard some shots. Pow, pow, pow! Like that. Maureau, the guy Marcus was meeting, got hit and went down. Then a little later we saw that one of the bullets hit Brother Antoine too. He was out by the sidewalk, close to the street."

"You said several shots rang out. How many?"

"I'm not sure, three or four. I guess four." Georgie shrugged and looked down at his hands.

"Do you know who was hit first? Maureau or Brother Antoine?"

"I don't know. At first I didn't even know Brother Antoine was there. Maybe Brother Antoine. But I really don't know."

Lauren looked down at her notepad as she wrote. "Did you see the shooter, or shooters, or anyone with a gun?"

"Nope."

"Do you know the direction the shots were coming from?"

"Nah. Couldn't tell." Georgie shook his head.

"Could you tell if the sound of the shots were in front of you, or behind you, or maybe to one side or the other?"

"Maybe to the right side, and kinda behind me? I'm not really sure."

"Did you have a gun that night?"

"Uh uh. No, I did not." Georgie glanced up at Lauren, directly meeting her gaze.

"Before the shootings, did you know either of the two men that were killed, either Brother Antoine, or Mr. Maureau?" Lauren checked her list of questions.

"No, not really." Georgie folded his arms across his chest. "I met Maureau once at his house with Marcus, but that was all. I been hearin' Alicia talk about Brother Antoine, but I don't know him."

"Are you a bodyguard for Marcus?"

"No, I ain't no bodyguard, but sometimes Marcus asks me to do stuff for him and I do it. And I don't know why you're asking these kinds of questions. What does this have to do with these two murders?"

"I'd just like to try to understand the relationships among all of the parties."

"Uh huh. Well, two guys got shot. I didn't do it. I didn't see who did it neither."

"Do you know what Louis had in the brown paper bag?"

"Nope."

"Did you see him take anything out of the bag?"

"No, I didn't."

"Did you see Louis do anything at all after the shooting?"

"Right after the shots were fired, Louis started running toward that big green box. You know. What's it called? A transformer, I think. It's just right there, right in the middle of the two buildings. He ran by there, and then I saw him lean over for just a second. I couldn't see what he was doing then he kept on running down toward the river. I don't know why he was running like that. The rest of us, we went back to Mama Ruby's."

"How big is the transformer?"

"I'd say it's up to here on me." Georgie stood up and put his hand up to his chest.

"So, that's about five feet high? How tall are you, Georgie?"

"I'm six-foot-three. So, yeah, I'd say it was five foot, all around."

"Five-foot, square?"

"That's right."

"So, it was big enough for someone to hide behind?"

"If they squatted down, yeah."

"Did someone call the police that night?"

"I guess someone did. Maybe a neighbor."

"Do you know whether Louis had a gun?"

Georgie shook his head. "I wouldn't know."

"Who had guns that night?"

"Sam Maureau did. I saw him pull his."

"What about Marcus?"

Georgie shrugged.

"Was that a yes, or a no, or a maybe?'

"A no."

"Anyone else?"

"I don't know. It was dark."

"Did you see anyone pick up a gun from the ground that night?"

He shook his head.

"There are some missing casings from that night. Casings are the coverings for bullets. They found some from the shot that hit Brother Antoine, but they didn't find any from the shots that hit Mr. Maureau. Did you see anyone pick up anything from around his body?"

"I didn't, but I really wasn't paying attention after the shooting. I just went back to Mama Ruby's."

"Do you remember seeing Tamika Jones that night?"

"Nah. I don't think so, even though she's usually around if Marcus is."

"Do me a favor." Lauren ripped a sheet of paper from her notebook and handed it to him. "I'd like you to draw a circle where each person was standing on the night of the murders, then identify the location of the transformer with a square. I'd also like you to label the circles. Make sure you include the people who were shot."

Georgie took the paper and carefully drew and labeled seven carefully arranged circles. He placed the square to the side of the circles, several inches away. Then he drew the apartment buildings to show that the transformer was approximately in the middle of the two buildings in the common area.

"And do you remember anyone changing positions, or moving before or after the shooting?"

"Just Louis, like I said."

"Alright. I don't have any more questions, unless you do?" Lauren glanced at Emma.

Emma nodded. "I have a couple." She glanced down at her notes.

"Do you remember what happened to Marcus after the shooting? Did he move, run to Mama Ruby's apartment, or what?"

"I don't know. I don't remember seeing him." Georgie shrugged.

"Do you remember whether Louis still had something in his hand after he ran by the transformer and started off toward the river?"

He shook his head. "I couldn't see what was in his hand then."

"That's it, unless you have anything to add. We'll be in touch if we need to ask you anything else." Lauren closed her notebook.

Georgie stood up, nearly knocking over the flimsy lunch table, and sauntered out of the small room. He turned and waved before he headed down the hallway and out of the front door.

Emma stood up and paced across the room while Lauren gathered her belongings. Lauren was cold and didn't put Georgie at ease. She was struggling with how to tell her. Teachable moments didn't always pan out so well.

"Lauren, your questions were good, just as they were when you interviewed Dwayne. I especially liked your question about the direction of the sound of the shots. Because of that, we have useful information we didn't have before."

Lauren smiled for the first time that day and continued to pack her bag.

"But Georgie is an unusually easy-going guy."

"What do you mean?"

"I thought you were about to jump down his throat during most of the interview. And there were a few times you were lucky he answered your questions. It's true that anyone out there that night could be a suspect, but we're depending on witnesses in this case. So we need him. Making him feel uncomfortable is the last thing we'd want to do, and some of your questions could have done that. And some of your questions weren't even relevant. I think he took everything pretty well, but that should be attributed to him, not you."

"I got some good information from him."

"You did. Some of your questions were the right ones, but after you asked him whether he was Marcus's bodyguard, he stopped answering your questions. Why do you think he did that?"

Lauren shrugged.

"Because they were offensive, and, from his response, he thought you were trying to implicate him in the murder of Sam Maureau. Everyone is entitled to respect, and you forgot that during the interview. Georgie's a high school kid, but he's got a lot of savvy and composure. I'm guessing he's had to think his way out of more jams than you and I will ever see in a lifetime. I think you could have softened your approach."

"I don't think that's a fair appraisal."

"I'm sorry you feel that way. You might not realize it, but you're missing empathy—an ability to relate to your witness—and you're going to need it to be a really good lawyer. At the very least, you've got to understand that there are two sides to every story, and the jury may see the side you don't want them to."

Emma thought she detected an eye roll as Lauren made her way to the door. She placed her hand on the knob and turned around to look at Emma before she walked out.

"I worked hard on those questions."

Emma nodded. "It showed. But you didn't see Georgie's willingness to help us and to help Louis. For all we know, he risked his life to be here. To be able to understand someone else's perspective or goals, you've got to be in touch with your own humanity. I don't think you're working out well here, Lauren. I've decided to take you off the case."

"You're what? I can't believe it." She slammed the half-open door shut. "You think Georgie knows what his goals are, or what he wants to do with his life?" Lauren didn't bother to hide her smirk. "You were so lucky to have someone like me on this case."

"I'm sorry things didn't work out, Lauren. I had hoped we could work together, and even greater hopes you could help us put together a solid defense. But you have to be able to see someone from their perspective, not yours, if you're going to represent them. You need to understand what motivates them. You have a problem with that. More troubling, you aren't even willing to try."

Lauren turned the knob and walked out of the door.

Chapter Nineteen

E mma barely had time to check her notes before both Melissa and Alicia showed up for the next interview in the thrift shop's tiny back room. Emma quickly glanced over Georgie's testimony and underscored the most important lines. Melissa and Alicia entered the room together, chatting about Alicia's latest school project. Since Alicia had met with them earlier, Emma didn't think this interview should take long.

Alicia, dressed again in her school uniform, was calm and seemed eager to help. Emma cleared her throat and gestured for Alicia to take a seat across from Melissa.

"We've gotten the okay from your Aunt Juanita for you to speak to us about the night of the shootings without her, which we thought would make you feel more comfortable. Did she speak to you before you came out here today?" Melissa clicked her pen in preparation for Alicia's response.

Alicia nodded. "Yes, she said to go ahead and tell you everything about that night. But..." She hesitated. "I don't really know if this is important." Her bottom lip trembled. She took a deep breath and continued. "That night, after we finished up the scholarship forms, I walked Brother Antoine to the front door and stepped on to the porch to say goodbye. I stayed up on the porch and watched him walk a little ways, like I said." She blinked and tears rolled down her cheeks. "I saw Louis separate from the group and start running with something in his hand, like I told you earlier. He was running toward the center of the grassy area. That's when I thought I saw a little red light, like one of those lasers, I think, on Brother Antoine. Then I heard shots. I turned toward the sounds of the shots, and when I turned back around, I saw that Brother Antoine had fallen in a heap on the sidewalk." She brushed the tears from her face with the tips of her fingers. "When he fell, I ran down toward him."

"Could you tell the direction the laser was coming from?"

"It looked like it was from the middle of the green area, or halfway between the two buildings. Maybe right where that green box is."

"The transformer?"

"Yes. The electrical box."

"Where was the red spot? Was it on Brother Antoine, or near him?"

"It was on him."

"Where?"

"At first it flashed on his arm. Then the sidewalk curved, and then it was on his chest." She sniffed.

Emma pulled a tissue from her purse and handed it to Alicia. "Did you hear talking or other sounds coming from the transformer area?"

Alicia shook her head. "No, I didn't."

"Could the shots have come from that area?"

"They could've, but I can't be sure."

Emma paused. "You said that you remembered seeing Louis run toward the river?"

"Yes."

"Did he stop anywhere during his run?"

"I don't know. I couldn't see very far because of the buildings. Plus, it was dark."

She hesitated and covered her eyes with both hands. Her hands were shaking.

Emma handed Alicia a tissue. "We can stop if you'd like."

Alicia shook her head.

Emma flipped through her notes. "Is there anything else you need to add about that night? Something that would help Louis?"

She shook her head but hesitated for another minute before continuing. "After I heard the shot and ran down to the sidewalk, my aunt screamed at me to come back. By that time, Louis had already passed that electrical box.

That's when I saw him running out toward the river."

"Did Louis have anything in his hand after he passed the transformer?"

Alicia shook her head. "I don't know. He passed under a light, but I can't be sure. Maybe."

Emma raised her index finger. "One more area of questioning, then we'll be done. Dwayne said you were at your Grandmother's for dinner the night of the shooting. Do you recall anything unusual about that night? Was a meeting going on while you were there? Anything like that?"

Alicia paused. "I think there may have been a meeting, but I didn't pay much attention to it. Usually, meetings are on Sundays, so, I guess it was sort of unusual. The room in the back had the door closed. Then they all came out for dinner, but everything seemed okay."

* * *

Emma climbed into her car, thankful the rain had finally stopped. But it was one of those sloshy days. The gutters and drains throughout the city were overflowing and water rushed at top speed down the street. They'd only barely avoided a flash flood. New Orleans was below sea level, and could flood in as little as fifteen minutes. A neighbor had told her horror stories of cars floating down the street after a few minutes of heavy rain. So, she was thankful the downpour had subsided. A few more minutes could have been disastrous. And now, Emma could even see the sun glowing behind one of the clouds.

The day had been pretty successful. Bits and pieces of new information had filtered in from Georgie and Alicia, which might add to the overall picture. She'd have to ask Louis whether he ran to the transformer after Maureau and Brother Antoine were shot, and if he did, she needed to know why. Was he dropping off or hiding a gun? Seems like a strange place for that. And what about the red lights Alicia thought she saw? Could they be as innocent as car lights passing by from the street behind them? She didn't think so, but the only thing to do was to get one of the students to drive back out to the Redemption to check out the transformer and see what would be visible from Juanita's porch. The most intriguing question to Emma was whether there might have been someone hiding behind the transformer. Someone with a laser sight attached to his gun. If so, how could they prove it without Alicia?

Emma pulled out onto Carrollton and prepared to turn left on to St. Charles Avenue. As she turned on her blinker, she noticed a police car in her rear-view mirror. She was stunned when the blue lights on the car began to flash and craned her neck to see who they were after. Certain they were in pursuit of someone else, she pressed her foot to the accelerator to proceed forward. She jumped when she heard a blaring beep and an amplified command to "Pull over." Shaken, she jerked her car over the curb and parked partially in the median, her heart beating rapidly.

A tall, overly muscled police officer approached her car and tapped on the window. She rolled down the glass.

"Can I help you, Officer?" Emma attempted a smile, but the left side of her face was quivering, and her hands were shaking. She didn't know why she was so frightened. She didn't know why she'd been stopped. Surely it was a mistake.

"Get your license, proof of insurance, and registration, and step outside of the car."

"Step outside of the car? Why do you want me to step outside of the car, Officer?" Emma was frantically searching for her registration. She never knew where she put things like that. She would bet it was at home and not in her car.

"Are you refusing to get out?" The officer started to open her door.

"No! I'm coming out right now. I can't find my registration, though. Here's my license and proof of insurance." Emma opened the car door and slid out, steadying herself. A fine mist of perspiration broke out along her hairline. She handed the documents to the police officer. She made a mental note of his badge, No. 4962, and scanned his shirt for his nametag. It had been removed. It should have been over his right pocket.

"Can you tell me why you stopped me, Officer?"

"I suggest you stop talking, Ms. Thornton, or you'll find yourself in handcuffs and at the precinct quicker than you can blink those pretty brown eyes." The officer had a reddish, rugged complexion with deep pitted acne scars. His deep blue eyes were nearly buried by his blonde eyebrows, which were in stark contrast to his completely shaven head.

Traffic had slowed down as drivers made their way around Emma's and the police officer's cars, which blocked a section of the road. Emma attempted to make eye contact with drivers in cars that passed by, hoping they would be able to bear witness to her dilemma. No one seemed to notice.

The officer walked around to the back of her car and popped open the trunk.

What the hell?

"Officer, do you have a warrant to look inside my trunk?"

"Do you have something to hide?"

"No, but I'm not sure why you stopped me and I know you don't have probable cause to look in my trunk. I'd like to know what's going on here. I'd also like to know your name."

The officer grabbed Emma's arm and pushed her up against her car, squeezing her arm until it hurt. Emma winced. She noticed some of the cars were driving by very slowly. Some drivers were obviously watching the officer.

"You see this, Ms. Thornton?" The officer pulled out a bag of white powder from his pocket. "I just found this in your trunk. I can put it back in my pocket this time, but next time you're stopped, you won't be so lucky. Do you understand?"

Emma stared at the officer.

"Do you understand?" He squeezed her arm even tighter.

"What's your problem with me, Officer? I'm afraid I don't get it."

"Then I suggest you figure it out in a hurry, Ms. Thornton."

The officer released her arm, returned her driver's license and insurance card, and climbed back into his vehicle. He was gone in a matter of seconds.

Emma slid back into her vehicle, her legs feeling as if they'd liquefied. Hands shaking, she started the car and began the drive down St. Charles toward her apartment. Although her body was trembling, her mind was racing. What was the cop up to? And why was he after her? Was it related to Louis's case, or was it about Juanita? Other than her students, she hadn't mentioned anything about Juanita's run-ins with the police to anyone but Ren.

The first thing she needed to do was to identify the abusive officer. Then she needed to figure out what he didn't want her to know.

Chapter Twenty

Emma trudged up the stairs to her apartment and unlocked the front door. The boys would be home at any moment. She needed to pull herself together before they arrived. She threw her keys on the dining room table and fell onto the couch. Maddie and Lulu flew down the winding staircase to greet her, their nails clicking like dueling typewriters. She welcomed their cold nose nudges and friendly kisses and hugged their necks in return.

Seconds later she heard the door of the building slam, and the boys stomping up the stairs to the apartment. They laughed as the keys jangled, unlocking the front door. The sounds were comforting, as if her world were back to normal and nothing horrifying had happened that afternoon. She could almost forget the police officer and his threats.

"I'm over here, boys," she shouted as they ran in. "Come tell me about your day."

They ran over to the couch and crowded in with the dogs, a jumble of blue jeans and wagging tails, each landing a kiss on her cheek. She hugged them both in return, a little tighter than usual.

"It was okay," Bobby said.

"Yeah, nothing great happened, but it was fine."

"There's protein bars for you out on the counter, and sports drinks in the fridge."

The twins tore into the kitchen to grab their snacks.

"Do y'all have any homework?"

They mumbled a reply as they ran up the winding staircase to their room.

141

"I'm coming up there in fifteen minutes. That gives you some time to relax before I check up on your assignments." She sat up from her reclining position on the couch. "And I need fifteen minutes too," she said to herself and the dogs.

Emma stood up, walked to the kitchen and poured herself a healthy glass of white wine, then walked back to her spot on the couch. She grabbed the phone and dialed Ren's number. He picked up immediately.

"You're not going to believe what happened to me today."

"I hope it was a good thing."

"Nope, but the boys are here, so I'm going to speak softly." She paused. "I was stopped by a police officer today. He asked me to get out of my car and popped the trunk. Then he pulled cocaine out of his own pocket and threatened to throw it in the trunk of my car and arrest me for possession. He told me I'd better figure out what was going on or he'd stop me again and finish what he'd started." Emma rubbed her free hand on her thigh to stop it from shaking.

"Did you get his name?"

"I asked him for it, but he wouldn't say. And he wasn't wearing a name tag. But I got his badge number. I thought I'd call Scott and tell him what happened. Think he'll tell me who the officer is?" Emma slipped out of her shoes.

"He should be able to since you've got the badge number. But you shouldn't have to go through Scott to get his name."

"I should just be able to ask for it, right? Is there a general policy on the identification of police officers? It looks like he pulled his name tag off deliberately."

"The name tag's part of the uniform. He shouldn't have removed it. There's probably a fine or disciplinary action the department could take against him for doing that. I don't know NOPD policy, but police officers ought to produce their name and identification when asked, unless they're undercover or in the middle of an investigation. Getting his name should be a pretty simple thing. Also, you could file a claim against him for harassment. Since you don't have his name, use his badge number. Ask for his name in the complaint. You'd get their attention that way."

"I can also file a criminal action against him for battery since he pushed me around. I wish I knew why he was after me." Emma piled all of the pillows at one end of the couch.

"When you break it all down, it'll be your word against his. Do you have any proof of what he did?"

"Why would I make something like that up? But to answer your question, I don't have a photo, or any concrete evidence. Just my testimony. But that's something. I might end up with bruises on my arms from where he grabbed me. I can take a photo of that." Emma pulled her feet up.

"You might do better to have Scott pursue this internally than you'd be if you file a criminal charge against the cop. That way the officer wouldn't know you were acting against him, and you'd be a little more protected than if you openly initiated a claim."

Emma looked up and could see Bobby descending the staircase, notebook in hand. She anticipated a question about homework soon. "I need to wrap this up. I don't want the kids to hear me. But, I'm not afraid to file a charge against this guy. And ultimately, putting everything out in the open could save me, don't you think? But, I was going to speak to Scott anyway, so I'll go down there tomorrow morning. Can you give him a call and pave the way for me?"

"Sure."

Emma felt a hovering presence. She sat up, turned, and saw Bobby behind the couch, history notebook in hand. "Just a minute, Ren."

"Bobby, go to the dining room table and sit down. I'll just be a minute, okay?"

"I just need to ask you a question about how to do a timeline for my history project."

"We'll work on that in a minute. I promise. Let me finish my conversation and I'll get right with you."

Bobby trudged over to the dining room table, scraping the chair loudly along the wooden floor, and flung himself into the seat, propping his chin into the palm of his hand. Emma ignored his sullen gaze.

"Wish I knew what was going on with that cop. I've never even seen him before. Louis's case is the only one I have where the police are involved. Of course, there's the situation with Juanita. What happened to her is remarkably similar to what happened to me."

"How's that?"

"You know, I told you about it. Some cops had been pushing her around because they wanted her to pay a protection fee, and she refused. And they also threatened to plant drugs somewhere in her shop if she didn't pay up. No one tried to get money from me, but the threats are the same."

"You're not Juanita's lawyer, are you? Or did you ever give her advice about how to handle the cop's harassment?"

"I'm not her attorney, but I told her she should check up on her complaint. Ask them where they were on the investigation."

"Maybe she told someone, either police officers down at the station, or some of the guys that patrol the streets in her area, that you suggested she follow up. It'd be a good thing to know."

"I guess. But she was assaulted by those cops before I'd even met her. When it happened, she immediately drove down to the police station and reported the incident herself. Juanita's fearless. As far as I know, she doesn't even have an attorney."

"Did you tell anyone about Juanita, either Scott, or anyone else?" Ren said. Emma could hear him pacing.

"No, of course not. I haven't mentioned Juanita's situation to anyone, except you. Have you told anyone about it?" Emma sat back and made room for the dogs on the couch and rested her feet next to Lulu. She heard Bobby clear his throat in the dining room.

"No. I wouldn't have any reason to mention anything about Juanita to anyone else," Ren said.

"I didn't think so. We went down to the 6th District to pick up autopsy and ballistics reports in Louis's case. You were with us when we did that. And then Josh ran down there, trying to trace some license plate numbers for a few unmarked cop cars. God, that could have done it, huh?"

"Maybe. There's a serious problem in the police department, or you wouldn't have been assaulted today. Josh's search could have put someone on notice you were looking into their activity."

"Yeah."

"You need to be careful. You don't know what you're doing, or who you're dealing with, and you're poking into the business of some dangerous people."

Emma finished up her conversation with Ren with mixed feelings. She was relieved to have escaped the officer and his intimidating threats without an arrest or worse. But she was in jeopardy, and she didn't know why. One thing she was certain of was that she couldn't allow her students to interview fact witnesses any longer in Louis's case. It had become too dangerous.

She turned to face Bobby and his timeline.

* * *

Dean Munoz was in his office, as he often was in the early morning, before class. Emma had made a special effort to catch him before he'd started his day, right in between his first cup of coffee and his dash to teach Evidence, his first morning class. She only had fifteen minutes.

Emma rapped on the Dean's door. "Got a minute?" She smiled at the dean's intense review of the books piled on his desk. The dean knew the contents of those books like the back of his hand. Emma wasn't concerned about interrupting him.

He looked up and nodded. "Always for you." He gestured toward the empty chair in front of his desk and scrutinized her face.

"I can tell something's wrong. What's happened?" Dean Munoz put his pen down and closed the case book he was reviewing.

Emma folded her hands in her lap and told him about the officer's assault.

"Good God. What do you think that's all about?"

"I have no idea. My first thought was that it had to be related to Louis's case. And my second thought was that the students should stop interviewing fact witnesses immediately. I'll contact them all and stop the interviews today. Don't you agree?"

"Yes. The students can't be put at risk."

"Good. But I wouldn't think it would be a problem if the students continued to research issues for the case, or speak to experts."

"Depending on where they meet them. If they met the experts here, on campus, or at the experts' offices, it should be okay. You said you think the officer's assault had something to do with Louis's case. How are you making that connection?" The dean pushed his chair out and grabbed a memo pad.

"It's just a hunch at this point. We've had very few contacts with the police department since the case began. One was made by Josh about an investigation we're conducting of some of the department's license plate numbers. That might be enough to prompt the assault right there. But it's all eerily similar to a situation with one of Louis's aunts. She was threatened by some cops at her shop on Magazine Street."

"You're thinking it's a little too coincidental for the incidents not to be connected?"

"Yes." Emma squinted her eyes and stared out of the window. "I think I should keep the students away from the precinct."

The dean nodded. "I agree." He looked at Emma. "And now...what about you?"

"If you mean I should restrict myself too, my answer is absolutely not. Other attorneys would run into the same problem I have. So, what's the difference? I know the case; I know the players. I've faced that cop and know what he and his car look like. I've even memorized most of the numbers from his license plate."

"It's dangerous, even foolish, Emma."

"I'm going to speak to McEnroe, one of the officers at the department's internal affairs section today, right after we finish up here. I think he'll take care of the problem."

* * *

Emma parallel parked in front of the 6th District station and fed the parking meter, pouring every quarter she had into the machine. The sun baked her back as she climbed the steps to the double front doors. Scott should be in at this time of day, but she was prepared to wait for hours if she had to. She didn't have a class until later in the day.

Her wait was shorter than she'd feared it might be. Within forty-five minutes, he appeared, hand extended, apologizing for the delay. She was glad to see him.

Scott waved her back to his office located down a long dark corridor and invited her to sit in a small chair next to his desk. The office was dimly lit and void of decoration, with the exception of a few awards from the police academy, including the Academic Excellence Award. He listened patiently as Emma described her encounter with the police officer, stopping occasionally to take notes. She included concerns about Josh's research at the 6th District on unmarked car license plate numbers.

"Has anything else happened you're concerned about, Emma?" Scott paused, pen in hand.

"There's one more thing. A similar assault was initiated by a police officer against a shop owner, Juanita Bishop, on Magazine Street. She reported it." Emma frowned and crossed her arms.

Officer McEnroe nodded. "I think I know the case you're talking about."

"The threats in her case and in mine are similar. But I have no idea why anyone, let alone a police officer, would be threatening me. I don't have a shop. I don't need protection. They aren't trying to force me to give them protection money. The officer thought I already knew what his threats were about, or should be able to figure it out. And I don't have a clue." Emma shrugged.

"Right now, I don't either. To be safe, perhaps you should stop working on your murder case. What is it? The Bishop case? Perhaps you could pass it on to another attorney, just to be on the safe side." Scott frowned as he reviewed his notes.

"Is that your recommendation? I was hoping you would look into the police officer who assaulted me instead." Emma hoped she didn't sound snide, but she'd expected a different reaction.

"We will. We'll get right on it. But I'm concerned about you. Until we can track this officer down and see what he's up to, it would work in your favor to be less visible."

"What do you mean by less visible?"

"You should pull back on working so hard on the Bishop case until we have a better understanding of what's going on."

Emma shook her head. "I don't buy that. I'm just doing my job, and I've reported what this officer has done to me. I don't do drugs, there will never be any evidence of drugs in my bloodstream, so why should his threats about planting drugs in my car be a concern to me? I want to proceed with Louis's case, but I won't do anything foolish. I trust you can quickly figure out who the officer is. You've got the badge number. So, I'm going to go downstairs and file an official report against Badge Number 4962."

"You don't have to take drugs to be found guilty. In fact, some dealers never touch the stuff. But if the officer was throwing down a baggie of cocaine, my guess is that it was at least twenty-eight grams, or enough to charge you with possession with intent to sell. If that's the case, you wouldn't be legally protected by a clean drug test if that bag was found in your car. I understand your desire to fight this. I just think it would be better if the officer doesn't know you're proceeding against him. But it's your call."

Emma paused for a moment. "Can you get me his name?"

"I can do that for you. There are over a thousand officers in the NOPD, so I don't know who he is off the top of my head, and I don't have a roster of officer badge numbers here in my office." Scott leaned over his desk to get a better look at Emma. "Don't worry. We'll figure out what's going on here. I don't know what's motivating this guy, but, hopefully, our investigation will tell us. That could require hours of work, and we may not know what he's up to for months. That's one reason I was concerned about you."

"You don't need to know that for me to file the complaint though, right?"'

"Nah. You've come to the right place. Go ahead, fill out a complaint form, explain everything in detail. You can file it downstairs, or you can leave it with me, whichever you want to do. If you leave it with me, we'll have all of the details of your complaint so we can conduct an investigation, and if you want us to file the report for you, we can."

* * *

Emma was glad the day was over. The boys were staying after school for play rehearsal. She didn't expect them until seven o'clock which was when a friend's mother said she'd drop them back home. She'd done her grocery shopping and had time to make dinner for once. The sun was starting to set, giving the sky a warm pink glow. She felt relaxed for the first time since her encounter with the police officer. Her shoulders lowered involuntarily, and she took a deep breath. She couldn't wait to get home.

Emma pulled into her parking space and grabbed her grocery bags from the back seat. She stepped toward the front door, keys in hand, and stopped when she heard dogs barking overhead. Startled, she looked up and saw long, floppy, brown and white ears hanging over the eaves of the house from the second floor. All of the windows of the apartment were wide open. The dogs were on the roof, again.

Emma felt panic clutching her throat as she opened the front door. She threw the groceries on the landing and flew up the stairs to her apartment. The door was ajar. Her heart was pounding so fast she thought she was going to throw up. She pushed the door open with a shaking hand.

The place had been completely ransacked. Chairs and tables were overturned, contents of desks were strewn about, the leg of her favorite antique French writing desk was broken, pantry items were on the floor, and drapes were fluttering from the opened windows. Emma ran up the spiral staircase to the boys' bedroom, and back to their bathroom, where there was access to the roof. She climbed halfway out of the opened bathroom window and called for Lulu and Maddie. The dogs wagged their stumpy little tails and tiptoed back from the edge of the roof to the window for a hello nuzzle.

"Come on in, girls." Emma whistled the dogs in and closed the window behind them, and hugged their necks. They were excited to see her, but didn't want to leave her side, refusing to drink water or eat a treat Emma offered them. She knew they were upset.

Then she noticed the twins' room. The contents of their closet and chest of drawers had been thrown on the floor. Everything. Every single thing the boys owned. Shoes, and pants, and shirts, and underwear, books and sports equipment piled on top. She hadn't even looked in her bedroom yet and was dreading it. She'd eventually assess whether anything had been stolen, but right now she was upset. And shaken. It was obvious that someone wanted her to feel that way.

Emma sat down at the top of the stairs and put her arms around both dogs, hugging them close. Just having them there to hang onto for a moment made everything better for a little while. She was relieved Lulu and Maddie hadn't been hurt when they were on the roof. Maddie, especially, loved to chase squirrels, and could have easily been tempted to jump. She was also grateful her boys weren't home. But she suspected the vandals chose a time to invade her apartment when no one but the dogs were there. It was obvious she was being watched.

She walked to the phone on the nightstand next to Bobby's bed and picked it up to call 911.

Chapter Twenty-One

Emma put leashes on Maddie and Lulu as soon as the police officers completed their inspection of her apartment, and left. The dogs were skittish and needed a walk to help them calm down. They nearly took Emma's arm off as they dove down the stairs, shivering in anticipation of a romp with squirrels. She opened the downstairs door and was startled to see J.C. and Cornelius standing on the sidewalk next to her car.

"Well, hello. What are you two doing here? Aren't you supposed to be home this time of day?"

"Yeah, but we saw somethin', and we wanted to tell you about it.." J.C. clasped his hands behind his back.

"Want to walk with me and the dogs down the block for a bit? The girls need to do their business and get a little exercise. They've had an upsetting day."

The boys nodded and scurried along beside Emma who was being pulled, Iditarod style, down the street by Maddie and Lulu. Lurching forward for nearly a block, the dogs finally stopped for a minute to sniff a patch of enticing weeds. Emma caught her breath.

"So, guys, what did you see that was so important you risked your mom's anger to tell me about?"

J.C. cocked his head to the side and looked up at Emma. "We thought you'd like to know we saw one of those cars again, one that we saw following Brother Antoine earlier. This time it was going down Magazine Street, and so we followed it on our bikes. It wasn't that hard to keep up with 'cause traffic was jammed up and slow that time of day. The car went all the way down Magazine and turned down by the expressway. There's a little park there. It's where Prytania turns into Camp? That's where he stopped. He went up to that statue of that old lady that's in the middle of the park and stuck under the very bottom of the statue was a brown bag. He pulled that out and left."

"Huh. Wonder what that's all about." Emma tugged at Maddie's leash to prevent her from getting too close to the street.

J.C. shrugged. "We don't know. And he didn't open the bag, so we couldn't see what was inside. But we thought you'd like to know."

"What was the guy wearing?"

"Just a regular police uniform."

"You didn't get a name or badge number or anything, did you?"

Cornelius shook his head. "Nah, we were too far away."

Emma knew the park the boys were describing. She passed it every time she drove to the central business district. The most unwelcoming park in the city, it was a tiny, barren, treeless space that no one visited. There were no benches, no shade, and no amenities to speak of, with the exception of the statue. Paying homage to Margaret, who dedicated her fortune to the orphans of New Orleans, the statute was directly in the middle of the park. Still, it might make an adequate hiding spot for small things, especially since it was vacant year-round. She'd check out the place on the way to see Louis tomorrow.

Emma and the boys walked back to her place.

"Before you go, there's one more thing. We had a break-in today. The first piece of furniture I bought here in New Orleans was broken. It's an old French desk I really love. Do you think your grandfather would take a look at it?"

The boys looked at each other and shrugged.

"Sure," Cornelius said. "We could tell him about it. He usually comes by and looks at the stuff. And if he thinks he can fix it, he puts it in his truck and takes it to his shop to work on it there. He says his customers like it better that way. Want us to take a look?"

"Okay." Emma smiled and let the boys in the front door.

They climbed up the steps with the dogs and unlocked her apartment door. J.C. and Cornelius walked in while she unleashed Maddie and Lulu and watched them bound around the apartment, happy to be free.

Emma walked over to the desk, which had been tossed over on its side, and showed the boys its broken leg. They examined it, flopping the broken piece back and forth with a serious look on their young faces.

"We'll tell Pop about this. I don't think it will be too hard to fix, but he needs to see it. He'll call you and set something up. That's usually what he does. Maybe we can help fix it too."

"I'd love it if you'd work on it with your grandfather. Maybe you could show Billy and Bobby how you do this work. I'd bet they'd like to learn too."

"Sure! That'd be fun. I'm sure Pop would agree."

Emma gave them her phone number and sent them on their way so their mother wouldn't worry.

She needed to put some order in her place before their friend's mother dropped them off from play practice around 7:00.

* * *

It only took Emma an hour and a half to tidy the boys' bedroom, but once she was finished she was drained, emotionally exhausted. She felt violated. She didn't know how she was going to explain what had happened to the boys. And she felt guilty. This was her fault. She'd brought this danger to her family. She didn't know how to undo the harm she'd done.

She started on the rest of the house, and managed to straighten the living room, dining room and most of the kitchen when the twins walked in from their school's play practice. She knew they could tell immediately that something was wrong.

"What happened?" Billy walked into the kitchen and looked around.

"Why's the desk propped up and why's its leg broken? And why are there pots and pans on the floor? What's going on?" Bobby dropped his book bag and stared at Emma. His cheeks were flushed, and he was breathing heavily.

"We were vandalized. Was anything stolen?" Billy flew up the stairs to check on their bedroom. Bobby followed.

Emma climbed the staircase after the twins. When she got to the top of the landing, she stopped and watched them checking the contents of their room.

"Nothing's been stolen, and now everything's back in place. So, your world's back in order," Emma said.

"What's going on, Mom?" Bobby's fists were clenched, his face flushed. Emma could tell he was trying not to cry.

"Here, come sit down." Emma walked over to Bobby's bed and patted a spot on each side of where she sat. The boys sat down beside her. She put her arms around their shoulders and squeezed.

"We had a break-in today, but no one was hurt. We don't know who did it, but I think they just wanted us to be afraid. So, the best thing we can do is not give them what they want, and not be afraid. Don't you agree?"

The twins nodded.

"Because being afraid or panicking never solves anything, right?"

"Right," the boys said simultaneously. But neither twin raised his head, or looked at Emma.

"But of course, we always have to be careful. Keep our doors locked. Make sure the windows are down, and that the dogs aren't out on the roof."

Each boy nodded.

"Do either of you have anything you want to say?"

"Sometimes it's hard not to be afraid," Bobby said. His eyes were watering, and his bottom lip quivered.

Billy nodded. "How do you know this won't happen again? Are we going to be okay to sleep here tonight?"

"I know it's scary, sweetheart. But I really don't think they'll come back, especially tonight. I called the police, and they inspected the apartment. They took pictures and fingerprints. They'll conduct an investigation and try to find the person who did this. They'll do their best."

The boys looked at the floor.

"What if we go to dinner at your favorite restaurant? Are you hungry?"

154

They nodded simultaneously.

"Hugo's for pizza?" Bobby said.

"Sure. Why don't you wash up and then come downstairs, and we'll go right away. I can pick up the rest of this mess later."

Emma went back downstairs while the boys got ready to go. She sat on the couch for a minute to rest her back, and, out of habit, picked up the telephone. Her fingers automatically dialed Ren's number. She hoped he wouldn't be home. She dreaded telling him about the break-in. But he answered.

"What? This is it, Emma! This has got to stop! Is there any sign of who did this? I mean, it could'a been that cop, or Marcus, or one of his guys. And why were the dogs on the roof? All the windows were open? If you're sure nothing was stolen, it was pure harassment. Someone's tryin' to scare you. Did they leave anything behind, or any hints about who they were?"

"No. But I'd just assumed it was the cop. Seems more his style, don't you think?" Emma glanced up the stairs to make certain the twins weren't coming down. "The worse thing is Billy and Bobby. They're so scared and upset." She felt her eyes watering.

"And you're sure nothing is missing?"

"Pretty sure. But I haven't gone through everything yet."

"I don't think you should stay there any longer. You need to leave."

"We could leave for tonight. Find a hotel room or something. But I can't sustain something like that for very long. We had such a difficult time finding a safe, affordable apartment in the city. The boys love this place. I'd hate to give it up."

"Don't you think you should re-think that 'safe' thing? You've just had a break in. Someone who knows where you live has it out for you and you need to get out of there for a while."

"I'm hoping this was a once in a lifetime thing. I hope I never have to worry about anything like this again." Emma leaned back on the couch and closed her eyes for a second. She could feel a headache coming on.

"That doesn't make any sense. Your kids have been threatened by Marcus. You've been accosted by a cop, and now your home has been vandalized. I understand you're trying not to panic, but I don't think you can rely on not being bothered by anything like this again. Have you told Scott about it yet? He'll need to know. It's got to be connected to the harassment from that cop yesterday."

"Or it could be. I'll mention it to him tomorrow. I've got to go by and see Louis too. Here come the boys. I've got to go."

* * *

A deputy escorted Emma into the small side room at Central Lockup. She pulled out one of the cold, metal folding chairs and sat down to wait for Louis. It wasn't long before she heard a familiar shuffling sound, and watched as Louis approached, his head pointed downward, toward his feet, as he moved to the center of the room. Emma stood up in an unsuccessful attempt to make eye contact.

"Hello, Louis."

Louis nodded once, but kept his gaze directed at his feet.

"We have some new information on your case. I need to hear what you think about it, and if you agree with what other witnesses say happened on the night of the shootings."

Louis sat down and leaned over, elbows on knees, hands clasped, and stared at the floor in front of him.

"We spoke to your cousin Georgie and another witness who said that, after the shootings, you stopped by the large electrical transformer in the middle of the common ground, on your way toward the river. Did you drop something off there? Can you tell me what you were doing?"

Louis cracked his knuckles. "I don't know what Georgie's talkin' about."

"Georgie also said he heard between three and four shots, not two. Do you agree with that?"

He nodded. "That might be about right."

"Louis, I want you to think about something. And this is very important. I know you want to do the right thing. Maybe you think you're doing that since you're young and you figured you'd be able to serve time in juvenile detention for these shootings. But you're not in juvenile court. The court and the prosecutor are charging you as an adult. Do you know what that means?"

Louis nodded. "I know what it means. And I know what they could do to me."

"Does that mean you know that if you're found guilty, you won't be free at age twenty-one, as you would have in juvenile court? If you're found guilty of the murder of these two men, you'll be sentenced as an adult. We received notice from the DA that the sentence could include the death penalty. Do you understand what that means?"

Louis looked at Emma directly in the eyes, suddenly losing his crusty, sullen exterior. His facial muscles collapsed, exposing something that looked very much like terror.

Emma waited a few minutes to allow Louis to absorb the full effect of what she'd said. He was young, and she hadn't wanted to overwhelm him with all of the possibilities of sentencing the first time they'd met. But it was time to discuss the reality of his situation. He needed to stop protecting Marcus and help her build his defense. He'd seen enough in his life to understand a set up.

Louis stood up and began pacing the room. He stopped suddenly and looked at Emma.

"How they gonna do it? Is it the chair?"

"Let's not go there right now. The thing to concentrate on is how we can make sure it doesn't come to that. You have to help us help you. And if we're going to help you, we need to know what really happened that night. Did you drop something off at the transformer?"

"You might try to help me, but I don't see how you really can. And are you talking about that big box 'tween Mama Ruth's place and Aunt Juanita's?"

"Yes."

"You gotta understand somethin.'" He sat back down and scooted his chair a little closer to Emma. He rubbed his forehead. Emma could see that he was beginning to perspire, and his hands were shaking. "If I say anything to you about that night, I could get killed. Either in here, or if I get out, I'm sure to get offed. There's no way I'll make it if I say anything about Marcus to you or anybody else." He wiped his face with his t-shirt sleeve.

"Can you tell me what you dropped off at the transformer, at least? Was it the brown bag Marcus gave you?"

He hesitated for a moment, then nodded.

"What was in the bag?"

"I don't know. Could have been money. I didn't see inside. But it wasn't a gun."

"Was anyone there when you dropped it off?"

He nodded.

"Who?'

"Some dudes. I don't know who they were. I couldn't really see 'em. They were all in black, and their faces were covered."

"Do you mean they had something over their faces, or did they have something on their faces, like black makeup?"

"They had somethin' over their faces."

"What was it? Ski masks?"

He shook his head. "No. It was big an' kinda lumpy. I don't know. It was dark, and I was runnin'."

"Do you recall seeing flashes of red lights or dots before Brother Antoine was shot?"

He shook his head. "No."

"The police only found one gun, and that was thrown through the window under your grandmother's apartment?

Louis nodded.

"So, the gun was found in the crawl space of your grandmother's place?"

"I guess." Louis shrugged. "I didn't throw it there, and I didn't find it either. But that's what I was told."

"How many men were behind the transformer? Could you tell?"

"I could see two, I think."

"Did you see anyone with a gun or holding a gun that night?"

"Not really."

"Are you sure about that? Didn't you see Mr. Maureau holding a gun?"

He grimaced. "Maybe."

"What about Marcus?"

"No. He didn't have one."

"Louis, I need you to be completely honest with me. You can't protect Marcus any longer. He's not protecting you. Do you understand that?"

"How do you know what Marcus is doing?" he whispered.

"What was that?"

Louis shook his head.

"You said you threw your gun in the river. Is that what really happened?"

He hesitated. "I didn't want to get caught with a gun, so I threw the one I had away. Like I said. After the shootings, I dropped off the bag and kept runnin'. I didn't want to have nothin' on me if I got stopped, so I ran down to the river and threw the gun I had on me away. But I didn't shoot anybody." He cracked his knuckles.

"Do you know who did?"

"No. I didn't see nothin'. But I'd think it might be those two dudes by that box."

"The transformer."

"Yeah." Louis nodded.

"And Louis, we can fight this death penalty thing. We just need you to be honest with us." She smiled. "How are you doing in here? Mr. Branson tells me you like to draw things, especially men's fashion. Have you been able to do any of that?"

Louis leaned over, placed his elbows on his knees and hung his head. Then he looked up at Emma. "Um, no." He hesitated, then shook his head.

"Do you want to say something, Louis?"

He nodded.

"Go ahead. What is it?"

"Some of the older, bigger guys in here," his voice dropped to a low whisper, and he looked around to see if anyone was watching him. "They're causing trouble."

"What sort of trouble?" Emma dropped her voice to follow Louis's lead.

"They're threatening me. Sayin' they want to have me. Take me. You know. Have they way with me. Especially at night. I hadn't had a shower a week, just tryin' to stay away from them." He looked around.

Emma had heard about abuse in the Orleans Parish prison, especially in Tent City. Louis was a boy, underage and hardly able to fend for himself against an abusive adult male.

"I'll see what I can do to get you help, Louis. Today."

As Emma was leaving the prison, she saw Jesse Branson, Louis's guidance counselor from Fortier High School, walking up the steps. She stopped to shake his hand.

"Here to see Louis?"

"Yeah. I've been stopping by every week or so since he's been in. He needs to know someone cares. Someone besides his lawyer, that is." He smiled.

"Good timing. I told him we received notice that he was subject to the death penalty, and he was upset. I'm sure he could use some reassurance. We're doing our best, but he needs to work with us. And we need him to be honest with us. It's not the time to protect others. Also, he just told me that he's being harassed by some of the older inmates. I need to see what I can do about that."

"I was afraid of that. Let me know if I can help. Also, you need to know that even though Louis told you about those inmates here, in Louis's world, no one rats out anyone, and if they did, the consequences of that are pretty dire. So, if he told you that inmates were after him, it must be pretty bad. Don't look for big revelations from him, or much of anything you can count on, realistically, about his case."

Emma nodded. "We got notice from the DA that they were going to pursue the death penalty in the case. Could you recommend someone for psychological testing? I'd like to be able to use the deprived background defense, as a mitigating circumstance. He should be checked out for a learning disability, too." She pulled a scrap of paper from her purse and fumbled around for a pen.

"Sure. I'd recommend Dr. Darlene Mitchell. She's insightful, thorough, and likes kids."

***

After Mr. Branson left, the guard walked Louis back outside to the open area in the prison and left him there. He immediately headed for the one place behind the laundry room where he'd been able to hide without being discovered. Everyone got two hours a day outside. So far, he'd spent most of that outside time in hiding. But at night, they did a head count, and he had to be in his cell. That's when Jenkie and Smoker came over and tried to mess with him. So far he'd been able to hold them off. He hoped that lady lawyer, Professor Thornton, could get him out of here, or at least away from those two.

He slipped behind the back wall of the laundry, between the wall and a wooden storage structure. He made his way behind several empty laundry baskets, sat down on the ground, and pulled out a small drawing pad which was tucked in his back pocket. He started sketching out some ideas he had for a jumpsuit. He could always think better when he was drawing.

He was scared. He was always scared, but now was different. Marcus would have him killed if he said anything about that night. He knew it. But if he didn't say what happened, he could get the death penalty. He'd feared that all along. Did that mean the electric chair? Of course, Marcus probably had people there in prison who'd kill him for doing nothing more than talking to an attorney. Marcus always said loyalty to the family was the most important thing. The Gangsta B's was always number one.

Louis put his notepad down and put his head in his hands. Tears rolled down his face. He was in big trouble.

***

"So, your apartment was torn up when you got home?" Scott McEnroe was jotting down notes as Emma spoke.

"That's right. Whoever did it was pretty thorough. Looked as if nothing was left untouched. And it happened so close in time to my encounter with the officer on Carrollton I thought the two incidents might be related. By

161

the way, do you have the name of that officer 4962 yet?"

"Not yet. I'm not sure what's taking the clerk so long. I'll check on it for you. We usually don't reveal the names of officers involved in police investigations, but we'll make an exception in your case."

"I appreciate it, Officer McEnroe."

"Call me Scott." He smiled. He could have made toothpaste commercials.

"Of course. I guess that means you're investigating the officer who accosted me?"

"I shouldn't say, but we have to look into situations like the one you described. I'm sure you understand."

Emma folded her arms across her chest. "Can you tell me why the internal affairs unit is investigating Officer Boudreaux's death, or why you wanted to speak to me about him? So many things are going on, and I'm beginning to wonder if they aren't all related somehow."

Officer McEnroe pressed his hands against his desk and stood up. "You've been here long enough to realize that New Orleans is a city with a fair amount of crime. Things happen every day, and they certainly aren't all related. The fact that the officer harassed you probably has nothing to do with Louis's case, and Officer Boudreaux's death probably doesn't either. So, if I were you, I'd just forget about it."

Chapter Twenty-Two

That afternoon Emma called the Orleans Parish Sheriff's office.

"I'd like to speak to Sheriff Degrasi."

"Who can I say is calling, please?"

"I'm Emma Thornton, a professor at St. Stanislaus University Law School. He's got one of my juvenile clients, Louis Bishop, in Central Lock Up. Louis is only sixteen. He's being threatened and harassed by older inmates. Something needs to be done about it before he's hurt."

"One moment please."

Emma was placed on hold for several minutes.

"Professor Thornton? We will have to call you back on that, but we will call you today."

* * *

Josh walked into Emma's cramped office space and sat in one of the Mid-Century chairs she'd arranged in front of her desk. Emma opened the sun faded drapes for more light and placed a copy of the autopsy reports for Sam Maureau and Brother Reginald Antoine on the seat of each chair. The office was hardly large enough for Emma, let alone two additional students. It was on the first floor, at the very back of the building, which Emma liked, since it was isolated, but it was far less prestigious than many of the other offices in the building. When Emma first moved into the space, the only furniture was a beaten-up desk, and a sad-looking metal filing cabinet. So Emma and her assistant raided one of the rarely used women's restrooms, and "borrowed" a set of office chairs and a cracked leather settee. They set the filing cabinet in the oddly shaped nook in the back, the office chairs in front of the desk and the couch by the wall next to the door. The effect was cozy and warm. Emma placed her diplomas on the wall and was happy there.

Josh picked up the reports. Emma gathered her copy of the documents she'd planned to use for the afternoon session and checked her watch.

"Melissa's late, which isn't like her. Something must have come up. We'll go ahead and start. But first, before I forget, someone needs to contact Dr. Darlene Mitchell, she's a child psychologist, and schedule testing for Louis for mitigation purposes. Josh, looks like you're it, since Melissa isn't here."

"No prob. I would have volunteered for that, anyway." He smiled.

"Good. She'll have to test him at the jail, so take care of those arrangements too."

Josh nodded.

"We have some new evidence, including evidence you and Melissa will review about our expert pathologist's interview and findings, and their measurements of the murder scene. Why don't you go over that in a minute?"

Josh pulled his notes out of his notepad.

"Melissa and I suspected Alicia might be more candid if her aunt wasn't around. So, we interviewed her again, and discovered that on the night of the shootings, she walked a few feet from the porch with Brother Antoine. She was able to see red laser flashes on his arm and chest before the shots rang out. Then, when she returned to the porch, she saw Louis running toward the river. She didn't notice if he had anything in his hands.

"Georgie was interviewed that same day. He said Louis handed off a paper bag to someone behind the transformer, then ran toward the river. Georgie didn't know what was in the bag, but said the bag was small, like the kind you'd pack a school lunch in.

"I interviewed Louis again, too. He corroborated Georgie's story and added a little more to his. Apparently he stopped at the transformer to hand off the paper bag. He didn't know what was in it, but said he handed it off to a couple of guys wearing black. He couldn't see their faces because they were also wearing something black on their heads.

"So. There were two guys at the transformer. Only one gun has been found, which has been associated with the shootings. That's the gun the police found under Mama Ruby's apartment." She paused. "Now that's some food for thought, huh? What do you make of that?" Emma sat back up, pulled out a notepad, and propped her elbows on her desk.

"Looks like our suspicion about missing evidence is on target. There are missing casings and if there were two shooters, there has to be another gun somewhere. And, I think it looks like the killing of Brother Antoine wasn't an accident," Josh said.

"I agree. But why do you say that?"

"The red dot that was described could have been a laser sight. They have them for handguns and rifles. And if that's what it was, I'd say the shot was aimed at him, and deliberate, not accidental as we've been thinking."

"Okay, but that changes everything, doesn't it?"

"If Brother Antoine was shot deliberately, maybe he was involved with drugs. Dwayne said there were rumors going around about him." Josh wrote down a few notes about Emma's findings and their conclusions.

"That's a possibility. It's something we hadn't considered before. You've heard me talk about J.C. and Cornelius, brothers around my kids' age. They loved Brother Antoine. He was their coach and role model. They were very upset by his death and said that for some time he'd been followed by an unmarked car. If Brother Antoine was involved in drugs, it makes sense that he'd be followed by the police. But it doesn't make sense that someone who works with kids, and who is doing everything he can for the community, would also be involved with drugs."

Josh nodded. "I guess so. But stranger things have happened. And, didn't Dwayne and Georgie say that Marcus left the area immediately after the gun was fired on the night of the shootings? They didn't know where he'd gone. No one else even mentioned Marcus or what Marcus did that night."

"That is interesting. Why do you think no one has a memory of Marcus from that night? We can use common sense to make an educated guess here."

"Because most of the witnesses we spoke to were afraid to implicate Marcus?" Josh raised an eyebrow.

"That'd be my answer. Did you and Melissa learn anything new from the pathologist, Dr. Roberts?"

"He confirmed what we thought. Maureau was shot three times by two different people. And none of the shooters were from a close-up range." Josh looked up from the autopsy report. "You've got superficial injuries on the right, then a fatal injury which entered on the right and exited on the left. Dr. Roberts said it's unlikely one person would have had time to get into the two different positions to have made the fatal shot as well as the two superficial shots because they were at completely different heights. He said the fatal shot came from ground level. So, he concluded that two separate people shot Mr. Maureau."

"What about Brother Antoine? Was that done by a third shooter?" Emma laid down her pen and looked up at Josh.

"Brother Antoine's shot to the chest was the first fired, and it took everyone by surprise. So, Dr. Roberts said one man shot Brother Antoine, from a distance, on his knees, then, after that, crouched down, aimed and shot Maureau. And the way he looked at it, the angle and distance from the transformer would be about right for all of the shots. But, absolutely the correct angle for the fatal shots. It's around fifty feet from the transformer to where Brother Antoine was shot, and depending on exactly where he was standing, twenty-five to thirty feet from the transformer to Maureau."

The phone rang. It was the sheriff's office. Josh got up to leave, but Emma put out her hand, indicating he could stay.

"This is Sheriff Degrassi's assistant. He told me to inform you that he would place Louis and two other juveniles housed at the Central Lock Up facility in one area on the second floor and have Deputy Maynard Johnson patrol the area all night long. Deputy Johnson is six feet, six inches. Sheriff Degrassi does not anticipate any problems from now on. They'll be protected at night."

"This should protect them at night, but doesn't do much to help through-out the day. I'll speak to Louis and will let you know if his problems continue.

If they do, please note that I'll have no problem whatsoever suing the Orleans Parish Sheriff's Department for this cruel and inhumane treatment of an underage inmate."

"I'll let the sheriff know, Professor Thornton."

Emma hung up the telephone and looked up at Josh's startled expression.

"Louis has been threatened and harassed by inmates at Central Lock Up. I had to do something."

They heard a knock. When Josh opened the door, Emma was surprised to see Melissa, whose eyes were red, and nose was puffy, obviously from crying.

Emma stood up to greet her. "Come on in. We've been discussing the autopsy report and some of the new evidence in Louis's case." Emma gestured toward the empty seat next to Josh.

Melissa dabbed her eyes. "I have some news to share." She sounded stuffy, as if she had a cold. "I got a call from Alicia about the time I should have been getting in the car to come down here. Her Aunt Juanita was found this morning in her shop. She'd been shot!" Melissa sobbed. "She's dead!" She dabbed her eyes. "Alicia is so upset. She doesn't know what she's going to do, but thinks she'll probably have to go live with her grandmother for the immediate future."

Emma felt the blood leave her face. She was dizzy and had to sit down. "Oh no! Not Juanita!" She put her head in her hands for a moment, then looked up. "Let's call it a day. We'll talk about all of the other issues later on in the week. Melissa, if you can, please stay behind for a minute."

Josh shuffled out of Emma's office as Emma threw her arms around Melissa.

"I'm so sorry. Does Alicia need anything? Is there anything we can do?"

"I think we should let the family have their privacy right now, but we should go to the funeral. I'll get all of the information and let you know."

* * *

Emma had no desire to cook. Instead, she stopped by her favorite restaurant for takeout and picked up lasagna for the boys, and Fettuccini Alfredo for her. She needed comfort food. She popped the lasagna and fettuccini in the oven to stay warm until the twins got home, opened the refrigerator, and pulled out a bottle of wine. Reaching into the cupboard, she searched for her best crystal goblet, poured a healthy portion of her favorite white Bordeaux, and sat down on the couch. She'd never felt more like crying. The dogs, sensing her sadness, curled up at her feet.

Juanita was such a life force. She loved fiercely, lived by her own terms, and was afraid of no one. Emma curled her hand into a fist and pounded the couch. No amount of wine was going to numb the horror of Juanita's death. Juanita was Alicia's role model, her safety net, the only mom she'd ever known. Juanita's loss was immeasurable, unfathomable. Without Juanita's protection, Alicia's life could be in danger, especially if Marcus discovered Alicia had spoken to Louis's attorneys. Juanita didn't want Alicia hanging around Marcus for good reason. But she'd already moved over to Mama Ruby's. She was certain to see him there.

Emma picked up the phone and dialed Ren's number. The phone rang a couple of times before he picked up. She gave him the sad news.

"Man, I can't believe it. Did you see that coming?"

"No. How could I? For one thing, I thought she'd be protected by the reports she filed against those abusive cops. I can't believe she's gone. It's just so scary and awful."Emma wiped a tear that had rolled down her cheek.

"Could be a random act by a crazy person, or something."

"That's comforting, especially since I was vandalized the other day. But I don't think so, do you?"

"Not really, no. And I'm not sure how those cops figure they can get away with something like this."

"I don't either unless they have more power than we realize."

"I almost forgot. I got a call from the NOPD police superintendent. He wants me to come in and talk to him about that internal affairs job. He said it was important to him to have someone who isn't from New Orleans for the position. They want some new blood."

"I thought you'd already interviewed with Scott."

"I did. But I have to interview with the superintendent, too. Sometimes you have to meet with several layers of folks. And Scott wanted me to meet a bunch of the guys that worked there to see how we all got along. I think I'd work under Scott. But the superintendent does the official hiring. That's how I understand it, anyway."

"So, are you coming down?"

"Yeah. He wants me there tomorrow, if I can get a ticket."

"I'd love to see you. And it would be great if you could stay a little longer, take a look at the gun and the other evidence and let us know what you think. Maybe you could even attend Juanita's funeral with me? Think you'd have the time?"

"I might be able to stay, but, like I said before, you can't really conduct a forensics exam on a Glock. I can take a look at the gun and the other evidence for you though."

"Good. I'd really like to know whether there's a night sight on the Glock they found under Mrs. Bishop's apartment."

Chapter Twenty-Three

Emma stared out of her office window, watching the soft breeze tease the Spanish moss in the mammoth live oak next door. She was expecting Ren's flight to arrive around 1:30. He'd managed to get a direct flight from Atlanta, a near miracle for last-minute air travel. His appointment with the superintendent was at four. They might even be able to grab lunch before she had to drop him off.

Ren promised he'd stay long enough to attend Juanita's funeral with her. She was glad; she needed his support. Juanita's death was tormenting her. She could see, now, that she shouldn't have urged Juanita to complain to the police a second time. If she hadn't, Emma was certain Juanita would still be alive. She rubbed her forehead. She'd seriously underestimated the police officers who had harassed Juanita—they were far more dangerous than she'd ever imagined. Cops who kill. She hadn't expected that. And she'd pushed Juanita right into their hands. She put her elbows on her desk, leaned her head onto the palms of her hands and closed her eyes.

She heard a knock and opened her office door. She waved Josh in, gesturing for him to take a seat.

"What can I do for you?"

"I finally heard from Tamika."

Emma's eyes widened. "That's a shocker. What'd she say?"

"I told her we wanted to speak to her about what happened on the night of the murders. She agreed to speak with us. When do you want to get together?"

"Like I said before, I don't want you or any of the other students meeting with fact witnesses, especially after what's happened to Juanita and to me recently. It's just too dangerous. I'd rather you guys stick with interviewing experts." Emma sighed. "I'm sorry. I know I asked you to set up the interview, but I've got to be the one that meets with her. I can't take any more risks with you guys."

Josh grimaced. "I think the situation we're in with witnesses is completely different than what happened to Juanita. Don't get me wrong. I understand where you're coming from, but Juanita was threatened first, then she complained a couple of times, and it looks like that's why she was killed. None of the law students will ever be in the same position, you know?" He paused and looked at Emma's clenched jaw. "But if you only want us to interview experts, that's okay with me. You're the boss." He smiled. "Do you want to schedule a time to meet with her?"

"I just can't take risks with anyone any longer." Emma raised the palms of her hands. "I'll meet with Tamika. But why don't you call her and set it up. Explain who I am and that you won't be there. See when she can meet and tell her we'll pay for transportation. I think it would be best if she meets me here. I don't want her to know about St. Francis's, especially since we've been interviewing other witnesses there."

* * *

Emma pulled up to the swooping 1960s overhang at the airport terminal, parked by the curb, and popped open her trunk. Ren threw his bag in and held out his arms. Emma leaned in for a peck on the cheek.

"Get a move on, Officer. They're about to blow the whistle at us."

Ren climbed in the car and closed the door as Emma started the engine.

"You made it off the plane in pretty good time. It's only 1:45, so we have a little time for lunch. I suggest we go downtown, close to NOPD headquarters on Broad Street." Emma made a left turn out of the terminal and stopped at the light.

Ren nodded. "Sounds great."

"I'm a little concerned about this interview, Ren."

171

"Why? I would have thought you'd be excited. I'm thinking about a move here."

"If you move here, and you're unhappy, I'm afraid you'll blame it on me. I couldn't take that."

"I haven't been offered a job. But if I am, and I decide to accept it, it will be because I've made up my mind that it's the best thing for me. Not us. Okay?"

"But I don't know if you're considering—"

"Whether I move here or not is something I'll decide in my own time and by myself. You'll have nothing to worry about. No blame will be coming your way for any decision I make. Promise." Ren squeezed Emma's shoulder. "Anyway, I'm thinking about moving here for the food alone, just in case you thought I was moving here for you. So, stop thinking about all of that, and start thinking about where we're going to eat."

* * *

Emma ran by the clinic office to check her mail cubby. Ren planned to find a way back to her apartment after his interview. She was free to finish up some work she'd started earlier in the day.

"Someone came by to see you. I knew you were coming in, so I had them wait in your office. Hope that's okay." Linda, the clinic's secretary, peered over her glasses at Emma.

"Who is it? I don't have an appointment this afternoon. I'm sure of it."

"She said you did. Her name is Tamika."

Emma sighed, grabbed her mail and walked down to her office. Tamika hadn't made an appointment, or at least if she had, Josh didn't tell her about it, and that wasn't like him. She would have preferred that Josh had set up a definite time for their meeting so she could have checked her notes first. And she wasn't crazy about unexpected visitors in general.

Her door was open and she could see a small African American woman seated in a chair in front of her desk. Her hair had been dyed a flaming fire engine red. Emma drew in a deep breath, walked into the room, and

172

extended her hand.

"Hi, I'm Emma Thornton. I'm guessing you're Tamika Jones?"

Tamika took Emma's hand. "That's right." She smiled. Tamika was tiny, fragile. So fragile Emma was afraid her bones could be crushed by a firm handshake. Except for the gray cast to her skin, and dark circles under her eyes, she had a childlike, wispy appearance, as if the slightest gust of wind could pick her up and carry her away.

"Cab ride cost $40 from my place."

Emma knew it was closer to $20.

"You took a cab here?"

Tamika nodded.

Emma sighed. "Do you have a receipt?"

"Driver didn't give me one. But that's what it was."

"Just so you know, we pay for the streetcar or a bus for witness transportation, not a cab. But I'll pay for it this one time." Emma reached into her bag for her wallet, pulled out a couple of twenties. She handed the bills over to Tamika, who eagerly grabbed them.

Emma walked over to her desk and sat down, placing her purse on the credenza behind her. She grabbed a notepad and pen, and swiveled around in her chair to face Tamika.

"Thanks for coming in. I understand several people saw you speaking to the police the morning after the shooting of Sam Maureau and Brother Antoine. Do you remember that?"

Tamika shrugged her shoulders and nodded.

"Do you remember giving a statement to the police that morning, or whether they wrote down what you said?"

She nodded.

Emma scribbled in her notepad.

"Did you read the statement?"

She nodded.

"Do you remember what you said that day?"

"I said I saw them two men get shot."

"Did you see who did it?"

"Well, it was dark, but it looked like Louis. He shot the men, then he took off runnin'."

"Did you tell them anything else?"

"Yeah. I said I saw Louis come back later and throw his gun under the building where his grandmother, Mama Ruby, live."

"What time did you see Louis do that?"

"I'm not sure the exact time, but it was later. A long time after the shooting." Tamika scratched at something on the back of her neck.

"Where were you at the time of the shooting?"

"I was right next door. In the building next to Miss Ruby. That's where I stay."

Writing furiously on the legal pad, Emma glanced up when Tamika stopped.

"No one remembers seeing you there that night. No one recalls seeing you on the porch, or anywhere where you could have seen the shootings."

"I could see from my bedroom. I watched the whole thing from my bedroom window." Tamika raised her chin and cocked her head as she gazed at Emma.

Emma drew a bird's-eye sketch of the area, and included four of the surrounding apartment buildings, along with the sidewalks and transformer.

"I want you to mark which building is yours with a T, and then mark where your bedroom window is."

Tamika grabbed the paper and studied it for several minutes, then carefully drew a T on one of the buildings. She circled the side of the building where her bedroom window should be placed.

"Now I want you to mark where Marcus, Louis, Dwayne and Georgie were standing with X's."

She placed the four X's in the middle of the page, next to the transformer.

"I'd also like you to mark where the victims were standing when they were shot with O's."

She placed Sam Maureau and Brother Antoine both close to the sidewalk in front of Mama Ruby's apartment.

"Finally, I'd like you to mark where you saw Louis throw his gun with a

174

triangle, and sign and date it for me."

Tamika put a triangle on one side of the building where Marcus's and Louis's grandmother lived. She signed and dated the paper.

"What was the weather like that night, Tamika?"

"It was hot."

"Do you remember whether it was rainy or clear?"

"No."

"Do you remember if the moon was out or not?"

"No."

"Can you tell me what you saw that night?"

"Louis, he was just out there with the others. Then he picked up his gun and aimed it at Mr. Maureau. I could see him pretty good."

"You said he picked up his gun. Where was his gun before he picked it up?"

"It was inside his shirt, kinda tucked in his pants."

"In the front or back?"

"I think it was in the front."

"Was there a streetlight in the area?"

"I can't remember."

"You don't know?'

"Not for sure. But I could see him. I know that much."

"Earlier, you said Louis shot both men. Is that really what you saw? Did you see Louis shoot Brother Antoine too?"

"I couldn't see Brother Antoine that good. But I know I heard a couple of shots. Maybe more. If Brother Antoine was shot, I'm sure it was Louis that shot him."

"How old are you, Tamika?"

"I'm twenty-three."

Emma was surprised. Tamika was waif-like in appearance, but on close inspection, her skin was dried and cracked. Her eyes were sunken. She seemed much older than her actual years.

"Have you ever been convicted of a crime?"

"What do you mean convicted?"

"Found guilty."

"I usually get off."

"You get your charges dismissed?"

Tamika nodded.

"How?"

"Sergeant St. Amant or one of those other officers just throw the charges away."

"Why do they do that?"

"I usually help them out with one of their cases."

"How do you help them?"

"It just depends on what they need. They might need someone to testify about some drug deal, or something like that. Or they might need a witness in another kinda case."

"Are you helping out one of the officers by testifying against Louis?"

"I didn't say that. I saw Louis shoot that man."

"What man did he shoot? There were two men out there that night."

"Far as I could tell, he got that guy named Sam. I couldn't see the other guy too well."

"Was Louis sitting, crouching, or standing when he shot Sam?"

"He standin', what else?" Tamika stood up. "I got to go. You need anything else?"

Emma watched Tamika walk out of her office and head for the front door of the school, twenty-dollar bills doubled up in her fist.

Emma pulled out Dwayne and Georgie's murder scene sketches and set them on her desk. She laid Tamika's drawing next to theirs. Dwayne's and Georgie's were nearly identical, but Tamika's was different. And she told a story of that night that was distinct from everyone else's. It was obvious she wasn't telling the truth, and equally obvious who she was lying for. Emma just didn't know how to prove it.

* * *

Emma opened the door as Billy and Bobby and their two canine companions barreled down the spiral staircase to greet Ren.

"Hi, guys!" Ren gave each of the twins a hug. Lulu and Maddie danced around the boys, each taking turns at nuzzling Ren's hand for a friendly pat.

"How was the interview?" Emma dried her hands on a kitchen towel, tossed it over her shoulder, threw her arms around Ren's neck, and nestled up to him for a kiss.

"Interesting. Got a minute?"

"Hey Ren," Bobby interrupted. "Want to go to the park and walk the dogs with us?"

"Just a minute, boys. Ren and I have a few things to discuss first. Then he's all yours."

Emma dropped her towel on the stair rail, grabbed Ren's hand and walked over to the couch. She pulled him down next to her. "What happened?"

Ren flopped down beside Emma and leaned back. "Like I said, my interview was with the superintendent. He was by himself. He's worried about a couple of groups in the department he thinks are corrupt, and he believes there's been a problem there for years. So, he wants to bring in someone new, someone from another state, if possible. That's why he's interested in me. He said I wouldn't answer to anyone but him."

"That's weird, isn't it? Wouldn't other officers mistrust you, immediately?"

"That's the thing. I'm telling you this, but no one would know. I'd be assigned to Scott, as everyone thought from the beginning. I'd still take orders from him. No one, including Scott, would know I'm reporting to the superintendent. Feels sort of creepy. I'm not crazy about it."

"You'd be an undercover cop for cops?"

Ren nodded.

"Wow. And since he hires all people in the department, he maintains control. So, nothing's ever given away. Interesting."

"Yeah. You've got it."

"Did he say anything about what problems in the department he was concerned about?"

"He did, but I can't say anything about any of that. I've already told you more than I should've."

"What are you going to do?" Emma grabbed his hand. "Will you try this out, or go back home to Jonesburg and become sheriff as you've always planned?"

"Jonesburg will always be there, but this is definitely more challenging. Plus, you live here. So, I'm thinking about it. My main problem with it is Scott. I don't like keeping things from a friend, but that's the job."

"This is a huge step."

"I know. But you've also told me about the problems with some of the police officers here in the city. I'd like to see what I can do to help. Mainly I'd like to be closer to you and the boys. We've been apart for four years. It's time to try this." He squeezed her hand.

Chapter Twenty-Four

Emma parked her car on the narrow, crowded street as close to the sidewalk as she could get. She and Ren got out of the car, stepping over mud puddles as they hurried to the church at the end of the block. The street was residential, filled with Victorian shotgun houses, some in good repair, painted in the pastel shades of the Caribbean, others with peeling paint and neglected lawns. This day the road was lined with cars. People in their finest were pouring into the modest red brick church to say farewell to Juanita Bishop.

Emma and Ren found a seat in the back pew. She could see Alicia in the front, dressed in black, her head bowed. Some of the boys Emma had seen at the Redemption were scattered around the sanctuary. She found Dwayne and Georgie, both in dress shirts and slacks. They looked well-groomed, respectful. She didn't see anyone who met Marcus's description anywhere.

By New Orleans' standards, the church was tiny. The simple oak pews were jam-packed. Even the cracked plaster walls of the sanctuary were lined with attendees, who spilled into the vestibule and collected outside in a line that wrapped around the block.

In contrast, the choir, by any standard, was huge. Dressed in purple robes with gold sashes that flowed down the front of the garment, they festooned the sanctuary with the boldness of their color and their sheer number. Standing on tiers, the choir filled the apse and served as the perfect backdrop for the torrent of floral arrangements sent by friends and family to commemorate Juanita's life. The choir director, a tiny man dressed in a matching purple suit and black horned-rimmed glasses, his hair perfectly coiffed, stepped into the area to the side of the choir where a multi-tiered organ stood. Facing the instrument, he played a run while simultaneously raising his free hand. Then he sat down and moved his elevated hand with a flourish. A woman stepped out and the sweetest sound pierced the silence:

"I am weak, but Thou art strong. Jesus, keep me from all wrong. I'll be satisfied as long as I walk, let me walk, close to Thee."

She was immediately joined by the rich, full-bodied sound of the choir: altos, sopranos, tenors, the deepest of bass, and the rich melodic burst of the organ.

The choir swayed to the rhythm of the sweet song.

"Just a closer walk with Thee. Grant it, Jesus, is my plea. Daily walking close to Thee. Let it be, dear Lord, let it be."

Emma dabbed her eyes, then scanned the sanctuary, eyes peeled for familiar faces. She was certain Mama Ruby was the white-haired lady sitting in the front pew next to Alicia. The emaciated lady sitting on the other side of Alicia must be her mother, and Juanita's little sister, Amy. Emma couldn't see either woman's face. Juanita had made it clear she didn't want Alicia to have contact with Marcus or anyone who associated with him, and that included Mama Ruby. Emma glanced at the grandmother, the woman who cooked for the family nearly every day. How could anyone find fault with that? But Juanita clearly suspected something wasn't right there. And Juanita's instincts were always on target.

The church was a sea of color. Wide-brimmed pastel-colored hats bobbed and weaved as ladies chatted behind fans before the priest made his entrance. The sun shone through narrow stained-glass windows depicting Jesus walking with a group of children, and another showing Jesus feeding bread and fish to a group of people. Emma was so distracted by the astounding red and purple hat on the head of the woman who sat in front of her, she nearly missed the officer sitting on the back pew, near the rear entrance. He was dressed in plain clothes, but Emma recognized him immediately. He was the man who had accosted her on Carrollton after she'd interviewed Georgie and Alicia.

When Emma saw the officer, she ducked behind Ren and nudged him in the ribs.

"There's the guy that threatened me the other day."

"Huh? Threatened you?"

"Are you asleep? The guy who threatened to arrest me for cocaine possession. The cop? Officer 4962?"

"Oh! My God! Why's he here?"

"I don't know. Curiosity? Maybe he wants to see who showed up at the funeral. And I never got his name from Scott." Emma's whispers erupted in a series of tiny staccato outbursts.

Just then the priest walked to the podium. Clearly Irish with the beautifully lilting accent of his homeland, he was an older man, with bright pink cheeks. He was so old Emma expected he'd be out of touch, unable to relate to the congregation. But she was wrong.

Dressed in purple silk robes with a black and gold sash around his neck, the priest stood at the podium and extended his hands outward in a gesture at once accepting and sympathetic. His voice rang out in a clear tenor. "Sister Juanita was a pillar of our community. There are people who are angels walking on this earth, and she was one." Ladies in the church nodded their heads in agreement. Emma heard an "Amen" from somewhere in the sanctuary.

"Not having any children of her own, she took in her niece, Alicia, and was raising her to be a perfectly wonderful young lady." Emma could see Alicia's shoulders move and knew she was crying. "Alicia is the recipient of a scholarship to attend one of our high schools here in town, and I have no doubt that Alicia will go on to do bigger and even better things.

"But Juanita helped others in ways you may not know. She helped the people who worked for her and the homeless on the streets. She didn't like unfairness and never backed down from a threat." He paused and looked out over the crowd. "Juanita didn't tolerate violence, or the exploitation of children. She did what she could to make our community a better place. We need more people like her."

The congregation shouted "Amen" and "Praise God," while the choir broke into "Amazing Grace." The priest said Mass, then turned to the family, and gestured for them to come stand in front of the altar. Juanita's mother, sisters, Alicia, and several of her nephews, including Georgie and Dwayne, all rose, shuffled to the front of the church, and gathered together to pay their final respects to Juanita, as the priest led them in a prayer vigil. The priest then stepped down to offer communion to the congregation, first offering it those family members who still remained at the altar.

Emma turned around to check on the officer, but his seat on the back pew was empty. Most of the congregation stepped into the communion line, but since Alicia, her grandmother, and her mother, Amy, had already participated in communion, they were leaving. Emma watched them walk down the aisle. Mama Ruby was as tiny as her daughter, but her russet skin had an under-glow of pink, and, even though she was in her eighties, her complexion was soft and supple. In stark contrast, Amy appeared drawn and brittle, much older than her years.

Ren stepped outside to check on Officer 4962, and Emma followed him.

"Please keep an eye out for the officer as he's leaving. If you can, get his license plate number or something we can use to identify the vehicle too." She squeezed his arm and scurried back inside the church to look for Alicia.

Minutes later, Emma caught Alicia's eye as she walked toward the exit. Emma stepped forward, arms extended. Alicia collapsed onto her shoulders in tears.

"I know this is hard," Emma whispered.

Alicia nodded.

"Are you still at your grandmother's?" Emma pulled back, searching Alicia's face.

Alicia nodded. "There's really no other place to go."

"Isn't there another relative, or a friend you could stay with?"

"Not really. The only thing left is foster care, and I don't want to do that. The only real problem at my grandmother's is Marcus, and I think I can avoid him."

"Can we talk sometime soon?"

"Tomorrow's Sunday. That would be a good day for me. Let's meet at the coffee house on Felicity."

* * *

Alicia had chosen the tiniest table in the shop, in the corner by the door. She waved when Emma walked in. Emma ordered a café macchiato and sat down next to Alicia.

"You've been at your grandmother's a couple of days now?" Emma pulled a scarf around her shoulders. It was cold in the coffee shop. Beastly hot outside and freezing inside. So typical.

"This was my fourth day there. Aunt Juanita was killed last Thursday, or at least they found her body Thursday morning." She grabbed a napkin from the table and dabbed her eyes.

"Can you tell me what happened, or is it still too upsetting to talk about?"

Alicia nodded. "Flo, Aunt Juanita's receptionist opened the shop early that day and found her in the back, in the office. She'd been shot." Alicia's mouth trembled. She grabbed another napkin. "She hadn't come home that night, but I wasn't worried. Sometimes she worked late and would fall asleep at the shop. So it wasn't that unusual."

"Do you think someone had been watching the shop?"

"I don't know." She shrugged. "Looks that way."

"Did you ever hear your aunt talk about an Officer St. Amant or any of the other officers who had harassed her?"

Alicia nodded. "Yes. She talked about them. And she filed a report against them. I know she did that."

"Do you know if anyone else in addition to those officers ever threatened her?"

She shook her head. "I don't know of anything like that."

"Do you know if anything was stolen from the shop at the time of her shooting?"

"I don't know. Not that I know of."

Emma paused and reached out to Alicia. "So, how are you? Are things okay at your grandmother's?"

"It depends on what you mean by okay. I'm getting by."

"Well, that doesn't sound so good. I know your aunt really didn't want you to hang around there. Do you feel safe?" Emma leaned back in her chair.

Alicia looked at Emma for a moment before answering. "Things are going on I didn't know about before."

"Like what?"

"Like kids doing stuff I didn't know about."

"Selling drugs?"

"No, not that."

"What then?"

"I think Marcus is paying for protection too. And he's using Dwayne and Georgie to carry it out. I'm just guessing, but that's what I think's going on."

"What exactly have you seen?"

Alicia looked around the room. It was filled with business people, college kids, folks in athletic gear, and a guy who appeared to be applying for a job. It seemed safe to talk. "I knew about the Sunday meetings at Mama Ruby's house. There's one today, a little later on. I always thought that was when Marcus handed out the boys' assignments for the week. And I thought he gave them the drugs they needed to distribute, too. But I was just guessing. He could be doing that, but I don't think so now." She shrugged.

"What do you think they're doing?"

"I'm not one hundred percent certain. But I think it has something to do with money and cops. This week was a little different because of the funeral and all. I didn't go to school on Thursday or Friday. I've just been hanging around 'cause I've been real upset." She took a sip of her drink. "Sat out on the front porch a lot. I think the guys forgot about me being there. One day I saw Dwayne and Georgie walk out to the transformer and leave a bag. There's a little space between the cement pad that the transformer sits on and the metal casing. A bag was shoved in that space. A while later, a police officer walked by and picked it up. I saw him open it up and take out something that looked like money folded up. Then he put the money in his pocket. The next day I saw them walking out toward Felicity Street. I'm pretty sure they stopped at that bench that's close by, before you get to Felicity. I guess that's another drop off place. I saw one of them bend down. Maybe they left it under the bench somewhere. But I didn't follow them.

After they got back, I saw a cop car stop by. An officer got out. I couldn't see much, but it looked like another drop off and pick up. I can't be sure."

"Wonder why there would be two drop-offs two days in a row?"

She shrugged. "Who knows? I'm telling you what this looks like to me. I'm guessing, but something's going on. And then Dwayne told me Marcus wanted to talk to me today."

"What about?"

"I'm not sure, but he asked Dwayne if I was good at math."

"Do what you can to avoid that. Come up with a sudden illness—suddenly remember homework you need to hand in—do whatever you need to do. Then see if I can come over and meet with Mama Ruby today."

Chapter Twenty-Five

Emma stared at the announcements on the bulletin board on the wall of the coffee shop. Someone had puppies for sale. Another person wanted to rent out a room in their house and had cleverly severed twenty little tear-away strips at the bottom of the page listing their telephone number. Several strips had been ripped off, leaving gaps reminding her of missing teeth.

She'd been waiting for nearly an hour, even though Alicia had promised that her grandmother would walk over for their meeting right away. Emma chose a table that gave her a view of the street and glanced out of the window in the direction of the Bishop apartment. Finally, she saw movement, and an older, silver-haired woman making her way toward the shop.

Ruby was by herself, obviously not the type of woman who needed hand-holding. Emma guessed her age as late seventies or early eighties, and could tell that she still maintained some of the beauty of her youth. But she walked with a stiff gait. Emma suspected Ruby had either worked hard or may have suffered from an illness or injury since her back was bent and stooped over. As she neared the shop Emma could see her bright, dark brown eyes and turned-up nose. She wore the slightest touch of makeup, and her silver hair was carefully coifed into a smooth twist. Emma greeted Ruby as she entered the shop and grabbed a café au lait for her.

"Thanks for agreeing to meet with me." She squeezed Ruby's hands and sat down across the table from her. "I'm so sorry for your loss. I know this is such a sad time for you and your family. We all loved Juanita."

Ruby's large brown eyes reflected the pain of the last few days. She nodded.

"It's the worst hurt of all. A mother should never have to bury one of her own. It's too much. I've lost too many. But I never thought I'd lose Juanita." Ruby's voice shook. She placed a handkerchief over her mouth.

Emma reached across the table to grasp Ruby's hand again. "I know this is a bad time for you and how much you must be hurting. Is it too early to ask you questions about the night the two men were shot outside your apartment?"

Ruby shook her head. "No, I expected you were going to ask me about that."

"Thanks, Mrs. Bishop. You can stop me anytime." She paused. "You may already know I represent your grandson, Louis. He's been accused of killing those two men. Their names were Brother Reginald Antoine and Sam Maureau. Do you know either man?"

Ruby shook her head. "No. I've heard my granddaughter Alicia talk about Brother Antoine. I think he helped her with a scholarship. I hear he was nice. But I don't know the other man."

"Did you ever meet Brother Antoine?"

"No, I never did."

"I'd like to talk about that night. Do you remember anything about that evening? Do you remember who was there?"

Ruby shook her head. "I don't recall that much. I think everyone came over for dinner. Alicia may have come over a little earlier and then left after grabbing something to eat because she had a meeting. Her meeting was with the brother. All of the boys were there, Louis, Dwayne, Georgie and Marcus."

"It was a Friday night. Do you all usually get together on Friday nights for dinner?"

"Well, I always cook. So, if they want to come by, they can. They usually do." She smiled. "I like it when they do."

"That night, do you remember anyone going out and then coming back in, or anything like that?" Emma took a sip of her coffee.

"Maybe. Louis may have done that. I'm not sure."

"Do you remember them all going out, then all coming back to the apartment a little later on?"

"I must have been in bed by the time they came back. I don't remember that."

"But, you remember them all going out?"

"I think so."

"You just don't remember them coming back inside?"

"No, I don't. Like I said, I was in bed, around that time."

"Do any of the windows in your apartment face the commons area?"

"The what?"

"The grassy area in front of your apartment."

"Oh. I'm a little hard of hearing. I couldn't make out what you said. The grassy area? Yeah. The living room windows do."

"Do you remember looking out of your living room window that night and seeing any of the boys outside in a group?"

"I didn't look outside for the boys. Wouldn't 'a had a reason to."

"What about gunshots? Do you recall hearing any that night?"

"No, but if I'd had my TV on, I might not 'a heard it. Kids are always getting on to me about my TV They say it's too loud. But I can't hear it unless it's turned up."

Emma looked down at her notes. "Mrs. Bishop, what can you tell me about Marcus's business?"

"Well, he has a pawn business he inherited from my son, Gerald. Gerald was Marcus's daddy. He had that business down on Louisiana for nearly twenty years. Had it until he died." She sniffed. "He was another one I lost. A beautiful man, gone before his time." Her body began moving in a swaying motion, as if she was in a rocking chair.

"You must be proud of Marcus for maintaining that business."

"I am." She stopped rocking and nodded. "He's done a good job."

"Who else works with him at the pawn shop? Do the boys?"

"I think the boys do a little delivery for him around here, but they don't work at the pawn shop. Now, Juanita was his bookkeeper, and a very good one. She did that bookkeeping for Gerald, too. Gerald always said that the pawn business is very tricky. You have to keep up with everything and show all items that come in every day to the authorities. That's very important."

"What authorities? Who do you have to report to?"

"You have to report it all to the police. You have to or they shut you down. Juanita took care of all of that. She worked on it at night, every night. She was saving all of the money she got from that to buy a house for her and Alicia." She brushed away a tear which rolled down her face. "She'd been saving for years."

"So, now, Marcus needs another bookkeeper, or accountant. "

"I guess he just might."

"Who worked at the shop with him?"

"I think he's still got a couple of guys Gerald used and a couple of new guys I don't know. You ought to go on by if you've got any questions. But I'm thinkin' he might ask Flo."

"Who's Flo?"

"She's the lady who worked the front desk there at Juanita's shop. She knew everything Juanita knew." Ruby nodded her head. "They were tight. Friends since they were kids."

"How could I find her?"

"She lives off of Carrollton Street somewhere. I don't really keep up with her, but everyone knows her."

Chapter Twenty-Six

Emma pulled up to the curb across from A Cut Above, and locked her car. Yellow crime scene tape was stretched across the front door of the hair salon and tied onto the doorknob. She pushed against the door and squeezed the handle. It was locked.

She walked to the store next door, entered, and found herself surrounded by lacy silk, and creamy satin lingerie in exotic blacks, rich reds, bright purples—more colors, fabrics and designs than she'd ever thought possible. Sitting in the corner on an overly stuffed chair in the shape of a high heel shoe, engrossed in conversation with the sales clerk, was Juanita's receptionist. The woman with chartreuse eye glitter and four-inch fingernails. The woman who Juanita had relied on every day to take care of her schedule, screen her calls, and protect her from unwanted visitors.

"Are you Flo?" Emma walked over and extended her hand.

"That's right. I'm Florence, people who know me call me Flo. Haven't I met you before?" Flo shook Emma's hand.

"I met you once at Juanita's hair salon. I'm the attorney for Louis Bishop, Juanita's nephew."

"Yeah. I remember. Juanita said you're okay. That you're not like all of them other people who say they gonna help and then don't. She said you really working hard to help Louis and all."

"Could we set up a time to talk?"

"Sure." Flo glanced up at Emma and smiled. "I got what I came by here for, so I guess we can talk now. Where you wanna go?"

"How about the coffee shop on the corner? We can walk there."

Flo paid for the tiniest pair of panties Emma had ever seen, gaping as she watched Flo hand the clerk fifty dollars for no more than three rhinestone covered strands held together by a tiny diamond-shaped piece of black velvet. The clerk carefully wrapped the undergarment in tissue paper, placed it in a bright red and black shopping bag twenty times the size of the item, and handed it to Flo, who headed toward the door. Emma had no idea how Flo managed to walk out of the store on her four-inch heels, let alone continue on to the coffee shop on uneven sidewalks and cobblestones.

"I halfway expect to see Juanita walking down the street, elegant robes flowing. I can't believe she's gone," Emma said as she opened the front door of the coffee shop for Flo.

Flo shook her head. "It just don't seem right." She stepped in and an arctic blast of air conditioning hit them in the face.

Emma walked up to the counter.

"Two coffees."

She turned around and watched as Flo walked to the corner of the shop and sat down at a table in front of the back window. A few minutes later she joined Flo, sliding her coffee cup across the table.

"Things are going to change now, you know?" Flo folded her hands.

"What do you mean?"

"Well, for one thing, Marcus's taking over the shop." Flo glanced down at a chip on her index fingernail polish, then scrounged around in her purse.

"You've got to be kidding."

Flo pulled out an emery board from the bottom of her purse and sighed. "Nope. It's not what Juanita wanted. That's for sure. She had a will and named me her executor. Alicia wasn't her actual child, but she left everything to her. The shop's just rented space. Juanita had paid through the month. But she owned the equipment. She owned her car, and her business, but that was it, really. She was saving up for a house. Alicia should own everything that was Juanita's. But now it don't look like she'll get it."

"Why not?"

"The will's missin'. Juanita kept it locked in her file cabinet in her office. The night she was killed the cabinet was broke into and everything was stolen, including the will." Flo paused and rubbed her head as if she was rubbing away an ache. "Juanita was Marcus's bookkeeper for the pawn shop, too."

Emma nodded. "I just found out about that. It's one of the reasons I wanted to talk to you. I was hoping to find someone who could explain what was going on. Juanita was always looking out for everyone else. I can see why she did the accounting for her brother, Gerald. But why did she continue doing the bookkeeping for Marcus? She didn't even like him."

"Uh huh." Florence looked around the coffee shop. "Looks like they got Juanita's books at the same time they got her will. Marcus's pawn shop ain't exactly a straight goods-in-and-goods-out sort of bookkeeping business. You know?" She leaned and looked over her shoulder, then took a sip of her coffee.

"What kind of books are you talking about? Her bookkeeping ledgers? They stole her ledgers?"

"Yeah. I guess that's what you call them. I called them the accountin' books. The books she wrote down all the comings and goings of the accounts in. You know." Flo swallowed hard and picked up her coffee cup again. Emma noticed that she'd begun to perspire along her temples.

"Have you seen these books?"

Flo nodded. "Talking about all of this makes me nervous." She glanced over her shoulder and out of the window.

"Do you think Juanita's death had something to do with the ledgers, or the accounting books?"

"Yeah." She nodded. "'Cause she kept more than one copy. Look, I really can't keep on about all of this. I'm gonna get myself killed, but just so you understand, she had to keep one set for the police, just about the pawn business. And she had to keep one for Marcus. And she kept one for herself, too. She called it her insurance. But she didn't tell no one about her copy but me. And that ain't so good for me."

"She kept three identical copies?"

"Well." Flo paused, clenched and unclenched her hands, then wiped the perspiration from her hairline. "The one she kept for the police was a little different. You know what I mean?"

"And Juanita kept up with all of that?"

"Juanita kept up with everything. She was a list maker. When she didn't understand somethin' or felt like things were just too much, she wrote everything down, made lists. She kept up with how much each business made, and kept a separate set of books for the pawn business, one for the drug business and a separate set of books for all of the payouts for the cops. She even kept a list of the people Marcus and the cops had identified as snitches, or people to watch. She listened, you know?"

"Snitches?"

"Yeah. They thought there might have been a couple of people working with the police. Spying on Marcus and them or something. I think that dead priest might have been one of the people on that list."

"Brother Antoine?"

"Yeah. I think so."

"You have a copy of the lists?"

"Yeah. Juanita kept copies of everything except that will. Well, I guess her lawyer had a copy of that. But she left everything else with me. Been carryin' the stuff around in the trunk of my car. And I don't want it. I sure don't want it in my apartment. I don't want it anywhere. And I don't know what to do with it."

"Is there any way I could look at it or get a copy?"

She nodded. "You can just have it. I got it all together in a box."

"Could I see it or get it from you sometime?"

"You can pick it up right now if you want to."

"Juanita trusted you with a lot. You must have been very close."

"Juanita's my girl. She and I been friends since junior high and we never had secrets. If she needed someone to know everything in case something went wrong, someone she could call if she needed to hide the books, or take them somewhere else, whatever, that was me. There's nothing I wouldn't 'a done for her. And she always had my back. When I had my son, she was there. If I needed money, same thing. When she worked for her brother Gerald, the pawn shop bookkeeping was a regular job, even though she worked nights. She got paid for it. But after he was killed, Marcus took over and everything changed."

"How was Gerald killed?"

"The shop was robbed. Guy shot him."

"Did they ever catch the killer?"

She shook her head. "No, they never did."

"How did things change after Marcus took over?"

"Marcus took over the pawn shop after his dad died and wanted to keep Juanita on as bookkeeper, but he'd been into drugs for a while by then, and she told him she'd help him only if he keep drugs away from the kids, especially Alicia. She said she wouldn't do nothing if he got the kids on drugs or if he had the kids selling drugs."

"I'm not so sure he held true to that promise."

"Juanita didn't trust him, but he knew she was watchin' him. She had enough information on him and his operation to put him in jail until he was a very old man. Same thing with those dirty cops."

"That's what got her killed."

She nodded and wiped a tear from her eye. "You right about that. He had to have found out about her keeping an extra copy of those books."

"How do you think that happened?"

"I think she popped off to the officers when they hassled her for the money they wanted from her, for protection, you know? Marcus was already paying them. And, then on top 'a that he bought stuff from them too. All those guns they stole on their drug raids. Marcus was buying them, then turning around and selling them to the guys he bought drugs from. The cops shouldn't have pushed Juanita for more. I think she got angry and lost her cool and told them she was keeping up with how much they were getting in payoffs, and how much they were selling." Flo shook her head, looked down for a moment, and grabbed a napkin to dab her eyes.

"I can't believe cops were selling stuff they'd stolen back to Marcus. That's crazy."

"This whole thing was crazy. And now, the one decent person involved is dead."

Emma cleared her throat. "I have to tell you something." Emma glanced down at her hands, which were folded in her lap. "I might have done something that contributed to Juanita's death."

Flo frowned, her eyes brimming with tears.

"I encouraged Juanita to go back to the 6th District and make another complaint about the officers' harassment. She was killed right after that." Emma clasped her hands. "I'll regret that for the rest of my life."

Flo was quiet for several seconds, then reached out and touched Emma's hand. "It isn't your fault Juanita was murdered. You just told her to do the right thing. To complain about the fact that nothing was being done about those cops. Who would'a thought that was gonna get her killed?"

Emma squeezed Flo's hand. "We've got to be extra careful with you and watch out for the bad cops. Problem is, we don't know who they all are. We know about St. Amant, the guy who came after Juanita. But, I don't know what he looks like."

"Me neither." She shook her head, brushed the tears that had fallen down her face.

"What about the other ladies in the shop? Are they trustworthy? Do any of them have any connection to Marcus?"

Flo shook her head. "I don't think so."

"Do you know who drew up Juanita's will?"

"Not right off the top of my head, but she told me. I think I wrote it down somewhere."

"See if you can find it. We can ask the attorney to file the duplicate will, and Alicia should be protected. I'd like to get Juanita's books and journals today, so, why don't you follow me to the law school where I work and I'll take them off of your hands."

Flo nodded. "Sounds good to me."

Emma scribbled down the address of the law school and handed it to Flo.

"There's one more thing." Flo glanced down for a second.

"What's that?"

"Juanita never said for sure, but I always thought she kept cash somewhere. And probably a lot. I don't have it and I don't know where it is, but I have a feeling that's one thing Juanita's killer was looking for. And I'm thinkin' that's why Marcus wants to take over the hair salon."

"Didn't she have a bank account?"

Flo nodded. "Sure."

"But..."

"I don't think you gonna find all her savin's in any bank account, if you understand where I'm comin' from."

"Because she didn't make all of her money at the hair salon."

"Right."

"She may have planned for her death, in part, but she didn't realize it would come so soon." She shook her head. "See you at the school in a few minutes."

* * *

Ren had started dinner by the time she got home. Even though he considered himself a one-trick pony, the one meal Ren could prepare was especially delicious. His mother's pot roast with potatoes and carrots, roasted to perfection, was usually reserved for Sundays. The tantalizing aroma teased Emma's olfactory senses as soon as she opened the street level door and started climbing up the stairs to her apartment. She knew Ren must have something to celebrate.

"Well, this is a surprise. What's the occasion, Deputy Taylor?" Emma removed the dish towel from his neck, searched his face, and gave him a kiss. She was happy to see a spark behind his soft brown eyes that matched his broad smile.

"How about celebratin' the fact that I'm no longer Deputy Taylor? I'm now NOPD Officer Taylor, reporting for duty, as of this very day."

"Oh my God, Ren. I can't believe it. This is so exciting!"

"I know! I couldn't be happier."

She wrapped her arms around his neck and gave him a hug. "Let's celebrate then!"

"First, I need to get the roast out."

CHAPTER TWENTY-SIX

"Billy, Bobby! Come set the table and feed the dogs!"

Emma heard the boys scrambling down the steel staircase, the dogs skittering behind, enjoying the cacophony of sounds. She hoped a full stomach would keep the dogs away from the table while they ate, but knew that was futile.

Ren proudly pulled the pot roast and vegetables from the oven, brought them to the table, and they all sat down filled with hope for a future together. The dogs circled the table even though they couldn't have been hungry, their noses searching and sniffing, like quivering periscopes.

Emma looked at the three men sitting at her table, enjoying their meal, their blonde hair glowing in the overhead light. Her boys could hardly be called men, but they were getting there. They'd grown up so much in the four years they'd been in New Orleans and were now almost as tall as she was. If only she could slow down time. She was happy they liked Ren. He fit in with the family as if he'd always belonged. Things were so easy with him. And her life had never been easy. She hoped those days were over.

"Did you go to Cooper's Antiques to work on the desk today?" Emma said as she passed a platter of carrots to Bobby.

"Yeah. It was cool, the wood putty stuff dried. We took off the clamps today and started sanding. Mr. Cooper let us do some of it," Bobby said.

"Were J. C. and Cornelius there?" Emma passed the potatoes to Billy.

Billy nodded. "They did some of the sanding too. It's really starting to look good."

"I appreciate the work you guys are doing. Sounds like a good thing to learn about, too. J.C. and Cornelius's grandfather sounds like a pretty good teacher." Emma smiled.

"Yeah, he is."

"I might want to work on some other stuff." Billy looked around the living room. "Like that old chair in the corner? Cornelius is bringing in his mom's bedside table. Mr. Cooper said we could bring some more stuff in to work on."

"I'm glad you two are so excited about this. I'll find something else for you." Emma laughed as she looked at their solemn faces. "I promise."

An hour and fifteen minutes later, the dishes were done, the boys were upstairs getting ready for bed, and Maddie and Lulu were in their beds dosing, filled with pot roast scraps. Emma pulled Ren to the couch.

He wrapped his arms around her and pulled her on top of him. He drew her close and kissed her until she couldn't breathe.

Emma sat up, gasping. "My goodness, Officer! You do have your ways!"

"I try." He smiled.

Emma pretended to fan herself. "Those boys might not quite be asleep yet." She peered up the spiral staircase. "So, why don't you tell me about your new position for now?"

"I really don't have anything to add. You pretty much know everything there is to know, and probably a couple of things you shouldn't."

Emma smiled. "When do they want you to start?"

"Right away. The chief wants me to come in tomorrow."

"You're kidding."

"I was surprised too, but they needed someone right away."

Emma propped her feet in Ren's lap. "What about all of your stuff, your clothes, furniture, and all of that?"

"I'll take a three-day weekend and go back to get it all pretty soon. They have something they want me to pay close attention to right now."

Emma sighed. "Okay. I'll stop fretting. I know you know what you're doing, and you know you can stay here until you have everything together. What kind of project do they have you working on?" She reached out and grabbed his hand.

"Now that I can't say."

"Well, Mr. Undercover Cop. I've got some information you might just find interesting."

She got up to pour them a glass of wine and told him about Juanita's bookkeeping endeavors and Flo's insights.

"So, Juanita's my hero." Emma took a sip of her wine.

"She was a strong woman. That's for sure."

"Part of the deal was that she'd do the books if Marcus kept the kids out of the drug business. But he had the kids dropping off money in bags. Or that's what Alicia thinks. She thought she observed that this past week. We don't know if it's something new, since Juanita died, or if they've been doing it all along."

"Well, you've been busy. Did Alicia actually see this?"

Emma nodded. "Yeah. Apparently, Alicia saw kids drop off a paper bag at the transformer by the Bishop apartment. Then she saw cops come by, pick up the bag, take out what looked to be a roll of money, and pocket the money."

"Are you sure she was close enough to see what was actually in that bag?"

"I think so. I don't have any reason to question her. We have the measurements somewhere, but I think the distance from where Alicia was and the transformer is about thirty feet."

"I don't know if you could see something like that at thirty feet. If the bag contains money, where did it come from?"

"Marcus. Alicia said Marcus has had meetings at Mama Ruby's every week, and the kids come out with these bags. At first she thought the bags contained drugs, but after seeing the cops pocket the cash, she realized the bags contained money."

"Well, now that Juanita is gone, anything could happen."

"That's what I'm afraid of."

Chapter Twenty-Seven

T he next morning Emma began pulling the ledgers and journals out of the boxes she'd thrown on the floor of her office the evening before. Juanita kept everything on paper. As far as Emma knew, nothing was kept on computer files.

The ledgers were organized by topic and by year. The ledger entitled "Pawn Shop Profits" began in 1980 and listed each item pawned, the loan amount, and each payment made by the customer, the number of times the customer was late with their loan payments, and whether the item was ultimately sold and the amount of the sale. Each item was photographed and reported to the police. Also, from 1980 through 1990, Juanita listed all loans Louisiana Avenue Pawn took out from the local bank. Paperwork for each loan was tucked into envelopes in the back of the ledger, along with all of the corresponding police reports proving the shop's compliance with local laws. Beginning in 1990, two new ledgers, identified as T. Bishop Sales, and NOPD payouts, were added, and the pawn shop ledger stopped showing bank loans. Instead, loans to the shop were made from the T. Bishop Sales account, and cross-referenced in both accounts.

Likewise, Juanita listed each cocaine purchase and source. Emma was surprised to see that crack was made and purchased in their Central City neighborhood in New Orleans. Marcus had a favorite "cooker" he paid in crack rocks. So, Marcus's costs would be the cocaine he purchased from outside the district, usually out of Houston, a little baking soda, and some ice or water. From that he made up to $800 an hour in crack sales for the past four years. T. Bishop Sales also made gun purchases and sales. Although

Marcus kept a few guns, most were sold back to his cocaine source in Houston.

Emma flipped through the NOPD Payouts ledger. Officers' names were listed for payouts and sales of goods, which was cross-referenced with the T. Bishop Sales ledger; among them was Officer Joseph St. Amant, the officer who had attacked Juanita. The most frequent and systematic payouts were those made for "protection pawn shop." The type of sale was identified, and the amount of payment to each officer was noted in the ledger. Emma was impressed with Juanita's meticulous notations.

She pulled out a plain, unmarked journal and opened it to the first page. Dates were at the top of the page. Names and observations were listed below. Juanita wrote that Ninja, a gang member known for his ability to get in and out of places undetected, was what Marcus called his "eyes." He was unobtrusive, unnoticeable, but observant. He reported his findings to Marcus at the shop nearly every night Juanita was there, and when she could, she wrote it all down in her journal.

Emma searched for Brother Reginald Antoine's name, which she discovered on September 13, 1993.

Ninja followed Georgie and Dwayne to drop off point. Brother Antoine seen talking to Officer Boudreaux.

Again, on May 27, 1994:

Ninja watched Brother Antoine talking to Officer Boudreaux after drop-off at Felicity Street. Boudreaux and Antoine go into coffee shop.

June 11, 1994:

Ninja said Brother Antoine and Officer Boudreaux spoke to Georgie and Dwayne at gym.

July 27, 1994

Ninja tracking Brother Antoine.

September 7, 1994

Marcus asked about Alicia's meeting with Brother Antoine on Friday night and about time they was meeting.

Emma closed the journal and ledgers, loaded them into a filing drawer in her office and locked the cabinet.

* * *

Emma watched Josh and Melissa walk through her office door and sit down in the chairs arranged in front of her desk. She asked Josh to close her office door. With the loss of Lauren, the group had become so small she could comfortably whisper in her small office space and still be heard. But she didn't want to take any chances.

"Everything we discuss in our meetings about the Louis Bishop case is privileged, especially evidence. But this week I came across some information which is more sensitive than usual, even potentially dangerous. I debated about whether I should share it with you, but you're third-year law students, close to graduation, and since this course exposes you to the actual practice of law, I decided to let you choose if you wanted to know this. It's no exaggeration to tell you that knowledge of these facts could be life threatening, especially in light of what happened to Juanita Bishop."

The duo nodded solemnly. Josh looked at Melissa and raised his eyebrows.

"If you don't want to know what I'm about to tell you, you can walk out now." Emma paused. "Are you two okay with proceeding?"

Josh and Melissa nodded.

"Okay. After Juanita was killed, I finally spoke to Mama Ruby. She told me Juanita was Marcus's bookkeeper, and that I needed to speak to her receptionist, Flo, which I did. Bottom line, I've got duplicate copies of the ledgers and journals Juanita kept when she was the bookkeeper for her brother's pawn shop, and when she was the bookkeeper for the next four years after Marcus took over. I've got evidence of loans made from his drug business to the shop, and what has been alleged as payouts to police, including gun sales. It looks like Marcus's been laundering drug money through the pawn shop, among other things." Emma watched Josh's and Melissa's jaws slowly drop as their faces registered their surprise.

"And it also looks like Juanita helped him by keeping a clean set of books for the police. She only did it, according to Florence, to get Marcus to promise to leave the kids alone. He swore not to involve them in his drug business if she did his books, and if she made all of the required daily reports

to the police for the pawn shop. She kept everything on the up and up."
Emma glanced down at Juanita's journal and flipped to one page.

"It looks like a pretty simple money laundering scheme. They used drug money as loan money for the pawn business. Any loan payback would be completely clean money. If anyone was late on a loan payment, the pawn shop would simply sell whatever was being pawned. So that was clean money too. It was easy to cover up since the pawn shop is a cash business.

"There is a complication, though. Marcus was good to his word. He didn't involve the kids in his drug business. But the police pressured him for pay-offs or "protection money"—presumably to keep quiet about his money laundering scheme. And Marcus had the kids make all of the drop offs, little brown bags of money, to the cops.

"Some of this is probably relevant to Louis's case. We won't know until we go through everything, so that's the first step. But you need to realize that Juanita's death could be related to the fact that she kept these documents. So, this work could be dangerous. If you're willing to do it, I'd like you to copy everything, each ledger and journal, page for page. I want to split the copies up too. I'll keep a copy here, and figure out somewhere else to keep the duplicates. After we review all documents, and decide whether they're relevant to Louis's case, we'll need to research how to get them into evidence."

"I think we might be able to get the ledgers in. They might be considered a regularly kept business record, and they'd be an exception to the hearsay rule," Josh said.

"That's a good argument. Some of the records were kept for the business, at least. As we review the documents, we'll need to keep in mind how we could use the ledgers and journals in Louis's case. Marcus wouldn't have appreciated Juanita's secret bookkeeping, that's for certain. But besides exposing Marcus's secret world, do they help us? Is it possible they might give us clues about what happened to Brother Antoine and Mr. Maureau the night of September 9th? Can they be used to prove Louis was not the shooter? Or do they help expose the actual shooter? If we decide they're relevant, they'll be subject to a document request by the DA, although he hasn't filed one yet. I want to understand everything there is to know about these ledgers before we reveal anything about them to anyone." Emma scratched down a few notes on a pad.

"It looks like Brother Antoine and Officer Boudreaux could have been involved in the drug operation or something illicit," Melissa said.

"I don't know how you got that. I realize Dwayne said he'd never met Brother Antoine, then Juanita said they had met, but that doesn't mean they were drug dealers." Josh flipped through his notes.

"Well, something's fishy. Maybe we should speak to Dwayne again. I think he knows more than he's saying," Melissa said.

"Maybe. Why don't you see if you can get him to come down here and answer a few more questions. Tell him we'll pay his fare on the streetcar or bus." Emma made a notation in her notepad.

Josh nodded. "I can do that. Whatever happened to Ren, our ballistics expert? He was going to take a look at the Glock they found under Mrs. Bishop's apartment. He said there might be a way to cast some doubt about whether it was the murder weapon."

"Just so you know, Deputy Ren Taylor is now Officer Taylor of the NOPD, but before he accepted the position, he looked at the report and verified what he'd said earlier. The gun they found under the apartment was a Glock. And he still doesn't believe anyone could do forensic testing on it."

"But we also think we have two shooters, based on our expert's testimony. We just don't have the other gun," Melissa said.

"Right, and Louis actually puts two guys dressed in black at the scene, but he didn't see them shoot or see guns in their hands. And don't forget Tamika's testimony that she saw Louis throw a Glock under the apartment."

"So, we have a gun with no real proof that the bullet or the casings found at the scene match up with it, Tamika's testimony that Louis threw a gun under Mrs. Bishop's apartment, our expert's testimony that there were two shooters, and Louis's testimony about the two mystery men." He paused, still reading his notes. "Wonder why Marcus was so curious about Brother Antoine's visit to Juanita's house?"

"That's a good question. Alicia is the only person left for us to ask now.

CHAPTER TWENTY-SEVEN

Can you two follow up with her?"

Josh and Melissa nodded simultaneously.

"I've also glanced at the ledgers, and the journals, but haven't carefully read any of them. Do you have the time to go over all of the accountings?"

Melissa and Josh nodded.

"Every word on these pages is important. The only thing that I ask is that the books not leave my office, except for copying. I'll get keys made for the two of you."

Chapter Twenty-Eight

T hat same afternoon Emma pulled up to the NOPD 6th District parking lot and locked her car. She pulled out a scrap of paper from her purse as she scurried downstairs to the clerk's office. She'd waited long enough for Scott McEnroe. He wasn't in any hurry to find the name of the officer who had assaulted her, and she had a feeling he wasn't going to. It was time she discovered what she could for herself. She also planned to ask the clerk about Officer St. Amant.

"Can I help you?"

"A few days ago I prepared a report about an officer who threatened me and left it with Officer Scott McEnroe. I had the officer's badge number, which is 4962, but I didn't know his name when I completed the report, and I don't know whether the report was ever filed."

"I can check for reports or complaints filed against that number for you."

"Thanks. Also, I need to check on an Officer St. Amant. A report was filed against him for harassment. I need to see his file, too."

"You filed the report against Officer St. Amant?"

"I didn't. But the underlying complaint is related to a case I'm defending." Emma put her bar card on the counter, hoping it would convince the clerk to let her see St. Amant's file.

"Okay. I'll get that file for you, too, then."

"Here's the badge number I was given for Officer St. Amant. I'm not sure it's correct." She handed the clerk a sticky note. "I need information on both officers' length of service with the NOPD, what unit they're assigned to, their current employment status, and the names of their partners."

Glancing down at the note, the clerk trudged to the back of the room, and searched through the filing cabinets for the next ten minutes. She emerged with two files.

"Here. Badge number 3178 is Officer Joseph R. St. Amant. Here's his photograph, and the precinct he's assigned to. He's been with NOPD for twelve years, and right now he's assigned to the Gun Search Task Force.

"Badge number 4962 belonged to Officer Sam Washington. Officer Washington is deceased. Badge numbers are unique here. His badge number hasn't been reassigned."

Emma scribbled down notes as the clerk spoke. "How did Officer Washington die?"

"He was one of the officers who was killed in a shooting a few years back."

"Do you know how that happened?"

"Nah. All those cases run together after a while."

Emma opened the St. Amant file and paused as she turned the page, her hand hanging in mid-air. The photograph of Joseph St. Amant, staring up at her from the file, the man who had threatened Juanita, and who had demanded that Juanita pay a protection fee to him and several of his fellow NOPD officers, was the same officer who had accosted Emma on Carrollton Street. He'd tried to hide his identity with a stolen badge from a dead man, but there was no mistaking it. Now that she knew who he was, she had to find out who was working with him.

"Who is Officer St. Amant's partner, or do you have that information?"

"We don't have that information here. You'd have to speak to his supervisor."

"Who's that?"

"I'd start with Sergeant Radick. He heads up the task force. Like I said, Officer St. Amant is a member. I believe Officer Washington was in the group too."

Emma glanced down at her notes. "What's the Gun Search Task Force?"

"I'm not sure. I think their goal is to get illegal guns off of the streets. But I don't really know what they do. I do know there's around a murder a day in New Orleans. Maybe more by now. But I think you'd do better to speak to Sergeant Radick about Officer St. Amant and the task force too."

"Is he here in this building?"

The clerk nodded. "Third floor."

"First, I need to amend my complaint. I'd like to file a report against Officer St. Amant."

* * *

Fifteen minutes later, Emma scanned the third floor for directions to Sergeant Radick's office, finally spotting an entire glass wall identifying the Gun Search Task Force, complete with a gold embellished logo. She opened the door to the office and approached yet another series of glass panes, designed much like bank teller windows. Emma wondered if the glass was bulletproof. A woman sitting behind one of the windows, her jet-black hair tightly curled close to her head, didn't look up as Emma neared.

Emma leaned down to the small half-moon shaped hole cut into the glass toward the bottom of the window and cleared her throat. The woman looked over her glasses at Emma. Her lips formed a thin red line of disapproval.

"Can I help you?" When she spoke the makeup along her lip line broke up in tiny encrusted, powdery fragments.

"I'd like to speak to Sergeant Radick and was told to look for him here."

"Why do you want to speak to the sergeant?"

"I filed a report against Officer Joseph St. Amant, who's one of the members of his task force. I'm an attorney and thought he should know about these claims."

The woman peered over her glasses at Emma again and stood up.

"Just one minute." She walked toward the back of the room and through a hallway, disappearing for several minutes, then reappeared and nodded at Emma.

"You can go in. He'll see you." She buzzed Emma in.

Emma walked down the back hallway to the sergeant's office and rapped on his door.

"Yeah. Come in." The sergeant sounded and looked like a Marine. His thick gray hair was high and tight, military style, shaved into a bristling brush at the top of his head, the sides close to the scalp. His office was extraordinarily neat and his uniform and shoes spit polished. He nodded toward a stiff, wooden chair in front of his desk. His name, Sgt. Jeffrey Radick, was carved neatly on a wooden placard placed prominently on his wall. Emma sat down.

"How can I help you?"

Emma explained her run-in with Officer St. Amant. "It was frightening and meant to ruin my life. But you could test me every day for the next several years and would never find cocaine in my system, so I'm not sure what he was trying to do, really. I guess what bothers me the most is that I don't know why he did it. Why would he harass me, threaten me like that? I've never even met him before. Plus, he was wearing Badge number 4962, and today I discovered that was the badge of a deceased person. He was obviously trying to hide his identity."

"I don't have any idea what's going on here, Ms. Thornton. I'm very sorry you've gone through such trauma. Believe me, I'll do my best to get to the bottom of it."

"What's the next step? I'll keep up with the status of my report, but can I call you to check-up on things? Something needs to be done about this, and it needs to be done soon." Emma hesitated. Juanita's death weighed heavily on her, and she knew she could be in as much danger, which was something she didn't take lightly. She inhaled deeply to calm her nerves. "If necessary, I have no problem bringing a lawsuit against Officer St. Amant and the police department. Something needs to be done about him. That man is dangerous." Emma clenched her hands together.

Sergeant Radick nodded. "We'll investigate, and if we find what you say to be true, we will proceed with a disciplinary action against Officer St. Amant. Everything happens in its own time."

"Isn't it my word against Officer St. Amant's word?"

"That's how it usually breaks down."

"Then how do you decide who's telling the truth?"

"Sometimes we analyze motivation, and sometimes we just never quite figure it out."

"Can you tell me the name of Officer St. Amant's partner, or the officer he usually works with?"

"Was he with someone the day he allegedly threatened you?"

"No. But he also threatened a friend of mine, and his partner was with him that day, or someone was. So, I'd like to have a name."

"I don't see how any of that's relevant to your case, but I'll see what I can find, Ms. Thornton."

* * *

On the drive home from the police department, Emma passed her street and drove a few blocks farther down to Louisiana Avenue. She parked across from Marcus's pawn shop. It was getting late, but Ren promised to meet the boys at home by 4:00. That morning they'd agreed that Ren would order takeout for dinner since Emma had a few errands to run after work. She knew he wouldn't approve of her Louisiana Avenue stop over.

The last time she'd paid any attention to the pawn shop was when she ran by with the twins. The lights were out that day, and the place looked closed and locked up. Plus, they were only there for a few minutes. Today she wanted to park across the street and watch for a while to see if there was any activity.

The pawn shop was about a block away from Magazine Street. Louisiana was a boulevard with a wide median separating two opposing double lanes. Although populated with charming Victorian homes and quaint bungalows, commercial shops thrived close to the Magazine intersection. One of Emma's favorite Italian restaurants was nearby. The pawn shop, an old clapboard creole cottage, had been a fixture in the area for years, even though Emma had never seen its doors open or noticed patrons entering or exiting.

She pulled into the parking lot of the fried chicken restaurant across from the shop and nudged her car closer to the sidewalk so she could get a better view. She grabbed her camera out of the trunk, hopped back in the car, prepared to wait.

Scrunching down in her seat, Emma took a few photos of the front of the place. It was warm in the car, and since it was the end of the day, Emma found herself fighting off drowsiness as she struggled to maintain her interest in what was happening across the street. It was worse than watching baseball on TV, which was like a sedative to Emma. She didn't know how detectives stayed awake during stakeouts.

A vehicle with a pulsating bass pulled in next to her in the restaurant's parking lot. The car, a black Mercedes G-Class SUV, had darkened windows and shiny chrome rims. The music coming from the vehicle was loud enough for Emma to hear clearly, the lyric "Whose world is this"? Her car's windows rattled with every boom. The driver of the SUV turned off the engine and got out. He was tall, muscular, feline. His long natural hair was tied back in a ponytail and flowed down his back. A pack of cigarettes was rolled up in the sleeve of his t-shirt, exposing intricate tattoos which cascaded down his biceps. A lit cigarette dangled from his lips. He threw it on the ground and stomped it out before entering the restaurant. Emma knew it was possible, both from Alicia's descriptions of him and the proximity of the pawn shop, that this was probably Marcus.

She also guessed Marcus didn't do his own surveillance, so he might not recognize her. She got out of her car and followed him.

A blast of cold air laced with the smell of stale grease hit her in the face when she entered the building. Marcus was in line, his phone crammed up to his ear. She stood behind him.

"Yeah. It's tonight. At the shop. 6:00. That's right. Keep it clean, no screw ups." He hung up and scanned the room, turned around and glanced at Emma, who didn't make eye contact.

He placed his order and stepped to the side to wait for his food. She walked up to the counter and ordered, then watched as Marcus retrieved his steamy paper bag from the pickup area, sauntered outside to his car, and drove across the street to the pawn shop. She grabbed her chicken nuggets and scurried back to her car, keeping an eye on Marcus as he parked in front of the shop. She didn't think there was an alley or a back entrance to any of the houses or shops on Louisiana Avenue. So, deliveries would have to come to the front door.

Twenty minutes later, a black van rolled up and stopped behind Marcus's car. Two men, with dark-colored jackets and baseball hats, got out and started unloading cardboard boxes. Emma pulled out her camera and began snapping photos. She estimated the boxes at thirty-six to forty-eight inches in length. She lost count after she'd tallied twelve. Zooming in on the faces of the men while they moved the boxes into the shop, she knew, even with their hats pulled down over their eyes, one was Officer St. Amant. The men lingered inside for about ten minutes, then drove off.

Emma tucked her camera under her seat and pulled out onto Louisiana Avenue to go home, anxious to see her boys, and to tell Ren about her day. He wasn't going to be very happy with her about some of it.

* * *

Two hours later, after they'd all eaten, and the boys had made their way upstairs, Emma loaded the last dish in the washer and closed the door. She turned to look at Ren, who was putting leftovers in the refrigerator.

"Let's go sit for a minute, okay?" Emma said.

Ren nodded and followed her into the living room.

"I ran by the 6th District today and discovered the officer who accosted me is the same guy who went after Juanita. Joseph St. Amant." She flopped down on the couch, moving some pillows so he could sit next to her.

"Yeah. I already knew that." Ren handed her a glass of wine.

"You've got to be kidding. Why didn't you tell me? I've been looking for his name for days." Emma sat back against the couch and crossed her arms.

"I only learned about it yesterday, after they'd hired me, for one thing. And for another, it's part of my investigation. I'm not supposed to talk about any of that. You know I'm not." He pulled her feet up on the couch and began massaging her ankles.

"Still, Ren. This affects me." She paused. "But you do know how to get on my good side."

212

CHAPTER TWENTY-EIGHT

"Yeah. I do." He smiled. "And I probably would have told you tonight, anyway."

"So, you're on to him?"

"Yes. And you're going to have to be very careful."

Emma sighed. "I went ahead and amended my report to show that he was the cop who assaulted me on Carrollton the other day. And I also went by Marcus's shop today."

"You what?" Ren looked up at Emma, his face becoming noticeably redder. "You can't do these things, Emma! It's way too dangerous to pursue a bad cop who's already threatened you, especially one who may have killed someone. Then, on top of that, you go off and follow a known drug dealer. What's gotten into you?"

"I had to do something. I couldn't just stand by and do nothing while St. Amant was getting away with harassing people, including me. And I was curious about that pawn shop, and what goes on there. I didn't think anyone would notice if I hung out a little while and took a few photos."

Ren shook his head. "That was way too dangerous. You could have been made, and you'd never know until it was too late. Why didn't you talk to me first?"

Emma paused and took a sip of her wine. She peered at Ren over the rim of her glass, judging his level of irritation. She inhaled deeply, reached out, and touched Ren's hand. "St. Amant was there delivering something in cardboard boxes." She told Ren about the various sizes of the boxes she saw being delivered, estimating the size of the boxes with her arms. "Don't you think boxes of that size could accommodate guns or rifles?"

Ren closed his eyes for a moment. "Good God, Emma. Sure. It'd be better to see your photos, to be certain. It also seems St. Amant wants something from you. We don't know what yet. Marcus and St. Amant both mean business, and messing with either of them could cost you your life. You've got to be more careful."

Chapter Twenty-Nine

Emma opened the front door to her apartment, startled to see J.C. and Cornelius sitting on the front steps.

"What are you two doing here this time of morning? You should be in school!" She closed the door behind her and sat on the steps with them. "What's up?" Emma had never seen them this early in the morning. They still looked sleepy. Cornelius had the residue of toothpaste in the corner of his mouth, but otherwise, they were cleanly dressed, and with backpacks crammed full of books and papers.

"We're going to be a little late 'cause we wanted to tell you something." J.C. looked down at his feet as if he were thinking about what he was about to say next. "We were riding our bikes down Magazine Street yesterday evenin', and saw Ninja's car turning down your street. Looked like he was followin' you. So, we turned down the street too. And, yeah, he stopped a couple houses away," J.C. said, nodding down the street. "We hung out as long as we could. And he was there watching your place the whole time."

Emma studied J.C.'s face. He was uncomfortable talking about Ninja. His face was ruddy with excitement or fear, she couldn't tell which, and he didn't want to make eye contact. "So, how do you know Ninja?" Emma said.

"We don't. We like his car." J.C. smiled, then looked down again. "But we've seen him around. Someone said his name one time. I don't remember who it was."

"I'm glad you let me know about him. But why did you think it was so important that you'd be late for school?"

"We were told that Ninja works for Marcus. So, we didn't think it was

214

good that he was hangin' out around your house." J.C. exhaled loudly, as if he was relieved.

Emma nodded. That's what he wanted her to know. Ninja was trouble, maybe even a threat. And she could be in danger.

The boys walked toward their bikes to leave, and she remembered something.

"Oh. What car does Ninja drive?"

"A 1975 Cutlass Supreme with chrome rims in candy apple red. It's sweet."

Emma watched the boys get on their bikes and waved as they headed off down the street. They would be nearly thirty minutes late by the time they got to school. She appreciated their warning. If she was being watched, chances were Flo was too. Deciding to pass on the same courtesy, she hopped in her car and drove toward the lingerie shop where she'd met Flo earlier, hoping to get some information about where she might find her.

A few minutes later, Emma pulled up to an unmetered spot on Magazine Street, parked, and hiked up to the lingerie shop in the mid-morning heat. She was disappointed to discover that it didn't open until 11:00, but noticed that lights were on at A Cut Above. She stepped next door, even more surprised to see that the yellow crime tape had been removed, and that the salon had been reopened. Emma pushed the door open, her eyes immediately watering from acrylic nail fumes.

The new receptionist was a little less glamorous than Flo, but her hair towered nearly twelve inches over her head, and ringlets dangled next to her ears, replacing the need for elaborate earrings. Her one piece of jewelry was a bejeweled nose ring worn in her septum.

"I'm looking for Flo, the former receptionist. Do you know where I might find her?"

The new receptionist shrugged. "She doesn't work here no more."

"Is the shop owned by Marcus Bishop now, or do you know?"

"I don't see how that's any of your business."

"No problem. I'm really just interested in finding Flo. Do you know where she is, or where she lives?"

"I do not. I don't know anything about Flo." She turned her back to Emma.

As Emma turned to leave, a woman from the back came up to her and pressed a piece of paper into her palm.

"That's where she stays. You can probably find her there." She smiled and went back to her station.

* * *

Emma searched for the address. She knew Richmond Avenue was off Carrollton Street, but wasn't certain where. There were so many one-way streets in New Orleans. After she'd been in the city a couple of years, she discovered that circling around in as many directions as possible was often more successful than taking a direct route, so she never worried about directions if she knew the general vicinity. In New Orleans, intuition often worked better than logic, even when looking for an address. She executed a turn down a street and noticed the flashing lights of police cars in front of an older, stucco apartment complex. The structure was classic, but the mold along the front wall looked permanent, a common problem in the city. The street sign at the corner indicated she'd finally found Richmond Avenue. She pulled up behind the police cars and checked the address on the slip of paper against the address of the apartment complex. They matched.

A group of people were gathered outside of the building on the sidewalk and driveway. Emma approached a police officer but was waved off. She turned to a man wearing a rumpled t-shirt and gym shorts. His fuzzy blonde hair was uncombed and his face hadn't seen a razor in days. She assumed he was a resident.

"Do you know what happened here?" Emma said.

"They say someone's been shot." He brought one open hand to his face. His thin, hairless legs were wobbly. Emma could detect the stale odor of beer on his breath. "Her place's been tore up. Lucy found her and called the cops."

"Who's Lucy?"

"That lady right over there." He pointed to a woman in a pink satin quilted robe, her graying hair still wrapped around pink foam curlers. If it weren't for the vivid color of her robe and curlers, she'd have been invisible. Her skin matched the tepid tones of her hair. Her eyes were lost behind the folds of her skin. She was speaking to several other people who had gathered.

"Do you know anything about the person who was shot? The apartment number, anything?" Emma said.

"Not really. They say she was one 'a them beauty shop ladies. You know. She had an upstairs place. That's all I know. That place right up there. I guess it'd be apartment 203."

Emma looked down at the slip of paper in her hand. The address clearly stated "2927 Richmond Avenue, Apartment 203." Her hands started shaking, and she felt dizzy. Not again. She couldn't believe it had happened again.

She thanked the man, and wrote down his name, Ed Stanley. Hoping she was wrong, she moved closer to Lucy to hear what she had to say.

"The place was a mess. Everything turned upside down. They was lookin' for somethin'. Maybe she was one of them drug mules. Maybe she was hiding drugs somewhere in the house or the walls of the place. They tore up everything."

Emma felt a wave of nausea rise from the pit of her stomach and fought the urge to sit down. Instead, she stepped closer. "Did you know the person who was shot?" Her voice wavered despite her efforts.

Lucy nodded. "I used to see her when she brought out her garbage. She liked all that fancy hair and nails and stuff, but she was nice. Always remembered my name."

"Did you know hers?" Emma could barely hear her own voice.

"Of course. Florence. But we called her Flo."

Emma felt her knees buckle, but she pushed on. "Is there anything else about what you saw you could tell me?"

"Who are you? Why should I talk to you?"

"I'm a friend. I'd just like to know what happened."

"There was feathers all over the place. So they must have used a pillow to keep things quiet."

"Do you know when this happened?"

"Nah. I don't know nothin' like that. I hadn't seen her for a while. It was garbage day, and it wasn't like Flo not to take everything out, you know? She was a real clean lady. There's clean people and those that aren't so clean." She looked over at Ed. "Flo was real clean and neat. You should have seen her nails."

"You knocked on her door to remind her about the garbage?"

"Yeah. And the door was open. So, I went in and found her. It was awful. Just awful." Lucy closed her eyes at the memory.

"One more thing."

Lucy turned around and glared at Emma.

"Did anyone else live with Flo?"

"If you were such a good friend of hers, wouldn't you know her son moved out months ago?"

"Could I get your telephone number in case I need to ask you anything else?" Emma handed Lucy a scrap sheet of paper and a pen.

"I guess, but I've already told you everything I know." Lucy scratched down her number and handed it back to Emma.

Emma plodded back to her car, unable to fully process what had happened. She slid into the front seat and put her head on her steering wheel to prevent another wave of nausea. Feeling as if she might throw up, she cranked the engine and turned on the air conditioner. Three people she knew, and to whom she had spoken about Louis's case, had been murdered. Two of them had probably been murdered over the ledgers Juanita prepared. The same journals and ledgers that were sitting in her office filing cabinet. But if the killer had known about the actual location of the ledgers, Flo wouldn't have been killed. Or at least Emma didn't think so.

But how could the killers have even known about Juanita's copy? Did Juanita alert them, as Flo suspected? Or was someone watching them? It was as if there was a camera watching their every move.

Chapter Thirty

Emma pulled up to her apartment. It was noon. She didn't have a class until 1:30 and wanted to grab lunch and relax before facing anyone. She was shaken by Flo's murder and needed to close her eyes for a minute. She trudged up the stairs.

The door to her apartment was ajar. She knew something wasn't right, especially since J.C. and Cornelius had alerted her to being watched. But she felt compelled to touch the door. It moved enough for her to step in.

Everything was quiet. The dogs didn't meet her at the door, and didn't bark, even though they always greeted her when she came home. If something was the slightest bit off, they'd bark, immediately. She hoped they hadn't escaped from an open door or window and had found their way outside to the street.

She tiptoed into the kitchen, then her bedroom, and poked her head into her bathroom. Every room on the main floor was empty. She found no intruder and no signs that one had been there.

She quietly began her ascent up the spiral metal staircase to the third floor, the boys' quarters. She crouched as she climbed, realizing how ridiculously vulnerable she was. Once she reached the top, she was able to see Maddie and Lulu in their beds, gnawing away at two huge ribeye steaks. She heard paper rustling and turned to see an African American man neatly dressed in a black jacket and baseball hat rummaging through a filing cabinet in the corner of the boys' bedroom. He looked familiar to her. Plus, the uniform he was wearing was identical to that worn by the officers at Marcus's shop several nights ago.

She wasn't sure what to do. Sneak back down the stairs and call the police, or confront him? Then Maddie stood up and wagged her tail. Eager for a pat on the head, Lulu bounded over to the top of staircase. Sensing the dog's movement, the man turned as Emma started back down the steps. In two quick strides, he grabbed her arm and crammed a gun under her chin.

By this time, the dogs were barking furiously, the steak forgotten. Maddie's eyes were riveted on the gun under Emma's chin and the man's neck, her eyes switching targets while her body remained poised, still at the top of the stairs, rigid, her muscles twitching, as if she were pointing a prey. Lulu's barking was relentless, becoming louder and shriller.

"Nothing's up here. So, you're gonna show me where you're keeping stuff. Those ledgers and other stuff too. Get back down the stairs." He started to push Emma, while at the same time jamming the gun even harder under her chin, so hard she couldn't swallow. Emma moved backwards, but the heel of her shoe got caught in the metal grating of the stairs and she fell, causing the man to jolt forward. At the same time, Maddie lunged toward him, heaving her body against his back, making him lose his balance and plunge down the metal stairway. His pistol discharged as he plummeted, his head banging against the metal treads. He landed in a tangled heap about halfway down the staircase, his neck twisted backwards at an odd angle.

Momentarily frozen in the same spot where the man had grabbed her, Emma peered down the staircase. The dogs continued down the steps after him, prodding his body with their noses. There was no response. Emma crept down the staircase, stepping over the fallen man's motionless body. She grabbed the dogs' leashes, quickly hooked them on to their collars, and ran out of the apartment and down the street, dogs in tow, reaching the nearest coffee shop within minutes.

She gasped for breath. "Can I use your phone? I've got to call the police."

* * *

By the time she got back to her apartment, the police had arrived, their blue lights flashing. She spotted Ren immediately. He walked over to her and enfolded her in his arms. Maddie and Lulu danced around them happily.

"What happened? Are you okay? We need to get you checked out. The EMTs and an ambulance are on the way." Ren held her so tight she could hardly breathe.

Emma laid her head against Ren's chest for a moment. When she came up for a breath, she looked up and shook her head. "It was awful. But, why are you here? I mean, how did you know?" She grabbed his hand and sat down with him on the curb.

"Your address came across the radio. I tried to call a couple of times, but no one answered. I wanted to make sure you and the boys were okay."

Emma shook her head. "I've been to two crime scenes today, one as a bystander and one as a victim. That's got to be some sort of a record." The dogs snuggled against her and Ren put his arm around her shoulders.

"I'm sorry, babe. What happened?"

"This guy was in my apartment when I got home for lunch. He looked familiar to me, but I don't know why." She stood up and began pacing. "How is he, by the way?"

"He's dead. Looks like he broke his neck, but we'll need the ME to confirm. Even though the gun discharged, the only thing he shot was the wall."

She sat back down on the curb and put her head in her hands. "Oh, man. I can't believe this. This is the second death of the day. I feel like throwing up." She took a deep breath. "I dropped by Flo's house earlier today and I discovered she'd been killed."

"Oh my God. What happened?"

"I thought I should warn her that I'd been followed yesterday evening. I thought it was possible Marcus might do the same thing to her. But when I got to her apartment, the police were there. She'd been shot."

Ren frowned. "I know that has to be upsetting for you. I'm so sorry."

"The police wouldn't talk to me, but the neighbor who found her told me what she saw. Feathers all over the place. That kind of thing. Guess they shot her through a pillow to muffle the sound."

"Sounds professional."

"You mean a hit?"

"Yeah. Looks like it to me. I think we have to consider that someone may be after Juanita's ledgers, and Flo was in the way of that. Which brings me to what happened to you today. Why do you think that guy was in your apartment?"

"He said he was looking for some documents Juanita kept and 'other stuff.' I don't know what the 'other stuff' is. He thought I might have it stashed somewhere in the apartment. I don't know who he was. And I'd like to know if he was a cop like I suspect."

Ren nodded. "Yeah. We're pretty sure the guy upstairs is James, or Jimmy Grant, St. Amant's partner."

"What? And you're just now telling me this?"

"He doesn't have any ID on him. No badge, no wallet. Guess he didn't want to be ID'd in case he was caught. But we think that's who it is. It's easy enough to verify."

"Why didn't you tell me right away?"

"Well, I am, really."

"Isn't that a little patronizing? Weren't you reluctant to tell me because I suspect St. Amant and his partner are connected to Marcus and to Louis's case?"

"You're upset, and you have every reason to be." He reached out and held Emma's hand. "Let's not think about this right now, anyway. You can tell me all about it later. The important thing now is that you're okay." He scooted the dogs over and pulled her close. Emma felt her eyes begin to fill with tears and looked down at her feet. She didn't want to lose control. Not now.

The Medical Examiner drove up in his SUV, and an ambulance pulled in next to him. An EMT slid out of the cab of the ambulance and Ren waved him over while the ME walked up the steps to Emma's apartment.

"This lady needs to be checked out. She's been through a rough time. Just make sure she's okay."

The EMT nodded and guided Emma over to his vehicle while Ren held Maddie and Lulu's leashes.

* * *

222

Emma waited on the stoop for Billy and Bobby to come home. The front door to the apartment was draped in yellow crime scene tape for the second time that month. She wanted to meet the boys so she could tell them what had happened, but she dreaded it. She hated herself for what she'd imposed on her family again. She'd put everyone in danger. But Flo had paid the biggest price.

She heard the bus rattling down the street, then saw the twins at the corner of Prytania climbing down from the bus steps, laughing and pushing each other as they started their walk home, their backpacks swaying as they ran. They waved when they saw her sitting on the steps, but sobered as they approached their building.

Billy pointed to the yellow tape draped across the front door.

"What happened this time?"

Emma sighed. "A man was looking for some documents and thought we might have them. We didn't. I walked in on him when he was looking, and Maddie didn't like the way he was treating me. So, Maddie pushed him down the stairs. He fell pretty hard."

"Is he okay?" Bobby's eyes looked like large circles.

"Well, the man fell backwards, in an awkward way, and when he landed, he broke his neck. So—that was it."

Billy and Bobby exchanged glances. "When he broke his neck, did he die?" Billy asked.

"Yes, he did, sweetie."

Just then a pair of NOPD officers opened the outside door of the apartment building and stepped around Emma to make their way down the steps.

"You can go on up now. We got everything we need." One of the officers grabbed the tape over the door and ripped it off. "We're releasing the scene." They nodded to Emma as they made their way back to their vehicle.

"What do you think? Do you want to go up, and have a family dinner in our place tonight, or do you want to go out to dinner somewhere else?"

As Emma asked the question, the officers left, and Ren pulled up, parked in one of Emma's spaces, popped his trunk, and grabbed a couple of grocery bags. The twins looked at each other and stood up.

"Let's eat here tonight."

Ren handed the twins a bag each, and they all walked into the apartment. Without even asking, Billy and Bobby took the bags into the kitchen and began putting away groceries. Ren started preparing dirty rice for dinner, peering at the recipe Emma had given him and the rice box for cooking instructions. Soon the place was filled with pungent aromas and the sounds of skittering dog feet.

Emma closed the door to her bedroom, filled her tub, then eased into the hot water for a long soak. She was more tired than she'd realized. The day had taken a toll.

She was shaken by the events of the day. Nothing like having a man invade your home and then die there. The whole thing made her shudder. But she also knew that if the cops or Marcus, for that matter, wanted her dead, she'd be dead. They didn't shy away from murder. Officer Grant's interest in other "stuff" intrigued her. They were looking for something besides the ledgers. What was it and was that why they didn't kill her? Would they come back to search again? How could she develop a plan for her family to keep them safe?

Nearly an hour later, she emerged, slightly pink, but far more relaxed, and ready for Ren's attempt at baked chicken and rice. He'd purchased the chicken, already baked, at a local grocery store and had made the rice as per her mom's recipe. He'd forgotten about vegetables, but that was okay. The twins didn't like them, anyway. She smiled. She was surprised at how happy she was to have him in her kitchen. Especially tonight. Nothing like trauma to strip away petty misgivings and expose the core of what really mattered. The boys and Ren, and now, even Maddie and Lulu, were Emma's core.

Emma asked the twins and Ren to sit with her in the living room after dinner.

"Guys, we need a safety plan. Things have gotten crazier than I ever thought possible. I get home at 4:00 because I don't want you two to be home by yourself any longer, for safety reasons. That will last through the foreseeable future. And we got dogs for safety reasons, too. But now, there are people breaking into the house when we're not at home. We can't protect ourselves from everything, but I'm going to get an alarm system installed for the apartment, as well as a camera system. It'll be pricy, but it will be worth it. Ren, do you have any other ideas?"

"That's probably all you can do. The alarm system and cameras are good ideas."

After the kitchen was cleaned, the boys climbed up the staircase to their bedroom. Emma and Ren sat on the balcony for a while, enjoying the remnants of the slight breeze from the river. She loved to listen to the traffic as it whooshed beneath them, mimicking the sound of the waves against the shore. It was soothing, especially if she closed her eyes. The rumble of the occasional streetcar nearly lulled her to sleep.

"Thanks for dinner."

"Glad you enjoyed it. Hope you're feeling better."

Emma smiled. "I am. Baths always help." She folded her hands in her lap and turned toward Ren. "Would it surprise you to learn that I've decided to sue the police department?"

"You what?"

"Yep. I have a case. St. Amant accosted me, but he's never been arrested. I asked Scott McEnroe for St. Amant's name, and he never gave it to me. Then I asked Sergeant Radick for the name of St. Amant's partner. He never gave that to me. St. Amant harassed me, threatened to plant cocaine on me, shoved me around, and might even be planning to do worse. And he's still out there. Grant, St. Amant's partner, tried to kill me, and I don't trust anyone to investigate that. I've been in danger, and no one, including your friend, Scott McEnroe, has done anything about it. I have physical and emotional damages. So—I'm suing."

"What are you really doing, Emma? This doesn't sound like you."

"I need to get their attention and I need information. I think a civil lawsuit may be the only way to get it. Plus, it allows me to go through the discovery process."

"What do you need?"

"Any information on St. Amant's and Grant's backgrounds. I think that might help me figure out what's going on here."

"What makes you think they're going to be any more willing to cooperate in a civil lawsuit?"

"Civil rules of discovery are broader and the compliance requirements are far more stringent. The courts will force them to answer my questions, eventually."

"Well, I can tell you a few things."

"Like what?"

"That St. Amant and Grant were in the Marines together, for one thing. Both were sharp shooters, a level above a marksman. I have their records."

"Sharp shooter. That's interesting. You have their military records?"

He nodded.

"I was going to file a subpoena or a Freedom of Information Act request to get their records, but that could take a while. I could start the process, unless you might like to share your copy." Emma raised her eyebrows and looked at Ren from the side of her eye.

Ren sighed and smiled. "I could make a copy for my personal use and bring it home. That's as far as I can go, though." Then he scooted his chair next to hers and wrapped his arms around her.

Chapter Thirty-One

G ood to his word, the next morning, Ren dropped off a copy of St. Amant and Grant's military records. When she arrived at the campus and pulled into the school parking lot, she turned off her car and sat for a few minutes, realizing that she couldn't allow her students to participate in Louis's case any longer. Any activity, the review of documents in her office, even behind a closed door, or the interview of a witness, was far too dangerous. She'd have to do all of the remaining work up on the case herself. She grabbed the records and walked to her office.

As she was sorting her mail, she heard a rapping sound. Josh stuck his head through her open door.

"Got a second?" Josh said.

"Come on in. I was just thinking about you and Melissa." She gestured for Josh to take a seat. "The last twenty-four hours have been awful. Flo, Juanita's receptionist, was killed, and Jimmy Grant, who was St. Amant's partner, broke into my apartment. He died when he tripped and fell down my staircase. The fall broke his neck."

"Oh, my God. I can't believe two people are dead. Why was Grant at your place?"

"Looks like he was there searching for Juanita's ledgers. And he threatened me before he fell. It was scary. So, I've decided it's too dangerous for you and Melissa to continue to work on Louis's case."

"They had something on the news about a guy breaking in an apartment and breaking his neck." He shook his head. "But I didn't know it happened at your place."

227

"You have to admit that's pretty newsworthy."

"I also didn't know the dead guy was a cop. And I don't remember hearing anything about Flo's murder. This is all so crazy."

"It is. I hope you understand why I don't want you and Melissa working on the case any longer." Emma folded her hands on her desk. "But that's not why you wanted to see me. What's up?"

Josh nodded. "I've been going over Juanita's books. She had a talent for detail. I've got to believe everything we need to know is there, either in her journal or the ledgers, but we have to figure out how to decipher it."

"Are you saying she put some things in code?"

"I'm not sure, but I think so." He raised his eyebrows as he spoke. "There are several references to Big Huey and Little Huey. These two give directions to everyone. And everybody, even Marcus, pays attention to them. Not sure what that's all about, but it's got to mean something."

"What kind of directions?"

"Right around the time of the shooting, there was a note that Big Huey was sending two men."

"That was it? Sending two men? Where was he sending them? Did she say?"

"It wasn't clear. Maybe it meant something to Juanita. Or maybe she didn't know, and she was just writing down what she heard. Here, let me show you." Josh walked over to the filing cabinet and grabbed the ledger from 1994. He opened it to September 8. "This says something about Big Huey. See?" He pointed to a line. "It's the day before the shooting. *Big Huey sending two men. Redemption.* Then it says, *Alicia meeting Brother Antoine.*"

"You can fill in the blanks, I guess. Someone's sending a couple of guys to the housing complex. It's not clear why, and they think it's important that Alicia is meeting Brother Antoine," Emma said.

"Big and Little Huey leave a few other instructions here and there. There's someone called Goldilocks too."

"Goldilocks?"

"Yep. Here." Josh flipped to September 15 and pointed. "It says: *Watch out for Goldilocks.*"

"That doesn't make sense to me, but mark it in case it shows up again and we can see if it makes more sense. Do you know if Melissa called Dwayne and set up a time for him to come in? I need to speak to him."

"I think she did. I'll tell her to come by and let you know what's up."

* * *

After her 1:30 class, Emma spent the next thirty minutes reviewing the military records of Officers St. Amant and Grant. There wasn't that much to them. Just a few brief type-filled governmental forms. The D-II 14. Both men had served time in the Persian Gulf Wars, Desert Shield and Desert Storm. They were in the Marine Corps Reserves and had been stationed out of New Orleans. Trained at Parris Island, they'd also been in Infantry together, and had each had passed the Marine Marksman Qualification Courses for Rifle, Pistol, and Combat. They'd completed advanced level training and were experts in long gun and pistol.

Their unit was activated in November of 1990, shipped off to the Persian Gulf, and was immediately thrown into Operation Imminent Thunder, where St. Amant and Grant both received the National Defense Service Medal. Honorably discharged in 1991, both had achieved the rank of E-7, Master Gunnery Sergeant, and each had plans to return to their previous employment with the New Orleans Police Department.

The officer disbursing their "mustering out" pay was a Sergeant Jeffrey Radick. The name was a surprise to Emma. Could it be a coincidence? Could their supervising sergeant on the police force and one of their sergeants during the Gulf War be the same person? This was strange. Maybe too strange. She knew it had to have some significance. Emma scanned the form down to the bottom of the page to check out who'd signed off on everything. The commanding officer signing the discharge papers was a Lt. Colonel William Cox.

She made a note in her calendar to run by the police station the next day and grabbed an envelope at the top of one of the piles on her desk. It was from Dr. Mitchell. It had to be Louis's test results. She tore it open and unfolded the report.

Louis had cooperated during the four-hour test. Emma was relieved to read that he was polite and responsive. He tested five years behind his grade level, which enabled his remedial placement, but more importantly, his intratest scatter indicated that Louis likely had a learning disability, and an attention deficit disorder. This was helpful. She picked up the phone and placed a call to Dr. Mitchell's office.

"Dr. Mitchell, thanks for sending me the results of Louis's tests. Looks like he has a learning disability after all."

"He clearly has some learning challenges, but he's a bright young man. He can learn, but has a little hyperactivity. If he has help focusing, he should have no problems succeeding. His main issue is a lack of stability in his life. He really doesn't have a home life, and at times, what he's had has been volatile. He's just a kid. He needs to know someone cares. Right now no one but his grandmother seems to. But I am impressed with that school counselor, Mr. Branson. He was right there with him during the test. I know his presence calmed him down; gave him confidence."

"He seems to care about Louis and the other kids."

"There's something else. The test scores show a twenty-point difference between his verbal and performance abilities on the Weschler. That can indicate some emotional disturbance, or an imbalance which could come from something like conflicts at home. The twenty-point differential could also come from the fact that he just has more aptitude with perceptional organization than with verbal skills. We really don't need to make too much of it. Also, I believe he did as well as he did because of Mr. Branson. Louis relaxed considerably after Mr. Branson entered the room."

"I'm glad to hear he's such a good influence. Did you get into the night of the shooting at all?"

"You asked me to test Louis for the guilt phase of the trial, to see if he knew the difference between right and wrong, and for the sentencing phase, to use in the mitigation of the death penalty. So, I had to ask a few questions relevant to the shooting, but not about the actual shooting, if that makes sense."

CHAPTER THIRTY-ONE

"Not really."

"I just asked him if a police officer were standing next to him and someone was also there who had made him very angry, would he carry through with his impulse and shoot the person. I also asked him if he would shoot someone if he'd been instructed to by an older person. Would he pick up a gun and shoot this person?"

"What was Louis's answer?"

"No. He said he would never shoot anyone, and would never shoot anyone in front of a police officer. That's the definition of sanity in the criminal context. Louis definitely knows the difference between right and wrong. His few learning disabilities may help you in the sentencing phase, but it won't help him with the guilt phase at all. But the truth of the matter is that any sixteen-year-old can be manipulated or influenced by an older friend or family member, like Marcus. Especially one offering money. Their brains aren't fully formed at sixteen, and they just don't have the ability to make the best judgments. It's called executive function, and it's not fully formed in a sixteen-year-old. So, that's what you're looking at here. It's not an inability to know the difference between right and wrong. Louis didn't have the ability to make good judgment calls. He was led by Marcus. Manipulated. That's why Marcus uses teenagers. They don't ask a lot of questions. Marcus buys things for them. Pays them a wage. He makes it tough for them to say 'no.' And I have a feeling Marcus isn't all bad either. That could be part of the problem."

"Would you be willing to testify to that?"

"I can't testify about Marcus because I didn't test him, or even speak to him, but I can give you all my findings about Louis. I've been doing my own research on these issues for years. It's a developing area in the neuroscience community, and I think it's going to take some time to be fully established. There are no peer reviewed articles in support of my position. But there will be, eventually."

"I'm not sure I understand what all of that means."

"All I'm saying is that I believe juvenile decision making can be compromised by a number of factors including emotion, peers, or other affective contexts. Here, Louis was manipulated by Marcus and that should make him less culpable. Right now science doesn't entirely back me up on that, but I believe it's heading that way. We're just not there yet, as a community."

"But it's your opinion he was influenced and manipulated by Marcus?"

"It is."

Emma hung up the telephone. She was relieved by some of what Dr. Mitchell reported, but wasn't sure how a jury would react to her testimony. So much depended on the individual jury members - whether they had children themselves, and understood how influenced kids were by others, or whether they were even capable of understanding how a young person could be manipulated with the enticements of money and a full stomach. She gathered a few documents and locked her office door. She needed to talk to the Dean. An updating of the Bishop case was long overdue.

Chapter Thirty-Two

"You have a visitor. A Dwayne Bishop," the receptionist said.

Emma walked down the corridor to show him the way to her office. She found him in the first-floor administrative offices, standing in a corner, thumbing through magazines in a rack attached to the wall. Dressed neatly in sparkling white tennis shoes, black jeans and an over-sized hoodie with a New Orleans Saints logo across the front, he seemed far removed from Marcus and his criminal world.

He followed Emma to her office and sat down across from her desk. Emma was still impressed with Dwayne's ease and confidence. Especially in such unusual circumstances. How many seventeen-year-old kids walk into a law school to discuss drug deals and murder?

"Thanks for coming in today. So much has been going on I'm a little surprised you're here, but it's good to see you." Emma flipped back her notebook and picked up a pen. "The last time we spoke you didn't have much to say."

Dwayne nodded.

"I hope you feel a little more comfortable talking today. But it's also important that you feel safe and do everything you can to stay safe."

Dwayne placed his foot on his knee, which began shaking, then laid his hands on top, as if to hold his jiggling foot still. He cocked his head. "Don't pay to talk."

"Keeping your mouth shut keeps you out of harm?"

He nodded.

"Is there anything you'd like to say before we start?"

Dwayne shook his head. "Nah."

"Are you here because you'd like to help Louis?"

He shrugged.

"Did you decide to come here today because there are police officers out there hurting people? Even people in your family?"

Dwayne nodded.

"Is this what you spoke to Brother Antoine about?"

Dwayne met Emma's gaze, but didn't speak.

"We've learned, through speaking to others, that on a couple of occasions, you were seen speaking to Brother Antoine. But when you spoke to us, you said you didn't know him." She paused.

Dwayne studied his hands, then looked up. "Yeah. I talked with him a couple a times. He wanted to know some stuff. You know. Stuff about some drop-offs. He'd been watchin' us."

"Drop-offs? What do you mean by drop-offs?"

Dwayne shifted his position in the chair, and leaned over, his shoulders scrunched up close to his ears, his elbows on his knees, his hands free to express what he was saying. "We don't have nothin' to do with drugs, if that's what you're thinkin'. We don't touch them, sell them, nothin'."

"Who are you talking about when you say we?"

"Me, and Georgie and Louis, mostly."

"What about Louis? His mom said she thought Louis was using."

"She's using, not Louis. He ain't on crack or nothin'. He's just a joker. A goof. He likes to have fun."

"So, what were you doing? What were you dropping off?"

"We were dropping off bags at places for people to pick up, sometimes at that electrical box out by Mama Ruby's, sometimes at a park down by Camp Street, sometimes at a little bench off of Felicity, sometimes as far as Louisiana Avenue. We weren't supposed to stay to see who was picking up, but sometimes we hung out around the corner and watched. We know them cops that picked up the bags."

"What do you mean you knew them?"

"We seen them around."

"Do you know their names?"

He shook his head. "Nah."

"Do you know what was inside the bags you dropped off?"

"Pretty sure it was money. Felt like money."

Emma jotted down a few notes on her pad. "You never looked in the bags?"

"Well, maybe a couple of times."

"And what did you see?"

He nodded. "Money. A lot."

"Did you do anything else for Marcus?"

"He wants us to be his eyes and his ears. Listen for things."

"What kind of things?"

"Like who might be stashing guns. Look, we're not supposed to know stuff, but we do. We know those cops make money off of Marcus and other people. They say for protection. But they're just pigs. They just want money and if they don't get it they do some hurtin'."

She made another notation in her notebook. "Have you ever seen them threaten anyone?"

"I heard they pushed my Aunt Juanita around. And I saw them shoving that lady who used to own the flower store one time. But she closed her shop." He paused and leaned over. "You need to talk to Georgie and Louis. They did some other stuff."

"Like what?"

"Well, Marcus used Georgie as a lookout, you know. He'd take Georgie with him on his drug runs, 'cause he wanted him to see if they had any guns stashed around, that kinda thing. So, Marcus would send his guys in to work on the deal, and he'd have Georgie there to scope out everything. He was just there as a pair of eyes. Most times people have guns right out in the open, just stacked up in their houses. The raids by those cops would happen right after one of their visits, but you'd never hear it on the news or anything. They did that to Maureau's old lady after he was offed. Broke in their place and took everything."

"By raids, you mean the cops bust the drug dealer and take guns from the drug bust?"

"They take everythin'. Anything that's worth somethin'."

"Then they'd turn them into the police station?"

Dwayne sat back in his chair and rolled his eyes. "You kiddin'? They sell what they take. They don't turn in nothin'"

"Where do they sell this stuff?"

"To Marcus, for sure. I don't know if they sell to anyone else or not. But I hear he buys it, then he sells the guns back to his coke supplier out in Houston."

"How do you know this?" Emma pulled back a sheet of her notepad paper and prepared to write.

He shrugged. "Word gets around."

"Why didn't the cops go to Marcus's pawn shop for their payment? Why did you have to leave bags all over town?"

"I wouldn't know that. Maybe Marcus didn't want cops hanging out at the shop all the time. I don't think they were there too much."

"One more question. Do you know a guy named Ninja?"

"That guy who works for Marcus? I don't know him, but he's always around, always checking up on things." Dwayne flicked a piece of lint from his socks.

"Were you worried he may have followed you here? He might know you spoke to me today."

He shrugged. "It's not a big deal. He don't know what I know. And I don't really know that much."

* * *

Emma heard Louis's tennis shoes shuffling toward the small, overly lit room where she was sitting in Central Lockup. Prison interviews, particularly when conducted solo, could be challenging. The overhead lights were penetrating, and often made the prisoner feel intimidated, even when he was in the company of his own attorney. Conversations held during confinement didn't come easy.

Louis's orange jump suit flashed between the bars on the interview room door as he shambled down the hall. The metal door squeaked as the guard pushed it open for Louis. She indicated he should sit across from her.

"Thanks for trying so hard with Dr. Mitchell on your tests, Louis. Your results will help us explain to the court why you don't deserve the death penalty. But let's hope your case doesn't even get to the penalty phase."

Louis nodded.

Emma pulled a pencil and a small notebook from her purse. "Do you have any questions about your trial or the testing?"

Louis nodded. "Am I gonna die?"

Emma took a deep breath. She felt dizzy, suddenly overwhelmed by the magnitude of the job. She'd also noticed that Louis's eyes had begun to well with tears. She needed to answer carefully.

"If the jury comes back with a unanimous or twelve-person verdict, where everyone in the jury agrees that you're guilty, you could be given the death penalty. But each juror has to approve the verdict. And we're going to do our very best to show that you're not guilty, and that you shouldn't be in here. You know that, and I know that. We'll do our best to convince the jury that you should never have been arrested. And, like I said, even if you're convicted, the test you took with Dr. Mitchell should help. We should be able to use those results to reduce your penalty. It's called mitigation."

Louis nodded, but his eyes were clouded, unfocused.

"Do you understand, Louis? What did I just say?"

"Twelve people gotta say I did it, or I'm not guilty."

"Well, the judge would call a mistrial. So the DA could try the case again. It would be better to win the case and get a verdict of not guilty. The problem is that you and Marcus know more about that night than anyone, and Marcus isn't talking. Marcus wasn't the one arrested, and he certainly doesn't have to worry about the death penalty. You've given us some information that was pretty helpful. Do you have anything else you'd like to add about that night? Is there anything you're not telling us? I need to know everything you know. We've got to fight hard to get you out of here."

Louis shook his head.

"Look. This is where we stand. We have a doctor, a pathologist who will say that there were two shooters that night. But then there's Tamika's testimony that she saw you throwing a gun, a Glock, under your grandmother's apartment. She also says, and this isn't as clear, that she thinks you shot Sam Maureau. What she said was that you aimed your gun that way. But our pathologist will say that the bullets were shot from a distance. Not close up, and you were standing close to Mr. Maureau. But, also, a bullet which came from a Glock, has been recovered from one of the victims. Are you following me?"

Louis nodded.

"But Glocks have an unusual problem. You can't tell one bullet or casing from another when they're discharged. In other words, they know the bullet came from a Glock, but no one can prove if the bullet recovered from Brother Antoine was fired from the Glock they found under your grandmother's apartment." Emma paused to see if Louis was paying attention. He raised his eyebrows, wrinkling his forehead. If Emma didn't know better, she'd think he was in pain.

"Do you have a question?"

"You mean they pulled a bullet out of Brother Antoine, but they can't say it came from that gun from under Mama Ruby's place?"

"That's right. We don't think it can be proved."

"Well then, why am I locked up?"

"Because Tamika said she saw you throw the gun under the apartment. The gun found there was a Glock, and could have been used to kill one of the men. Maybe both. And because others say that you stopped next to the electric box in the middle of the common area with something in your hand. You saw two guys dressed in black at the transformer, but even you admit you didn't see anyone shooting either Brother Antoine or Mr. Maureau." Emma glanced at Louis, who was staring at his feet. "Did you see anything else that might help prove who shot Brother Antoine or Mr. Maureau?"

Louis took a deep breath and exhaled slowly. His hands were shaking. He cracked his knuckles and shook his head. "No."

"The case against you isn't that strong, and we think we can raise reasonable doubt about your guilt, but others could also testify against you. I know you'd like to protect Marcus, but you can't afford that right now. You have to save yourself. You've been indicted for two counts of murder. Marcus hasn't been charged with anything. And your trial is coming up soon." She paused and looked at Louis, who had lowered his head. "You didn't do this, did you? You didn't shoot either Mr. Maureau or Brother Antoine."

He shook his head.

"I never thought you did. We've got to get these charges dropped. What happened to Marcus after you heard the shots? What aren't you telling me?"

He shrugged and shook his head. "I don't know. Marcus told me to start runnin' at that box as soon as I heard the shots. So that's what I did." Beads of sweat gathered around his forehead and began running down the side of his face. "It was hard to see. I thought I saw somethin' movin' and I ran at it. The closer I got, the better I could make things out. Then I could see two guys."

"What happened to Marcus?"

"I don't know. I passed the bag to those guys and kept runnin'."

"Are you sure? Marcus was right there. Where did he go, Louis?"

Louis turned away from Emma.

"This is your life you're messing with. Did you see anything else that night you can tell me about?"

He slowly nodded. "Maybe."

"What do you mean, maybe?"

"I started runnin'. When I got to Felicity, I could see a car down by the coffee shop, across the street, right before you get to Magazine. And there was someone in it. I could see the street light shining on the guys inside."

"What did the car look like?"

"It was a plain white car. But the guys inside were cops."

"So, you think it was an unmarked cop car? You're sure about that?"

"I'm sure. They were just watchin'. They watched me run down the sidewalk. I ran all the way down the road to the river. They didn't stop me. They didn't do nothin'."

* * *

The aroma of Ren's spicy white bean chili wafted down the stairwell. He was becoming quite the chef, and Emma had no complaints about that. She opened the door to the apartment, threw herself on the couch, and propped up her feet. She yelled up at the boys.

"I'm home, guys! Are you working on your homework? I'll be there in a minute."

"Okay! Yeah, I've got to make a map," Bobby shouted down the staircase.

"And I've got math and science," Billy said, outdoing his brother's volume.

Maddie and Lulu bounded over and shoved their noses in Emma's face, eager for a pat on the head. Ren walked in the room, scooted the dogs over and sat down next to her.

"Hard day?"

"Long one. But I got some good information. Some I might even be able to share. Did you realize Sergeant Radick was with both St. Amant and Grant during the Gulf War, operation Desert Storm?"

"Yeah, Radick's an old military guy. Little Huey."

"What?" Emma sat up and removed her shoes.

"He and Superintendent Cox both served in 'Nam together and were in the Battle of Hue. They are always talking about that battle. Guess it was one of the longest and worst in the war. Cox was a lieutenant then, and that's when Radick made sergeant. They were both kids. They started calling them Big and Little Huey, sort of an American version of the name of the battle."

"How do you know this stuff? It's weird that they're still together." Emma sat back against a multitude of couch pillows.

"I get to look at personnel files, remember?" Ren reached over and filled up Emma's wine glass. "Cox's an interesting guy. After 'Nam he went to law school and applied for some federal positions. Either CIA or Secret Service, I can't remember. He served for a while, but he was always in the Marine Reserves. Got called up for the Gulf War in 1990. Cox was the commanding officer for both Grant and St. Amant during Desert Storm, too, but Radick was an administrative officer. HR. He gave out the checks. A year later, they were all discharged, and all ended up with the NOPD. Grant, St. Amant and Radick had been with the force for years, but Cox is new. When the NOPD superintendent position came up, he applied and got it."

Emma propped up her pillows and grabbed her wineglass from the coffee table. "What did Radick do in Vietnam? Did he see combat there?"

"I don't really know." He shrugged. "I guess I just assumed he had."

"So, I'm guessing that the Gun Search Task Force group is the subject of the internal investigation." Emma looked at Ren from the corner of her eye. "Can you tell me if you've targeted either Radick or Cox?"

"You know I can't talk to you about any of that." Ren stood up to check on dinner.

"Well, I think I need to talk to you about something."

Ren sat back down on the couch. "Yeah?"

"Yeah. Or maybe I should just show you some documents at my office. Those ledgers I've been talking about? That might be better. Why don't you come by my office tomorrow afternoon? The boys have a late rehearsal again." Emma said as she stood up to check on the boys' homework.

Ren stood, then pulled her close. "I can be there around 6:00, but I think I need a kiss before I check on dinner."

Chapter Thirty-Three

Emma, home for a late lunch, pulled out from her parking space in front of her apartment, drove down the end of her street to Magazine and took a left. She scanned the area, checking for any sign of a car that may be following her as she drove toward Felicity Street. She didn't have any classes scheduled for the remainder of the day and knew that Ren would be home to check on the boys by 4:00. She wouldn't be long, but she needed a better understanding of what Louis did on the night of the shootings, and where he ran. If cops were watching him as he said, she needed to know just how far away they were. She was lost in thought as she drove.

She parked next to the coffee shop on Felicity, threw her purse in the trunk, and locked up. She crossed the street so she'd be on the same side as Louis had been that night. Staying on the sidewalk along Felicity, she walked to the midpoint between the Bishop building on the left, and the building where Tamika lived on the right. Juanita's building was across from Tamika's, and another building was in front of Mama Ruby's, forming a square. The transformer was in the center. Emma was standing approximately three hundred feet from the transformer, and she was across the street from where the cops would have been watching that night. There were enough overhead lights to see Louis easily. They would have been able to hear shots, and they may have seen some activity as well, even in the dark.

She continued to walk down Felicity. It was a long street, a little over half a mile from the where it crossed Magazine Street to the River. The late afternoon sun pounded on her head, and the heat which rose from the asphalt made her fight for every breath. Relieved she wasn't burdened by her purse, she was soon cursing her pointed-toe shoes.

She made the curve around Tchoupitoulas Street and crossed over to the wharves along the river, walking up to the edge of the dock. The wind blew wildly. She looked out over the river and its swirling currents. Gulls squawked overhead and brown pelicans soared, spreading their wings before landing on a nearby pier. She thought about sitting down for a minute but even though this section of wharf was isolated from the shipping channels, it was an industrial space, built for commerce. It smelled of diesel fuel and petroleum, and didn't welcome visitors. She looked up the river and could see warehouses, buildings, and ships. There were commercial docks at First Street, and Louisiana, and even farther down on Napoleon. But the wharf at Felicity was either abandoned, or wasn't regularly occupied.

Except for flocks of birds. Since it was September, hundreds of species were heading south for the winter along the Mississippi River flyway to Mexico and South America. Emma looked up and saw a flock of Swallow-tailed Kites headed to parts unknown. As a child, she'd studied birds with her grandmother, who kept a worn, green leather field guide on her coffee table. They'd consult the book religiously every time an unfamiliar species popped up in the back yard. Emma had learned to discern flight patterns and wing shapes and could recognize most species.

Emma stood on the wharf and shielded her eyes against the sun as she watched the sky darken with passing flocks. The air was filled with the sound of birds calling and ripples breaking against the pier.

She spun around when she heard a scraping sound.

"Well, if it isn't Professor Goldilocks." Officer St. Amant was dressed in civilian clothes, a black jacket and a black baseball hat. Emma could see his blue eyes beneath the brim of the hat. He pulled a gun out from the back of his pants and started to walk toward her. "I need those ledgers, Goldie. And that gun. And you're going to take me to where you're hiding 'em."

Emma's mind was in a whirl. So, she was Goldilocks. And what gun? They were also after a gun? But she'd always known one was missing.

She scanned the wharf. Except for a rusted oil drum, she had nothing to hide behind, and nothing to run toward. St. Amant was a brute. She knew what he'd done to Juanita, and she didn't want to wait around to see what was in store for her. Plus, he wanted something from her. He wasn't going to kill her outright. He'd wait until after he had what he wanted. Her only hope was to outrun him. She kicked off her shoes, flinging them in his direction, and bolted down the dock.

Charging along the bumpy cement surface of the wharf, she was well ahead of him for the first three hundred feet, or so, but soon the soles of her feet began to ache. The concrete pier was poured unevenly and had jagged edges, and certain sections of the wharf were higher than others. Emma had scuffed her heel and toes several times already, and both had started to bleed. She turned around and could see that St. Amant was gaining on her. Even though the bulk of his weight slowed his body movements, he was powerful. He pounded after her, charging down the wharf.

She could see that ahead, ships were moored for loading and unloading. Grain elevators were poised, booms outstretched, next to the ships. She knew the river was nearly two hundred feet deep at the French Quarter and guessed the ship channels had to be at least fifty. And treacherous. She should keep away from the edge of the wharf.

She looked back. St. Amant was only a few feet away. She could hear his tortuous breathing. Then, tripping on an uneven section of the dock, she fell, hurting her toe, and losing valuable time. She picked herself up immediately, but it was too late. St. Amant grabbed her and shoved his gun against her throat.

Emma pulled away from St. Amant, struggling away from the gun, then elbowed him in the gut. He pulled her closer without flinching. She wriggled out of the jacket she was wearing and ducked away from his grip. Lunging forward, she prepared to sprint away, but St. Amant grabbed her arm. Pulling away from him with as much strength as she could muster, Emma slipped from his grasp, not realizing how close they were to the edge of the wharf, and lost her balance. She teetered for a moment, certain she'd be able to regain her bearings. Then realizing she hadn't, she scraped her hand against the wharf in a last-ditch effort to save herself as she fell, feeling a rush of wind before her body slammed into the murky Mississippi River.

* * *

J.C. and Cornelius followed Emma that afternoon, continuing their spying game, curious, as usual, about her comings and goings. They'd watched as St. Amant struggled with Emma, and as she fell from the wharf, standing completely still for a moment. Then they turned toward each other.

"Let's go!"

They got on their bikes and peddled harder and faster than they thought possible to Emma's apartment. When they arrived, they pounded on the outside door, but received no response.

"We gotta go on upstairs," J.C. said.

Cornelius nodded, looked around to see if anyone was watching, and tried the outside handle. The door was open. They flew up the stairs and pounded on the door to the apartment. Within seconds Bobby opened the door.

"Call the police! We just saw a man fighting with your mom, and she fell into the river." J.C. was nearly shouting.

Ren walked to the door.

"Oh, my God." He looked at the twins. "I can't leave you here by yourselves. Your mom would kill me. Come on!"

Within five minutes he'd called for backup, loaded J.C., Cornelius, Billy and Bobby into his truck, and headed out to the wharfs at the end of Felicity Street.

* * *

Emma's heart was racing. Although the fall from the pier was only a little over ten feet, the impact took her breath away. She was dizzy and her heart was beating so loudly she could hear it. It was a hot day, nearly ninety degrees, and the water was warm, but Emma was cold, and had started to shake uncontrollably. She realized she must be in shock. Trying not to panic, she treaded water, and concentrated on breathing, extending each breath by a count of six.

She didn't have much control when she fell, but she'd tried to land as close to the wharf as possible, making certain not to fall backwards, or knock herself out on the dock or piers. The water was deep enough to break her fall safely, and, as soon as she got her bearings, she swam underwater to the supports under the wharf. She knew St. Amant would be searching for her, looking for her to emerge. She clung to a slippery piling.

Totally immersed in toxic river water, Emma was surrounded by the smell of petroleum byproducts and dead fish. When she emerged, she exhaled forcefully, hoping she hadn't swallowed anything. A frothy yellowish substance was making its way toward her. The underbelly of the wharf was teeming with old tires, rusted bicycles, wooden spools, rusted, rotting baby carriages, rusted metal objects that must have been buoys, blobs of Styrofoam and any number of fishing rods, and plastic bottles. Everything was covered in rust, slimy film, or algae. It was a minefield of hazards.

Emma hooked her foot into a crevice in one of the concrete pilings and pulled herself up high enough to be able to look downriver, away from the industrial section. She could see that the river became shallower along the shoreline as it approached the Central Business District and the French Quarter for a little while, at least. She also knew that with St. Amant lurking overhead she needed to wait, but she didn't want to wait too long. It would be dark at 8:00. She didn't want to be in the water or on the street at night. Either could be as dangerous as her stalker.

* * *

They found St. Amant further down the wharf than J.C. and Cornelius had remembered. He was nearly to the docks at Louisiana Avenue, standing at the end of the wharf, staring straight down at the water.

Ren parked five hundred feet from where St. Amant was standing, turned around, and looked at each of the boys.

"I have to get out. Listen to me and do exactly what I say. Your life depends on it. Get down on the floorboard of this truck and do not move. Do not raise your heads or anything else, no matter what happens. Not for any reason. There could be gunshots and raising your head could get you killed."

Ren slid out of his truck and moved toward St. Amant, who was still at the end of the pier, pacing back and forth, scanning the water.

The wail of a siren broke the silence. St. Amant spun around, and spying Ren, and the backup officers who were exiting their car, ran down the pier at a breakneck speed. Ren, who was several years younger, and many pounds lighter, sprinted after him, catching up with him almost immediately. He tackled him about the waist and brought him to his knees. St. Amant fought back, ramming Ren with his elbow, then his fist, but Ren held his own, grabbing one of St. Amant's wrists, then the other, forcing them to his back, and handcuffing them together.

"You got the wrong man. You must be new. I can tell you don't know who you're messing with," he snarled, then stood, chin up, chest out, never changing his posture, even in handcuffs. He refused to look at Ren as he was pushed into the squad car.

Ren ran back to the boys to check on them.

"Can you tell me where you saw Emma when she was fighting with the man?"

The boys tumbled out of the truck and ran to the dock. J.C. and Cornelius pointed to the place along the wharf where they'd last seen Emma, and to Emma's shoes. Ren and the boys called her name. There was no response. Ren called dispatch and requested a boat and divers to search for Emma. He picked up Emma's shoes and put them in his car. He felt sick to his stomach. She had to be okay. That's all there was to it.

"J.C., I need to get you and Cornelius home. I know it's about time for your mom to start worrying about you two."

"I don't want to leave. I want to stay and look for Mom," Bobby said, his face red and blotchy from trying to hide his tears.

"Me too." Billy's eyes were beginning to well. "I've had Red Cross life guard training. I can get in the water and look too."

"Yeah, me too," Bobby chimed in.

"Look, guys. I'm sure your mom's okay. She grew up on the water. She knows what she's doing. And the police department has professionals who do nothing more than look for people in the water. It's their job. Your mom wouldn't want you to be out here at night, and it'll be dark soon. She'd want you to be in a safe place, and get a good dinner. So, we're going to do that."

"We don't want to," Bobby said.

"I know. I don't want to go either." He hesitated for a minute, looking at the ground. Then he looked up. "Here's what we'll do. I'll stay. I'll get one of my friends, one of those officers over there, to take all of you to J.C. and Cornelius's mom's or his grandad's house. Who would be home now J.C.?"

"Right now our Pop would be home. Our mom might not be." J.C. looked at Cornelius who nodded in agreement.

"Do you think it would be okay if Billy and Bobby stayed there for a little while?"

Both J.C. and Cornelius nodded simultaneously.

Ren put his arms around Billy and Bobby. "I'll help find your mom and as soon as we find her, we'll come and pick you up over at Mr. Cooper's. Would that make you feel better?"

"I guess so." Bobby wiped a tear that had fallen off of his chin.

"Yeah. At least someone would be here looking for her," Billy said.

"We're going to find her. I'm sure she's fine. She just can't hear us. That's all." Ren motioned to one of the Officers.

"All four boys need to be dropped off at the residence above Coopers' Antiques on Magazine Street. The grandfather of these two young men lives there. Do you know where that is, or do you need the street number?"

"I got it."

"Make certain Mr. Cooper is there before you drop them off and explain the situation to him. Tell him I'll get there to retrieve Billy and Bobby as soon as possible." Ren looked at the twins. "With their mother. And thanks,"

The Officer loaded the boys into the back of his squad car. J.C. and Cornelius, arms draped across the twin's backs, tried to offer some comfort. Billy and Bobby couldn't hold their tears back any longer, and were both crying as the officer pulled away from the wharf.

* * *

Emma knew there was a storage facility that faced the river on the other side of Felicity. She thought there might be steps in front of the warehouse from the wharf to the river for loading, but she wasn't sure. She'd waited nearly an hour under the wharf, but she'd been moving nearly the entire time, slowly making her way down the river. She thought she might have heard sirens and stopped moving at one point, but couldn't be certain. It was hard to hear with the waves lapping against the pilings, and the sounds of the ships upriver. Her back began to ache, and she was afraid she was going to start cramping. She continued swimming between the pilings, toward downtown, searching as she made her way for those steps, or for any way out.

The river was busy that day. Ships were docked at the Louisiana Avenue wharf, loading and unloading. There was also a breeze that produced a slight chop. Emma was aware that any movement she made also created a series of ripples that would be obvious to anyone observing from the wharf above. She was certain that St. Amant was on to her, and equally certain he was watching. She didn't want to give away her location or destination, although she was afraid she already had.

The river was filled with debris. In addition to the partially submerged items under the wharf, there was even more rubbish that drifted by on top of the water. Each time an item with some heft floated her way, she picked it up and tossed it in the opposite direction, creating an impressive, but misleading ripple. Bread crumbs on the water to lead St. Amant in another direction. Or so she hoped.

She didn't stop moving, piling by algae encrusted piling, slowly, surely, endlessly. Then she saw them. Rusted steps, slimy with the same green algae. Nothing had ever looked quite as beautiful to her. Nearly weeping with relief, she swam, head up, dog-paddle style, to the decaying ladders. She kept an eye out for St. Amant as she swam. Finally, she dug her toes into the mossy carpet coating and pulled herself up.

By that time, it was nearly dusk. She thought she should have enough time to get home safely before it got too dark. The breeze hit her wet clothes, causing her to feel chilled. She began shaking uncontrollably. Wrapping her arms around herself, she turned the corner from the back of the storage facility to cross Felicity, still on the lookout for St. Amant.

Flashing blue lights of several police vehicles lit up the corner of Felicity and Tchoupitoulas. An ambulance stood ready and waiting behind the police cars with an open back door. Officers were gathered around the ambulance talking. One was smoking a cigarette. She crossed the street, hobbling on the road in her bare feet, and approached the group.

"Officers!" She waved at them as she crossed the street and approached. "Could I get some help? Another police officer, an Officer St. Amant, threatened me. I ended up in the river, thanks to him." Her teeth were chattering so hard she could hardly speak. "I fell right about there." She pointed to the wharf. Her wet sleeve clung to her arm. The officers stared at her. "I've had a tough time of it this evening." She was shivering from her wet clothes and the breeze from the river. "Do you know Officer St. Amant?"

The officer who was smoking nearly choked.

"You wouldn't be any chance be Emma Thornton, would you?"

"Yes. I am. How would you know that?" Emma paused and looked around.

"Uh, Ren?" one of the officers directed his question to the back of the ambulance.

Ren stepped from the back of the vehicle. When he saw Emma, he stopped for a moment, riveted by the very wet Emma. Then he ran, in three bounding steps, and threw his arms around her.

"I knew we'd find you! I knew you'd be okay!"

Emma coughed. "Well, I think I found you, actually." She pulled back from Ren and smiled. "And I'm cold. Got a jacket or something?"

Ren flew to the back of the ambulance and grabbed a blanket, then scurried back and threw it across her shoulders.

"You need to get in the back and let them check your vitals and all of that. They're going to want to take you in to the hospital after all you've been through. And I'm going to want to hear just what went on. But first things first."

Emma smiled. "Thanks. But I'd rather have a ride back to my car. I'm ready to get home and see the boys."

"Uh, no. You're going to the hospital to be checked out like Ren said." The EMT said. "In fact, you need to have a seat in the back of the ambulance right now." He nodded toward the open door at the rear of the ambulance. "We need to check your body temperature, blood pressure, and do some blood work. You've been in the water a long time."

"I'm fine. Just a little shaky. Is there any way I can let the boys know I'm okay?"

"I'm sure they'll let you use the phone at the hospital."

* * *

On the way to the hospital, Emma tried to close her eyes and relax. The full impact of everything hadn't quite hit her. She was nervous, on edge. Jumpy. But all she could think about was Louis's case. She couldn't calm down and she couldn't get warm.

She hoped St. Amant had been caught, and arrested, but she doubted he'd ever talk. Were Radick and Cox the leaders in this scheme? The ledgers indicated it, but she still wasn't sure.

But her main question was about Marcus. Where was he at the time of the shooting? Where did he go? Someone must have seen him.

Her mind was racing.

* * *

Emma leaned back on the narrow hospital bed and pulled several layers of blankets over her shoulders as high as she could. She still couldn't get warm, even though the blankets were heated. The lights in the room were so bright she couldn't relax or sleep if she'd wanted to. She'd sent Ren to go get the boys, so she didn't want to sleep, anyway. She couldn't wait to see them. Other than a little bruising from the fall, she was fine, except for some dehydration and exposure issues from staying in the water so long. They wanted her to rest, but that seemed impossible.

She heard the sound of running feet. Then Billy and Bobby's smiling faces appeared at her doorway. They flew into room, and hugged her neck. Ren was right behind them with purple tulips, her favorite flower. He handed them to her and tenderly kissed her forehead.

"Is that all I get?"

He bent over and kissed her lips while the boys made faces behind his back.

"That's more like it."

"Man, you had us scared. Don't ever do that again." He pulled up a chair so he could sit down next to her and hold her hand.

"I think I might need a hug, too."

Ren reached over to hug her and Emma felt her body ease for the first time since she climbed out of the water.

"Yeah, Mom. What were you thinking?" Billy frowned.

"I didn't do anything. I was just there at the pier checking out a few things and was attacked out of the blue. That's not my fault. By the way, do you know what happened to St. Amant? Did they get him?"

"Yeah, he's been arrested."

"Ren got him, Mom! He chased him down and tackled him!"

"What? How did that happen? And how does he know about it?"

"That's a story for another day. Let's get you home. You need a nice bath and bed."

Chapter Thirty-Four

R en talked Emma into waiting until the morning to get her car.
"There it is, down a few feet from the coffee shop. Thank
goodness. Looks like it's still in one piece." Emma pointed out her
car's location to Ren.

Ren pulled up next to Emma's car. She leaned over and gave him a kiss
before hopping out of his truck. She was feeling much better, ready to
face the day after last night's hot bath and a good night's sleep. She waved
goodbye to Ren as he drove off.

Her car was parked a half a block from Mama Ruby's house. She'd like to
drop by to speak to Alicia, but knew she couldn't. She wouldn't want to put
her in danger, for one thing. Alicia was probably being followed, just like
Flo had. She couldn't risk it.

She pulled out her keys to open her car and felt something tap her on the
back. She turned around, shocked to see Alicia.

She quickly checked the area. "You really shouldn't be here. It's not safe
for us to be seen together. But if you want to talk, run down to that church
at the end of the block. I'll pick you up there." Emma started her engine and
watched in her rear-view mirror as Alicia walked to the end of the block
and turned in the direction of the church. Emma made a U-turn and drove
down the street, keeping an eye out for police cars, or other suspicious
vehicles. She pulled up in front of the church, motioning for Alicia to get in.
Alicia crawled in the front seat as Emma pulled away from the sidewalk.

"That was pretty obvious if anyone was watching."

Alicia buckled on her seat belt. "What's going on? Your car's been in front of the coffee shop all night. Maybe even longer. What happened?"

"It's a long story. Let's just say I was chased by some bad guys. The same guys who I suspect killed your Aunt Juanita."

"Oh my God! Are you okay?"

"Yeah. But I was thinking. There's something not quite right about the story of the night of the shootings. I never have heard anyone say exactly what happened to Marcus. And someone had to have seen him that night, although no one admits to it."

Alicia hung her head.

"I always got the feeling you might know more than you were saying. And some things you told me didn't make sense. You said you walked Brother Antoine out to the porch, and watched as he walked down the sidewalk, right?"

Alicia nodded.

Emma pulled up to a red light and stopped. "Then you said while you were still on the porch you saw red lights on his chest and turned when you heard shots. You said you turned toward the shots?"

"That's right."

The light turned green, and Emma continued down Magazine Street. "Then you ran toward Brother Antoine, but your aunt called you back. And you said you saw Louis run toward the middle of the green space while holding a bag. You said you saw him run away from the electrical box, toward the river, but you didn't think he was holding a bag then. Did I get the correct sequence?"

Alicia glanced at Emma. "Yes, ma'am."

"The problem I'm having is that I don't think you could have seen those red lights from the front porch. You would've only been able to see his back from that angle. And, no one runs toward the sound of gunfire."

Alicia stared at her clasped hands.

"Your aunt wanted to shield you, didn't she?"

Alicia sniffed. "Yes, she did."

"I promise I'll do everything I can to protect you, Alicia. But you have to tell me what really happened that night."

Alicia looked up at Emma, then down at her hands again. "Well, you're right. Some of what I said wasn't exactly true. I walked Brother Antoine down the sidewalk a little way that night. I could see Louis running out to the electrical box about that time, and Marcus too. Louis had something in his hand. I was right there with Brother Antoine when the laser lights were on him, and when he crumpled down. I could tell he was shot. My auntie screamed for me to get back up on the porch. I was scared, but I looked out in the yard to see where the lights were comin' from. Then Louis took off again toward the river, but this time he had something else in his hand. Marcus started running back the other way. I saw Marcus throw whatever he had under Mama Ruby's buildin'."

"What did Louis have in his hand?"

"It was hard to see."

"Did it look like the same shape as before?"

"No, it was different. It looked like it might be a gun."

"What about Marcus?"

"Looked like he had a gun, too."

"So, Louis and Marcus took the guns from these two guys. Marcus threw his gun under Mama Ruby's apartment and Louis ran toward the river with his."

"Yes, that's what happened."

"Great." Emma sighed.

"I'm going to have to break a promise to your aunt. We'll need you to testify, Alicia. But first I'm going to do what I can to get some protection for you. You aren't safe right now." She turned down 6th Street and made the loop down St. Charles to drop Alicia back off at the church. "You can't afford to let your guard down like I did yesterday."

Emma pulled around and dropped Alicia off on the street behind the church, not noticing that when she stopped to let Alicia off, a candy apple red 1975 Cutlass Supreme continued down the street.

* * *

"Surprised to see me so soon?"

Louis sat down in a metal folding chair in front of Emma and nodded. There were dark circles under his eyes, and a gray cast to his skin, as if he wasn't getting much sleep.

"I've got a couple of quick questions. I've been speaking to a few other witnesses and have been told that on the night of the murders you dropped off the paper bag, then you picked up something else from one of the men there. I was told it looked like a gun. Can you tell me anything about that?"

Louis stared at his hands.

"I know this is tough for you, Louis. But protecting Marcus isn't working for you anymore. You've got to talk to me." She reached out and touched his arm. "Did you take a gun from one of the guys out by that box?"

"Yeah. But I ain't protecting Marcus. I'm protecting me." Louis stood up and began pacing around the room. "Marcus ain't the only problem, you know."

"Can you tell me why you took the gun from that man? Did Marcus tell you to?"

He nodded and sat back down in his chair.

"Do you always do everything Marcus tells you to do?"

His eyes began to well. He rubbed his tears away with the palm of his hand.

"I didn't mean to upset you, but I need to understand what was going on that night. Your life is at stake here."

"My life was at stake that night, too. Marcus said throw that guy's gun away, throw it in the river. He said if I didn't he'd take everything away from us, from Mama Ruby. I had to."

"But you were the one they set up. Marcus, and Tamika, and the police all ended up blaming everything on you."

He nodded and wiped his nose with the back of his hand.

"So, you need to save yourself."

"Yeah." He nodded and sniffed loudly.

"And the gun you threw in the Mississippi River wasn't your gun, was it?"

He shook his head. "I didn't throw it away."

CHAPTER THIRTY-FOUR

Emma raised her eyebrows. "What? But that's what you've said all along."

"Marcus told me to, but I thought I might need it 'cause he might try to pin everything on me. So, I didn't want to throw it in the river."

"Marcus took the other gun, right?"

He stared at his feet.

"That's what I've been told. Is that correct?"

Louis turned his head away from Emma.

Emma hesitated for a moment. "This is important."

Louis nodded. "He took it."

"Then what happened?"

"He ran down to Mama Ruby's place."

"And?"

"He threw it under her apartment. There was a little door there, or a window that was open, I think. He threw it in that."

"Then he set you up, knowing that Tamika would lie for him."

"Guess so."

"Where's the gun that you took that night?"

"I don't know. I put it in my pocket and started runnin'. I tripped, and it fell out of my pocket. I looked for it, but it was dark, and I couldn't find it. I knew those cops were watchin' me, so I just kept runnin'. I thought I'd go back the next day and find it. But when I went back and searched, it wasn't there."

Chapter Thirty-Five

Emma finished up her afternoon class and ran to her office to freshen up for the faculty party. Most law school faculty events were excruciatingly stiff affairs set in the middle of the day with foamy green punch and overly sweet, sugary white petits fours, but this one was deliberately set in the late afternoon to celebrate the long and illustrious career of a colorful, and much-loved colleague. It was catered, there was a bar, and champagne was served. Everyone anticipated a good time.

By the time Emma arrived, the toasts and testimonials had already begun and the slide show was the next thing on the agenda. It would go on for hours, but Emma, who only yesterday found herself plunging into the Mississippi River, was exhausted, achy, and emotionally spent. She quickly found a seat. Although she had no problem with the testimonials of the Dean and Father Alfonso, she found the long-winded accounts of others tedious and more than she could tolerate for very long. After listening to more than an hour of tributes while she sipped on a glass of white wine and nibbled on tasteless hors d'oeuvres, she started looking for an exit. Once the lights were dimmed for the slide show, she made her escape through the back door. She knew no one would miss her.

* * *

Emma's office door pushed open without a key, even though she would have sworn she locked it as she was leaving. She stepped into the dimly lit room, scanning the small space for anything unusual. The lamp cast a golden glow on the desk, but it was approaching dusk, and the corners of the room were shadowy. Still, all appeared to be clear.

As she stepped toward her desk to retrieve her notes, a hand reached out from behind the door, grabbed her wrist and pinned her arm behind her back. She felt cold metal at her throat.

"I need those ledgers, Professor Thornton."

She recognized the voice immediately, and tried to turn her head, but her assailant dug the gun deeper into her neck.

"I don't know what you're talking about," Emma said. She cursed herself for waiting to move the ledgers from her office. She should have found another storage place for them days ago.

"It's not time for games. Let's see what's in that filing cabinet. Give me your keys."

The nasal twang of the voice couldn't be mistaken. "Officer McEnroe?"

She heard the sound of the hammer of a pistol being cocked.

"I could just shoot you and find the key myself. Now. The key to the cabinet." He pushed her out into the middle of the room. He followed and extended his hand.

Emma grappled with the keys, fumbling to find the tiniest on the ring. She hesitated for a moment, and then threw the entire bundle into a dark corner, somewhere behind the door. Taking McEnroe by surprise, she ducked, then scrambled toward the door in an effort to escape. But McEnroe, a tall man, athletic, and powerfully built, caught up with her in one easy stride, and grabbed her by her hair.

"Not so fast." He shone his flashlight in the corner behind the door. The keys sparkled in the light. He motioned for Emma to pick up the keys, then, finally releasing her hair, shoved her, his gun at her neck, toward the filing cabinet. He scratched through the jumble of keys with one hand until he found the correct one and opened the top drawer.

"You lied, Professor." He spat out the word "professor" as if it was a disease. "You did know what I was talking about, because here they are. Juanita Bishop's duplicate set of ledgers."

"Why are you so interested in them?"

"Shut up and pull the ledgers and other books out, one at a time." He jammed the gun in her neck even deeper.

"You're going to have to let up on the gun."

He moved the gun a fraction of an inch from her neck, and she stepped forward and removed the first ledger, then set it on the desk.

"I don't think you've thought this thing through. It's not that dark yet. What makes you think you can get away with this? There are people upstairs, security guards all over campus. Students are milling about, especially in the library."

"I told you to shut up. The party upstairs is so loud no one will hear anything that goes on down here. The only reason you're alive right now is because I need something else from you."

"I should have realized you were involved when you were so unwilling to help me with St. Amant. You and Radick, both."

Officer McEnroe motioned with his gun for her to continue to unload the filing cabinet.

Emma pulled out another ledger and placed it on the desk. "Big Huey and Little Huey, Superintendent Cox and Sergeant Radick. They served in Vietnam together, at the Battle of Hue. So that's their nicknames. Radick, at least is in on this with you."

McEnroe laughed. "You got some of this wrong, Professor. Radick and Cox may have served in Vietnam, but Radick was never in a battle. He's always been an admin guy. He was HR during the Gulf War and had a tidy business fixing up dishonorable discharges. That way they could get jobs when they got out. Charged a reasonable fee for it, too. St. Amant had his court martial erased."

"You were in the Gulf War too?"

He nodded.

"So, I'm guessing both you and Grant also had a little help from Radick."

"Well, aren't you the clever one."

"Did Radick blackmail you guys to do the protection and gun smuggling work?"

"I wouldn't call it gun smuggling. And you need to keep unloading that cabinet."

Emma pulled out another ledger and stacked it on top of the others. "But he blackmailed you, right?"

"You're still talking too much."

"But then greed took over, didn't it, Officer McEnroe? You must be making a lot of money."

"There's nothing wrong about taking guns from criminals."

"You've got to be kidding. What about the murder of Brother Antoine and Sam Maureau? And what about Lionel Boudreaux? And we can't forget about Juanita Bishop and Florence Cronin. And what about illegal sales to drug dealers?"

"That's enough." He shoved her with the butt of his gun. "Where's that other gun? The one that's missing from the night of the shootings. Louis ran off with it. You've either got it or you know where it is."

"I don't know anything about a gun. I figured there were two shooters, and I know only one gun was found. But I don't know where the other gun is. I wish I did."

"You're lying. You hid the ledgers and you're hiding the gun." He pointed the muzzle of his pistol at the ledgers and motioned for her to speed up.

"Marcus knew that Alicia and Brother Antoine were planning to get together, and he must have told you. Then you set up the whole thing with Radick, who set up the sharpshooters. Superintendent Cox wanted you to protect Brother Antoine that night, but instead, you and Radick planned his murder."

McEnroe pointed the gun back at her "Can you feel your pulse? Just keep talking and you're dead." Emma swallowed. "Pull that last book out of the filing cabinet and put it on the stack."

He was so close Emma could feel his breath on her neck. She shivered.

"Pick everything up and come with me, or I can kill you here, in your lovely office. It's your choice."

"How do you think you can walk out of here with a gun at my throat?"

"Take off your jacket."

"What?"

"Take if off and hand it to me." Emma pulled her jacket off and gave it to McEnroe.

He draped Emma's jacket over the end of his arm so it covered the gun and aimed it at her back.

"Now pick up the ledgers." He motioned for her to open the door.

Emma waited for McEnroe to come as close to the door as possible before turning the handle, then popped the door open in an attempt to knock McEnroe off balance, but he stopped the door with the toe of his boot.

"Nice try, Professor. Now let's go."

"You know there are cameras right there." She pointed to a camera in the corner of the hall. "There's no safe way out of here for you. You won't get away with it."

McEnroe shoved Emma into the hall.

She glanced up at the fire alarm, estimating it was twenty feet from where she was standing, at the end of the corridor.

Seconds later, Josh Delcambre stepped out of the elevator and walked down the hallway to Emma's office carrying a large ledger.

Josh waved at Emma. "Professor Thornton! I just finished…"

As soon as Emma saw Josh round the corner, she threw the ledgers she was holding at McEnroe and started to run toward the fire alarm in the upper corner of the hallway. McEnroe lunged toward Emma, but missed. Emma continued running toward the fire alarm.

In two strides McEnroe reached Josh, who was nearing Emma's office. He grabbed Josh by the coat and pulled him close, cramming his gun into Josh's throat. He looked up as Emma's hand stretched toward the alarm in the corner.

"Pull that fire alarm, Professor, and the kid's dead."

Emma froze. She saw Ren creeping around the same corner Josh had emerged from, gun raised. He ducked behind a display shelf used to store the school's weekly newspaper, then peered out from the cabinet. She flinched as Radick emerged from the opposite corner of the hallway. *Radick!?!* Radick moved toward Emma, his pistol also raised. Ren took aim at Radick's chest and pulled the trigger. Emma watched Radick fall as Ren's shot rang out.

McEnroe spun around to look at Ren, who was still crouched behind the cabinet, bringing Josh with him. "Don't do it, friend. You move and this kid's a goner. Don't come after me, don't call the cops, nothin'. You do anything at all, and he's dead. I'm taking him and the ledgers and I'm out of here." He leveled his gun at Josh, then pulled him close.

"Pick up the books." He shoved Josh toward the ledgers.

Josh bent over and picked up as many ledgers as he could carry.

Ren kept his gun aimed at McEnroe.

Using Josh as a shield, McEnroe pushed him toward the exit. "Now move. Out the door." He kept Josh close to his body, still using him as a shield. McEnroe swung Josh around so that they were both facing Ren, and stepped backwards, toward the double doors leading outside, his gun at Josh's back.

Ren lowered his gun. As he and Emma watched McEnroe and Josh back through the front doors of the law school into the dusky night, he pulled his portable radio from his pocket, and made one more call to dispatch.

Five seconds later, gunfire rang out. Emma ran to the front picture window of the law school as students, cleaning staff and faculty began gathering behind her. Scott McEnroe lay in a crumpled mass on the front steps, bleeding from numerous gunshot wounds. He wasn't moving. Josh Delcambre was standing on the steps about five feet away.

"St. Amant and Grant weren't the only sharp shooters on the force." Ren laid his arm across Emma's shoulders and drew her close for a moment. Emma collapsed against him, allowing herself a moment to cling to Ren, to catch her breath, to shut her eyes against the horrors of what had just happened.

Ren walked outside to check on the SWAT team and to report again to dispatch. Emma followed and stood next to Josh, trying not to look at McEnroe's shattered body as officers carrying assault weapons approached Ren.

She reached out to Josh. "Can I call your wife to come and get you?"

Josh nodded. "I think the EMTs want to see me first, but, sure."

Emma tried to ignore the crowd gathering along the sidewalk and behind the closed glass doors as she walked back inside to call Josh's wife. She hoped the party was still going on upstairs undisturbed. Somehow, she didn't think that was possible.

* * *

Emma found her way back to her office and watched as paramedics checked out Sergeant Radick. Police officers lurked nearby, ready to question him as soon as they got the okay. She wished everyone would clear out from the front of her office.

Radick's wounds were serious, but there was a possibility he might recover. The paramedics brought in a gurney and whisked him into an ambulance waiting by the front door. The hovering officers followed. After they were gone, Emma's office was back to normal. Almost. There were bloodstains on the floor by her door, and ledgers were strewn along the hallway. Her office was a crime scene. She was certain that within minutes she'd be asked to leave.

She called Josh's wife, who was at home. She'd soon be on her way to pick up her husband, who was shaken up but not injured. Emma knew the Dean would be down soon and she wasn't looking forward to the meeting.

She heard a knock and turned to see both Dean Munoz and Ren in her doorway.

"You okay?" Ren's face was ashen.

"Or are you single handedly trying to destroy the reputation of the law school in one evening?" The Dean smiled, but when he saw Emma's face he stepped into the office and reached out to her. "I was kidding, you know."

Emma sighed and nodded. "I didn't expect any of this tonight."

"What happened?" The Dean sat down in one of the chairs across from Emma.

"I'm sorry guys, but I've got to mark this place off with tape. You've got to step out of here. I know the Dean has a few questions for you, Emma, and so do several of the officers, including me. So, why don't you go over to one of the front offices, and I'll come find you in a little bit?" Ren pulled the tape out of his back pocket and walked over to Emma to give her a hug.

CHAPTER THIRTY-FIVE

Emma nodded and grabbed her purse.

Ren frowned. "I'll send the paramedics over to take a look at you. If they tell you to go to the hospital, then that's what we'll do. You've had a shock. It wouldn't hurt to get checked out."

She and the Dean plodded down the hall to the clinic's administrative offices. The door was open since the director was there, working late. They sat down on a couple of the plush chairs in the waiting room.

"Do you need anything?" The Dean leaned toward Emma.

She shook her head. "No, unless you could erase the last thirty minutes."

"Who was that who was killed out front? Wasn't he a police officer?" Dean Munoz propped his elbows on the arms of his chair.

Emma nodded. "Yeah. An old friend of Ren's, McEnroe, an officer in the internal investigations unit. Weird, huh?"

"What happened?"

"McEnroe was looking for Juanita Bishop's ledgers I had stored in my filing cabinet. I think I told you that Juanita did the bookkeeping for Marcus's pawn shop for years. The ledgers showed that Marcus was working with a group of cops, including McEnroe, and Radick, the other guy that was shot. They took protection money from Central City businesses, even Marcus. And they also took guns from citizens, most of whom were drug dealers, during raids. They turned around and sold the stolen stuff to Marcus. Marcus then sold the guns to his drug suppliers in Houston. I suspect he used the guns as a tradeoff for cocaine purchases. They were corrupt.."

"Who, the cops?"

"Yeah. And worse." Emma leaned her head against the palm of her hand.

"Does any of that have anything to do with Louis Bishop's case ? It doesn't seem to." The Dean leaned toward Emma.

"It does." Ren said as he walked into the office. "We're pretty sure we can prove that Officers St. Amant and Grant, the guy who broke his neck when he fell in Emma's apartment, were the sharp shooters who killed Brother Antoine and Maureau."

The Dean turned around as Ren entered the room. "You've been working on the case too?"

"Yes, sir. My unit's been investigating these officers for a while. I've been looking into my old buddy McEnroe, the guy who was shot outside. But in looking into him, I also ended up following up on St. Amant and Grant. Those two were nearly inseparable. They were highly skilled shooters, and we got them on a few brown bag pickups."

"Brown bag pickups? I bet it was awkward to look into an old friend."

"It was, but Emma was up to her ears in this. I wanted to do what I could to figure out what was going on. Plus, I've always hated a crooked cop, friend or not. We knew Brother Antoine was working with Lionel Boudreaux. He'd discovered Marcus's protection money drop-offs to the cops. Those were the brown bag pickups. The best thing we could figure is that the target on the night of September 9th was Brother Antoine. Maureau was a cover-up. They wanted us to think it was a drug deal gone bad. Instead, St. Amant and Grant were there to execute both men. Antoine was killed because he was acting more like an undercover cop than anything else. Only he wasn't."

"Yeah, Brother Antoine was an informant. And Juanita's ledgers back up everything Ren just said," Emma said.

"They killed Officer Boudreaux too?" The Dean raised his eyebrows.

"Looks that way."

"I've finally convinced Alicia Bishop to testify about that night. Her testimony helps Louis. And Louis should testify against Marcus, but they both need protection. Louis will also testify that McEnroe and Radick watched everything from their car on Felicity Street that night. But Marcus also had a role." Emma scooted down in her chair and propped her feet up on a coffee table in the waiting room.

"I don't think you're going to have to worry about some of this, Emma. I don't think the DA will want to pursue the charges against Louis when he sees the evidence we have against the four police officers."

"I hope you're right. But what about Marcus? If he's not arrested, Louis and Alicia will be in jeopardy. He's certainly threatened Louis."

"If the ledgers are as detailed as you say, we've got him on several charges, even without the kids' testimony. If Radick survives, my guess is he'll talk.

When he does, he'll have something to say about Marcus and that night. If that happens, the kids shouldn't have to testify."

"I hope you're right."

"Is there any actual evidence that puts St. Amant at the scene of the murder that night?" Dean Munoz folded his hands in his lap.

"I think Josh said there was something in Juanita's notes about a meeting that night. Plus, there was a notation about St. Amant's payout for that hit. That should be in the ledger." Emma rubbed her head.

"That's excellent, then." The Dean smiled. "Good work."

"It's all thanks to Juanita. By the way, I found out a few days ago, after we got Louis's test results, that his counselor, Mr. Branson, wants to foster him when the timing is right for that. If his mother doesn't have an objection, I think he'll make it happen." Emma rubbed her forehead again. Her headache wasn't going away.

"What about the girl, Alicia?"

"We need to work out a plan to protect her, too, which means keeping her away from Marcus and his gang. Father Alfonso was working on getting her a scholarship to Our Lady of Fatima High Academy in Grand Coteau, and it looks like it's going through. The school is thrilled she applied. And it's a boarding school, so she could live there, and would be away from New Orleans and the Gangsta B's. Her aunt would be so happy."

Emma reached out and squeezed Ren's hand. "When do you think you'll be able to call the DA about this case? I'd like to speak to him tomorrow."

"I'll call him first thing in the morning. Let's get you checked out with the EMTs and get home."

Chapter Thirty-Six

A week later, Emma, excited to learn that Alicia was accepted to Our Lady of Fatima Academy in Grand Coteau, made plans with Ren to drive Alicia to the school since Mama Ruby's vision was too poor for long distance driving. They decided to leave from Emma's apartment Monday morning at 8:00. Ren had taken off from work for the day to make the drive with Emma. He'd never visited any of the bayous or parishes south of New Orleans and was looking forward to seeing the lush terrain. Even though they were in the middle of a semester, the school had acknowledged that the circumstances and Alicia were exceptional. Plus, they were impressed with her test results. The trip would take approximately two-and-a-half hours, one way. Emma wanted to make it back to New Orleans before Billy and Bobby got home. She also wanted to see Louis at the Parish Prison when he was released that afternoon.

Ren met Emma at the coffeehouse around the corner from her apartment at 8:10 with two steaming cappuccinos in go cups. They drove to Alicia's grandmother's place, anxious to beat the morning traffic. Making good time for a workday, they arrived at Mama Ruby's within fifteen minutes and rapped on the front door of the apartment.

Alicia was dressed casually in blue jeans and an oxford button-down shirt. Emma realized she'd never seen her in anything but her school uniform or her "Sunday best." Alicia seemed more relaxed, almost cheery, and motioned for them to come inside. Small, dimly lit, but neat, the living room had obviously been tidied in anticipation of guests. The windows were covered with venetian blinds that might have been hung shortly after the building's construction in 1942, but Emma could tell they'd been washed and dusted on a regular basis. A brown corduroy couch placed along the wall facing the courtyard, was worn, but comfortable-looking, and sat directly in front of the TV. Emma easily imagined several grandchildren crammed on its cushions watching their favorite show. A cracked leatherette recliner with a lopsided seat and broken springs sat next to the couch. Cozied next to the recliner was a basket filled with magazines, a rolled-up shawl, various eye glasses, and something that looked suspiciously like parlay sheets. It was obvious Mama Ruby had laid claim to the recliner and the surrounding area.

"Come in. Would you like some coffee, or something else to drink?" Alicia directed Emma and Ren toward the couch.

"We just need to grab your things and get going, but I'd like to say 'hi' to your grandmother first, if she's up." Emma smiled. "I'm guessing you're all packed?" Emma looked around for Alicia's bags, spying one next to the door.

Just then Mama Ruby emerged from the back of the apartment. Emma had forgotten how tiny she was. She was pushing a rolling suitcase, dressed to perfection in navy blue sweat pants and a matching top, with spotless white tennis shoes. Her silver-white hair was pulled back into a smooth twist. Every hair was in place.

"Mama Ruby! You don't need to be pushing that thing! Here, let me do it!" Alicia rushed toward the woman.

"Don't be silly, girl! It's one last thing I can do. I'm so proud of you!" Mama Ruby looked up at Emma and Ren. "She's our pride and our joy, you know."

Ren walked over and extended his hand toward Mama Ruby.

"It's so nice to meet you. You have an incredible granddaughter, I know why you're proud of her." Ren smiled. Mama Ruby accepted his handshake and handed the suitcase over. Ren grabbed the rolling bag, Alicia grabbed a duffel bag next to the door, and they both walked out to load the car.

Mama Ruby turned toward Emma. "Good to see you again. Alicia showed me those pamphlets from the school where she's goin'. Looks like they even teach horseback riding. And the place is so beautiful with those tall buildings and beautiful gates. I'm so proud of her going to a school like that." Her eyes welled with tears.

"Well, she earned it, Mrs. Bishop. She's made excellent grades, and scored very high on her tests, so the Sisters are excited to have her."

She brushed her eyes with her fingertips. "I keep thinkin' about that night when those two men were killed. Everything coulda been so much different."

"What do you mean?"

"She didn't know what was goin' on, not about anything, really. But a few days before it all happened, I heard Marcus tell her to have Brother Antoine at her house that night, the night of the shooting, and at what time. Said she needed to do what he said or she and her Aunt Juanita would start having trouble. She was gonna have Brother Antoine over anyway, so she just made sure it was at the time Marcus said, you know? Then, after Brother Antoine was shot, she knew what Marcus had done, and she ran down the sidewalk, then over here, and stood in front of my house, down on the sidewalk there, with Juanita steady yellin' at her to come back. Alicia was so upset, fussin' and cryin', yelling 'Why, why?' and that kind of thing. She was there on the sidewalk when Marcus ran by and threw the gun under the house. She screamed at him and said, 'You killed him. You killed Brother Antoine.' Marcus dragged her inside the house. I thought he was gonna kill her right then and there."

"What did you do?"

"Well, I was about to yell at him when Georgie and Dwayne got in between Marcus and Alicia. Dwayne said he'd walk Alicia home. Then Marcus told her she'd better keep her mouth shut, or he'd kill her Aunt Juanita in front of her and then he'd kill her, too."

"Do you know if Juanita knew about Marcus's threat?"

"She didn't have to know the exact words. She knew enough about Marcus to know that's what he'd do."

"And that's why Juanita didn't want Alicia to talk to us?"

"That's right."

"Did Alicia realize that Marcus had something planned that night for

Brother Antoine?"

"I don't think she really thought about it until the shootin'. You know how kids are. They get so tied up in their own world, they don't think about things like that. So, when Marcus asked her to do him a favor, she just did it. She had Brother Antoine come over at 8:00 like Marcus asked. Didn't think anything about it."

"What did Marcus do after the boys walked Alicia home?" Emma kept an eye on Ren and Alicia through the front window. They were arranging and re-arranging the suitcases to fit in the trunk. They'd be awhile.

"He just got in his car and drove off."

"Have the police questioned you about that night?"

Mrs. Bishop walked into the kitchen to get a cup of coffee. "Yeah, they did. Want a cup?"

Emma shook her head. "Did you ever tell them about Alicia?"

"No, never. She shouldn't ever be brought into this." Mama Ruby added some sugar and cream to her coffee and walked back to the living room. She sat her cup on a side table and sat down in the chair next to it. She gestured for Emma to sit next to her.

"Does anyone else know she saw Marcus throw the gun under the house, or that she was told to have Brother Antoine over at her house that night at 8:00?" Emma perched at the end of the couch, ready at any moment for Ren and Alicia to return.

"Someone might. But no one's talking. No one wants Alicia in this. Marcus shouldn't have done what he did."

"Marcus's been indicted now, you know. They got him on several drug charges, sales of stolen weapons, criminal conspiracy, and accessory to murder before and after the fact. So, he's going to serve time."

"I hate to say it since he's my grandson, and I love him, but I'm glad to hear it. He has some good in him, but he needs to pay for the things he does that are wrong."

"Marcus ran the family, didn't he?"

"He thought he did. But now he's gonna realize he didn't. That he was wrong." She sniffed. "His daddy, my son, had a good business down there

271

at that pawn shop, but Marcus had to go and mess it up. He was always about doing more and making more money, but in ways that were bad, underhanded, you know? He's where he needs to be now."

Ren and Alicia walked back into the apartment. Alicia looked at Emma. "Ready to go?"

Emma nodded.

* * *

The drive to Grand Coteau, a few minutes outside of Lafayette, Louisiana, over marshy and bucolic countryside, was captivating. Emma had never driven that far south in the state. Long bridges curved through miles of swampland and marsh grasses where elegant white ibis roosted in stands of cypress. Emma counted as many as ten birds in one tree.

Our Lady of Fatima Academy was an imposing structure with lush green lawns mowed to perfection. The iron gates were majestic, with ornate scroll work and brass pulls. The buildings were multistoried brick Greek Revival structures that seemed to breathe academia. Girls on horses trotted by in jodhpurs and riding boots. Emma glanced over at Alicia.

"What do you think about all of this? The horses, and riding boots, fancy buildings, and shining brass gates?"

"I think that if my grades and test scores can get me into something like this, then I must be doing okay."

"I think you're right."

Ren pulled up to the administration building. Emma and Alicia slid out of the car and began walking up the front steps as he parked. Taking advantage of Ren's brief absence, Emma reached out to Alicia.

"This morning your grandmother gave me some new information about the night of the murder of Brother Antoine. Some information that affected you. I think she felt comfortable talking about it since Marcus will be indicted now, along with the police officers."

Alicia looked at Emma from the corner of her eye, which began to brim with tears.

"I shoulda known better. I knew something was wrong when he said I had to have Brother Antoine at my house at a certain time. Why would he do that? But I didn't think he could have a reason to hurt him. I never in a million years thought something like that would happen." She wiped away tears as she walked up the steps.

"Why didn't you speak up about Marcus throwing the gun under your grandmother's apartment?"

"I was afraid, I guess." Alicia stopped on the steps and turned toward Emma. "He was always getting everyone else to do his dirty work. He used me to set up Brother Antoine, and that's not fair. Marcus hides behind everyone and everyone always protects him. I guess I did too. But this time people protected me also. That was new for him. And now I'm the one with the money."

"What do you mean, you're the one with the money?"

She hesitated. "Mama Ruby didn't tell you about that?"

"No, she didn't. What money are you talking about?" Emma motioned for Alicia to sit down at the bench at the top of the steps and sat down next to her.

"My Aunt Juanita's." She wiped tears from her face again. "She left it to me. Told me to get it if anything happened to her. I know Marcus wanted it, and that creep Ninja was following me around trying to see if I'd lead him to it. So, I hid it. I sneaked it in Mama Ruby's place the night Aunt Juanita died. There's a place in the wall of Mama Ruby's bedroom, behind her vanity, where the plaster caves in a little. We put the money there and covered it back up with the furniture." She smiled at Emma. "We didn't think he'd go looking in her bedroom, and he didn't. Aunt Juanita was saving all her money for a house, but she said if anything happened to her, I was to get it for college. I wanted to make sure Marcus didn't get his hands on it."

Marcus had seared Alicia's hatred of him by killing people she loved. Alicia was a good girl, a person with pure motives. But Marcus had mistaken her virtue for weakness.

"Would you testify against Marcus if we need you to?"

"I would. I'm tired of being afraid of him."

"I don't think you'll have to. They should have enough on Marcus and the police officers without you, thanks to your Aunt Juanita."

Alicia broke into one of the widest smiles Emma had ever seen as she started to stand up. "And you think Marcus will be convicted?"

"It looks that way. All you'll have to worry about from now on will be making those good grades I've been hearing about."

"That's no problem. I've just got to figure out where to put my money. It's not really safe right now." Alicia sat back down.

"Where is it?"

"It's in that duffel bag in the trunk of the car."

"You're right. That's not safe. If you'd like me to, I can contact your aunt's attorney. I found his name in one of her journals. He can get the will probated, the money deposited, and get an account set up in your name."

Alicia nodded.

"I'll keep in touch with all of that, and he'll be in touch with you too."

Alicia smiled. "That sounds good."

"One thing, though. Stay out of New Orleans, at least until things stabilize. Keep in touch with your grandmother. She'll know what's going on and when it might be safe to return. But, don't forget, you can always call me." She pressed her card in Alicia's hand.

* * *

Ren and Emma returned to New Orleans just before 2:00. Emma knew that Jesse Branson was picking up Louis from Orleans Parish Prison that afternoon, and Ren had agreed to wait at the apartment for the boys while she dashed off in hopes of meeting Jesse and Louis. As they pulled up to her apartment, Ren opened the door and turned around to face her before leaving.

"One more thing. I was going to wait to tell you, but I can't. I'm pretty excited." Ren's face was flushed and he was grinning.

"What is it? You look like the cat who swallowed the canary."

"Well, nothing like that. But I got an apartment. Right down the street from you and the boys!" His smile got even bigger. "I can move in, first of the month. I already gave them a deposit. I've got time to go back to Georgia to pick up my things and drive back down over a weekend. Maybe next weekend." He paused. "Well. What do you think?"

Emma laughed and hugged him. "I'm very excited. I can't wait to have you close by. And an official resident of New Orleans!" She gave him a kiss. "But now I've got to go if I'm going to catch Jesse and Louis before they head out. We'll celebrate when I get home."

* * *

Emma drove into the Central Lock Up parking lot, unsure of where to go. She understood released inmates departed from a large door somewhere along the side of the prison. She was driving around the perimeter searching for a parking space when she saw Jesse. He was leaning against his car, arms folded, staring ahead at the prison walls. She pulled into a space and walked up the gravel path toward him. He turned as she approached.

"Didn't know you were coming here today. I'm so excited about picking up Louis I got here early. A couple of days ago I spoke to an old high school friend of mine, Todd Germaine, who made it big in New York in the fashion industry. He's impressed with Louis's drawings and is going to let him work in his shop downtown in New Orleans, after school, and on weekends. Who knows, he might use a drawing or two. Maybe it will even go somewhere." He grinned.

"That's incredible! Even if it doesn't lead to a design job, Louis will be in a great environment. One that will encourage him to keep drawing and use his talent. Wow. Does he know?"

"He knows Todd likes his drawings. I haven't told him anything else. We've got to establish some house rules. It's going to be an adjustment for both of us, especially Louis. I'm not sure he's going to like my interference. But I've been so excited about the whole thing I haven't been able to sleep."

"I don't think Louis will think you're interfering. No one's ever paid this much attention to Louis. Marcus just barked orders at him. Mama Ruby cares, but she's overwhelmed by too many grandchildren and too many mouths to feed. By the way, Marcus was indicted yesterday, along with the police officers."

"That's a relief." Jesse exhaled. "What are the charges?"

"Some drug charges, and accessory to murder, among other things."

"What about our fine upstanding cops?" Jesse said.

"St. Amant was indicted for three counts of murder in the first degree, and Radick isn't getting off lightly either. He got indicted for criminal conspiracy, accessory to murder, and attempted murder. They won't see the light of day for a while. Radick, the injured officer, taped everything, and ratted on everyone, from Marcus to his fellow officers."

"Does that mean Louis won't have to testify?"

"Probably. The DA would rather not use Louis or Alicia if he can avoid it since they're juveniles. It's easier on everyone."

Jesse nodded. "I heard the residents in the 6th District are protesting against the cops who killed Juanita Bishop. They've been harassing everyone in that district for so long. People are tired of the abuse."

"I don't blame them," Emma said.

"I'm so glad the charges against Louis have been dropped."

"Yeah." Emma nodded. "The first and second-degree murder charges have been dropped. And that was all they'd filed against him. They wouldn't have let him go if they'd planned on bringing new charges."

Several prisoners departed from the sally port entryway at the front of the building. Jesse and Emma searched the group. Louis wasn't there.

"Louis changed his story about the gun he picked up from those two men by the transformer that night. Did he tell you about it?" Jesse folded his arms against his chest.

"He did. He mentioned something about it the last time I visited him."

"I don't know what I think about all of that."

"You think he made it up?" The afternoon sun was in Emma's eyes. She scrunched up her face.

"It's hard to tell, but Louis has been manipulated by others for so long I think it's just second nature for him to do what they want or what he can to protect them," Jesse said.

"And he's told so many stories about that night. Wonder if we've heard any version of the truth. I still think he has more to tell us—especially about that gun."

Emma saw the gates slide open and Louis exit the prison. She waved to him. He tried not to smile, but she could see that he was excited to be leaving.

Louis walked up to them, his head held a little higher than usual. He bumped Jesse's fist and tilted his head toward Emma.

"Louis, before you head out with Mr. Branson, let's meet at that coffeehouse down by your grandmother's apartment. See you in ten or fifteen minutes."

* * *

Emma arrived at Felicity Coffee first, grabbed a table, and pulled a couple of chairs over. A few minutes later, Jesse pushed the door open and walked over to greet Emma. Louis followed, stopping to read the menu on the wall of the shop.

He wandered back to the table where Emma sat, still distracted by the large menu.

"What would you like, Louis?" Emma pulled her wallet out of her purse.

"One of those coffees with ice."

"Do you want a flavor, like chocolate, or vanilla, or hazelnut?"

"Chocolate."

She stood up. "I'll order it for you. Mr. Branson, what do you want? My treat."

"I'll have the same."

"Well, that'll be three, then. I'll be right back."

Emma walked to the counter, ordered three iced coffees with chocolate and returned a few minutes later with frosty glasses and three straws. Louis's eyes widened when she sat his in front of him.

"Louis, all charges against you have been dropped for now, but there's still the issue of the missing gun. You told me you lost it the night of the shootings, when you were running down toward the river. Did it really happen like that?"

Louis concentrated on his iced coffee. He didn't look up at Emma as she was speaking.

"It's important that you tell Professor Thornton the truth, Louis." Jesse Branson set his drink down and leaned toward the young man.

Louis looked out of the window.

"The police could still charge you with aiding and abetting the murder of Brother Antoine and Sam Maureau, or as an accessory for the role you played that night. Mr. Branson is correct. It's important that we know everything." Emma pulled her notebook out of her bag.

"That night Marcus told me to give those two guys that bag of money. Then he said to take one of their guns and go throw it in the river. But he wanted me to say it was my gun. That way no one would know who did the shootin'."

"Marcus wanted you to cover up who did the actual shooting?"

Louis nodded.

"And at the same time make it look like you might be a suspect." Emma tried to make eye contact with Louis, but he stared at his drink. "At first you told me you had your gun, and you threw it in the river. Then you said it was someone else's gun, which you threw in the river. Then you changed your story, again. You said you had the gun from the actual shooters, but you lost it. I have a feeling that was a lie too. Am I wrong?"

Louis cracked his knuckles.

Emma could tell he was upset. "Did you lie to me again?"

Louis stared at the table. His face collapsed in tears. "'Cause I know Marcus's got people who'll kill me if I talk to you. And if his people don't, the cops will. If I tell you what happened, and if they find out I got the gun, they'll kill me. I know it."

"So, you didn't throw it away, because you thought you might need it to prove you didn't shoot Brother Antoine or Mr. Maureau that night?"

Louis nodded.

CHAPTER THIRTY-SIX

"But the difference is now Marcus is in jail. Does that make you feel safer?"

He nodded. "Yeah. But he could still have someone get me, even from jail."

"But one of the police officers was the shooter, right? Not Marcus. The gun isn't evidence against Marcus. And all of the police officers who did any of the shootings are in jail or are dead."

Louis looked up. "That's right. Marcus told me to pick up the gun and run it down to the river. But that's all. He didn't shoot anyone."

"Do you feel safer about showing me the gun?"

"I think so." He hesitated. "One of the guys at that electric box fired it. I got it from him that night and left it down by the river."

* * *

They could have walked, but Emma insisted they all pile in her car. She drove to the end of Felicity, made the turn at the end of the road around the bend at Tchoupitoulas, and parked next to an abandoned warehouse. She locked up after everyone exited her car and crossed the street to the wharf where Louis and Mr. Branson were standing.

They were waiting in almost the same spot where St. Amant had confronted Emma a few days ago. The sun was at a similar angle, and the breeze was blowing just as it had that day. Emma could feel her muscles tensing and her breath quickening.

"Do you have something to show us, Louis?"

"Yeah, I think." He walked over to an empty oil drum on the wharf, the same container Emma had seen on the docks when she was face to face with St. Amant. He flipped the barrel on its side. The lid had been removed, the rim was ragged with razor sharp cut marks. Underneath the barrel, lying on the cement wharf, was a nondescript steel-gray pistol with night sights. Louis bent down, picked up the gun and handed it to Emma.

"It's a Glock 22. Standard issue for the NOPD," Jesse said.

Emma flipped it over. "Here. Look at this." Scratched on to the bottom of the grip were the initials 'St.A.'

"Those initials have to stand for St. Amant. This was St. Amant's gun. I'd bet my last dollar on it. There's a serial number. And I'm sure the gun would have been checked out to him. This must be the gun which was used to kill Brother Antoine. And it could also have been the gun which discharged the fatal shot to Mr. Maureau."

She looked up at Louis. "Louis, you've just handed me what the police have needed all along to convict St. Amant. If you agree to let me turn this in for you, which is what I advise, I believe the DA will drop any future charges against you for the murders. Marcus asked you to hide the gun. But if you bring it to the police, you'll not only give them what they need to solve a murder, you'll have stood up to Marcus and those corrupt officers, which is something men twice your age have been afraid to do."

Louis grinned. "You can take it in. This ain't about Marcus anymore. This is about me."

"I couldn't have said it better. I'm so proud of you. From what we can tell, St. Amant is the man who killed your Aunt Juanita, and he was the man who killed Brother Antoine and a few other people too. I know how scary it's been to put your life on the line. You've been in real danger."

She reached out and grabbed both of Louis's hands and squeezed them.

"You've been so brave. Now I've got to get this gun to the police. And you've got to start this new life of yours."

Louis and Mr. Branson piled back into Emma's car and she drove them back to the coffee shop where Mr. Branson's vehicle was parked. She pulled into the lot and put her car into gear and turned off her engine. As Mr. Branson opened the car door, Emma walked out and handed Louis her card with her telephone number.

"I hope you never need this again. But I'll always be there for you if you do. Sometimes life takes a surprising turn. I don't think either you or Alicia would have believed a year ago, that your life would have taken the path you find yourselves on today. But I'm beginning to believe in redemption, and you, Louis, are a big part of it."

Footnote

*On February 28, 2005, the day before *Roper v. Simmons* was decided, seventy-one people were on death row for crimes committed while they were juveniles. All were aged sixteen or seventeen at the time of their crimes; they'd been on death row from six months to twenty-four years. On February 29, 2005, the Supreme Court of the United States held that the death penalty for juvenile offenders younger than eighteen violates the U. S. Constitution's prohibition against cruel and unusual punishment.

But today all states have transfer laws that allow or require young offenders to be prosecuted as adults for more serious offenses, regardless of their age. Four forms of transfer laws are:

- Statutory Exclusion - State law excludes some classes of cases involving juvenile age offenders from juvenile court, granting adult criminal court exclusive jurisdiction over some types of offenses. Murder and serious violent felony cases are most commonly "excluded" from juvenile court.
- Judicially Controlled Transfer - All cases against juveniles begin in juvenile court and must literally be transferred by the juvenile court to the adult court.
- Prosecutorial Discretion Transfer - Some categories of cases have both juvenile and criminal jurisdiction, so prosecutors may choose to file in either the juvenile or adult court. The choice is considered to be within the prosecutor's executive discretion.
- "Once and adult, always an adult" Transfer - The law requires prosecution in the adult court of any juvenile who has been criminally

prosecuted in the past, usually regardless of whether the current offense is serious or not.

https://www.sdxncsl.org/research/civil-and-criminal-justice/juvenile-age-of-jurisdiction-and-transfer-to-adult-court-laws.aspx

Acknowledgements

This story was inspired by my love of a city, and the time I spent there working with troubled kids and families. Fond memories with my own family are also reflected in moments in Emma's kitchen, Mardi Gras parades, and the family pets' errant escapades on the roof of our apartment. New Orleans is a warm city. One cannot help but love it, and it will love you back with the richness of its cuisine and heritage.

I'd also like to acknowledge Jamie Hubans Desporte, and Brian Swanner who have lent their considerable photographic inspiration and great shots of New Orleans to the project. Brian Swanner's photography graced the cover of the book, which turned out beautifully. Brian is an architect in New Orleans. I appreciate the time he took from his busy schedule to take photos of the city. Thanks to my children Laura Desporte Akin, M.D. and Charles Desporte, Jr. for their continued inspiration, particularly for their youthful New Orleans days. I recalled many of Laura's high school moments while writing these pages. Also, thanks to Carolyn Jarboe, Monica Hardy, Elizabeth Whitaker, and Aleta Magana for their friendship and our days in the great city.

Thanks also to Mari Ann Stefanelli for her continued guidance in all things writerly. And thank you to my beta readers. I'm not sure how I'd do this without them. My beta readers are my ninety-two-year-old dad, O.W. Tolbert, Jr.; Rip Sartin, Pat Pennington King, Liz Humphrey, Carolyn Jarboe, Monica Hardy, Norma Nixon Schofield, Jay Shaw and Juli Stewart.

Thanks also to the very careful reading of Luz Molina, good friend, excellent lawyer, and professor/ advisor extraordinaire. The world is a better place with Luz in it.

Brittany Yost's insights were also invaluable. We all need an awakening to cultural differences, and sometimes we need more help than we realize.

Thanks also to the readers of the very first draft of the manuscript, writing group members: Dawn Abeita, Dawn Major, Katherine Caldwell and Nicole Foerschler Horn. Their insights helped shape the story.

I'm grateful to Harriette Sackler and the team at Level Best Books, including Shawn Reilly Simmons and Verena Rose, for guiding me through the publishing process one more time. Harriette has proved yet again than she has more patience and kindness than I'd ever thought possible in the publishing business. She, Shawn, and Verena are a remarkably brilliant, talented trio. I am lucky to be involved with this group and am thankful every day for them.

Several other people have also read the book and reviewed it. Specifically, I'd like to thank authors Ellen Byron and Brian Coffin for their willingness to read and comment on this work. Their kind and encouraging words are so appreciated, and their talent and dedication to their craft will always be an inspiration.

I'd like to thank the entire writing community, especially the members of Sisters in Crime, Guppies, and Mystery Writers of America, as well as the Atlanta Writing Club, and Broadleaf Writers Association for all of their support, and the education they provide for new writers.

Finally, I'd like to thank my family, who continue to be my inspiration in this life.

About the Author

C. L. Tolbert grew up on the Gulf Coast of Mississippi, a culturally rich, beachy stretch of land with moss covered oaks and unforgettable sunsets. Early in her career, she earned a Masters of Special Education and taught children with learning disabilities before entering law school at the University of Mississippi. She spent most of her legal career working as defense counsel, traveling throughout the country in litigation for corporations and insurance companies. She also had the unique opportunity of teaching third-year law students in a clinical program at Loyola Law School in New Orleans where she ran the Homelessness Law Clinic and learned, firsthand, about poverty in that city. The experience and impressions she has collected from the past forty years contribute to the stories she writes today.

After winning the Georgia State Bar Association's fiction writing contest in 2010, C. L. developed the winning short story into the first novel of the Thornton Mystery Series, *Out From Silence*, which was published in December of 2019. Her second novel in the series, *The Redemption*, is set in New Orleans where she lived and worked for twelve years. Retiring after thirty years of law practice, she lives in Atlanta with her husband and schnauzer Yoda. When she's not writing, she visits her children and grandchildren as often as possible.

Visit C.L. Tolbert at www.cltolbert.com, and on the following:
  www.Facebook.com/cltolbertwriter
  www.instagram.com/cltolbertwrites
  www.twitter.com/@cltolbertwrites

CPSIA information can be obtained
at www.ICGtesting.com
Printed in the USA
JSHW021743290722
28601JS00001B/29